BLOOD FOR BLOOD

BLOOD FOR BLOOD

Julian Gloag

HOLT, RINEHART AND WINSTON
New York

First published in the United States by
Holt, Rinehart and Winston, 383 Madison Avenue,
New York, New York 10017.

Library of Congress Cataloging in Publication Data
Gloag, Julian.
Blood for blood.
I. Title.
PR6057.L6B5   1985   823'.914   85-8741
ISBN: 0–03–006012–5

Printed in the United States of America

ISBN 0-03-006012-5

Contents

BLOOD FOR BLOOD

1 Funeral

'Speke,' I said, 'Ivor Speke.' And I spelled it.

The plump young blonde raised her pencil, hesitated. 'Affiliation?'

'Affiliation? Well, I'm a member of the NUJ, if that's what you mean.'

'You a journalist?' Her chilliness matched that of the cloistered corridor in which we stood.

'No—well, yes, in a manner of speaking. I—'

'You representing the NUJ?'

'Repres—no, of course not. I'm not representing anyone.'

'Member of the family of the deceased?'

'No no. I'm just a—'

'Excuse me, madam, may I have your name? I'm representing the *Chronicle*.'

'—a friend,' I finished to the empty air. Once, I might not have had to spell my name.

I moved on slowly, half-sorry the interrogation had not been prolonged. I loathed funerals and, after the last one seven years ago, had sworn I'd never go to another. On the long early-morning drive across southern England, from Eastbourne to Bath, I had listened to my Mozart cassettes and managed not to think about the occasion at all. But now it was unavoidable.

1

I paused at the entrance of the chapel, belatedly remembering to remove my hat. Except for an empty pew at the front,
obviously reserved for the family, the chapel was almost full,
and ushers were unfolding extra chairs. I was placed at the
back and dutifully knelt for a few moments in the conventional
attitude of prayer, trying for appropriate thoughts. But all that
came to my mind was Vivian, who'd accepted traditional
religion with a fond tolerance, laughing at me when I crossed
myself with holy water at St Denis and, when I'd muttered
that it was simply a matter of *politesse*, laughing even harder.

To my left was a large alcove with the altar at the back and
in front a raised tomb-like structure of marble on which the
coffin would be placed. The low stone pulpit was a little to one
side of the recess. Facing me, the wall was one enormous sheet
of float glass, with an engraved cross in the centre. The crematorium was on the side of a hill with a view giving across miles
of grass or some early crop of bright spring green down to a
small river and then up to a distant range of wooded hills.
There was not a human habitation in sight. It was a strong
gusty day at the end of April and the clouds drove high in the
sky, casting cupfuls of glittering sunlight here and there over
the landscape. The sense of rapid movement and the audible
buffets of the wind against the glass emphasized the stillness
within the chapel itself, where the only sounds were the occasional cough and the creaking of the chairs as the latecomers
settled themselves.

Covertly I examined my fellow mourners in the pews on my
right. I knew a few of them, some from the Club, some from as
far back as Cambridge—Alva Norman, the *Gazette*'s literary
editor, elegant but fidgety, Hugo Pulteney with the bland,
half-asleep look of the higher civil servant, Shepperton Keith
of the Tavistock, shaggy and unkempt but fully alert, Cyril
Grayling the solicitor, solemn-faced and silver-haired, and Phil
Wood, the publisher, white with grief or a hangover; there
were the Club Secretary and several legal faces—Vivian's
fellow barristers—a well-known judge, and then, among all
that male solemnity a smattering of marvellously pretty
women, like birds in a petrified forest. These would be the girls
whose names—Sue, Charlie, Gina, Val, Veronica—now and
again casually cropped up in Vivian's conversation. But who
would have imagined a crop of such beauty?

The organ gave a preliminary blast. As we rose, I noticed at the rear an exceptionally tall, stiff individual with a small black moustache and, making no concession to mourning, a striped tie—a soldier perhaps, or a headmaster.

The coffin was of some black wood with silver mountings, heavy, for the bearers were bowed under its weight and out of step, failing to find any rhythm in the shapeless Church of England dirge the organ emitted. Behind the clergyman, a small bustling man with a chestful of medals that clinked as he walked, came Lady Winter, in face and carriage unmistakeably resembling her son, and behind her, seven elderly straight-backed women—the Aunts, of course. These were the sisters of Vivian's father, a diplomat who, according to Vivian, had joined the Foreign Service in order to escape them. The ironic result was that Vivian himself had been largely brought up by females. Perhaps that had accounted for his extraordinary sweetness of nature, an old-world almost spinsterish innocence which somehow made even the most misanthropic of his friends feel unusually likeable. Yet there had been nothing soft about him.

We sat for the psalm, and I allowed the beauty of the language to lull me without understanding. I'd only once heard Vivian in court, at the trial of Foxton, the financier; I'd been struck, though not surprised, by the steely, silver-tongued skill with which he unravelled that old crook's complex swindles. Later that week at the Club, he'd said, 'There's nothing much to it, Ivor. You mug it up beforehand and the next day you've forgotten the lot.' No one, not even Foxton, could have borne Vivian any malice. And yet someone had. . . .

Barrister Slain at Home
The body of Vivian Winter, QC was found early yesterday afternoon in the kichen of his flat at Alderney Court, SW. The discovery was made by his mother, Lady Winter. The cause of death was multiple stab wounds inflicted by a sharp instrument. 'There is no doubt that this is a savage and brutal murder,' said Detective Chief Superintendent McQuade of the CID, in charge of the case.

'. . . and fade away suddenly like the grass. In the morning

3

it is green, and groweth up; but in the evening it is cut down, dried up and withered. . . .'

On the near slope the sun shone and the wind rippled the gleaming blades, pressed them down, shook them, let them start up, then brushed them flat again.

(It had been Vivian's gentle, unsentimental understanding that had kept me steady after that other death seven years ago. 'Look,' he'd said, 'I always spend Christmas abroad. I'm going to Venice this year. Why not come with me?'

'I couldn't. I couldn't possibly leave Marion.'

'I think you could. I think you should. You need to be alone—so does she. You're not doing each other any good. You know what it will be like sitting round the Christmas tree without Henrietta. I shan't bother you—all I ever do is drink, read a bit, potter round a few of the sights.'

'Well, I don't know. . . .' But I had gone, and Vivian had been as good as his word—better. We had stayed at the inn on the island of Torcello, sometimes taking the *vaporetto* into Venice, but more often sitting drinking in the garden among the orange trees under the pale winter sun. We had connecting rooms beneath the eaves, and twice I had woken crying out in nightmare and once been seized by uncontrollable weeping. Each time Vivian had sat up with me, drinking brandy, gently reminiscing about old cases, until the dawn had crept stealthily into the room and soothed me into a dream-free sleep. He had helped me to blunt the sharpness of my grief there on Torcello, to put out—or at least to bank—the self-inflicted fire of rage that had shaken my hand and blurred my eye.)

The Order-of-Service card fluttered in my fingers; I stilled it by pressing my hand to my knee and trying to concentrate on the eulogy.

'. . . eminent Queen's Counsel . . . Recorder of the City of . . . indefatigable labourer in the cause of prison reform . . . one still so young, so full of high promise, cut down in the flower of. . . .'

Cut down! Where had they dug up this tactless donkey of the cloth? I closed my eyes and the tears swelled under the lids and ran warm down my cheek. There was a shuffling of feet and I opened my eyes and stood up. Slowly, operated by some unseen mechanism, two long curtains closed across the alcove where the coffin lay, blood-red velvet decently concealing the corpse.

'...delivered from the burden of the flesh....'

The mutilated flesh, the blood, the white bone, astonished eyes.... I shook the images from my head. In the old days the coffin had trundled creaking straight into the furnace. When did they do the burning now?

'We give Thee hearty thanks, for that it hath pleased Thee to deliver this our brother Vivian Charles Alexander out of the miseries of this sinful world.'

('Vivian, isn't there a kind of casual blasphemy about the idea that God actually engineers the killing of the innocent?'

'Not necessarily. It's the essential precondition for the exercise of His compassion, isn't it?')

I turned my head and found the military headmaster staring at me—had he never seen a tear before? I looked away. It was the end now.

'...and the fellowship of the Holy Ghost be with us all evermore. Amen.'

'Amen.'

I was almost the last to leave. The walkway leading down to the car park had a low wall on one side against which were propped a mass of wreaths and fresh-cut posies, but otherwise was open to the weather. The wind rumpled the hair and tugged at the clothes of the assembled bodies. Lady Winter, flanked by the Aunts, stood a little aside on a grassy mound.

'Hello, Ivor. A sad occasion.' Phil Wood had regained something of his normal ruddy colour.

'Yes.'

'I thought it went reasonably well—in a conventional way.'

'Yes.'

'Damned tactless hymn—all that about *latter years*. Good God, Vivian was six months younger than me.' He was fiddling with his breast pocket—surely he wasn't going to smoke a cigar now? 'How are you getting back?'

'Driving.'

'Can I cadge a lift? Or are you going straight home?'

'Yes, but that's all right—I don't mind dropping you off in town.' And yet I did mind—I was looking forward to a quiet and solitary drive.

'Good. We could stop off and have some lunch on the way. Well, I'd better go and say my piece to Lady Winter. Coming?'

5

'In a minute. I'll see you in the car park.' I turned to the distant hills, hoping my back would discourage other contacts. The wind thrust at me, whipped the air from the nostrils, strummed and poppled in the ears, dried my cheeks. It had been sagacious of the municipal authorities to site the crematorium on a hill; the very nature of the place seemed to evoke atavistic rituals more ancient and sacred than Christianity knew of: pyres built high on lonely crags, bodies exposed on rocks to wind and sun and rooks and eagles. . . .

The Aunts had retreated from the grassy mound and Lady Winter was guarded now by a little coterie of males—Alva Norman gave me a nod, Hugo Pulteney gazed blankly through me, but Cyril Grayling unexpectedly put out his hand.

'Hello, Ivor. Nice of you to come. You know Hugo, don't you?'

'Yes. Hello, Pulteney.'

'Hello, er. . . .'

'Speke,' I said.

'Well, yes—but I'm awfully sorry, I'm afraid I've forgotten your name.' And this was the man they said would be Head of the Treasury one day.

I moved on. 'Lady Winter, my name's Speke. Vivian and I—'

'Yes of course. Ivor, isn't it?' Close to, she was even more strikingly like Vivian, though the features had been set in the face with a rougher hand; she had the high-bridged nose, the deep-set clear blue eyes and, though the rest of her hair was white, the same thick black eyebrows. 'Thank you for your letter.'

'It was nothing, I. . . .'

'Oh no. It was much the most just of any I have received.' She smiled, and the severity of her stare dissolved. 'Vivian always spoke highly of you. He was so pleased when you agreed to take your Christmas vacations together. It's never easy to find a completely congenial companion, is it?'

'No—very rare indeed. I shall miss him a great deal.'

'Yes.'

'I wondered—if there is anything I can do to help. . . .'

'Do you often come up to town, Mr Speke?'

'Once a week—on a Wednesday.'

'Then would you come and have tea with me the day after

tomorrow?'

'With pleasure. Where?'

'At the flat—Alderney Court.' She gave me Vivian's quick ironical little smile. 'You didn't think I should run away, did you?'

I shook my head.

'Good. At four-thirty then. I shall count on you.'

Of course I would not have expected her to run away or to keep herself safely shuttered in Bath with her sisters-in-law, and yet it took a special sort of steel to stay on in the place where your son had been brutally murdered. After our loss, Marion and I had left the flat on the day of the inquest and had returned only once—to pack up and move out forever.

My peppermint green car stood out flashily amidst the soberly expensive colours of the other vehicles. As I approached it I saw Phil waving his finger at a sandy-haired man in a raincoat.

'No I bloody well won't give you my name or my address,' he was saying loudly. 'One of your women did all that when I came in—and a damned nuisance it was, too. Ah, Ivor—there you are. This impertinent twit of a—'

'Calm down, Philip. He's only doing his job.'

'Is it his job to go nosing into one's private affairs? What am I?—a politician that I can be badgered and hectored at will by—'

'If it was a woman,' said the man, totally unflustered by the onslaught, 'it certainly wasn't one of us.'

'Are you telling me I don't know the difference between male and female?'

'Hold on, Phil,' I said. 'Maybe he isn't a reporter at all.'

'A reporter!' Raincoat grinned; with his ginger head and ruddy complexion, he had the cheerful air of a butcher's boy.

'Do you have a problem here?' The soldier-schoolmaster had come upon us unawares.

'These gentlemen think we're reporters, sir,' said Ginger, suddenly sober.

'I see. Well, I am Detective Chief Superintendent McQuade and this is Detective Sergeant Roughead.' His voice had the faintest touch of the Scottish. 'As a matter of routine, we're asking the names and addresses of anyone attending the funeral.'

'Why?' said Phil bluntly.

McQuade looked at him. He had dark, almost black eyes and the white, slightly translucent skin of the true Celt. 'As you are no doubt aware, sir, we are investigating a case of murder. Any assistance you can render to the police will be appreciated and we will be calling upon you in due course. Meanwhile, I'd be obliged if you'd give your details to the Sergeant.' He gave us each a careful glance, then turned on his heel and was gone.

Phil made some inaudible mutter. We both 'obliged'. Names, addresses, phone numbers, relationship to the deceased—'friend. Friend.'

'Thank you very much, gentlemen,' said Ginger. 'As the chief said, expect we'll be in touch with you before too long.' And he gave us an unexpected wink.

2 *Home*

'So what are we—suspects?' Phil said grumpily and then, as I bumped the car too fast over one of the concrete ramps, 'Christ, isn't it about time you turned this old rattletrap in for something manufactured in the twentieth century?'

'Sorry, but you asked for the lift,' I said firmly, 'so you'll have to put up with my driving.' Phil's own licence had been suspended for three years when he was caught racing his Mercedes through Croydon at 110 m.p.h. with half a bottle of whisky inside him, but he still imagined he owned the roads.

'Sorry, I'm being ungracious. Mind if I smoke?' he asked, already in the act of lighting a cigar. 'The fact is I'm upset.'

'Aren't we all?'

'Yes yes. But I mean—those policemen. Where were you last Wednesday night?'

'After that lunch of ours? I drove very slowly back to Leeching and slept it off. What about you?'

'You know I went back to the flat. Much the same sort of thing. Wish to hell you'd stayed.'

8

'But I thought you were going down to spend the night with an author in Portsmouth.'

'Plymouth. I was. I think on the whole that's what I shall say.' He smoked in silence for a bit. I said nothing. Friendship is based on what you don't say, not what you do. I didn't want to know.

'We should swap alibis,' he said.

'Come off it, Phil,' I said, exasperated.

'Alright alright. I know you think I'm in bad taste. I am. What else do you expect from a publisher?' He laughed. 'By the way, have you given any more thought to that book idea?'

Phil was not my publisher—publishing a friend's novels, he asserted, was a misplaced charity—but he had been on at me for years to write a 'serious' book and had urged me again at our drunken lunch.

'No,' I said shortly. In the last few days I'd had room in my mind only for Vivian.

Even now, after I had dropped Phil at his office and crawled out of London, I thought of little else. I only began to feel easier after I had turned off the A22 at Polegate and taken the winding lanes that climbed gently up into the Downs. My cottage was half a mile from the village of Upper Leeching, set back up a steep unpaved driveway that required nicely calculated acceleration to avoid a skid in wet weather.

I switched off and got out. It was still blowy and the clouds were moving fast, but I had the feeling it would clear before nightfall.

When I bought the cottage ten years before, it had been mean and dark, with too few windows, dry rot, loose flints and broken slates. In the burst of sudden but brief affluence on my mother's death, I had remodelled it, painted, patched, re-pointed, pierced windows, and old Jeremiah Pleach had found me a load of almost perfect 'duchesses' and had reslated the roof. Yet Marion had never liked it and, ironically, it was only when I was entirely alone that it became my home. No longer new, it had a lived-in look and pleased the eye—or pleased my eye.

But the garden was bedraggled. I laboured at it regularly and joylessly (like so much else), but I was no gardener and it showed the lack of a loving hand. I breathed deeply and caught a hint of the sea—that faint scent of the familiar that I

9

had missed on the hillside at Bath. The smell of the sea was the scent of loss. The nagging vestiges of my irritation with Phil were dissipated. Vivian was dead, and this was a place accustomed to dealing with loss.

I lived and worked in the kitchen, which was two rooms thrown into one, painted white, with wide oak boards, stripped beams and comfortable furniture of a variety of woods and hues. Even the refrigerator and the wood-burning stove were brown. The stove, which stood in the chimney breast, had an agreeable, though entirely false, old-fashioned look, for it was a model of fuel-conserving efficiency, not only good for cooking but also providing hot water and central heating for the whole house. Knowing the animal sentimentality to which solitary people are prone, I had resolutely refused to have a dog or cat; instead, the stove had become something of a pet.

'Good old girl,' I murmured, lifting the lid. She was still alive from the morning and I fed her a couple of stout logs. The property had included two and a half acres of scrubby woodland, so I was never short of fuel—wood chopping and long walks over the Downs or along the cliffs were my only forms of exercise. Self-sufficiency had become a minor fetish; often at night I dispensed with electricity, reading or writing by the light of the big kerosene lamp with a frilly shade that stood in the centre of the table.

I made a pot of tea and looked round for the tea cosy. As usual I had used it to cover the phone on the Welsh dresser. Now, as I lifted it off, the phone rang, as though on signal to spoil my silence. Hadn't I had enough of people today?

Nevertheless, I picked it up—it might be, who?—the police asking for 'help in their enquiries.' Or one of my fellow mourners wanting to hash over the obsequies, as Phil Wood had tediously done at lunch between mouthfuls of fillet steak. But it was only Phyllis Pleach asking if she could come up tonight to do the typing rather than tomorrow morning. I said yes, of course, come right away, although I rather resented interruptions of routine. Yet, in order to attend the funeral, I had been forced to alter it myself—finishing my weekly review on Sunday night instead of, as usual, Monday, tonight.

It lay now, three neatly hand-written sheets, beside the pile of review copies; the top one was the new Desmond Sheen, *Bloody Mann*. It was a clever book, and Mann, the chief protagonist, was of such unmitigated nastiness that his death was greatly to be desired—if only it had not been so accurately gory. I was touchy about blood—if I cut my thumb, it was not the pain that made me wince, but the sight of the blood. But the blood in crime fiction, by definition, should be unreal. In my standard lecture on the subject, I compared fictional blood to a vaccination which prevents the spread of a taste for killing among the general population—or to a prolonged methadone treatment unhooking the addicts from the real thing. I didn't believe it. Readers were children amusing themselves with fire (there was even a series called *Murder for Pleasure*); that it was a false fire made it no better. It made it sicker (why not *Romps with the Bomb?*) and a decent society would have nothing to do with it.

I drank my tea quickly, irritated at these prevarications. Then I took a cigarette from the slate box on the mantelpiece which I kept full for visitors, like the whisky decanter on the dresser. Or so I told myself—but I couldn't name half a dozen visitors in as many years, except for Phyllis, and Jim the postman who sometimes drank a cup of tea with me, and once Mrs Helmsley-Clinch who'd barged in canvassing for the Tories and stalked about my kitchen with frank inquisitiveness ('Miserable patch of garden you've got out there,' 'Mantelpiece needs dusting,' 'Nice piece of Meissen that, pity it's cracked,' 'What d'you want all those knives for, going to set up as a butcher?'). And, though I claimed not to smoke, the cigarette box often needed replenishing; the decanter too.

I needed—deserved—a drink now, having drunk nothing at lunch. But as I started to get out the ice, Phyllis Pleach passed the window and tapped on the door. I put the ice back and let her in.

'Ivor, I'm sorry to bother you on a Monday, but—'

'That's all right—it's all ready for you.'

'You see, I've got to take Dad in to a doctor's appointment in Eastbourne—it's a specialist and I just couldn't get another time.'

'Nothing serious, I hope.'

'It's his arthritis. They're thinking of a knee-cap operation, but the problem is....' Her large serious grey eyes lent a calm beauty to her otherwise undistinguished features. But, though I hardly listened, I detected the worry in her voice and face.

She had worked for me for five years, yet still retained that curiously unremitting admiration some people have for writers. It formed a barrier to intimacy which at the beginning I had once or twice wanted to break, but now I was used to it, had become perhaps too confirmed a solitary to welcome any untoward invasion of feeling.

'Shall I take it inside then?' she asked finally, picking up the copy and the books.

I nodded. 'Inside' was the study, formerly the front parlour, lined with old review copies, and furnished with a table, a chair, a typewriter and an old TV set. I seldom entered.

'Anything for me to do on the novel?'

'No.'

As soon as she left the room, I made myself a whisky. What Phyllis had referred to was my effort at formula romantic fiction, in which *The Heroine is always young . . . she has a good figure, and is often petite and slight of build. . . . In spite of her fragile appearance, she is independent, high-spirited and not too subservient. She should not be mousey or weepy . . .*; a kind of Utopian limbo where the characters have no character and nothing ever happens—neither life nor death. *Naturally when she dresses up she is stunning. Her outfits are described in detail. . . .* It was this that had caused me shamefacedly to seek the advice of Phyllis, who enthusiastically invented 'outfits' and who was typing the manuscript free of charge. I had promised her a share of the proceeds, in the improbable event that there were any. Although, God knows, I needed them—the *Gazette* just about paid for my food and the last remnants of my mother's legacy were running out.

I was able to treat *Love's Loose Strife*—Phyllis had invented the title too—as a joke between us, except when she called it a novel. Once I had written real novels. Once I had lived a real life. Both had vanished in the gap between sham love and artificial crime.

The whisky was making me maudlin, as it usually did, and I was glad when Phyllis came back.

'Is it all right?' I asked her.

'Of course—more than all right. It always is.'

'Have a drink?'

'I'd love to, but I must be getting back. Dad will be wanting his supper.'

12

'I'll walk you down to the village then. I could do with a pint anyway. How is Jeremiah, apart from the arthritis?'

'He's apt to be a bit crotchety. Not having anything to do makes him. . . .'

I listened with half an ear as I put on the metal-studded boots that had saved me from many a fall on slippery turf and slick chalk. One of the mysteries about Phyllis, who had a degree and had taught English for a year, was that she'd not married but chose to live with her father, admittedly a man superior to any she was likely to find in the village. But what happened to her emotional energies? I had a suspicion they went into writing, poor lass.

'Come on,' I said, taking my shooting stick from the rack.

Though it was still light enough to see clearly, she took my arm at the steep part of the path.

'I read about your friend. I was so sorry.'

'Did you?' I was surprised she was even aware I knew Vivian—but, of course, I must have talked of our holidays together. 'As a matter of fact, I've just been to his funeral today.'

'How sad for you.'

'Oh, it was very tasteful.' And then, perhaps to correct my off-handedness, I began to tell her about it—the beauty and the banality, the falseness of sentiment, the truth of feeling. Maybe I always talked to Phyllis more than I knew; at any rate I was sorry when we reached her cottage.

'It was him you went to Paris with at Christmas, wasn't it?'

'Yes, that's right.'

'Why was he murdered, Ivor?'

'Why?' The clouds had almost cleared away and the sun was sinking behind the curve of the Downs. 'I have no idea.'

As I watched her enter the cottage and then made my way to the Green Bough, I felt a sense of bewilderment that I had not thought to ask *why? Who*, yes—obviously some maniac. But even a maniac would have reasons, and what could Vivian of all people ever have done to harm anyone?

Constable Fred Fletching and Judge Towner were the only customers.

'Hello, Ivor—what will it be?' said the Judge. 'No no, let me do this. A pint. Hamish—a pint for Mr Speke. And another for the Force—and one for me too.'

'Good evening, Hamish.'

'And good evening to you, sir. Three pints of the best it is, sir.' Hamish, short and dark, with an enormous beer belly that seemed quite independent of the rest of him, filled the order with clockwork dexterity. 'There we are, sir, that will be one English pound and ninety-five pence.'

When Hamish had first taken over the Green Bough, the betting had been that he wouldn't last six months—he evinced no interest in the community or, apparently, anything else, and his impersonal suburban bonhomie set everyone's teeth on edge. But he had already lasted five years, absolutely impervious to the fascinated dislike of his customers, among whom there was some competition to provoke him into new depths of ghastliness. But I hadn't the heart for the game this evening.

'You look a bit fagged tonight, Ivor—all that gadding about in town wearing you down?' The Judge smiled—it was the convention that I kept a mistress, or maybe two, in London and used the country merely to recuperate from wild nights of gaiety and vice.

'My own back garden's good enough for me,' said Fred Fletching dutifully. 'Haven't been in London since goodness knows when.' Large, red-faced, flaxen-haired, in his youth Fred had once been an extra in a terrible British movie about the Count of the Saxon Shore—as a Saxon raider. He still looked the part—but underneath the heaviness of feature and deliberation of manner, there was an astute and observant mind; it was said he had several times refused promotion in order to stay at Upper Leeching.

'Don't talk to me about gardens,' said Towner.

'Having problems?' I asked. This was a customary conversation that dwindled in the winter, then renewed itself with pristine vigour in the spring.

'Nothing but. This damned sciatica—can't stoop, can't stretch.' Years of sitting on the bench were finally being paid for by a stiffening of the judicial spine. 'My yew hedge looks like a Chinaman's beard. Mrs Helmsley-Clinch is the same—thinking of tearing up her herbaceous borders and putting in a lot of shrubs! I ask you!'

'That's bad,' Fred said gravely.

'Bad? It's the beginning of the end—before you can say Jack

Robinson, Leeching will be no more than a Garden Suburb. Truth is, we're a lot of old crocks these days.'

I said, 'What about Old George, wouldn't he help you out?'

'Oh yes, he's always willing to lend a hand. The trouble with George is he won't take payment—getting a bit past it, as well. Old Jeremiah's the same. They want to do it their way, and you want it done your way. Result—impasse. No, what we need round here is a vigorous young chap who'll take orders.'

'Well, don't look at me,' I said.

'Why not? Healthier than all that pen-pushing. Better paid too, probably.'

'Charity begins at home,' said Fred.

I laughed. 'Yes, I know, my patch is a disgrace to the village.'

'Oh, I don't know about that—and it's out of the way a bit, isn't it?'

'Out of sight, out of mind?'

'No, but serious now, Ivor—if you're going to be gone more'n a night or two, you let me know and I'll keep an eye on the place. There was that burglary at Mr Hurst's house when he was away up North to his mother's funeral, and there been two out Ditchling way lately—all isolated houses.'

'Ought to keep a dog,' said the Judge.

A dog, I thought as I walked home. Better than talking to myself—or to a cast-iron stove.

I did not pause at the house, but went on up the hill, shedding the beer on the stiff climb, shedding the moroseness of the day.

The wind had blown out and when I reached Beachy Head the moon silvered an almost flat calm sea. The Channel was scattered with the lights of passing vessels—the arrogant glare of tankers, the decorated trimmings of coasters, and the comfortable gleam of the Newhaven–Dieppe ferry. But they moved silently and the only sound was of the swell washing softly far below at the base of the cliff and, inland, the low of a cow and the quarter-hour strike of a church clock.

I had planted my shooting stick as close to the edge as possible. Sitting on it, I half-closed my eyes and was soothed into a dreamlike dizziness where to slip from the cold heights to the sea's moonlit glimmer would be a delectable temptation, falling a consummation.

It was an unusual calm for April—an angry month, and yet one when there were the least suicides (life giving the lie to literature?). And anyway, it was only the women who tended to let themselves topple; the men favoured a running jump. Both sexes usually left wallet or handbag some distance from the cliff edge, but not often a letter—perhaps because there was no one left to care.

I stood up and pulled my stick from the turf. I walked home at an even pace—it's no good hurrying downhill after two weeks of rain. When I reached it, I changed my boots (the cleats scarred the floor), bolted the door and closed the shutters. I poured half a tumbler full of whisky and drank it slowly, standing beside the stove for warmth.

Why had he been killed? *Why* did he die? *Why* were they sacrificed?

I refilled my glass and then, when the lights began to blink at me, made for the hall and pulled myself up the stairs. I crossed the little landing and unhooked the key from its place above the lintel and unlocked the door.

The room was pink and white—a rose-coloured carpet, flowered Laura Ashley walls, a crib, a chest of drawers, a stool, a small table, a rocker, all white, lined damson curtains to give the early morning sun a roseate light, a bear upon the pillow and a mobile above of coloured glass and small bells from which no sound had come for seven years. A child's room.

I locked it up again, but could not lock up the nightmare that would follow as surely as sentence upon crime.

3 No Tea Party

'I hope you weren't expecting cucumber sandwiches and buttered scones?'

'No no. I mean. . . .' Then my adolescent sense of confusion dissolved under Lady Winter's smile. 'Well, yes, I suppose that's just what I was expecting.'

16

We both laughed, and I was able to look at her more closely. In a plain black wool dress with a black enamel and seed pearl mourning brooch at the collar, she seemed smaller and frailer than I remembered.

'And tea—do you really care for tea?' she said, leading the way down the hall. I found myself obediently accepting the suggestion that I did not like tea. 'Good. I detest the stuff. I've had to spend a great part of my life drinking quantities of it in the most unsuitable places. My husband was a diplomat, you know.'

The large, airy sitting room was done in primrose and varying shades of grey—dove-grey walls, silvery carpeting, a long couch of battleship-grey suede, curtains and upholstery of yellow velvet, with gleaming pieces of mahogany and a black and gold Empire bookcase against one wall. Its elegance surprised me, for Vivian had had little sense of colour or eye for design.

'We shall have whisky. Perhaps you would be kind enough to pour, Mr Speke?' She indicated a decanter and two cut-glass tumblers and a Bristol blue jug of water on the side table. 'Neat for me.'

So she had arranged it all beforehand. I smiled to myself, but poured dutifully; it was a long time since I'd had my decisions made for me, but I could certainly do with a hair of the dog.

'You've not been here before, I think,' she said, as I handed her a glass. At the crematorium her hair, pinned under a black hat, had resisted the tugging of the April bluster, but now as she sat upright in the wing chair, there were wisps and strands adrift like flags of an inner turbulence.

'No,' I said, taking a seat on the couch.

'No. Of course Vivian liked to keep his life in compartments. He used to entertain here a little, usually a small dinner party for his legal friends and their wives. That would be on a Thursday, the day I come up to town, you know, so that I could be his hostess. On Fridays he would sometimes come back with me to Bath for the weekend—if he wanted domesticity. We are very domestic in Bath, Mr Speke.' She smiled.

'But more often than not he spent his weekends here, sometimes with one of his women friends, though naturally I didn't enquire—and hardly ever a sign of them. They must all have been most neat and discreet ladies. Vivian did not believe in early marriages, as I expect you knew.'

'No. No, I didn't.' But it didn't surprise me. Despite the chattiness of her tone, I sensed this was no idle gossip or attempt to break the ice.

'Yes. It's often the bachelors that are the most fond of women. And of course there was the club, a very different ... kettle of fish. Not just yours, where the attractions are clear, but the other one, the athletic one, where he played squash— he seemed to get on well there too, although the members are mainly businessmen, I understand. And then there was you— your holidays together. I believe, you know, that you were his only *close* friend.'

'Oh surely not. Well, I mean, I don't know about other friends. Certainly we were close, yes—though there were a lot of things we *didn't* talk about.'

'Precisely. That's what I meant about compartments. Some people thought it odd, but on the whole I think it quite wise not to mingle different sorts of love.' She drank some whisky.

'Perhaps. I hadn't considered it like that.' It was rather like an examination when one does not quite grasp the terms of the question, but must answer all the same. I wanted a cigarette. 'I see what you mean in a way—if you mix styles too much, you end up with no style. For me variety isn't really desirable—isn't the spice of life—it's a distraction. I see it as disjointedness, symptomatic of some basic inability to get it together, which causes discomfort—even guilt.'

'You are talking as a writer.'

'Maybe. Partly. Perhaps that's why I'm not really a very good writer. I try too hard to impose a control I don't feel. But that didn't apply to Vivian—he carried his unity around with him.'

'He was always self-confident, even as a little boy.'

'I can imagine. I've never known anyone so unaffectedly self-possessed, certainly.'

She nodded. 'And yet, I wonder if you didn't feel that he wasn't quite himself these last few weeks? In Paris at Christmas, for instance, what was he like?'

'Much the same as usual, I think.' I took my first swallow of whisky. We'd been to the Orangerie, and I'd hauled him out to St Denis, but otherwise we'd mostly sat in cafés, drinking, watching the passers-by hurrying against the bitter cold, reading the English newspapers.... 'Well, I'm not sure, but there was one—'

I was cut off by the ringing of the front door bell.

'What a nuisance. I expect it's the wing-commander next door collecting for his charity. Dreadful man with a moustache. Would you be kind and send him away?'

But it wasn't the wing-commander; it was the policemen from the car park.

'Mr Speke, isn't it?' said the ginger-headed one. 'That's a bit of luck, we wanted a word with you.'

'Is Lady Winter at home?' asked the other one.

'Yes,' I said, feeling like the butler, 'but—'

'Good.' They stepped inside. So I shut the door and led them into the sitting room.

'Lady Winter, I'm sorry, but it's the police.' I made an effort of memory. 'Mr McQuade and Sergeant Roughneck.'

'Roughead.' His chuckle died at a sharp look from Lady Winter.

'I'm already acquainted with them. Mr McQuade, would it not have been possible to telephone before arriving unannounced on my door mat?'

'I'm sorry to trouble you, Lady Winter, but—'

'It is inconvenient.'

'I shan't bother you but a minute.' He returned her stare unflustered. Roughead made a movement towards the couch, then checked it. They were not to be asked to sit down.

'You'll recollect,' McQuade said, 'that in our search of the flat we found no diaries, no address book, no private papers belonging to Mr Winter at all—except for the strictly legal ones. You undertook to look for anything of that nature at your house in Bath. Were you successful?'

'I was not. I should have informed you if I had been.'

'Quite. And you still do not recall whether or not he possessed an address book—or a pocket diary?'

'I imagine he had an address book. I believe he did. He may have left it in Chambers.'

'No, he did not.' Most men in the circumstances would have been shifting about on their feet—Roughead was—but McQuade remained utterly still. Of course Vivian had an address book and a diary, both crammed with his tiny precise writing—I'd seen him consult them many times.

McQuade had gone on to something else. '... at what time you remarked the absence of the knife?'

'As I have never been aware of its presence, I could hardly remark its absence. I do not spend my time in the kitchen. As I've already told you, Mrs Blaine informed me one was missing.'

'Who's Mrs Blaine?' I asked, interest overcoming trepidation.

'Mrs Blaine is what is nowadays called household help. She is a good cook, but she's the sort of woman who will clean the silver with steel wool. Frankly, Superintendent, I should not be surprised if she hadn't purloined the knife herself.'

'Mrs Blaine is dishonest?'

'All servants are light-fingered.'

'She might have made off with the address book too?' Dryly.

'Don't be ridiculous.' Frosty.

'Then I am to take it as a general sociological observation, rather than a formal accusation?'

'Take it in any manner that pleases you.' She *must* have known that Vivian kept an engagement diary, as well as an address book—then why was she lying? And why was she being so extraordinarily offensive to the police?

'Thank you, ma'am. Now, with your permission, we'd like a word with Mr Speke here.'

'I hope you don't mind, Lady Winter,' I said placatingly, seeing the snap in her eye, 'but it might be better to get it over with. It won't take long, will it, Mr McQuade?'

'Not long, sir.'

'Very well. You may use my son's study. You know where it is.' And then, as we turned to go, 'Superintendent. While I am of course anxious to help in your enquiries, I do hope you're not going to make a habit of calling upon me without warning at any time of the day or night.'

McQuade merely inclined his head.

The study was small, dark and stuffy. A single window giving on to an airshaft was draped with old brownish velvet curtains; the walls were lined with glass-fronted bookcases; there was a green filing cabinet, two worn blue leather club chairs, a writing table surfaced with ink-stained pink leather to which was clamped a flexible reading lamp painted scarlet.

A half-size Victorian longcase clock standing in one corner had stopped. It was a depressing room, but then Vivian was strangely indifferent to his surroundings; abroad we had generally stayed in the shabbier hotels.

'Phew!' said Roughead, opening his notebook and perching himself on the arm of one of the club chairs. I took the other, and McQuade sat down at the desk and switched on the lamp. Under the sudden light, his face was a study of contrast—high pale forehead, broad cheekbones, pointed chin, neatly clipped moustache, sedately smooth-lying black hair, impenetrably deep-set eyes. It carried impassivity to the point of caricature, yet there was a sense of vibrancy beneath the mask.

'Sorry,' I said. 'Yes. Since Cambridge. We were at the same college. We weren't great friends. He was a lawyer and I was an historian—but we had interests in common.' I tried to think what, but my memory failed. 'And we both rowed—though Vivian was the athlete. I just did it for the exercise.

'After Cambridge? Well, we rather went our different ways. I don't suppose I saw him more than twice a year, if that. We met at the occasional party, he came to my wedding—that sort of thing. Until about ten years ago when we found ourselves members of the same club. We saw each other a bit more after that—oh, I dare say two or three times a month. I usually dine at the club on Wednesdays and Vivian made rather a habit of turning up then too, when he wasn't off on circuit or something.

'No, we never went to each other's home. It wasn't that kind of—of friendship.' I felt slightly discomfited under the steady gaze, by a vague sense of betrayal. 'I don't want to give you a misleading impression—we knew each other quite well and we were, well, fond of each other. He was one of the kindest men I know and he was very good to me when—when I split up from my wife. You don't happen to have a cigarette, do you?'

'Ginger, give Mr Speke a cigarette.'

Ginger—I was pleased. 'Thanks, thank you,' I said, taking a cigarette from the inscribed silver case on which I caught the words *for gallantry*.

'Would you describe Mr Winter as a sociable man?'

'Highly sociable—I sometimes wondered if there was anyone he didn't know. He had enormous charm, you see, and.... Women? Well, yes, I think he did. He was rather inscrutable about his private life, you know. But I'm sure he did have quite a number of "lady friends," as you put it. *What?* That's a pretty offensive suggestion, Superintendent, what—'

'Don't get worked up, sir. It just so happens Mr Winter's murder bears some of the marks of a homosexual killing—the peculiar savagery of the attack, for one. So I am bound to ask you whether you know of any involvement of that kind.'

'Absolutely not. To anyone who knew Vivian Winter, it would be a ludicrous idea.'

'I see. Well, that's very clear. But now, can you think of any reason why anyone would have killed Mr Winter?'

'No I can't. I've thought about it—but it just seems impossible. . . . Enemies? I should have said Vivian didn't have an enemy in the world.'

'Now what about his court cases, did he ever talk to you about them?'

'Not often—only if there was something amusing or *outré*. Oh. I see what you mean. Well, his criminal practice was intermittent, I believe. He only took a criminal case when he felt particularly strongly about it—and always for the defence. He never prosecuted—or so I believe. I suppose someone he defended who was convicted all the same might hold a grudge.' I drew on my cigarette. 'Or the injured party to a case in which he got the accused off, but. . . .'

'But what?'

'But for *that*—to commit such a brutal murder. They would have to be insane.'

'Maybe. But in my experience the brutality of the murder has no necessary connection with the mental condition of the murderer. Injustice, whether real or fancied, can provide a powerful motive for revenge among men not ordinarily considered dangerous. Is there any case at all of Mr Winter's that might fall into that category, as far as you know?' It was a long speech for McQuade and the tinge of Scottish somehow increased its earnestness.

'No, I don't think so.' But there was one at the back of my mind—Bateman. Yet Vivian had never talked about it and, anyway, Bateman was safely in Broadmoor.

'Depressed?' Well, he had been broody that day in Paris, but it might have just as well been indigestion as the news. Admittedly he *had* looked in his address book and gone off and

22

phoned, but. . . . 'No,' I shook my head, 'he was the most equable of men. I suppose that means if he had been worried, he wouldn't have shown it; on the other hand, I'm sure he had no inkling of—of anything like this.'

'Quite. Well, thank you, Mr Speke.' There was a tiny movement of the facial muscles, no doubt intended to do duty as a smile.

'Is that all?' I was surprised.

'Just one or two questions about where you were on the night of the murder.' Ginger grinned cheerfully. 'Nothing to worry about. Let's say from about eight o'clock on April 14th to two the following morning?'

'I was at home—at Upper Leeching. Is that when it happened—during the night?'

'Probably around eleven p.m. You were at home all day, were you?'

'No, no. I came up to town as I usually do on a Wednesday, did my business, then drove home.'

'Right. Half a minute, you said earlier you usually had dinner at your club on Wednesdays, with Winter. Why not this time?'

'It was out of term, you know—I assumed Vivian was still in Bath. Besides, I'd had rather a heavy lunch and decided to get back early. I must have arrived home about six-thirty.'

'Six-thirty. See anyone, talk to anyone, any phone calls?'

'I'm afraid not.'

'You live alone, Mr Speke?' It was McQuade now, leaning forward a little.

'Yes. My marriage was dissolved five years ago, but we'd been separated for two years before that.'

'Any children?'

'We had one daughter.'

'And she is in custody of the mother?'

'She died. In an accident. Seven years ago.'

'What sort of an accident was that, sir?'

'Does it really matter? Oh well. She—she fell.' My voice shook slightly, it always did when I mentioned Henrietta—and my visit to her room last night, with its consequent nightmare, had not helped my equilibrium. Other people put flowers on a grave, I got drunk and played with a teddy bear. 'She fell from a second-floor window onto a concrete patio. She broke her neck.' McQuade was expressionless. And suddenly I remembered the young policeman—PC Buckby, he'd been called—who stayed with us for hours afterwards, making tea and giving Marion a gentle easy comfort which I had not been able to, then or ever.

'Do you pay your ex-wife alimony?'

'I make her a small monthly allowance—though I'm not obliged to do so.' And this month, I realised, I'd forgotten to write the cheque.

'You're a novelist, I understand?'

'I was. I haven't written anything for a long time. I do a weekly review for the *Gazette*.'

'And that's your main source of income?'

'I do a bit of hacking, and now and again I'm asked to give a lecture, but the *Gazette*'s what puts the bread on the table, yes. Why?'

'Well, sir, you have a house to keep up, you make an allowance to your ex-wife, you run a car, belong to the London Library and a rather exclusive club—I just wondered how you could afford all that on what you earn.'

'I'm frugal, Mr McQuade.'

'Quite so. And the holidays abroad? Or did Winter pay for those?'

'Certainly not,' I said sharply; nevertheless I felt winded. I should have told them about the holidays. It was not just that I had been caught out, but my private affairs had been delved into (though, God knows, I had nothing to hide), and I felt soiled and just a little bit frightened. 'If you must know, I had a small amount of capital left me by my mother.'

'Now, your wife—what's her name, by the way?'

'Marion. Ex-wife. Marion Caroline Bland—she's reverted to her maiden name.'

'Miss Bland. How well was she acquainted with Winter?'

'Not very well. As I said, he was at our wedding—we may have all three dined together once or twice. I don't—'

'But she did not accompany you on your holidays abroad?'

'No. They were later—after we'd broken up.'

'Now, this is a personal question, Mr Speke, but I'm bound to ask it. Did your breaking up with your wife have anything to do with Winter?'

'With *Vivian*? Of course not.' I stared at him. 'I told you—

24

they hardly knew each other.' Yet it wasn't quite the point. Supposing I had resisted Vivian's urgings and not gone to Venice that Christmas, leaving Marion untended and alone with her grief? Supposing.... 'What?'

'I said,' McQuade was watching me closely, 'were you aware that you're a beneficiary under Vivian Winter's will?'

'Am I?' I was mildly surprised. Vivian was very well off, but like most rich men he was not extravagant. I was touched. 'I suppose that makes me a suspect?'

'Yes.' McQuade missed any hint of irony. 'Anybody left money by someone who is subsequently murdered is automatically suspect. And there are quite a number of beneficiaries under Winter's will.'

'Oh come on,' I said, slightly irritated, 'one doesn't murder a friend for the sake of a legacy.' I was sorry it was money; I should have preferred something personal—an object, a book or a painting, the broken clock in the corner.

'It's not my business to disclose details, but I am talking about substantial sums.'

What did this Scotsman consider substantial? Enough for a new car perhaps?

'Substantial,' he repeated. 'Were you aware that Winter made an entirely new will only a month ago?'

'No. Is that significant?'

'It is always significant when a man at the height of his career, in apparently excellent health, with no obvious worries, suddenly takes it into his head to put his affairs in order—in, I may say, an entirely new order. You have no idea why he decided to do so?'

'No. I . . . no. But you mean,' I grappled with the idea, 'you mean that maybe he knew he was—in some kind of danger?'

'It's a possibility, isn't it, Mr Speke?'

Suddenly he and Ginger were on their feet. I rose too and followed them out of the dim little study.

'You might be interested to come in here,' McQuade said, pushing through a swing door.

It was the kitchen, ugly with worn brown linoleum and shabby yellow paint, dirty windows and an ancient cooker—good enough for Mrs Blaine.

'It was in here?'

'Aye. Where I'm standing now. You'll note the knives in

yon rack—we reckon the murder was committed with the one that's missing.'

I recognized it—it was the twin of the set in my own kitchen.. A rack of five Sabatier kitchen knives—Vivian had bought a pair of them one Christmas in Marseilles four or five years ago (at a reduced price) and presented one to me. It was the only gift I had ever received from him—we didn't exchange presents—and even that, I thought sadly, I had paid him a franc for, so as not to sever our friendship.

I turned and pushed my way into the hall.

As I let the policemen out of the front door, McQuade said, 'And you'll let us know, Mr Speke, if anything occurs to you? Anything, maybe just a little thing you think of no significance.'

'Yes, yes of course I will.' Watching them walk to the lift, I wished suddenly I was going with them. I hated this flat—with its bizarre mixture of the elegant and the tawdry, the sordid and the high-minded, cut-glass decanters and blood on the kitchen lino.

In the sitting room, Lady Winter said, 'I do apologise for the interruption. Please help yourself to a drink.'

I did, and took a cigarette from the silver box. Outside it had grown darker and started to rain.

'Did that McQuade creature tell you you were under suspicion?'

'Yes.' As I sat down, my heart gave—surely she didn't think that I was a passenger in one of Vivian's secret compartments?

'Don't let it upset you, Mr Speke. I've no doubt I am myself a suspect—Medea, you know. The police mind plods, so naturally it steps into bogs. In this case, I'm afraid, Mr McQuade is not averse to seeing dirt where no dirt is.'

'Why? Why in this case, particularly?'

'Because he bore a grudge against Vivian. Oh he won't show it of course, but Scotsmen like that don't easily forget an injury—it's that disagreeable mixture of Calvinism and Celtic savagery, I expect. It goes back to that Bateman business—did Vivian ever talk to you about that?'

'No. He didn't talk to me about it, but I do remember in Paris. . . .' We were drinking Guinness and I looked up to see Vivian staring out at the boulevard, *The Times* on his lap, his face icy as the street outside.

'I'm sorry, Ivor, I've got to go back to the hotel and make a call. I shan't be long. Order me another Guinness.'

I picked up the discarded *Times*; the news on the open page had the bland quality peculiar to holiday periods, except for one short item, roughly as follows:

Christmas killer foiled
It was learned yesterday that Harold Henry Bateman, of Haslemere, Surrey, has been charged with the rape and attempted murder of Jennifer Thrush, 21. Miss Thrush was savagely assaulted in a field on the outskirts of Haslemere on Christmas Eve. Despite several knife wounds, she managed to crawl to a nearby road where she was picked up by a passing motorist. Miss Thrush is now in Guildford General, where her condition is listed as serious.

It will be recalled that a year and a half ago Mr Bateman, also 21, was acquitted of the murder and rape of Madeleine Jane Hodder.

'... I remember Vivian was rather quiet for the rest of the day,' I said. 'But where does McQuade come into it?'

'He was in charge of the investigation into the murder of the Hodder girl, and Vivian, who was defending Bateman, handled him rather roughly in the witness box.'

'So, in consequence, you'll think he'll drag his feet?' It had not been my impression.

'No. *Because* this was a particularly shocking murder and *because* Vivian was who he was, I'm sure the police will make their best efforts, but I'm equally sure they'll not be averse to unearthing any little unpleasantness. And *that* is likely to divert their attention and misdirect their energies. Of course, Hugo Pulteney, my godson, you know, will interest himself as much as he can from the Home Office, but he's not a man of great imagination—and imagination is what we're going to need.'

'Which is why you're talking to me?' I asked wryly.

'And because you are an observant man.' She gave me, not the vivid Winter flash, but a gentler smile. 'And Vivian always said you were tenacious—a survivor.'

'Obstinate, more likely.' But I felt a little prick of pleasure. 'So, what exactly is it that you want me to do?'

'First of all, I want you to think—to imagine. Not *who* so much, as *why*. As a newspaperman, you have access to files and you can make enquiries which ordinary people cannot. Secondly, as a start, I'd like you to come to the inquest.'

'The inquest?' I was plunged back seven years—the inquest. I remembered the kindly face of the coroner swimming out of the horror—*and I'm sure we all extend to Mr and Mrs Speke our deepest sympathy in this tragic accident, for which no blame attaches....* And afterwards the cold descended and wrapped me like a fog—and wrapped me still.

'... tomorrow at ten o'clock. It will be adjourned of course, but there will be some evidence of interest.'

'Ten,' I repeated numbly. 'Very well.' I stood up, hardly knowing what I was doing.

She too was on her feet. 'I know this is painful for you, Ivor—I hope I may call you Ivor.' She put out her hand and lightly touched my arm. 'I'm not asking you to do it for me—but for Vivian's sake. *We* must protect him now.'

'Yes. I understand.' Of course, that's why she'd lied to McQuade about the diary, to protect Vivian—but to protect Vivian from what? All I wanted was to leave, to get away to think, or not to think.

'You see, Ivor,' she said in the hall, 'you are the only other person to detect that Vivian was worried. And perhaps only you and I can guess what enormous disruption there must have been inside for Vivian to show a trace of perturbation. He was always equable—that was his strength.'

'Yes.' Except in court, perhaps. 'Lady Winter, did Vivian ever talk to you about the Bateman case?'

'No. He often talked to me about the law, but never about the cases he really took to heart.' And I heard the faintest trace of sadness in her voice. It was his heart that we all wanted—and none of us ever got.

'Tomorrow, then.' I took her hand.

'I shall be expecting you.'

Outside the rain was steady now. It was too late for the London Library, too early for the club. A grey time in a grey world. Bareheaded, I set out in search of a pub.

4 Inquest

Lady Winter preferred to stand.

I had arrived just as the proceedings began and slipped quickly into a seat at the back, next to Shepperton Keith.

'How are you, Ivor?' he said, giving me an examining look and the professional handshake.

'I feel like hell,' I murmured.

'Of course, of course.' He nodded gravely, and I hadn't the heart to tell him it was not a psychological trauma, but a simple hangover. I had crawled my way through several pubs, then back to spend the night at Phil's flat in Stonehouse Mansions. Phil, I remembered, had gone home to the country for his daughter Isabelle's tenth birthday party, but all the same I'd been angry at his absence and used his whisky to drink myself to sleep.

'... Amelia Irene Winter of 21 Alderney Court and Slaydon Hill House, Slaydon Hill, Bath.'

She was entirely composed, her hair confined by a black hat, and the severity of her costume only emphasized by a small white rosebud at her shoulder (a white rose buttonhole had been Vivian's daily touch of dandyism). The long face, grey hair and heavy black eyebrows hinted at how Vivian might have looked if he'd have lived to become a judge—bewigged, tight-lipped, wisdom tucked into the vulnerable pouches of flesh under the brilliant eyes. The contrast with the plump, florid countenance of the fussy little coroner was absolute.

'The Yale was locked but not the mortice—as was our custom when at home. I noticed nothing unusual. I went almost immediately to the kitchen to make myself a cup of coffee. My son was lying on the kitchen floor on his back. His right arm was flung out with the fist clenched; otherwise, it was a posture of repose. Yes, the shirt and cardigan were badly stained. I realised at once that he was dead.

'I immediately telephoned the police. It was 12.15—I remember looking at my watch. My train from Bath had been a little on the late side.'

'And what, er, did you do then?'

'I made myself a cup of coffee.'

There was a faint stir in the courtroom. I glanced at Shep Keith, but he was unmoved. Of course he had attended hundreds of inquests probably and yet ... yet why had she said it?

'No, there was no sign of a struggle or anything of that kind. My son had evidently been working on a brief; there were a number of legal papers on the desk in his study and a half empty bottle of claret. Yes, it was his custom to work late—he would open a bottle of claret after dinner and continue working until it was finished....'

She had stood there, boiling the water, pouring the milk, stirring the sugar while he lay ghastly at her feet. And yet what did we expect those suddenly bereaved by violence to do? To cry, to shriek, to tear their hair?

'No,' she was saying, 'on the contrary, the signs were that he was not expecting a visitor. He was wearing flannels, an open-necked shirt, an old grey cardigan and leather slippers. My son was rather particular about his dress and would certainly never have received anyone when he was wearing slippers.'

'Yet the fact is that he did admit a visitor at a late hour. Would that not suggest that the person he admitted was known to him, probably well known to him?'

'Nothing of the kind. My son was an hospitable and a charitable man—I cannot imagine him turning away any plausible person who had, or said he had, a claim upon his attention. That's not the question. The question is, how did the person get into the building?'

'Quite.' The coroner's face grew redder—he didn't much care for being told the questions. 'We shall be listening to evidence on that point later on. Now, Lady Winter, had Mr Winter in the weeks before his death received any threatening letters, phone calls—anything of that nature?'

'Not to my knowledge.'

'Would he have been likely to tell you if he had?'

'No.'

'I see. Then just one final question, m'lady. Have you been

able to form any conclusion as to the possible identity of your son's assailant?'

'Only that it must have been a maniac.'

The coroner puffed out his cheeks. 'And why is that?'

'Because my son was a man entirely without personal enemies.'

Lady Winter moved slowly across the well of the court and, as she took her place between Pulteney and Cyril Grayling, I recognized the set look of her face. Seized by the sudden sickness of memory, I closed my eyes and immediately I saw Marion's face, inconsolably stony beneath a black felt hat from her church-going youth and retrieved from an old hat box where it had long been laid away with lavender bags as though in expectation of this very disaster. I smelled the lavender and saw her grief-clarified countenance more stark than I had seen it then, wrapped in the miasma of my separate desolation.

And I smelled myself too—the stale sweat of yesterday's solitary whiskies. And Henrietta's smooth child smell, warm even in death.

'Ivor, are you all right?' Shep's hand was on my arm.

'Yes thanks. Just a touch of. . . .'

'Why don't we step outside for a breath of air?' Grey face, grey hair, soft grey eyes disguised by the thick lenses.

'No, I'll be okay.' I raised my head to concentrate on the proceedings; yet he kept hold of my arm, and I was grateful for it.

'. . . in other words, from the base of the throat to just below the navel, I found sixteen quite separate and distinct wounds, several of which would have been immediately fatal.' The pathologist was tall and cadaverous, his voice sonorous but without expression. 'Each wound was seven inches in length exactly, in width tapering from one and a half inches at the point of entry to less than one-sixteenth of an inch. They were inflicted with a sharp single-edged blade of those dimensions.'

'Would not the evenness of the wounds and the fact that not one overlapped the other suggest that they had been inflicted with a degree of deliberation?'

'Very possibly.'

'In other words, not the kind of wounds one might expect from a frenzied attack?'

31

'I would hesitate to conclude that the nature of the wounds entirely precludes such a possibility. Frenzy is not a scientifically precise term.'

'Perhaps not, but I imagine we are all quite clear in our own minds what it means.' The coroner nodded his fat round head two or three times as though expecting applause. He was enjoying himself. 'Now,' he said with a frown, as if coming down to business at last, 'let me ask you this. Was there much blood?'

'There was considerable initial effusion, mainly. . . .'

The nausea rose in my throat and the neat green courtroom tipped sideways. I opened my mouth. And then my hand was caught and squeezed hard. 'Breathe,' I heard.

I didn't want to breathe, I wanted to put my head under the blanket or thrust it into the gas oven or. . . .

'Hold on!'

And somehow I held on, against my will which urged me to relax, turn with the dizzy world, fall. . . .

'. . . agree with those of the Police Surgeon. The indications are that the deceased met his death between ten p.m. on April 14th and two o'clock the following morning. These are the absolute outside limits. In all probability, give or take half an hour either way, the time of death was at midnight.'

April sunlight suddenly filled the court from the big square windows high on the south side. It seemed to me some kind of signal—perhaps that the worst was over. From thereon everything was speeded up.

The pathologist was dismissed and Albert Ralph Trubshaw, the porter at Alderney Court, was called. A little gnarled, sleepy-eyed man, he was deaf enough for the coroner to be able to shout at him. He deposed that both entrances to the building—the main entrance and the Figgis Street entrance—were locked at ten p.m. The residents had keys, but no one else could enter unless let in by the porter. He had admitted no visitors on that particular night. The main entrance was kept under constant observation. No, he would not have seen anyone coming in by the Figgis Street entrance and taking the stairs rather than using the lift in the main hall. He couldn't be in two places at the same time, could he? Certainly he recalled locking that door as usual on the night in question.

I gently detached Shep's hand. I was breathing and holding on all right now. And as McQuade was called, I felt comforted—we were near the end.

I looked for some hint of the savagery of which Lady Winter had spoken, but in his dark suit, white shirt and fresh striped tie, McQuade was an ordinary, civilized figure—even the Scottishness had disappeared from his voice. The unflinching dark stare could give qualms, I thought, only to the guilty.

He described briefly his actions on being called to the scene and confirmed Lady Winter's description of the state of the flat. The police, he said, were pursuing various lines of enquiry, which for obvious reasons he would prefer not to specify, and at this time would like to ask for an adjournment to allow them to gather further evidence which they would present to the court at a later date.

The coroner huffed and puffed a bit to assert his dignity, then obediently adjourned the inquest until such date as, etc. etc.

I stood, slightly dazed, with the others.

'Sure you're all right now, Ivor?'

'Yes thanks, Shep—thanks.'

'Well, come and talk to me some time.' He shook my hand rapidly and was gone. As I turned, the spectators parted and Lady Winter came directly down the aisle to where I stood and shook my hand.

'Thank you, Ivor, for coming.' She smelled faintly of lavender. 'I think it went very well, on the whole, don't you?' Behind her on either side, Pulteney and Grayling stood guard—like a couple of heavyweight goons in an old gangster movie.

'Yes. I suppose so. Yes.' I felt a ridiculous smile coming to my lips, and fought it down.

A burly man, on his way out, swung round. 'Ah—Lady Winter!' he said, seizing her hand and pumping it. 'My most sincere condolences.' He had an immense curling moustache and explosive cheeriness of manner. ''Fraid I've been a bit dilatory, but we feel it deeply, you know, Mrs Posey and I. Deeply. If there's anything we can do, as neighbours you know—only too glad.'

'Nothing.' She withdrew her gloved hand. 'It is a kind thought though.'

'Only too glad, too glad.' He saluted and backed away.

'Oh dear,' Lady Winter said. And her bodyguard, which had closed up, relaxed.

'Your Air Force neighbour?' I enquired, this time allowing myself to smile.

'Quite. Ivor, I hope to see you soon—very soon. I know you won't forget our little conversation. If anything occurs to you, please don't hesitate to come along.'

'Yes, of course.'

I waited a few moments, then followed the tag end of the crowd into the street. The sun was warm and there was a smell of spring in the air.

'Hello, Ivor. I see you're in favour.' It was Alva Norman, immaculate in black, with a stiff white collar—odd to see him without a bow tie. 'I'm hungry. Are you hungry?'

'Yes,' I said. 'Ravenous as a matter of fact.'

'Then let's get a cab to the club.'

5 Singed Eyebrows

We washed our hands slowly and carefully, side by side in the marble washroom. Alva made a *moue* as I combed my hair with the communal comb. Then we went upstairs.

Apart from Eddy, the bar was empty—if any room could be called empty with a hundred-odd actors pinned wide-eyed on the walls.

'Morning, gentlemen.'

'Morning, Eddy. What will it be, Alva?'

'Oh, a pink gin, I think.' He took a handful of nuts and strolled over to the window.

'Two large pink gins then, Eddy.'

'Right you are, Mr Ivor. In or out?'

'Out, please—and some ice.'

'Right. How's your father then—still enjoying himself down there in the South of France?'

'He's quite well, I think, though I don't hear from him very often.'

'Wouldn't care for it much myself—I'd feel isolated among all those foreigners.'

'Isolated is the last thing he feels, I believe.'

'Ah, but then Mr Speke always did have the knack for friends, didn't he? We miss him. A lot of the members still ask after him. That will be two pounds exactly, Mr Ivor.'

This conversation was repeated almost word for word five or six times a year. Actually, my father was a surly old man who'd never had much use for other people. The only time I'd visited him at Méthamis he had outdrunk me, outwalked me and regularly beaten me at chess every evening. 'Not much good for anything, are you?' had been his parting words. 'Nothing I can do for you. I'm a poor man—a very poor man.' I rather relished the irony of being clothed in his bogus popularity.

I handed Alva his glass. His large, mobile face was more than usually lugubrious and, as he drank, his tall elegant frame shuddered.

'My God, what an absolutely ghastly performance,' he said.

'Why did you go?' I was curious; my guess was that he was even more squeamish than me.

'To cure my unbelief. There's a part of me that simply doesn't accept he's dead.'

'And did it—cure you, I mean?'

'No. I suppose it was one degree less grating than that frightful funeral, but that's about all that can be said for it. I can't stand hypocrisy.'

We looked down on the fitfully sunny street. A taxi stopped at the door and a fat man got out.

'Alva, what did you mean by saying I was *in favour*?'

'Well, you are, aren't you? You got a handshake and a chat, didn't you? All I got was a cool nod. I'm obviously *persona non grata*. I wasn't even invited to partake of the funeral bake-meats.'

'Nor was I.' But I refrained from mentioning that I had been asked to tea.

'Weren't you?' It seemed to cheer him up momentarily. 'That just shows you—she's gone over to the other side.'

'What on earth are you talking about?'

'Oh for God's sake don't be dim, Ivor. Haven't you noticed Greaser Grayling and that damp stick Pulteney clinging to her like chewing gum to a boot sole?'

'Well, yes—but after all, Pulteney's her godson, isn't he? And Cyril is Vivian's solicitor. It seems fairly natural—rather decent of them, in fact.'

'Decent? You've spent too long in the country. They're hoping to lay their sticky fingers on some of the Winter millions.'

'Oh don't be ridiculous!'

'I may be ridiculous, but I'm not a fool.' He took my empty glass from the hand. 'Let's have a drink.'

I watched him stride athletically across to the bar, like a superb tennis player subtly gone to seed. Alva and I were on affable rather than intimate terms and I had always considered him a lightweight, yet, like Lady Winter the day before, he was giving me a disconcerting feeling of unworldly innocence.

I took a chair in the corner. 'You can't really mean millions,' I said when Alva came back.

'Why not?' he said, lighting a cigarette. 'Two, at least, I should think—maybe three. You'd be amazed what a lot of money there is in bicycle pumps.'

'Bicycle pumps—was that it?'

'Something like that—something to do with air. I don't suppose you ever met Vivian's papa—Sir Donald, frightful old smoothie. He had a sort of oily diplomatic flatulence—couldn't tell you whether he wanted one lump or two without making a paragraph out of it. Amelia of course didn't drink tea. I remember once. . . .'

The bar was filling up, and I listened with only half an ear to Alva's reminiscent gossip. The gin had begun to bite and the members were swarming. What would the club be like without Vivian? I had little in common with these people, no stock of jocularity, no anecdotal vein, only the slow wit of the countryman I had become, murmuring of seasons and the sea and deeply anti-social. Perhaps I was more like my father than I chose to imagine.

'. . . and my people were as poor as church mice, but it was always I who paid for the teas, dear mean old chap that he was. I—'

36

'Mean? Vivian? Vivian wasn't mean.'

'My dear Ivor, did he ever stand you a meal?'

'I don't recall.' It was true he'd always chosen the cheaper hotels where there was a choice, but that was out of consideration for my pocket, not his. 'Alva—how well did you actually know Vivian?'

Alva blew twin plumes of smoke through his nose and cocked an eyebrow at me. 'We were at the old Col together.'

'Were you?'

'You *are* inquisitive. Oh, I don't mind. I used to worship the ground he trod on in those days. I detest the water, you know, but I became a wet bob because he was one—and I got quite good at it. I was bow to his stroke at Henley one year. We lost because I caught a crab when we were leading by a length fifty yards from the finish.'

'I'm sorry,' I said fatuously.

'I'm the sort of person who seems to put a curse on those they love. Do you know what I mean?'

'Yes,' I said slowly, 'I know what you mean.' We had accidentally taken a shocking plunge into the waters of distress. Alva's eyes were closed—against smoke or tears.

'You are the most *damnably* serious man.'

'Yes, I'm sorry. Give me one of your cigarettes, will you?'

I put the cigarette in my mouth and took a match from the fat glass holder in which the non-safety matches stand head-up, like tulips in a vase, and struck. There was an explosive plop and a great spear of flame shot upwards. I fell back, barely conscious of a sudden total silence in the bar.

And then they were laughing. Alva was doubled up.

'He lit the whole bloody torch.'

'The man's dazed.'

'He's scorched the ruddy ceiling.'

'Ha-ha-ha-ha!'

'Give the man a drink!'

Eddy beside me, 'Are you all right, Mr. Ivor?'

'Of course he's all right—get him a drink, Eddy, on me.'

'Very good, Sir Frederick.'

'What happened?' I said feebly.

Alva dabbed at his eyes with a handkerchief. 'You ignited the entire holder! Glorious—I've been waiting for that to happen for years.'

'But why?'

'You're supposed to strike down, old man—not up. I say, your eyebrows are singed—you look like the very devil. Are you sure you're all right?'

'Oh yes—quite.'

Eddy was back with a silver tray. 'Sir Frederick, Mr Hayes, Mr Palamountain, and Mr Wilshaw,' he said, placing four large pink gins on the table.

The faces at the bar were still smiling and nodding. I stood up, bowed, lifted a glass and drank.

'Well, Ivor, I take it all back—about you being so serious. I haven't laughed so much for months.'

'Thank you,' I said, sitting. 'I suppose I am now the club clown.'

'You will be if you drink all that. I'd better give you a hand. And you'll need a light.'

My eyebrows felt slightly brittle to the touch. I looked up and there was a distinct scorch mark on the ceiling. 'Alva,' I said abruptly, 'what do you think of the idea of my writing a book?'

'*Aren't* you writing a book?'

'No no, not a novel,' I said, unwilling to confess to the depths to which I had sunk in that line. 'I mean a serious work of non-fiction.'

'About what?'

'Well, I haven't thought exactly—it would rather be up to me.'

'Sounds as though some publisher has been getting at you. Hypocritical lot, publishers—"do whatever you like," they tell you, and when you do, they don't want to pay for it.'

I thought about Braithwaite, who could say in the same breath, 'Ivor, this is the best thing you've ever done. But I'm afraid we can't go above seven hundred on this one, old man'; Braithwaite with his penchant for ravaged lesbian poets, left-wing politicos, and illiterate millionaire hacks (maybe one day he'd find all three rolled into one); Braithwaite with his fat bottom and beautiful wife and spittle-spraying bray of a laugh. At least they hadn't let Braithwaite into the Club.

'. . . so long as it doesn't interfere with your Crime Column,' Alva was saying. 'I know we pay you a pittance, but if it's a question of money, I expect I could get you another five hundred. I don't want to lose you.'

'That's very touching, but I hardly think I'm indispensable to the *Gazette*.'

'Little do you know. Getting hold of you was one of the best things I ever did as literary editor, and I intend to keep you.'

'I've always wondered how you came to pitch on me in the first place.'

'Have you?' He smiled. 'Well, I don't suppose there's much harm in telling you now—in fact I think I'm absolved of my promise not to. You owe it to Vivian. Mind you, he only suggested your name, although he was quite pressing about it, as I remember. I was dubious—I knew your work of course, admired it very much, but I didn't think there would be a hope in hell of your accepting.'

Vivian again. I stubbed out my cigarette and took another of the pink gins. 'I was in rather a bad way at the time.'

'Were you? I thought as much. At least Amelia got *that* right. Vivian was a charitable man—always willing to put in a good word or lend a helping hand, so long as it didn't cost him anything. All right all right, protest registered.' He held up his hand. He frowned. 'But the point is, it makes nonsense of this business about not receiving visitors in his "working clothes," as though he were some kind of a builder's labourer.'

'I don't think the maniac theory holds much water, either.'

'Of course it doesn't. Any one of us could have rung him up at midnight. "Look here, Vivian, I know it's late and all that, but I'm in a bit of a hole, could I come up and have a chat right away?" He'd say, "All right—where are you?" "Just round the corner in a phone box." "Right," he'd say, "use the Figgis Street entrance—I'll pop down and open the door for you." Now he's not going to put on his white tie and tails for that, is he?'

'No, of course not.' It had a startling ring of reality. I wondered how often he'd done just that. 'You're saying it's likely to have been a friend who murdered him.'

'Who else? And I haven't got an alibi—have you?'

'No. But it's a contradiction in terms. What friend would wish to kill Vivian?'

'Oh my dear boy.' And he gave a sad little shrug.

I looked away, out of the window. The sun still shone, though it had started to rain. But I saw no rainbow. I had set my hand to the door of one of Vivian's secret compartments, but I had no desire to open it. I began to understand why Lady Winter had got rid of the address book.

6 A Curious Coincidence

'There you are, ducky—eleven pages of it. Everything we've got on Mr Bateman.' Her perpetual cigarette waggled inelegantly from the corner of her mouth as she spoke.

'Thank you, Molly.'

'I thought you were on the literary side.' Molly had been at the *Gazette* time out of mind and had the memory of an elephant; with her heavy grey folds of flesh, she looked rather like an elephant too.

'Well, yes.'

'What do you want with all that muck then?'

'I'm not sure myself.' I took a chair in the corner of the little library, turning my back on Molly's watchful eye.

Harold Henry Bateman had been brought to trial for the murder of Madeleine Jane Hodder on the night of July 4th. The prosecution's case as outlined on the first day of the trial seemed a very strong one. Madeleine Hodder was a first-year student at Sussex University; during the vacation she was working as a barmaid at the Drum and Monkey in Haslemere. An only child, she lived with her parents a quarter of a mile from the pub. On the evening in question she left the pub as usual to return home, and was never seen alive again.

When Madeleine had not returned by midnight, the Hodders became worried and Mr Hodder rang the pub and various friends with one of whom it was thought she might have decided to spend the night. At one o'clock Mr Hodder informed the police of her disappearance and left the house himself to look for his daughter. Some two hours later he discovered the body half-hidden in a ditch beside a track, locally known as Carter's Lane, about three-quarters of a mile outside

40

the town. She had been stabbed nine times in the chest and abdomen and had been sexually assaulted after death; the autopsy later revealed that she had been six weeks pregnant.

Bateman had been arrested two days later when one of the Drum and Monkey's regulars identified him as the fair-haired young man he had observed walking away from the pub with Madeleine at closing time. The rest of the evidence was circumstantial: bloodstains of Madeleine's AB group on Bateman's trousers, partially washed off; semen stains on a pair of his underpants; two cigarette ends of Bateman's special mentholated brand found a few yards from the scene, and, a littler lower down the lane, a clear imprint of Bateman's heel on a patch of moist ground where a freshet trickled across the path. The wounds had been inflicted with a sharp double-edged blade, such as a dagger or a dirk; Bateman had been in the habit of carrying a dirk, which he claimed to have lost some days before. He had been acquainted with Madeleine who had several times refused to go out with him, referring to him as 'a public school pest'. Finally, Bateman had no provable alibi for the time of the murder. On the whole, the evidence seemed damning.

But in law almost nothing is as it seems. Bateman, described as 'handsome and upstanding', had evidently made a good impression in the witness box. The son of a retired brigadier and chairman of the local magistrates, he had been educated at Haileybury and spent a year as an officer cadet at Sandhurst, from which he had resigned because he was 'in principle opposed to violence'. Vivian had not attempted to refute the circumstantial evidence, but under questioning had skilfully drawn from the boy an ordinary explanation for each item.

Bateman had admitted knowing Madeleine casually and having once asked her out. On that particular evening, after leaving another pub, he had accidentally encountered her and walked her to the corner of the road in which she lived. He had then gone straight home, made himself some sandwiches in the kitchen—in the course of which he had cut his thumb quite badly with the bread knife, making 'an awful mess of myself'—and had then gone to bed (his parents having already retired).

He knew Carter's Lane well and had passed along it that very afternoon, as he often did, on his way to the woods at the top of the hill which was an excellent place for bird-watching, his principal hobby. He never smoked in the woods but it was quite likely that he had smoked in the lane on his way there and back. The dirk, which had been lost, he carried as a useful tool for cutting branches in order to construct hides for bird-watching. The semen stains were a result of masturbation. Bateman had an explanation for everything and he remained quite unshaken under cross-examination.

One of the less pleasant innuendos of the case for the defence was the clear suggestion of Madeleine Hodder's promiscuity. Two students from her university were produced, each admitting that he might have been responsible for her pregnancy. Yet perhaps a clinching argument for Bateman's innocence was that the bloodstains on his clothing had no significance, for—a fact which Vivian brought out with aplomb—he shared the same uncommon blood type as Madeleine.

The jury took scarcely more than ten minutes to arrive at a unanimous verdict of Not Guilty.

It was not a perverse verdict and yet it must have left more than a lingering doubt. Bateman's answers sounded to my ears like the exasperatingly convincing excuses of a practised liar. But even a practised liar was not necessarily guilty. A dash of rain against the window made me look up. Not far away the soot-streaked dome of St Paul's squatted sad and diminished by the high-rise office buildings that disfigured the City.

I went over to Molly's desk. 'Can I cadge a cigarette?'

'Sure. There we are, ducks. Keep the packet, there are only a couple left anyhow.' Her large grey eyes regarded me sorrowfully. 'Turns your stomach, does it?'

'Yes, a bit.'

'If you ask me, they should have hanged the little sod.'

'He was acquitted, you know.'

'Pah, you've only got to take one look at him to see he was guilty as hell.'

Back at the table I lit a cigarette and opened the folder of glossy prints. Hastily skipping the more macabre, I found an obviously posed shot of Madeleine Hodder; her even-toothed smile was posed too, I thought—too pretty for the rest of the face: dark hair cut very short, a small rather pointed nose, strongly marked eyebrows and intense, deep-set eyes. It was a face of obvious intelligence and character.

42

Bateman had the sort of good looks that had gone out of fashion with Leslie Howard—well-bred and wistful, with a dimpled chin and a little too much nose, but harmlessly conventional and giving away nothing. The two faces had nothing in common except youth.

Bateman's second trial—for the rape and attempted murder of Jennifer Thrush—revealed the treacherous animal beneath the bland mask. To his plea of Guilty had been added an impressive array of expert psychiatric testimony (some of it, predictably enough, from Shepperton Keith) to prove that abnormality of mind had substantially impaired his mental responsibility for his actions. Incidents of violence, which, if they had been revealed at the first trial might have made all the difference, were now paraded forth with earnest authority: he had stabbed the matron at his school with a pair of scissors; at Sandhurst he had attacked an under-officer with a bayonet; more recently, he had been involved in a knife fight at a pub in Milford.

It had been at this same pub that Bateman had been arrested on Christmas Eve, only two and a half hours after his attack on Jennifer Thrush.

The facts were not in dispute. Jennifer lived at home and, since leaving school, had worked in a local stationery shop. Her father was a carpenter and odd-job man. Her mother had worked as a daily woman for the Batemans for sixteen years; as children, Harold and Jennifer had frequently played together.

It was the custom for the Thrushes—mother, father and daughter—to be invited to the Batemans' at six o'clock every Christmas Eve. Brigadier Bateman served rum punch, Mrs Bateman mince pies, and presents were exchanged. This year, Jennifer had been given a box of six embroidered Irish linen handkerchiefs. At seven Mr and Mrs Thrush had left, Jennifer staying on for a few minutes to help Mrs Bateman prepare the stuffing for the next day's turkey. Just before seven-thirty, Harold had escorted her home. Less than half an hour later she had been picked up by a passing driver on the Milford Road, half-conscious and bleeding from seven deep stab wounds which had, miraculously, missed the vital organs.

Bateman was deemed to have committed the crime while the balance of his mind was disturbed and was sentenced to be confined during Her Majesty's pleasure.

I laid down the page and stubbed out my cigarette. Surely no sane woman would have trusted herself alone with Bateman after the Hodder trial—no sane woman *except* Jennifer Thrush, who knew him from childhood, for whom he must have been almost a brother. But others would have known better—his father, his mother.

And Vivian. He must have known, must have at least guessed that his client was guilty of the Hodder murder. Of course he had been bound to use his talents—in Vivian's case, not just an astute legal mind, but an impression he always gave of irrefutable logic and patent sincerity—to make doubt out of truth, to put a face of innocence upon the face of guilt; but to what extent does professionalism absolve a barrister from moral complicity in concealing a crime, and had Vivian not guarded a little guilt in one of those secret compartments away from the daylight?

As soon as I asked myself the question, I had the answer. Sitting in the Rotonde that bitter winter morning, reading of Bateman's second arrest, what had struck Vivian white-faced had been remorse. By his own efforts he had released a monster upon a trusting world to commit a second crime hardly less terrible than the first—maiming, not murder, seven wounds to nine for Hodder, yet. . . . I paused. Seven and nine—sixteen. With a flush of adrenalin I recalled the pathologist's words that morning—'I found sixteen separate and distinct wounds. . . .' What did it mean? Probably just one of those curious coincidences—almost certainly. Almost. But if not, what?

Outside a pigeon was fluttering foolishly at its own reflection in the window, but the new *Gazette* building has no ledges for perching and the bird flew heavily off towards St Paul's.

Had the moral complicity come home to roost in Vivian's own body? I was being over-imaginative, as one says to children afraid in the dark. But that's what Lady Winter had hired—asked—me to do: imagine. And we were in the dark. And suddenly I was afraid.

I closed the folder carefully and took it over to the desk.

'Molly, can I use your phone?'

'Go ahead, ducks.'

I got an outside line and dialled. As it rang, I knew that, if she didn't answer, I would let it go. But she was there all right, and she would be delighted if I came to tea—about five o'clock. She asked no questions—no vulgar curiosity at Alderney Court—but all the same I felt burdened with her expectation. And I had such a pathetically small scrap of information to offer—not even information; a hint, a guess, a vagueness.

'Feeling better, are we?'

'What? Oh—yes. I mean, no. I. . . .'

For the first time, Molly smiled. 'You want to make up your mind, love,' she said.

7 Outmaneuvred

'Going to visit her ladyship?' asked the moustachioed man squashed uncomfortably against me in the tiny lift.

'Er, yes,' I murmured, wondering if I was going to be asked for a donation.

'Thought so. Never forget a mug. Saw you talking to her ladyship after the inquest, right? Or am I wrong?'

'Quite right. Wing-Commander Moser?'

'Posey, old man. Squadron-Leader—retired. One of the Winter crowd, eh? Depressing business. Gives you a thirst. How about a snifter? What say?'

'Say no—I mean, no thanks, not just at the moment.'

'All right, old man—if that's how you feel. Another time. Very'd be glad to see you.'

The old iron cage ground to a stop. 'Very what?'

'*Very*—the wife. Mrs Posey—likes a bit of company. This is our stop.' He slammed back the grill and pushed open the door. 'You first. Going to be a bit on the quiet side round here in the future, eh?'

I stepped into the passage. 'Is it?'

'You bet.' He gave me a wink. 'Mum's the word, eh?'

'Oh—well, goodbye.'

'Jolly good show.' And he marched off to the other end of the passage. But as I rang the bell, I was aware of him observing me from the half-open door of his flat.

'Ivor—how nice of you to come so soon.' She gave me her hand and I was surprised at the strength of her grip; yet beneath the warmth of her welcome, I thought I detected a note of inquiry, and again I felt uneasy at the meagreness of my information.

The afternoon was overcast and the sitting room had an almost sacerdotal dimness. Lady Winter sat in her high-backed chair and I took my by now accustomed place on the couch. On the sideboard stood a glass vase of tightly-budded white roses, and next to it, a decanter—of sherry this time. I had the impression I was not to be offered any until I had delivered a satisfactory report.

I had difficulty finding my voice. The room was so soundless that the silence seemed to have a tangible quality, and when I spoke it was rather like shouting in church.

'I've been doing some digging into the Bateman case,' I said baldly. 'Or, rather, cases. I wonder how much you remember of the details of the trials?'

'Very little. I never followed Vivian's cases unless he asked me to. I only know the general outlines. I was interested because Brigadier Bateman was an old friend of my husband's.'

'Was he indeed?'

'Ronnie Bateman was military attaché in Ankara when my husband was First Secretary there before the war. He had an extraordinarily dull wife.'

'I see.' I cleared my throat; I'd been smoking too much, yet I badly needed a cigarette now. 'I take it you don't read the *Gazette?*'

'I'm afraid not,' she said, as though I'd asked whether she was in the habit of riding her bicycle naked through the streets of Bath.

'In that case, would you mind taking a look at these?' I stood up and handed her the *Gazette* cuttings. 'Or, rather, read them fairly carefully. Shall I turn on a light?'

'That won't be necessary.' And, holding the pages at an angle to catch the light from the window, she began to read.

I sat down again and looked at the silver cigarette box on the table, reluctant to open it without permission. I felt like a schoolboy—and had a ridiculous schoolboy impulse to giggle. *An extraordinarily dull wife*! Or had she said *life* and I had misheard it? But that was even more absurd; the life of a soldier couldn't be all that dull. Lady Winter's asperity bespoke no particular malice, yet in my heart of hearts I too felt that dullness was a sort of crime—a crime against life. Perhaps the maternal dullness had so blanketed the boy that he could only cut himself loose with knives. Better to have one's child murdered than to have him a murderer. Yet that was nonsense—Vivian was dead, and Harold Bateman was alive. But how had the Brigadier felt when his son was freed? Vivian had let the side down, Vivian bore the responsibility. Perhaps the old man had decided to visit his son's guilt upon the head of his old friend's son—a soldier, knowing all the details, accustomed to planning, used to killing, ruthless, tough, determined. Mad. A military monster with a dull wife.

Lady Winter turned another page and the little noise brought me to my senses. I rubbed my eyebrows, still brittle from the singeing. How could she possibly read in this twilight? I longed for light, for a clean breath in this stifling air, for a. . . .

'That is very interesting, Ivor.' She laid the cuttings on her knee and gave them a little tap with her fingernail.

Had she got it? Her eyes were invisible in their shadowed sockets. I waited anxiously.

'It's the stabbings of course. Nine and seven to Vivian's sixteen.'

'That's it.' I drew the cigarette box towards me. 'May I?' At her nod, I took a cigarette. 'Of course it's probably no more than a curious coincidence, but if not. . . .'

'If not?'

'Then it was intended.' I struck the match, a kindly light amidst the encircling gloom. 'Of course, again that may not mean very much—after all, the details are all there in the paper. Anyone could have read them.'

'Anyone could have read them. But only the murderer used them. Why?'

'Two reasons I can think of. One is just as a complication, a little red herring to send the police jogging off down the wrong path, trying to find a connection with Bateman that doesn't

47

exist. The second is that it was a kind of sign manual, a rather esoteric one I admit—but an indication that such a connection does indeed exist.'

'And what would be the nature of that connection?'

I didn't object to her cross-examination; it was leading me round to questions of my own. But I don't think well sitting down, so I stood up and began to perambulate slowly.

'I think it must have to do with an idea of retribution. That ties in with the fact that the murderer went out of his way to advertise a connection at all—in however recondite a manner. If I am right and this is some warped idea of justice, then justice has to be seen to be done too—hence the sixteen stabbings. I know it sounds far-fetched, but—'

'On the contrary, Ivor, I don't find it far-fetched at all. It is the first piece of sense I have heard in the whole business. Presumably Bateman would have been the murderer's first choice, but he, I imagine, is unavailable for execution, locked away in some "safe" place. No, I understand it quite well. A life for a life.'

'Two lives,' I murmured.

'Two?'

'Madeleine Hodder was pregnant.'

'So she was. So where does that leave us?'

'Well, it leaves us with the people who might have a motive for exacting retribution.' I stopped and tapped some ash into the ashtray.

'The Hodders—and, I suppose, the Thrushes?'

'Well yes—but they're very ordinary people. Thrush is a carpenter and—'

'Knows about sharp tools.'

'—and Hodder's a milkman, I believe.'

'You mean the association with cows exempts him from normal human emotion?'

'Normal?'

'Natural human feeling, then. We won't quibble.'

'All right. But the point is, would people like Hodder and Thrush have the organizing ability and determination, the cleverness, if you like, to carry out this sort of crime?'

'We can't tell till we've met them. But you can't have it both ways. You can't say on the one hand, this was an act of retribution, but on the other, there's no one, having the motive, who's capable of performing the act. Not if you take it seriously.'

I hesitated, stubbed out my cigarette and sat down. 'I'm not sure I do take it seriously. Not yet.'

'What do you mean?' Sharp.

'Lady Winter, when we talked yesterday afternoon, you asked me to consider, not so much *who* murdered Vivian, as *why* he was murdered, that is to say, the motive. There are three—three motives—I can think of. The first is sex— passion, jealousy, humiliation, something of that sort, which is rather suggested by the nature of the attack itself. The second is money—someone who owed Vivian money or was refused it or expected to gain it by his death. And the third motive is retribution—vengeance, if you like—which I'm naturally more inclined to, as I think you are, because it is a public motive rather than a private one and because it must involve someone of whom we know nothing, a stranger, a seriously disturbed personality. I would say, a maniac. In that sense it's the least unattractive motive, but also—except for this one rather tenuous piece of quasi-evidence—the least likely.' I paused, unable to judge her reaction in the crepuscular dimness. 'May I go on?'

'Pray do. But first I think you might pour us each a glass of sherry.'

I obliged with alacrity; at least I hadn't had my head bitten off. I sipped the sherry—it was good, dry, with a taste like the smell inside an empty cigar box.

'What I want is to be in a position to discount the other motives,' I said, returning to the couch. 'Perhaps all I'm asking for is reassurance. Lady Winter, did you destroy Vivian's address book and engagement diary?'

'Yes. I did.'

'May I ask why?'

'For the same reason I destroyed much of his correspondence. It was his private life. The dead deserve as much decent privacy as the living, wouldn't you agree? Besides, they might have caused a great deal of unnecessary unpleasantness to those concerned. Vivian would have hated that.'

'Yes.' I drank some more sherry and wondered how much further I could push it. 'But still, don't you think there might have been someone in the address book, someone he might not have seen for years, who felt, well, rejected, ill-used, with whatever neurotic basis, angry and vengeful?'

'Do you think that, Ivor?'

'Frankly no.' I was relieved at the opportunity to be honest.

'Love may not always be wise, but I don't think, with regard to Vivian, it would ever have been murderous. And also I doubt whether a woman would have been physically capable of this crime.'

'No, probably not.' But jealousy, I thought, was not confined to women, and for a fleeting moment my mind went to Alva Norman. 'Yes, well. Then that leaves the question of money.' I was suddenly embarrassed—and angry at myself for such conventional prudishness—and quickly lit a cigarette, but the flare of the match seemed only to illuminate my awkwardness.

'Vivian's money?' she gently prompted.

'Yes. McQuade told me that I'd been left a small legacy, and when I rather jokingly asked him whether that made me a suspect, he said yes, it did—that anyone benefiting under a murdered man's will is automatically suspect. And he went on to say that there were quite a number of beneficiaries. So I— well, the point is—I mean—'

'You want to know who they are?' There was a hint of amusement in her voice.

'No!' I said, a little too loudly. 'Not at all, I—'

'Nothing could be easier.' She stood up. 'I shall ring Cyril Grayling at once and tell him to send you a copy of the will. Then you can see for yourself.'

'No, really. . . .' I, too, stood.

She touched my arm lightly. '*Calmez-vous, mon cher.*' And then, as she left the room—for the phone was in the hallway— I was sure I heard her laugh.

I filled up my glass and went over to the window. The rain had settled in steadily, and in the premature twilight the garden below looked as drab and gloomy as my own. There were no swings, no sandpit; perhaps children were forbidden at Alderney Court, the garden reserved solely for dogs and the elderly. I drew on my cigarette and my features were reflected redly back at me from the window pane. Why had Lady Winter found my mention of the will so amusing? Because, of course, it was ridiculous to imagine anyone would have

50

murdered Vivian for money. Who, except Grayling, would have even known the terms of the new will?

'Ivor—Cyril would like a word with you. He needs your address.'

'Right.' I put my glass down and went into the hall.

After I had given him the details, Cyril said, 'You know, professionally speaking, I don't really approve of this.'

'And unprofessionally?'

'Oh well—we have to obey orders, don't we?' He gave a laugh of exasperated amusement. 'Anyway, good luck. I shall see you on Saturday.'

'What?' I said, but he had put down the phone.

Lady Winter was seated at a bureau in the corner of the sitting room, writing, illuminated by a single lamp.

'Ivor,' she said over her shoulder, 'would you mind drawing the curtains.'

I did so with a feeling of foreboding, as though I was closing myself into a situation not of my choosing. I switched on the lamp beside the couch and sat down and tried to drink my sherry tranquilly. I knew in my bones I ought to get up and go. But I knew I wouldn't.

'Here we are, Ivor.' She held out an envelope.

I accepted the missive gingerly; it was addressed to *Brigadier R.T.W. Bateman, CB, DSO, The Old Rectory, Upper Lane, Haslemere.* My heart sank.

'What's this?' I asked insouciantly.

'It's just a brief note of introduction. I've said you are an old friend of the family and a writer. You'll like Ronnie. I think you should see him first—he'll be of great help, I'm sure.' She went over to the sideboard and poured more sherry.

'First?' I said to her back.

'Before Hodder and Thrush—I think you should definitely have a chat with them.'

'Hold on a minute. I—'

'It's got to be done, hasn't it?' she said, turning to me with a brilliant smile so like Vivian's that I was weakened by the tugs of seductive memory. 'And you are so obviously the man to do it—a newspaper man and—'

'Reviewer,' I muttered.

'All the better—then you won't frighten them off. I think you should go down tomorrow, before anyone else will have made the connection. One must strike while the iron's hot, don't you agree?'

'Well, I . . .'

'And then I suggest you come to dinner on Saturday evening. I have invited Cyril, and Mrs Blaine will be on hand to do the cooking—and, despite her faults, she is an excellent cook. We shall have a council of war—and you must stay the night.'

'That's most kind of you, but, look, really you know,' I was moved to protest, 'I'm not at all good at that sort of thing. I've never interviewed anyone in my life.'

'Nonsense. You are very persuasive, Ivor, and, I may say, extremely good at eliciting information.' She laughed and, crossing the room, sat down with a brisk sweep of skirts.

'Honestly, I'm not at all sure I'm your man. I—'

'Ivor, we are agreed that Vivian was not murdered over any piffling matter of money or vulgar sexual involvement. He was killed for a reason—as a scapegoat, a symbol—as much in the line of duty as a soldier fallen in battle.'

'Yes—well.' In a moment of clarity, I saw her on the other side of the fence—if she had been Mrs Hodder, what an avenging angel she.

'The truth *must* lie there!'

'All right, I'll give it a go round,' I said wearily; I didn't think truth was so easily found lying about on the surface.

'Splendid. Then perhaps you will stay to supper—a scratch meal, I'm afraid. But there's a Harrods game pie in the larder and there's still a good stock of Vivian's '70 Lafitte. Do you play chess?'

'Oh—a little, passably, not very well.'

'Good, then we will be on equal terms.'

I shall always remember that evening—the pie with Mrs Blaine's own potato salad, the perfume of the wine (we drank two bottles) which smoothed the sharp edges of my unease, but most of all the chess. We played on one of those marquetry tables with a chess board inlaid; the set itself was of the most intricately carved ivory, white and red, a gift, she told me, of some minor Chinese warlord beheaded a month later ('Of course if he'd lived, we'd have had to give it back, but one cannot be bribed by the dead').

Under the light of the single lamp, I covertly watched Lady

Winter. And in that island of silent combat, girt with darkness and shadows, there was a curious bonding. I, too, began to feel there was truth available, there was an answer if only on a level as unconsciously primitive as the game we were playing.

Myself, I am a stolid, conventional player and after a dozen moves, I began to feel I had the game within my grasp. Just before each move, Lady Winter had the odd habit of pulling her chin—a classic gesture of sagacity—but her actual moves. had no discernible logic and no relation at all to my rather obvious strategy. After twenty moves or so, I had both her bishops and three pawns to a knight and one pawn of mine, and I had her queen in jeopardy. This she blandly ignored—or didn't see—and as I took the queen, I gave a little grunt of satisfaction and sympathy.

She raised her head and gave me such a look of steel, I blushed, faltered. And then she moved—moved her king's knight, but I didn't see it because she smiled a smile of glittering intimacy so that I turned away, turned to the solace of the non-combative gloom, even the familiarity of my nightmare—ghosts riding, death at hand—being preferable to such a victory.

'Check,' she said, 'check mate.'

I looked down in astonishment. 'Yes,' I said slowly, 'you're quite right. I didn't see it.'

8 Soldiering On

The drive down the Portsmouth Road had been much faster than I had expected, so it was not yet nine when I parked in front of the Drum and Monkey—and I couldn't decently call on Brigadier Bateman before ten. I bought a town plan and twenty cigarettes from the newsagent and decided to retrace the route Harold Bateman and Madeleine had taken on her last night.

It was a bright, crisp morning. Just below the brow of the

hill I passed the top of Upper Lane where there was a large house screened by a high fence and a row of Lombardy poplars; this I took to be the Old Rectory. Further on, beyond the last of the houses, there was a turning to the left marked *Carter's Lane* in white paint on an old wooden board. After the first hundred yards it was little more than a track, with hedgerows close on either side and untrodden grasses wet from the night's rain. I marked the shallow ditch where Madeleine's body had been found, then, climbing a mossy stile, entered a pine plantation. Set in regular rows, the trees were of almost full growth and little of the bright April sunlight filtered through the furred branches. No noise, no movement—no birds here. Did the police not know pine woods were no place for an ornithologist?

Soon the plantation gave way to a straggle of brambles and slender birches and young bracken, and then I was in the open, on the edge of a great meadow—Wightman's Mede—that stretched down the valley. Beyond, the last tip of Surrey and the great expanse of Sussex lay wide and fair in the sun. White sheep were delicately embroidered on the green fields, cows moved almost imperceptibly, a hawk rose high. It was a scene of placid domesticity, with none of the underlying sense of turbulence and melancholy the sea brings to the coastal lands. Beachy Head is a natural destroyer, but this place ought to have been a stranger to violent death. And yet it was here, perhaps on this particular spot, that Jennifer Thrush had been dragged down, stabbed, and violated. I half expected to see traces of blood on the bracken.

I turned away abruptly and a sudden flutter of birds took twittering flight, rose swiftly, wheeled twice, then resettled a little further off.

I pushed back the way I had come, climbing the stile, and lighting a cigarette in the lane. I threw it away, hardly smoked, at the Old Rectory gate and, straightening my tie, I went up the curling driveway, my sodden trousers clinging clammily to my ankles.

'Is the Brigadier expecting you?'

'I have a note for him.' I handed Lady Winter's letter to the middle-aged woman who had opened the door. Round-faced and rosy-cheeked with greying hair and a ready smile, this, I guessed, was Mrs Thrush. She invited me in and asked me to wait.

I wiped my muddy feet on the mat. The house was a large, badly proportioned late Victorian mansion, the last of a type built in expectation of an unending supply of domestic servants. But inside it was spacious and airy, with a high arched window at the head of the stairs and a gallery running round two sides, a squat mahogany clock ticked softly from a wall bracket, and on top of a large mediaeval chest stood a gleaming copper vase filled with irises and yellow tulips. The hall had that peculiarly tranquil smell which comes from the mingling of woodsmoke and furniture polish and coffee and fresh-cut flowers.

'Mr Speke? I'm Bateman. Do please come in.'

My picture of the mad soldier, heavy faced and sinister eyed, instantly vanished—the Brigadier was a small, quick, lithe sort of man with an alert and humorous look.

'Sit sit. Cigarette?'

I accepted one and settled myself into a deep leather armchair on one side of the fireplace as the Brigadier took the other. The sunlight, falling full into the book-lined room, rendered almost invisible the flames of the log fire, but I was glad of their warmth.

'Amelia tells me you're a writer. Should I know your work? Dear me, how clumsy that sounds.'

'That's all right. I wrote three or four novels some years ago, but I'd be surprised if you'd heard of them.'

'Chucked it, eh? Not a very lucrative enterprise, I imagine. And yet, you know, your name seems to ring a bell. You don't contribute to *Country Life* by any chance?'

I laughed. 'I'm afraid not. I do a certain amount of book reviewing for the *Gazette*.'

'Of course, how very stupid of me. I.W.J. Speke—you do the thrillers, don't you? And excellently well, if I may say so. How most interesting.'

'I'm not sure I'd call it that—not most of the time.'

'Wouldn't you? Would you not? No, they're rather a sorry lot these days perhaps. Though I must confess I'm extremely partial to Dick Francis—my only cavil there is that his heroes seem so curiously anti-social. You know what I mean?'

'A chip on the shoulder?'

'Exactly.' He gave a quick pleased laugh. 'Still, my dear

chap, I'm sure you didn't come down here to listen to my views about detective stories. Tell me, how is Amelia?'

'Bearing up pretty well on the whole.'

'Umm. A woman of very decided character, Amelia. Terrible business that—terrible. You knew Vivian, of course?'

'Very well. I was at Cambridge with him.' I drew on my cigarette, then threw it into the fire. 'As a matter of fact, it's to do with Vivian that I wanted to talk to you, sir.'

'Is it?' He stared at me; his eyes were of a strikingly vivid pale blue. 'Fire away.'

'Well, sir, it's no more than a possibility of course, but Lady Winter—Amelia—has a theory that Vivian's murder might have a connection with what happened down here. I'll try to put it as succinctly as I can. You see....' As I talked, the intentness of his gaze never wavered, giving me, oddly enough, more confidence in the substance of what I had to say.

When I had finished, he got up and went over to the window and stood for a while looking out and softly jingling the change in his pocket. The only sound in the room was the stirring of the logs and the ticking of the brass carriage clock on the mantelpiece.

'Well,' he turned and came slowly back to the fireplace, 'I'm not sure there's a great deal in it. But if Amelia thinks so, that's good enough for me. She was always the brains of that outfit.' He took a cigarette and lit it and began to smoke in swift short puffs. 'Of course, you'll want to see for yourself. You won't get much from Billy—Billy Thrush. He's a deaf-mute, you know—a competent workman, but not very bright. I hardly think he'd know how to go about buying a railway ticket to London, let alone getting there. No, I think you can give Billy the go-by. As for Mrs Thrush—that's the good body who let you in—frankly I don't think she'd be up to planning much more than the next meal. She's a woman entirely without malice in her make-up—you can take my word for that.'

I nodded and then, as he looked at me, 'Yes,' I said firmly.

'Come,' he said, getting up and walking briskly to the window. As I came to stand beside him, he put his arm through mine. 'There they are—that's Billy Thrush, and my wife.' He pointed to the two figures on the lawn—Mrs Bateman, tall, rather angular, something regal in her stance; she had a sheaf of gladioli on one arm and was gesticulating with the other as she talked to a short, stolid man who was totally fixed in concentration on her.

'He hears nothing, you know, and his lip-reading is elementary, but in a curious way he seems to absorb everything one says.'

As the sun clipped behind a cloud, a shadow crept across the garden. At the same moment Mrs Bateman finished her instructions and, turning, saw us at the window and smiled. It was a smile of pleasure and reassurance—from one gentle person to another. A dull woman she might be, I thought as the Brigadier vigorously waved back, but a decent, kindly, vulnerable one.

'There's something brittle about our kind, Speke,' he said meditatively. 'Frankly, I don't know what would have happened to Anne if Jennifer had died. We can take the initial shock of loss or disaster all right, far better than the Thrushes of this world, but when it comes down to surviving after the event, they have it over us every time. Perhaps it's because they don't feel the need to ask questions. Whereas we go on asking—"Why did it happen?", "What if I had done this or that or the other?"'

'We ask,' I said, 'but we don't talk.'

'Ah—then you know what I mean.'

'I lost my only child. Several years ago now. It was an accident but. . . . She was just a little girl.'

'And it gets no better?'

'No. It hasn't. Not for me. Perhaps it might have if . . . if I had talked.' Yet it wasn't what I meant. For I had talked, to Vivian, to Shep many times at ten pounds an hour. Suddenly the sun returned and, as the garden was sharpened with clean bright light, my body was suffused with the fresh pain of Henrietta's death.

'Here,' said Bateman, 'come along and sit down.' He led me back to the chair.

'I'm sorry,' I murmured.

'My dear fellow.' He shook his head. The sun was full on his face and he raised a hand to shield his eyes from the glare. 'My son, you know, was a boy without any of the normal vices—he smoked a little, but never took any kind of drugs the way they do these days even at the best schools, hardly drank, didn't bet or gamble or anything like that, didn't go out with the girls, drove the car like an old lady. I'm not saying he was a sissy—he was tough in his way, very fit, and he always had this streak of recklessness. But no inner strength. LMF, as we call it in the army.'

'LMF?'

'Lack of moral fibre. Where does moral fibre come from? Is it bred? I don't know. Hal was the child of our middle age—Anne was forty-three when he was born. We had given up hope—so perhaps in the event we expected too much. I don't think we cosseted him though—and we certainly didn't neglect him. And as far as I know, there's no bad blood in the family. Yet the moral responsibility must lie somewhere. But where, Speke, that's the problem—where?'

'God knows.'

'Does He? I've always had the conventional man's belief in the Deity, but that's no help to me at all now. In fact, it seems to me perfectly ridiculous. As a magistrate, I believed in justice as something one could get reasonably close to, but in all conscience, I could never sit on the Bench again.' He stayed quite still, shading his eyes.

'Is that because of the verdict in the Hodder trial?'

'You mean, did I know Hal was guilty?' He lowered his hand and regarded me with his piercing blue gaze. 'Yes, I knew all right—so did Anne in her heart of hearts. Of course, we had no *proof*. But it had all the hallmarks, you see. Hal panicked easily—he'd never have made a soldier. I fancy he tried to kiss Madeleine, she slapped him and he—well, over-reacted, we call it nowadays. I blame myself for instructing my solicitor to brief Winter—but, an old friend of the family, don't you know. He could hardly refuse. And now you tell me that possibly he was engulfed by that selfsame violence.'

'It didn't occur to you that Vivian might get him off?'

'No,' he said sadly.

'What did you do?'

'It was a nightmare. We tried to get him committed—he wouldn't do so voluntarily—but it was no soap with the trick cyclists, not after that verdict. We tried to keep an eye on him the whole time—unobtrusively of course. I gave up my public duties, my wife her voluntary work. But of course Hal resented and hated it, so in the end we sent him off to a cousin of my wife's in South Africa for a year.

58

'When he came back last December, we told ourselves it had worked. He seemed more confident, stronger in himself, less nervy. There was one unpleasant incident when he came home after closing time quite badly beaten up—a pub brawl, I expect, though he wouldn't say. We put it down to youthful high spirits, I'm afraid.'

'And of course Jenny Thrush was the last person in the world you thought he'd harm?'

'Quite. Of course I should have known better. An old soldier—always guard your flanks. But we were pleased, do you see, that Christmas Eve. We could almost pretend things were back to normal. Normal. What's difficult for people like us to accept very often is that there's no such thing as the normal—if by that one means a peaceable, easy, decent flow of life. One simply has to keep soldiering on.'

'Yes,' I said, 'yes. I wonder—what can you tell me about the Hodders?'

'I know Hodder slightly. He's our milkman, you know. I'd occasionally have a little chat with him. I'm a great believer in chats—as you can see.' He smiled a little sadly. 'Gives you the feel of what's going on—and I used to be on the Council before all this. Hodder's a remarkably intelligent man, leftish, you know, so he'd never have voted for me, but I used to get a lot out of him. He's a notable chess player—county champion once, I believe. His wife's a nice woman, a bit nervy, works in the local bakery.'

'How do they feel about it?'

'I don't know. We tried to do what we could of course, but quite understandably they didn't want anything to do with us.' He flicked some ash into the fire. 'Have you thought about how you're going to approach him, by the way?'

'Well no—not exactly.'

'Then if I may make a suggestion, why not say you're writing a book?'

'About what?' I was startled.

'About all this. About what the trail of violence does to people. After all, you're a writer.'

'Yes,' I said, rising to my feet. 'Yes.'

Bateman stood up at once. 'My dear fellow, of course, you'll want to be off.'

'I thought I'd try to catch the Hodders at lunchtime.'

'Good idea.' He led the way into the hall. 'It's just about eleven—you'll probably find Hodder in the pub at the bottom of the hill. He'll have finished his rounds by now. He once told me, after all that milk, he couldn't wait for his first pint. Did you have a hat? No hat.'

We stood on the front step. The sun had warmed the day and filled the air with the odours of spring.

'Goodbye, sir. And thank you for all your help.'

'Help? My dear chap. I should have said the boot was rather on the other foot. I enjoyed our chat a great deal.'

We shook hands and he held on to mine a moment longer than necessary. 'Look here, Speke, if there's anything in this theory of yours—and I'm by no means convinced—still, if there is, you ought to take care.'

'All right, sir, I'll take care.'

'Splendid.' He let go of my hand. 'Please give my kindest regards to Amelia.'

'I shall.'

When I was halfway along the drive, he called out, 'Just go straight down.'

I turned and gave a little wave to the old soldier, firm-lipped and straight-backed, on his doorstep.

9 Vision of the Future

'What's done's done. It's no good moping.' Hodder drank some of his beer. He looked so startlingly like his daughter that I'd spotted him at once without having to ask at the bar—the same dark, intelligent good looks, the pointed nose, the slightly quizzical regard. 'I see too much of that round here.'

'Too much moping?'

'Living in the past. Couples rattling around in their big houses, central heating going full blast, swimming pool, sculp-tured garden, a Jag for the boss and a Mini for the wife—and all they do is moan about things not being what they used to be. They're living in clover but from the way they talk it might be a bed of nettles.'

'People like the Batemans?'

'Oh, the Brig's okay. He's a doer—I like a doer. And he's fair—by his standards. He doesn't fight dirty. I don't blame the Brig. I ran against him for the Council a couple of times— fair clobbered me.' He smiled. 'Thinks I'm a Commie.'

'Are you?'

Hodder laughed wryly. 'Soft left is about as far as I go. But they don't understand nothing round here. You talk about free milk for the kids, and they're on about the totalitarian state destroying private compassion. See, in my job you want to keep the customers happy, so I always have a smile and a bit of a joke ready. Well, a couple of days after Maddy died I was back at work—I'm not one for sitting at home—and they all expected me to have a long face and be bowed down with misery. But you can't change your ways, you know, and whatever I feel inside, I've got a cheerful nature. And every time I'd give them a grin I could hear them thinking, "That Wally Hodder's a heartless bastard." Talk about compassion!'

I wondered if this was a trace of the paranoia I was looking for. I said, 'But that doesn't apply to everyone, surely—the Brigadier, for instance?'

'No—not him. You know what he did after the trial? Him and his wife came round and paid us a call, to express their sympathy.' He finished his beer, then sighed. 'Only Edna wouldn't see them.'

'Let me get you another?'

'Thanks, I won't say no.'

I ordered two pints of Director's bitter—curious name for a beer; the only directors I knew drank whisky or claret.

'Cheers.'

'You mentioned your wife—how's she taken all this?' I offered him a cigarette.

'It hit her hard. No thanks—don't smoke. She's a bit on the religious side—not fanatic, but a regular churchgoer. Or was. She hasn't been inside the church since it happened. I've often noticed with church people—they think religion buttons everything up, so they don't have to worry about the important things too much. But when they're really up against it, all that faith and comfort seems like so much piss and wind. Then they're worse off than the rest of us. It's partly the shame. In my view, that's mostly what religion's for—to make you ashamed of things you can't help, aren't responsible for. Like being alive.' He laughed sharply. 'I sound like Maddy.

'No, but I'm serious. If you're a victim, that's God's will— you deserve it, so don't make a protest, don't rock the boat or Noah might fall out of the Ark. In our system it's only the rich and the criminal classes have rights—never the victims. Not that Edna was ever one for protesting anyway—she was always quiet like. But she can't accept it neither. Underneath, she's angry, but she can't show it.'

'Angry—or guilty?'

Hodder stared at the drifting smoke from my cigarette, then raised his hand and brusquely brushed it away. 'Both. Yes, I guess she thinks it was all her fault somehow. She never got on too well with Maddy, didn't understand her. Maddy was really bright and knew it and didn't mind showing it. She always said what she thought—straight out. She had views on everything, she did.

'She could be terribly sarcastic—very keen on politics she was—but most people didn't mind. She had a way with her, you see. She was lively—bored with all this, couldn't wait to get to college. Well, Mum—Edna, that is—didn't take to that. She *loved* her of course, but she couldn't appreciate her like I could—not in her nature, you might say. And that's what makes it hard on her now. She feels she ought to have done something different and if she had, it wouldn't have happened—and now it's too late. I tell you, Mr—Mr—'

'Speke.'

'Mr Speke, I tell you she's right down.' He frowned, giving me a critical look; his eyes were a very dark brown, but there was something about him that reminded me of the Brigadier. 'I haven't talked to anyone like this. It's a good job you're a stranger. And then there's another thing. Maddy was always free and easy with everyone, but she liked the lads. I'm not saying she was promiscuous, but she'd got herself fitted up with one of these coil things—lot of good they seem to be!— and she didn't have any hang-ups about sex. But when it came out at the inquest she was pregnant—that was a terrible shock to Edna, terrible.' His face grew pinched and for a moment lost

62

its ruddy outdoor tan. 'It was as though it was almost worse than her being dead.' He lowered his eyes and shook his head.

Away to our right a fruit machine clattered noisily as someone won the jackpot.

'And how did you feel about it?'

'Me? I just thought how bloody annoyed Maddy must have been—after taking all the proper precautions. Of course she'd have had an abortion—she wasn't ready for kids, that wasn't in her plans. And she wouldn't have said anything about it to those two lads at college, whichever one of them it was responsible. She was proud,' he said bleakly, 'she was a proud woman. I sometimes think if she'd just given in to Bateman, told him, "Okay, go ahead, if it means so much to you," then he might not have killed her.'

'But he had a history of violence, you know,' I said carefully. 'I don't think there's any doubt he was a killer.'

'Yeah—you're right. But it sort of goes round and round in your head.' He drank the rest of his beer slowly. 'I tell you, it's a silent house I live in now—and it used to be full of noise and life—and what with Mum in despair about her fallen daughter, I'm beginning to lose the sense of Maddy, of what she really was.'

I stubbed out my cigarette in the tin ashtray. For all his sagacity, the Brigadier was wrong—*these people* had no special remedy for loss. The only difference was that Hal Bateman was alive and could not be made dead, whereas Maddy was dead and all Hodder's valiant battling could not keep her alive.

I stood up. 'Listen, I'm going to have a whisky—the same for you?'

'All right.' Hodder seemed relieved. 'Thanks.' Then, when I returned with the drinks, he said, 'Listen, I've been moaning away to you all this time, but—'

'I did ask for it.'

'So you did. Well, I hope it's done you some good.' He smiled. 'I've always been a talker, that's why being a rounds-man suits me. But it's Edna that really needs to talk now. Have you done much of this—interviewing people like us?'

'No. This is my first attempt. Why?'

'Oh. The thing is—I was wondering if you had any ideas. I've tried the obvious things—young Dr Gilbert, all he did was talk to her like a kid and give her a lot of tranquillizers, and the vicar, she was downright rude to him; I got hold of a psychiatric social worker and a woman who called herself a bereavement counsellor, if you can believe that. But Edna wasn't having any of it. I can't say I blame her, but,' he made a gesture of angry impatience, 'there must be something or somebody who could help!'

'If you like,' I said hesitantly, 'I could try to have a talk to her.'

'You'd do that?' he said in surprise. Then he shook his head. 'No, mate—it wouldn't work.'

'Why not?'

'No. Not with a—with a stranger. She'd clam up.'

Class, I thought—the wrong class. I didn't press it. I was relieved—I was being spared the worst of it.

Hodder raised his glass. 'Cheers,' he said with a quick grin.

'Cheers,' I echoed, and sipped my drink. 'There's something I haven't asked you yet—Harold Bateman. How do you feel about him?'

'Me? Personally?' He shrugged. 'Well, I'm angry— naturally I'm angry. But that won't bring Maddy back. And the way I look at it, he wasn't responsible—you've got to agree with the law there. Then he was at a public school, wasn't he? I reckon they all go a bit potty at those places—I'm dead against them myself. The poor sods think it's a privilege, but I reckon they ought to be saved from themselves. I mean, it's a completely artificial environment, isn't it? It can't fit them for real life. Sorry, mate, I expect you went to one yourself, didn't you?'

'Yes, I did.' I smiled. 'But, you see, in a public school, uselessness is considered to be a positive value.'

'Doesn't surprise me,' he said wryly. 'Well, it helps to explain Bateman, doesn't it? Maybe underneath, all he wanted was to be shut up again. I'm not one for blaming individuals—it's the system that's fucked up.'

'Is the system to blame for getting him off—or do you think it was Winter's fault, the barrister who defended him?'

'Winter, him that got killed? That's a bloody strange coincidence, isn't it—I mean, a bloke like him? But no—he was just doing his job. Of course it's the system that's wrong. We ought to have a system like they do in France: not where you try to

64

pin it on someone and it's a sort of a gamble whether it comes off or not, but where you try to get at the *truth* of what really happened. When you come right down to it, it wasn't *just* that kid Bateman's fault. He was abnormal—must have been to do a thing like that. But where does the blame lie? That school of his, his Mum perhaps and the Brig too, for all I know—or something wrong in the genes. Maybe Maddy even had something to do with it. But how can we ever know if we don't try to find out—all of it? And if we don't know, how can we ever do anything about it in the future? The future's got to be better than this!' He'd been leaning forward earnestly, now he sat back and looked around, perhaps suddenly conscious of his vehemence and the one or two curious glances it had attracted.

He turned back to me, half-apologetically. 'I'm not a spirit drinker usually. Clouds the vision.'

'The vision of the future?'

'That's right.' He laughed his first easy laugh, without irony or rue. 'It will get better. That's what I keep telling Edna. I'm not expecting paradise tomorrow. But we're not that old, you know; we're young enough to have another—just about. But she's frightened, you see—right off sex as well. And she doesn't work no more—just sits looking at that sodding telly. Doesn't do the cooking, neither.' Smiling, he stood up. 'So I'll have to be off to get the dinner. Nice meeting you.'

'Yes. Look, I'm enormously grateful to you for—'

'It was my pleasure. It's done me a power of good. I don't hold much with the media, but I suppose writers are different.'

'Poorer,' I said.

He smiled in ironic disbelief as we shook hands.

10 The End of Strife

I always work badly under pressure. Demands of time, money or expectation seem to touch some deep core of laziness in my soul, and the louder the sound of the winged chariot, the more idle I become. So at ten-thirty on the Saturday morning I was still dawdling over my second pot of tea and had only got as far as arranging the review books in two piles—five probables and three possibles—when the postman banged on the door and thrust it open.

'Recorded delivery for you,' he said, producing a well-bitten piece of pencil.

'Morning, Jim. Come in and have a cup of tea.' I signed the slip and took the letter which was headed Pemberton, Stoddard, Keystone & Grayling, with an address in Lincoln's Inn.

He glanced round my kitchen, where he'd drunk tea a hundred times before, as though inspecting a café of dubious hygiene. 'All right,' he said, 'but it'll have to be quick.'

Jim was tall, fat and sweaty and his unfailing surliness was one of the small pleasures in my life. I fetched him a mug and, pushing aside the pink folder containing *Love's Loose Strife*, filled it with milk and tea and added five lumps of sugar. 'What's new?' I asked.

He grunted and drank his tea thirstily. 'Know anything about kites?'

'Only that they seem to give a great deal of innocent pleasure for very little effort.'

'Little effort, my elbow. My eldest nipper had his birthday this week. The old lady bought him a kite. Can he get it to fly? Not nohow. It might as well be made of lead.' He held out his mug for more tea. 'I tell you, it's a pig.'

'Pigs may fly.'

'Eh, what's that?'

'Maybe there wasn't enough wind?'

'Bloody great gale Wednesday afternoon—or hadn't you noticed?' As he drank, the liquid seemed to be immediately transformed into great beads of perspiration on his forehead.

'Well, you need space for trailing it too, I believe. Why don't you try Beachy Head—people don't seem to have much trouble up there?'

'Beachy Head!' He wiped his face solicitously with an ancient grey handkerchief. 'I got better things to do with my Saturday afternoons than running about after a piece of paper in the sky.' He got up. 'I must be off,' he said accusingly, as though I had been deliberately hindering him in his appointed round.

'How was the tea?'

'I've had worse,' he said over his shoulder as he lumbered out, leaving the door open.

I didn't bother to shut it against the faint April breeze carrying a gentle hint of the sea. I tidied away the breakfast debris and then slit open the thick brown envelope. The Will consisted of six or seven foolscap pages bound with green tape, to which was attached a letter from Cyril:

Dear Ivor,

As instructed by Amelia Winter, I am sending you herewith a copy of Vivian's Last Will and Testament.

I am sure I need not emphasize that the contents of this document are entirely confidential and should be disclosed to nobody, least of all the beneficiaries.

Yours sincerely,
C.F.W. St. D. Grayling

I put the letter aside and looked gingerly at the 'document,' whose meaning, I could see at a glance, was guarded and hedged about by peculiarly legal unpunctuated verbiage. The last will I had handled had been my mother's—a matter of twenty lines or so, handwritten in plain English on a will form obtained from the Citizens' Advice Bureau. One clause flashed in my memory—'To my dear granddaughter Henrietta, to be held and invested for her until she is twenty-one, two thousand pounds.' I had invested it in gold, the price of which had almost immediately doubled—a benign omen, we had happily thought, for the future. But there was no future.

I got up and, taking a cigarette from the box, lit it with a kitchen match. I saw my kitchen—my living room—with an eye as jaundiced as Jim the postman's. Planning it for convenience and simplicity, I had achieved only bleakness. It lacked the grace of Amelia Winter's sitting room or the easy, used feel of the Brigadier's study. For years I had existed in this place blindfold, waiting for a presence that would never come. How much worse if Henrietta, like Maddy Hodder had survived till twenty-one, only to be murdered and foully violated. The courage of a Walter Hodder shamed me. Anger swept through me, anger against Hal Bateman, against the unknown murderer of Vivian, against the killers, the cutters-off, the life-refusers—anger against myself and my own futility.

The phone rang and jerked me out of my trance of rage.

'Yes?' I answered abruptly.

'Ivor? It's Eleanor—you do sound cross.'

'Eleanor?'

'Eleanor Wood. Where have you been? I've been trying to get you for days.'

'Eleanor—oh. I'm sorry. Round and about. In town mostly.'

'That sounds mysterious. I just wanted to say we're expecting you for lunch tomorrow—Phil couldn't remember if he'd invited you or not.'

'Not. Lunch. Well ... who's going to be there?' The last time I had innocently gone to lunch at Wriston, there had been an appalling writer from *Private Eye* who talked about nothing but the sexual proclivities of literary notables—enough to put one off lust for a lifetime.

'Don't worry.' Eleanor laughed. 'You won't have any competition. Just Phil and Isabelle and me. Not very exciting, I'm afraid.'

'No no—that's fine.'

'Good. Tomorrow then—one-ish. And I do rely on you to get Phil away from the pub by two-thirty at the *latest!*'

Lady Winter tonight, the Woods tomorrow—that put paid to the weekend and to my Crime Column. Hesitantly, I rang Phyllis Pleach. Once when I'd had scarlet fever and been forbidden to read, Phyllis had not only read the books for me, but had wound up writing a couple of reviews. I put the proposition to her; she sounded delighted and grateful and agreed to meet me at twelve at the Green Bough—somewhat to my surprise, for she was not normally a pub person. But it suited me very well. I needed to get out. I'd have my lunch there, then walk over the Downs or up to the Head and let the sea breezes sweep me clean of lament and memory.

It was after eleven, so I poured myself a glass of sherry and sat down to study Vivian's Will.

I waded through a thick preliminary undergrowth of jargon, in which the word 'trust' kept popping up like so many scared

68

rabbits, but the real matter of disposal only began towards the bottom of the second page. A hundred thousand pounds, the house in Bath and the flat at Alderney Court were left outright to 'my mother, Amelia Irene Winter.' There then followed a roll call of the Winter aunts: Emily Blanche, Agnes Mary, Sophia Florence, Matilda Sybil, Gertrude Agatha, Elizabeth Alice, and Lilian Dorothea—each of whom received a hundred thousand pounds. I turned the page.

To Veronica Jane Ashe of Lissom Cottage, near Blakeney,
Norfolk, the sum of Thirty Thousand Pounds.
To Geraldine Jasperson of 171 Camden High Street,
London NW1, the sum of Fifty Thousand Pounds.

My glance slid rapidly down the list, drawn inexorably to my own name:

To Ivor William James Speke of Upper Leeching, near
Eastbourne, Sussex, the sum of Eighty-Three Thousand,
Three Hundred and Thirty-Three Pounds.

I half-rose, then fell back, winded. Behind the house the hill rose, now steep now gentle, the footpath a grey-white thread across the green turf where gorse and broom lay sprinkled with yellow flower and the sun shone with easy morning pride. Eighty-three thousand, three hundred and ... what a strange sum, what a bizarre amount, what a very curious figure.

I went to the door and stood there breathing deeply, making my mind a blank, feeling the sun.

When I turned back to the room, the Will lay on the table, the teapot on the hob, the phone on the dresser—everything as before, yet everything changed. Everything changeable. I picked up the glass and drank the sherry. I felt delicate and tender.

I put on my boots, took an old haversack from the back of the door and filled it with the week's books. Haversack on shoulder and armed with my shooting stick, I made my way slowly along the footpath to the village. A Guernsey cow raised its head and gave me a laconic glance. The vicar, a thin pale priest with a contrary manner, greeted me with that special heartiness reserved for pagans. In the High Street, Mrs

Helmsley-Clinch gave me a vigorous wave from her ancient Daimler.

Phyllis and I arrived at the same moment and we entered the bar together. She had done something different to her hair and, wearing a dress of pale green and white-striped gingham and with an unusual touch of colour in her cheeks, she looked enchanting. I felt a flush of pride as Fred Fleming gave a slow wink and the Judge nodded approvingly.

'Morning,' I said generally.

'And a very good morning to you, sah—and lady!' answered Hamish, smelling powerfully of after-shave. 'And what will it be this morning? A pint of Harveys—ah, and I think I know what this young lady would like.' He waddled off mechanically.

'How is your father?' I asked—immediately annoyed with myself as Phyllis's smile faded.

'I think they've decided not to operate. I'm glad in a way—he hates hospitals, but ... well, it just means more and more painkillers and....'

'More pain?'

She gave a little nod. 'It gets him down, irritated—and underneath he's just sort of fading.'

'I'm sorry.' The notion of Jeremiah's great frame—the confidence, strength, the perfect balance—dwindling was distressing.

'Here we are, sir. That will be one English pound and ninety-five pence exactly.' Hamish set my pint on the counter together with a tall glass of orange-coloured liquid.

'What on earth's that?'

'That, sah, is an orange blossom, sah.'

Judge Towner and Fred and I laughed simultaneously.

'A great favourite with the ladies,' said Hamish with his formal smirk.

'Come on, Phyllis,' I said. We went over to a table in the corner and I unloaded the books from my haversack. 'Shall we get on with it?'

'Yes please.'

'Number one's Bleddisloe—bound to be the same old stuff, but he's good on the clergy and it's always well worked-out. And this is the new Swedish fellow, "In the Tradition of Sworval and Van Meerloo"—he's hardly been dead five minutes and already he's a tradition. Let's just hope it's not too interlarded with gloomy chunks of Scandinavian sociology. Hamilton Gouse is the American whose last one was first-rate. *The Blooding* is undoubtedly vile, but somebody in Hollywood has already paid a fortune for the film rights. Now....'

Paid a fortune for the film rights? I looked up, seeing not the parlour of the Green Bough, but the blackened wood interior of the little bar in Amsterdam, just off the canal, which Vivian and I had immediately chosen as our base. Hour after hour we'd spent there—three, four years ago?—keeping the bitter dampness at bay with hollands (*oude* for him, *jonge* for me) and herring snacks and occasional drafts of lager.

Having just swapped my *Gazette* for his *Times*, I'd turned directly to the publishing column. 'Good God!' I'd said.

'What's up?'

'Listen to this: "Following its unusual success in America, Ben Blatter's historical World War II thriller, *The Hump of the Camel*, has been bought for $200,000 by TBS Studios, LA, who are reported to be planning a major production early next year. Is Blatter the new Le Carré?"'

'Well?' Vivian's quizzical smile. 'Is it any good?'

'Any good? It's the most absurd farrago of badly written, ill-informed anachronistic and unconvincing rubbish I've ever read. I didn't even bother to review the damn thing—all about a Franco plot to take over Ireland. Two hundred thousand dollars! I ask you!'

'Your commercial judgment doesn't seem to be any too good,' Vivian had said, smiling. 'Is that considered to be a lot of money?'

'It's a bloody fortune.'

'Oh come—at the present exchange rate, it's about eighty-three thousand pounds, give or take a hundred or two. What real difference would that make?' There was no mockery, only a genuine interest. He really didn't know—wanted to be enlightened.

'Freedom,' I'd muttered, embarrassed as a vicar explaining sex to a confirmation class. It was the only time—and only for a moment—I'd felt Vivian, with his puzzled, slightly amused expression, to be an utter stranger.

'Ivor?'

71

'What?' I was back in the pub—tobacco smoke, beer smell, murmuration of the regulars, piped strains of the Blue Danube, and Hamish's computer-like enunciation.

'Are you all right?'

'Yes, yes. Where were we? Oh yes, *Bodleian Bodies*—a coy academic teaser by Leo Leotard of all people, with his face all over the back of the jacket. The other three are probably also-rans, but you might take a quick glance. Otherwise, that's it.' I lit one of yesterday's remaining cigarettes, trying to keep my mind away from the Will.

'You detest all this, don't you?' she said, giving the books a swift little caress.

I was not surprised, although I had tried never to give her a hint of my true feeling. 'Yes,' I said.

'Why don't you give it up then?' Her grey eyes regarded me with unerring seriousness. 'If it's just the money, I don't mind—'

'No,' I said, 'no.' It wasn't the money—not now.

'It's not good for you, Ivor.'

'Oh?' I smiled. 'What should I be doing then?'

'You ought to be writing, really writing—not this. Not contemporary romances either. You oughtn't to be stuck away in this little village where nobody reads books or cares about them. Where nobody knows your name. Not *you*.' Her colour was higher, her eyes graver, her tone more eloquent than I remembered. I was surprised by a sudden pulse of desire in me—a hope, an opening, a promise. For a moment I was on the point of confiding in her, but something—long habit, old ice—held me back. And after all, what had I to confide?

On my way out of the village I stopped to buy cigarettes and a cheap throw-away lighter. In the long run it may kill, but meanwhile tobacco is an instrument of tranquillity. Had Wordsworth smoked? I was going to need calm—calm that evening for Lady Winter and Cyril, calm with the Woods tomorrow, calm in the face of a changed life ... maybe.

I had eaten nothing at the pub, but I was not hungry, so I passed the cottage and, pushing through the tight little hawthorn hedge at the back, made my way up the hill. It was a mile and three-quarters to the Head—fourteen furlongs exactly—and I made it in just under half an hour.

Although it was lunchtime, there was a fair number of

72

people on the clifftop; I avoided them by moving 'dangerously' close to the edge. It was a clear, calm and now almost windless afternoon. The sea was a velvety grey and the few visible ships appeared to be stationary. It was a scene of peace beyond time and movement, the real busy-ness of maritime commerce being disguised by distance, just as, I thought, the placidity of my own existence disguised a long laborious struggle.

Yet Vivian had set me free from all that—I could drift, desultory now if I liked, just like the lone yacht down there with flapping sails. I could move back to town, furnish a sitting room as elegant as the Winters', or buy a villa in the Vaucluse and pay a weekly visit to my father. Divested of care, I could travel.

Easier said than done.

I turned away from the indifferently dreaming sea and watched a boy attempting to get a kite aloft—Jim's son perhaps, for all I knew, although he had a look of iron determination quite foreign to the postman. He ran again and again across the springy turf and, again and again, the wafts of air were just sufficient to lift the kite, then, failing, let it fall. Jamming my stick into the ground, I walked over to where he was momentarily resting.

'Can I lend a hand?'

Too out of breath to reply, he just nodded. I lifted the serpent's head at full arm stretch while he stood ten yards away with the string raised and taut. 'Go!' I shouted at the first true tug of wind and leapt clear of the tail. By luck, the gust held steady and he raced without a stumble and the kite rose, swung downwards once, recovered, then soared smoothly upward. The tail was all of forty foot long and made of some multi-coloured translucent material that rippled and glittered in the sun. Like a playful bird, it swooped and darted, only to rise proudly higher, magnificently flaunting plumage and prowess.

'How much line have you got there?'

'Eight hundred yards,' he said. And we looked at each other and laughed.

I retrieved my stick and went home with a smiling step. Even from my back door I could still see the splendid glitter riding in the sky.

Inside, I removed my boots and sat down to a serious

perusal of the Will. The dispositions fell essentially into four parts: (1) the money, real property and chattels left to Lady Winter, who was also the residuary legatee; (2) the sums left to the Aunts; (3) legacies to named inviduals; (4) bequests to institutions—£50,000 each to the Club, the College, the Howard League for Penal Reform, a church in Bath, the National Council for Civil Liberties, the Prisoners' Aid Society, etc.—a roll-call of liberal decency. The total money amounts added up to just under a million and a half. But it was the third category that interested me most. I read it with great care:

Veronica Jane Ashe (address in Norfolk)	£30,000
Geraldine Jasperson (Camden Town address)	£50,000
Georgina Deidre Maynard (12 Ember Road, Putney)	
	£15,000
Cicely Albertine Quinn (85 Prince's Square, Harrogate, Yorkshire)	£30,000
Joanna Marigold Claudia Salisbury (23 Chandos Gardens, London, NW9)	£150,000
Estelle Jacqueline Soley (45 Riverside Road, Bathwick, Bath, Avon)	£30,000
Ivor William James Speke	£83,333
Sheila Eileen Wantage (37A Bilberry Street, Eastbourne, Sussex)	£15,000
Eleanor Felicity Wood (Wriston Manor, Near Heathfield, Sussex)	£100,000

This was not the Will of a mean man, and I was pleased at the refutation of Alva Norman's cynicism about the self-interested protectiveness of Grayling and Pulteney, neither of whom figured. In fact, puzzlingly—though flatteringly so—I was the only male beneficiary. Of the other beneficiaries, Eleanor Wood was the only one I knew, or had even heard of. But why Eleanor, rather than Phil? And who were all these women—old family retainers, distant cousins, lovers (members of that funeral bevy of beauty)? But surely here was no cause for alarm, even of suspicion—nothing but innocent generosity.

I did not for a moment believe a woman would have killed

Vivian. But had a husband done so in a jealous frenzy? Perhaps, if Vivian's famous discretion had failed—but then it was not done for money. For surely Vivian's discretion had not lapsed sufficiently to tell anyone the contents of the Will—new and freshly made. Of course he'd only have had to drop a hint—'you'll be well taken care of when I'm gone, my dear'— to be passed on—'well, at least someone loves me enough to take care of me, even if you don't!'—and the trick would have been done. Betrayer could have been turned into benefactor with one stroke—sixteen strokes.

I shook my head impatiently and went to the door. Sex *and* money, then? I could not imagine it. I couldn't visualize Phil Wood, say, plotting, planning—executing. But had Eleanor been aware of the legacy? It shouldn't be too difficult to find out—with a little probing at tomorrow's lunch table.

The kite in the sky had vanished now, and I felt a vague sense of dismay. What was I setting myself up as? Hadn't I decided I was not the man to investigate all this? Hadn't I been saddened enough by the Batemans and the Hodders? Wasn't I carrying a thoroughly negative report tonight to Lady Winter and Cyril Grayling? What did I owe them anyway?

What did I owe them? Eighty-three thousand pounds odd.

Perhaps Vivian's money was not simply a gift of freedom, but also a legacy of bondage.

I turned back into the kitchen and noticed *Love's Loose Strife* lying on the table beside the Will. I picked up the pink folder and, opening the door of the Welsh dresser, shoved it in among all the other abandoned projects and failed ideas. Literary bondage, at least, was easily disposed of.

I went slowly upstairs to pack my bag and put on my best suit.

11 A Council of War

My best suit was not good enough.

Lady Winter had invited not only Cyril Grayling, but Vivian's law clerk, Mr Marsham, a remarkably clean-looking old gentleman. They both wore dinner jackets, and Lady Winter herself was splendid in a watered black silk gown, cut low to display an ornate necklace of rubies that glimmered richly in the candlelight.

'Ummm ummm. Most interesting.' Mr Marsham lifted the nutcracker and held it delicately in his palm as if weighing his weapon, then swiftly crushed a walnut. 'You are, if I may say so, a gifted raconteur, Mr Speke. A lucid exposition. Literature's gain is the Law's loss.'

I drank some port—my mouth was parched from talking and I should have preferred a whisky and soda.

Lady Winter was smoking a cigarette in an ebony holder and staring abstractedly at the six-branched candelabra—or perhaps into the dimness beyond. At her back the log fire softly stirred, and a little humming sound came from Mr Marsham as he chumped his walnut, his appetite quite undiminished by the extravagant meal we had just eaten. Mrs Blaine had fully lived up to her reputation as a cook, and it crossed my mind idly to wonder why she had not figured in Vivian's will.

'Yes, a jolly good show, Ivor.' Cyril took the cigar from his lips and nodded his carefully groomed head of silvering hair. 'But it doesn't get us an awful lot forrarder, does it? Hodder may be a bolshy but if the Brigadier vouches for him that's good enough for me. And Thrush is a mental defective, so—'

'Deaf-mute,' I said.

'Same sort of thing. Anyway, his daughter survived. In my book, what we're looking for is a madman.'

'Ah, but if we say only a madman could commit such a crime, we are allowing the nature of the crime to determine the mentality of the criminal.' Mr Marsham gave a small bland smile. 'And that is not good law.'

'Isn't that rather an academic point?' I said, taking a cigarette. 'Surely a criminal psychopath may appear to be as sane as you and I.'

'Appear, my dear sir, appear—but is not so. An important distinction. A pathological condition *ipso facto* excludes *mens rea*—that is to say, a psychopath is by definition suffering from a substantially impaired mental or moral responsibility for his acts.' Mr Marsham cracked another nut; he was enjoying himself. 'But retribution is essentially a *moral* act—indeed, our whole legal system, insofar as it's based on the concept of *mens rea*, is a retributive one. The guilty are, after all, *punished.*'

I said, 'If we're dealing with someone who has taken the law into his own hands, then we're talking about private retribution. What moral dimension can that have?'

'I have lived in countries, Ivor, where vengeance is regarded not as an aberration, but as a bounden duty.' Lady Winter spoke softly, her hands folded delicately on the table as if in prayer. 'Private retribution as a moral obligation isn't incompatible with civility—or sanity—it was once at the heart of it.' The strong black bar of the eyebrows above the deep-set eyes and the gems glinting barbarically at her neck lent an element of judicial ruthlessness to her serene certitude. If she could, she would destroy her son's killer with the same speed as she had destroyed his diary.

'Still is in some places,' Cyril said. 'Iran, for instance.'

'Dammit, Cyril, we're not living in Iran.' Why was I being so vehement? I took a slow swallow of port. 'You're saying—if I follow you, Mr Marsham—that Vivian's murderer may have been someone acting out of a considered moral judgment. What I am saying is that here, today, in England, any such judgment—such action—is the product of an insane distortion of the moral sense.'

'My dear Mr Speke, do forgive me, I was not intending to make a normative statement. But it is not helpful to characterize as insane a man whose motivation is, according to our concept of law, distorted. A throwback he may be, fanatical almost certainly—but if we declare him insane, we have lost all hope of a logical approach to his identity.'

'In other words, old man, we're barking up the wrong tree.'

Cyril laughed and, leaning across the table, lit my cigarette with his gold lighter. 'Still, you know, Toby, it leaves a pretty wide field. A lot of the chop 'em and top 'em brigade would be only too glad to put Harold Bateman out of the way—just haven't got the requisite guts, that's all.'

'I don't know,' I said slowly, 'I think somebody might have had a try. A week or two before he attacked Jennifer Thrush, Hal Bateman was quite badly beaten up. His father put it down to a pub brawl, but....'

'Why on earth didn't you say something about this before?' Cyril asked with a touch of truculence.

'It didn't seem to me particularly germane, besides....'

'Oh but it is most certainly germane.' Marsham pushed the decanter round to Cyril, then steepled his fingers—he'd finished with the nuts at last. 'The difficulty with the theory that Vivian's murder was one of retribution is that Vivian himself was not responsible for any loss of life. Therefore, if the theory is to hold water, he must have been the scapegoat for another's crime—presumably Bateman's. The attack on Bateman tends to confirm this—it was unsuccessful and, by the time another attack was planned, Bateman himself was unavailable. Hence the choice of Vivian as substitute victim.'

'What it means,' Lady Winter said, 'is that Vivian was murdered by someone who had at least tried to do this sort of thing before.'

'Exactly so.' Mr Marsham smiled, but I had the feeling he was slightly put out, as the singer in a duet might be when his partner comes in a bar too soon. 'At any rate, I do believe it would be foolish to assume that the desire for retribution must be limited to those who suffered as a direct result of Bateman's crimes. Now, of all the people in the country who might have been desirous of Bateman's execution, who would be most likely to actually take the matter into their own hands? Those who had at one time or another suffered a similar tragedy themselves, that is to say, relatives or connections of other women who were murdered and raped. Would you not agree, Mr Speke?'

'I—I don't know. I suppose so.'

'But, Good Lord, Toby, there must be hundreds of 'em!'

'Of murder *with* rape cases? Not at all, not at all.' Mr Marsham sipped a little port with relish. 'I'm no expert, but I seriously doubt whether there are much more than half a dozen such cases a year on average. We are an essentially law-abiding nation—whatever savage propensities may be lurking in the subconscious.'

Lady Winter smiled faintly.

'Yes, but look here,' said Cyril, 'six cases a year over a period of ten years multiplied by three or four aggrieved relatives apiece gives you well over two hundred possible suspects. You'd need a small army to investigate that lot.'

'You're looking at it the wrong way round,' Lady Winter said. 'The starting point is not the kin of the victims, but the murderers themselves. If anything has happened to any of them, then we've proved our point.'

'What do you mean "happened to them"?' I asked.

'I mean that they have been murdered—or died in unexplained circumstances.'

'And if they had,' said Cyril, suddenly much sharper, 'where would that get you?'

Mr Marsham said, 'It would merely tend to suggest that Vivian's murder—and the attack on Bateman—were not isolated instances. That, in other words, there is somewhere a morally outraged fanatic executing a retributive justice which society has failed to exact from murderer-rapists.'

'Well, why not go to the police—they should know?' Cyril was asking the obvious questions and I was grateful to him.

'I think that would be distinctly premature. If our hypothesis is correct—if one, or more, of these criminals has subsequently been murdered, then we would have something to go on. But the motive is, we must admit, bizarre and the hypothesis, at the moment, tendentious. The police might well be reluctant to treat the matter very seriously.'

'I can't say I'd blame them,' Cyril smiled sourly. 'So how do you propose to attack the problem?'

Momentarily disengaged from the argument, I covertly examined the three of them: Marsham sipping port, serenely unsullied by reality; Cyril, impatient, but keeping his usual heavily sarcastic style in check; Lady Winter, straight-backed, watchful, vivid with rubies, her silence sharp as steel. The log fire and candlelight, the ancestors upon the walls, the polished gleam of mahogany, the cigars, the port lent an air of artificiality to our talk of killing and rape and vengeance. Yet, just on the other side of the swing door there had been the agony of death, the violence of murder, the heart's blood of the man we loved dark on the kitchen linoleum.

'Here,' said Cyril, skidding a small white card to me across the table. I had seen Mr Marsham take it from his pocket, but had completely missed what was said. I was aware of them all looking at me as I picked it up and read:

1966 Horace Smith, convicted of the murder and rape of Michelle Turner.

1972 Kenneth Frederick Soper, convicted of the murder and rape of Frances Price.

1974 George Leonard Camrose, convicted of the manslaughter and rape of Anne Rourke.

I raised my head expectantly, observing an intelligent silence.

'They all received life sentences,' Mr Marsham obliged. 'But it's very much on the cards that they've all been released by now. In any case it would be interesting to know where they are now—if they're alive. I haven't put down any later cases Vivian defended—they're almost certainly still incarcerated, so not to our purpose.'

'You're selecting them as potential victims because of their connection with Vivian?'

'No no no no, my dear sir. On the contrary. It's very likely that our retributive killer, if I may so dub him, was initially impelled by a strong personal desire for vengeance, but by the time he came to Vivian my guess is that he was motivated by an entirely personal desire for justice—what he imagined to be justice. In the long run it will probably be necessary to look at all convicted murderer-rapists released in, say, the last five years. But you have to start somewhere.' He gave me his Toby-jug smile.

You. The pronoun fell like a dead bird out of the sky. In the sudden quiet a car's hooter sounded faintly—from a distant world of Saturday night traffic and pubs and people leaving cinemas.

Lady Winter began to speak—on cue, I thought. Of course. They'd set it up between them, maybe even rehearsed it— Marsham's exhaustive disquisitions, Cyril's straight man,

Lady Winter's flashes of eloquence. I was being subtly—not so subtly—maneuvered.

'Who?' I said, catching at something familiar. 'Did you say Shepperton Keith?'

'Yes,' she said blandly. 'I understand he's a member of the Parole Board and has been for some years. I'm sure you'll have no difficulty in getting most of the relevant information from him.'

'You know Shep pretty well, don't you, Ivor?' said Cyril, smiling. 'Didn't I see you talking to him at the inquest?'

'Yes.' There was a knowingness about that smile which suggested Cyril knew my relationship with Shep was professional as well as personal. No—I was imagining things. 'Fairly well,' I said firmly, only realizing as I spoke that I was committing myself—to what, thank God, I could not possibly foresee.

A few minutes later Mr Marsham made his courteous farewells and Lady Winter rose to show him out.

'Join me in the other room,' she said, 'when you've finished with your port.'

Cyril and I reseated ourselves. I took the decanter and filled my glass to the brim, drank, and filled it again.

'What the devil's all this about, Cyril?'

'Well,' he said, slowly lighting another cigar. 'Frankly, I think it's a bit of a wild goose chase—though you must admit old Marshers is fairly convincing. I wouldn't let it cause you any sleepless nights if I were you. But it's good for Amelia— gives her a focus, if you know what I mean. You and I can't possibly imagine what this sort of thing does to a woman of her calibre. She's a very determined woman of course, but all the determination in the world doesn't do you any good if you haven't got something to be determined about.' Cigar well-lit, he drew on it deeply. 'All in all, whatever you and I may think about it, we owe it to Vivian to do our best.'

'Then why don't you do it?'

'My dear Ivor—I'm a solicitor!'

'And I'm a beneficiary?'

'I didn't say anything of the kind.' Then he gave me that same smile again. 'Although I imagine it must be a pleasurable feeling to have an unexpected eighty-three thousand in your pocket.'

'I'm not so sure,' I said slowly. 'Cyril, what about all those other people in the Will—the women?'

'What about them?'

'Who are they?'

'Oh, just some of Vivian's lame dogs, you know.'

And that, of course, included me, I thought wryly. Was that perhaps why I had been chosen—a lame dog for a wild goose chase? 'It seems to me,' I said off-handedly, 'that some of them had a pretty good motive for murdering Vivian.'

'Don't be absurd, Ivor. One doesn't go about murdering one's friends and benefactors for the sake of a few thousand.'

'*One* doesn't—but *they* might. After all, we don't know who they are—or what kind of desperate need they might be in.'

'Put that right out of your mind.' He gave me a hard look. 'I hope you're not thinking of going round harassing these people, or anything silly like that. I don't have to remind you that information you have is confidential.'

'What's confidence when murder is at stake?'

He stared at me, then laughed abruptly. 'My God, you're ragging me! I never could understand that sense of humour of yours—too subtle, I expect. Not enough imagination.' He adjusted his face from the conciliatory to the sagacious. 'But seriously, how do you imagine any of the beneficiaries knew they were even mentioned in Vivian's will?'

I could imagine it all too easily; I only wondered why they were being so clearly marked off-limits. But I was thoroughly sick of Cyril and his heavy-handed manipulations.

I stood up. 'Come on,' I said, 'let's join her in the other room.' I needed a whisky and soda, and there would be no need of chess tonight. I had already been outmaneuvered.

12 An Unexpected Posey

The door of the flat closed and I turned off my goodbye smile. For a few moments I didn't move. My overnight bag was heavy in my hand and I had a headache. I'd slept badly—

because of the port perhaps or, more likely, because I'd been given Vivian's bed—and the old nightmare had woken me before dawn. Three weak cups of instant coffee and a single digestive biscuit had left me feeling bloated but famished.

I went over to the lift and pressed the button, and down in the depths the ancient machinery groaned, faltered, and was silent. As usual, I had been struggling, trying desperately to run, across a grey foggy marshland. As I struggled to move, so the mire struggled to hold me fast. Each breath, each sucking footstep was a terrible labour, as always. And as always at the back of my mind—a different terror—temptation plucked at me to falter, give up, sink and be swallowed. But this time for a single moment the fog parted and I saw the house—a tall dirty yellow house with all its windows wide open, like blind mouths calling. And I'd held out my arms and striven to shout, but all that came out was silence. And I'd woken then, my mouth parched with the mute cries and my face wet with beads of the sightless fog.

I jammed my shaking hand against the button again, but all that resulted was a solitary clang.

'Hello, old man—lift on the blink?' Squadron-Leader Posey, appearing from nowhere, rattled the gate fiercely. 'Somebody must have forgotten to shut it downstairs. Happens all the time.'

'You mean we'll have to walk?'

''Fraid so. You don't look up to much, old man. Here, come and have that drink.'

'Drink?'

'Well, I suppose it is a bit early—coffee then. I expect the wife's brewing up—she usually is. Women, eh?'

'It's very kind of you, but I really should....' But I had time to spare, and something Posey had said flickered in my mind—something he had hinted about Vivian's social life.

'Like you to meet the wife. She makes a damn good cup of coffee.'

That decided it. 'Well—but weren't you on your way out?'

'Just going to fetch the Sunday papers—that can wait. Come along.' He put a hand on my shoulder and I allowed myself to be propelled into the Posey flat.

'Very? Very! We've got a visitor! Sit you down, old man. There—that's a comfortable one.'

83

I took the proffered place—a venerable club chair with springs that immediately attacked the buttocks.

'Snug, eh?' Posey made a generous gesture.

The room was crammed with furniture ranging from wartime Utility to nineteen-fifty-ish bulbous, a peculiar mixture of threadbare austerity and flaccid luxuriance. And every surface, horizontal and vertical, was covered with RAF memorabilia—shell cases for pipes and pencils, ashtrays made out of engine parts, model aircraft, engraved plaques, coats of arms, a propeller above the mantelpiece, photographs of young men in uniform with arms about one another's shoulders.

'Very,' I said. I pointed at a huge picture of a Spitfire soaring into the sunset—or possibly the dawn. 'Did you fly one of those?'

'Eh? Oh, Very—Very, old girl, this is Mr Sleek. He's one of those writer johnnies.'

'Speke—Ivor Speke.' I pushed myself to my feet and took her hand. 'How do you do?'

'Hello.' She was totally unexpected—tall, slim, her Grace Kelly-ish good looks only slightly spoiled by a nose a little too long and pointed. I felt my headache clearing.

'Coffee? Yes, I'd love some coffee.' I realised I'd been holding her hand rather longer than necessary.

'I shan't be a minute then, it's nearly ready.'

It was as if it had all been arranged—Posey spying for hours through the peephole to catch me leaving. Ridiculous.

'No, I'm afraid I was a non-driver,' said Posey.

'What?'

'A wingless wonder.'

'Oh—the Spitfire.'

'Bit of a fraud, I'm afraid.' He laughed heartily. 'Still, I always say to myself, Frank, old man, they also serve who only stand waiting about, eh? Ha-ha.'

I smiled. 'Is that what you did?'

'Intelligence, actually—same thing really. Doesn't win you any gongs. Still, I could tell you a thing or two if I wanted—make your hair stand on end.'

'I bet you could.'

'Oh I could, certainly I could.' But he spoke in an abstracted way, as though the subject suddenly bored him. 'Only I can't

84

of course—Official Secrets Act and all that. I say, old man, would you mind if I popped out after those papers, after all? The *Sunday Telegraph* tends to get snapped up rather early around these parts.'

'No, of course—go ahead.'

'Right. Shan't be long. Very'll look after you.'

And she came in almost on signal as the front door slammed, carrying a tray laden with coffee pot, cups, hot milk, sugar bowl and a plate of ginger nuts—paraphernalia which she managed with deftness and speed. I noticed there were only two cups, and she noticed me noticing.

'Frank doesn't care for coffee. Do sit down. I expect he went to get the papers, didn't he?'

'Yes. Just the milk, thanks. Yes, and a biscuit.'

'He's a worrier.' She smiled. 'About world affairs, I mean.'

'Who isn't these days?' The coffee was good.

'I'm not.' She said it regretfully, and then her nose twitched—twice to the left, once to the right, a prehensile movement, like a small animal on the alert. 'I've read one of your books.'

I forced myself to stop staring. 'Have you?' That was a remarkable enough event in itself. 'Which one?'

'*Last Leavings*. Vivian lent it me. I thought it very sad. Is that right?'

'There's no right or wrong about these things, you know. Limpid irony was more what I was aiming for, but sadness will do. I didn't know you knew Vivian.'

'Oh yes.' The nose moved again, a snake's head dart—right and left.

'Your husband said the other day—'

'Frank's not my husband, you know.'

'Oh, I'm sorry.'

'We say we're married of course, although it's not really necessary these days. Frank's real wife went into a home just after the War—and Frank thinks it would be disloyal to divorce her.'

'I see.'

'But I'm sorry, I interrupted you.'

'It was only that your—that Frank suggested,' I gave a little laugh, 'well, suggested that there was rather an active social life going on across the corridor.'

85

'Did he? Frank's a great one for keeping tabs on things. I've always thought he's a spy, but he's never said and I've never asked. He'd think *we* were living in a social whirl if two or three people came in for coffee once a fortnight.'

'I don't think he quite meant that,' I said.

She stared at me without blinking, without answering. There was something statuesque, but at the same time wistful about her—perhaps she had been a model, whose career was destroyed by the nasal tic. 'Mr Speke—'

'Ivor, please.'

'Then you must call me Very. Ivor, do you think he suffered? Vivian, I mean. I couldn't—didn't read about it. Only what Frank told me.'

'It was very quick. We know that. I don't suppose he even had time to be surprised, let alone to feel any pain.'

'Thank you. I'm horribly squeamish, I'm afraid.'

'Does it matter to you a great deal?'

'Oh yes.'

'You must have known him well.'

She said nothing, but her nose twitched violently and she gave me such a look of despairing intimacy that I had to glance away. What, I wondered, would Vivian have made of this extraordinary room.

'Vivian thought it was so ghastly it used to make him laugh—but he liked the bedroom.'

It was my turn to be silenced. A faint blush touched her cheeks—not of embarrassment, but of pride perhaps. And why not? Her strange lop-sided beauty would have appealed to Vivian—would appeal to anyone. Did the nose twitch in bed?

'I expect that's what Frank was referring to.'

'He *knew?*'

'Oh no. I mean, in general. Frank's terribly jealous of course and frightfully nosy, but he's not very good at finding things out—which is mainly why I've always thought he might be a spy.'

I laughed.

'Would you like some more coffee?' she said, smiling at the pleasure of my laughter.

'No, no thanks.' Yet all the same I leaned forward and put out my hand to her—and then, as a key rattled in the lock and the front door banged, slowly withdrew.

86

'Hello hello hello, what have you two been up to then? Whoof!' He dropped a thick wad of newspapers onto the couch. 'Had to go all the way down to the Square for the *Telegraph*. Sorry to be so long.'

'We were talking about Ivor's writings.'

'Ah, I envy you penpushers. Don't have much time for reading myself, more's the pity.' He raised a finger and gave his moustaches a quick upward brush. 'How about that drink now?'

'Not for me thanks. I must be on my way.' I rose reluctantly, but I was in for a lot of drinking at the Woods.

'Sure?'

'Sure, thanks—I've got to get down to the country.'

'Where's that?'

'A place called Wriston.'

'Never heard of it.'

'Well, it doesn't figure very largely in world affairs.'

'Eh? What's that? Ha-ha! Can't say I care for the country much myself,' he said, as though dismissing an inferior brand of pickles. 'If you've seen one tree, you've seen the lot.'

'You like the seaside, Frank.'

'Do I? I suppose I do. But then it's flat, isn't it? No trees at the seaside!'

'Reminds you of an aerodrome, I expect?'

'What? I say, that's jolly good.' He clapped me on the shoulder. 'Well, I'll escort you to the lift, old man—in good working order now.'

I shook Very's hand. 'Goodbye.'

'Goodbye,' she said with a smile, but, although I waited a moment, her nose remained quiescent.

I followed Posey who was talking loudly about the inadequacies of the building. 'As for Trubshaw—about as competent as the man in the moon. Drinks, you know. All that stuff at the inquest about locking up—pure twaddle. Half the time it's open all night. Not that it makes much difference—any fool with a credit card and a twist of the wrist could get in. Now if I had Trubshaw in the Service . . .'

13 Wood Fright

'I wouldn't touch it with a greased barge pole, if I were you!'

I felt a nick of irritation at Phil Wood's vehemence—but then Phil was always vehement after five or six scotches and a large lunch. 'Why not?' I asked mildly.

'Christ, Ivor, where's your common sense? The old lady's off her trolley. It's as plain as a pikestaff. She's lived out of England so long she's just lost touch with reality.'

'You equate England with reality?'

'Funny man.' Phil puffed his cheeks and blew out a mouthful of cigar smoke. 'It's understandable enough—having your child killed is enough to send anyone round the bend, but—'

Eleanor made an abrupt angry gesture.

'What? What did I say? Oh. I'm sorry, Ivor—that was fairly unforgivable.' He stretched out a placatory hand.

'No—you're right. Henrietta's death did—send me round the bend a bit. But it was a long time ago. I've recovered enough sanity to see that Lady Winter is slightly paranoid—I recognize the symptoms. The difference is that I had no one to blame, except myself—'

'That's not true, Ivor,' Eleanor said quietly.

'—which meant I was left carrying the guilt. But Amelia Winter hasn't an iota of guilt—maybe because she does have someone to blame and she's hell-bent on finding out who. The really cracked part of it is that if she does discover the murderer, she won't want to hand him to the police—she'll want to kill him.'

Eleanor bent over and stirred the fire with the poker. 'Or get you to kill him for her,' she murmured.

Phil grunted. 'Fair enough. But then why is she trying to paper over Vivian's private life? You have to admit this theory about some nutter going around avenging murdered girls simply isn't credible. Devoted as I was to Vivian, there was obviously something nasty in the woodshed somewhere and it suddenly popped out and chopped him.'

'Well, that doesn't seem very credible either.'

'Oh yes it does,' Eleanor said. 'It does to me.'

'What exactly do you mean?' I said.

'You know perfectly well what I mean,' she said in that clear light upper-class voice of hers. 'Men.'

We laughed, but she hadn't intended to be funny.

'Eleanor,' Phil said, 'I admit you have an infallible knack for putting things in a nutshell, but do you think you could expand on that?'

She hung up the poker and turned to us full face, her colour heightened by the fire. 'You all just do exactly what you want without ever thinking there might be consequences—and when there are, you're taken utterly by surprise.'

'Surely you're not talking about babies?' said Phil in his best bewildered voice.

'No, Philip—I am not talking about babies.'

I said quickly, 'You think he ought to have expected something like this—the possibility of it?'

'He ought to have known you can't live your life on charm forever and get off scot free.'

'Is that really what he did?'

'Oh, we've got to admit that,' said Phil. 'It's what we all loved him for. Of course it was only one side of him, but I think Eleanor's saying that it was a potentially dangerous side. Vivian's sort of attractiveness—and mind you, I don't think it was simply superficial, I think it went deep—but it was the kind of attractiveness that can quite innocently provoke odd passions and secret jealousies and, maybe, murderous rage. I don't think we have to look further than that. And my bet is that old Lady W. knows it—but damn well isn't going to let on.'

I said, 'I'd never thought of Vivian as a man of passion—rather the opposite perhaps.'

'It wasn't his passion,' Eleanor said, 'it was the passion he aroused in others.'

'I see.' And Very Posey was a prime example, of course. Yet, in reality, was there any more to Very's devotion than a fantasy extrapolated from a few odd moments of conversation in the lift? 'People don't die for love,' I said, 'these days.'

'Why not? What else is worth dying for? Or killing for?' Eleanor stood up, as Phil and I exchanged an uneasy glance. 'I'm going to take Isabelle for a quick walk before tea. I expect you'd prefer to stay here with Phil, Ivor?'

'No no,' I said, recognizing the signal, 'I'll come too if I may. The fresh air will do me good.'

'Fresh air never did anyone any good,' said Phil, already comatose, 'it only makes you cold.'

It was cold. As soon as we got out of the valley, a sharp wind pierced us, making me shiver and Eleanor turn pale. Isabelle, gambolling ahead with Marigold the ancient spaniel, seemed quite unaffected. She was a pretty child, with her mother's high colour and dark good looks and, even at ten, the same easy, detached air of confidence with men.

'We had Marion here last weekend. She's doing very well at the Beeb—did you see that piece about her in the *Sunday Times* magazine the other day—'Coming Women in Television' or something like that?'

'No. I don't read that rag any more.' My foot slipped on a loose turf and I would have fallen but for Eleanor's hand on my arm. 'Ought to have brought my boots.'

'She's thinking of getting married again.'

'Is she?' We had reached the crest of the hill. I stopped to look down at the beech woods cut by a broad marl avenue banked with bracken. Isabelle was out of sight. 'Who to?'

'A TV producer. I'm sure one ought to know his name, but I didn't when she told me. And now I've forgotten. He was married to an actress who left him. He's got two children, teen-agers, who he's bringing up by himself.'

'Oh.' I looked down at her, conscious of the warmth of her arm against my side. 'Is she happy?'

'Yes, I really think she is—though it's never easy to tell with Marion, is it? You don't mind me telling you all this?'

'Of course not.'

'I just thought it was a coincidence. I mean, I've never heard you speak about Henrietta the way you did today—even casually. It's always been a taboo subject, hasn't it? Listening to you this afternoon, I thought—perhaps he's getting over it too at last. Marion must be, mustn't she, if she's thinking of getting married?'

90

'So it's time for me to marry, as well?'

'Of course it is. It's such a waste your being alone.'

Eleanor, I knew, had been waiting to say this for a long time, her natural directness strained at the leash for years. I said, 'When I could be making some nice girl happy?'

'I'm not thinking about nice girls, I'm thinking about you.' It was the declaration of a sort of love—the sort of love I'd sensed in Very this morning and yesterday with Phyllis in the Green Bough. I looked up to where the wind was tossing the newly budded branches and, further away, rippling the short grass of the meadows.

'Where's Isabelle?'

Eleanor raised her head and called in her high incisive soprano, 'Isabelle? Don't get too far ahead, darling!'

There was no reply.

'Well, not to worry. She must have taken the short cut at the bottom of the hill.'

We listened to the wind. Then far away below us came a cry—and then another. And I was running.

One moment I was standing there in the contentment of a placid Sunday afternoon, the next I was making a mad dash for life down the slippery track. And in my head I seemed to hear the swelling last wild cries of Maddy Hodder, to see in my mind's eye the dagger raised and stabbing down, the body thrashing left, then right, the twisted hair, the blood red on the bracken.

I slid and fell heavily once, but managed a kind of sideways somersault and was on my feet and into the stand of birches at the bottom of the hill. The thin boughs whipped my clothing and slashed my cheek and the yells were closer—running, running through a blur of tears and despair, I caught a glimpse of Isabelle's scarlet scarf and thrust through into a little clearing. She was crouched with her back to me, leaning forward, keening.

'Oh God oh God,' I muttered.

'Oh hello, Ivor.' She looked up with the clear eyes of surprise, then stood. Couchant at her feet, the dog was whining and growling and suddenly let out a high yelp. 'Marigold's been very naughty, she caught a rabbit and— why, whatever is the matter?'

I laughed. 'Nothing,' I said, then laughed again, caught in

an upsurge of ridiculous giggles.

'It isn't funny. She's been a very naughty girl, haven't you, Goldie?'

Eleanor came up in a quick rush. 'Oh, Isabelle, has she been rabbiting again?'

'Oh Mummy, I thought she was much too old and slow to actually catch one!' Isabelle was tearful now.

'Ivor, do shut up. Where is it, darling?'

I forced down my laughter. 'Over there,' I said, pointing to the edge of the clearing where the rabbit lay almost invisible among the old leaves. As Isabelle held Marigold by the collar, Eleanor and I advanced towards the animal. Except for an occasional shiver, it was quite still and looked at us with that expression of innocently wounded terror endemic to rabbits. Then its nose gave a quick Very-like twitch. All impulse of laughter vanished, and tears pricked my eyes.

'Why, the poor thing's in shock,' Eleanor said. But then, as she took another step forward, it turned and loped slowly away. 'Oh dear.'

We watched the white tail bobbing until it vanished among the birches, then turned back to Isabelle.

'If he can run like that he's bound to be all right,' I said.

'What makes you so sure it's a male?' the girl asked coolly. 'It looked like a doe to me.'

'All the same, I expect Ivor's right, darling. And I think you'd better keep Marigold on the lead for the rest of the walk.'

Positions were reversed now, girl and dog following us sedately—had some instinct suggested to Isabelle that her mother and I bore keeping an eye on?

'Are you okay, Ivor?'

'Yes of course—I suppose I ought to apologize for that bit of hysteria.'

'You have got it a bit on the mind, haven't you? This rape business, I mean.'

'Yes I—I have. Those talks with old Bateman and Hodder I told you about—it's hard to get it out of one's head.'

'I see that, but is it wise to think of making a book out of it?'

'Phil doesn't think so, obviously.'

'Phil's just afraid no one will buy a book about victims. I mean *you*—after all, you're a bit of a victim too, aren't you?'

'Sure you don't mean a lame dog?'

'It's the same thing. Won't it stir everything up again just as you're really beginning to get over it?'

'Psychotherapeutically, stirring things up is supposed to be a healthy first step towards sorting things out.'

'Bother psychotherapy—I don't believe a word of it. As for stirring things up—look at the way you behaved with that rabbit.'

I halted abruptly. 'That rabbit might have been your daughter.'

As I spoke, Isabelle and the dog ran swiftly past us. 'I'll be at the house, Mummy.'

'Put the kettle on, there's a dear.' Eleanor faced me angrily. 'That's a beastly thing to say, Ivor.'

'Is it? Well let's just get this straight—I don't really give a damn about the book, that's just a pretext. What I care about is Vivian. Vivian was murdered, Vivian was the victim, and I want to find out why.'

'I don't think you do—just the opposite. You want to prove his death was the act of a maniac—just like his barmy mother. I can understand it in her, but why is it so important to you to pretend his death had nothing to do with the way he lived his life? If I didn't know you better, I'd think you were queer.'

'We call it gay these days.' My irritation almost led me to challenge her directly with Vivian's legacy. Instead, I said, 'What exactly have you got against him, Eleanor?'

'Against Vivian? Don't be ridiculous. Why, if it hadn't been for Vivian, Phil and I would never have met.'

'I didn't know that.'

'Of course you did—you were at our wedding, Vivian was best man, he made a joke about it in his speech.'

'I don't remember.' I didn't even recall the marriage, which must have occurred in that happy patch of my life that ended seven years ago and had been carefully blanked out of my memory.

Eleanor took my hand. 'I was very fond of Vivian. When Brian walked out and left me, Vivian was an angel of goodness. I don't know what I'd have done without him.'

I saw the eagerness in her upturned face, the innocence in her dark eyes, felt the flow of her vitality, and I wanted to kiss her. But there was something I wanted more. 'Did you ever happen,' I said, 'to go to bed with him?'

She jerked her hand from mine. 'What an extraordinary remark!' Her cheeks were scarlet, her body stiff. 'Don't you dare ever say anything like that to Philip!'

I watched her stride away from me, and I was puzzled. Her answer sounded like an admission. But whether it was or wasn't, if she was so concerned to keep the nature of that relationship secret from Phil, she was going to have a lot of devious explaining to do when he found out Vivian had left her a hundred thousand pounds.

'Come on, Ivor,' she called over her shoulder, 'we don't want to be late for tea.' Like a nanny. Perhaps that was a clue to her reaction. While Phil talked freely enough about his own peccadilloes (to me, at any rate), I didn't think he'd be so open-minded about hers. Long ago, I remembered, Phil had been a Catholic and, beneath his indulgent condescension, he fully accepted Eleanor's maternal authority—she was for him the Immaculate Mother, to be kept free from taint at any cost. Even for a hundred thousand? It was a high price of course—but it still made her a whore.

'Coming!' I shouted. As I began to trot to catch up, I thanked God that Philip hadn't known about the money before Vivian died.

14 Professional Skepticism

'How are we?'

I smiled at that gentle inquiry—the invariable opening to our weekly sessions, which might still be going on if I hadn't soon realized the disease I was suffering from was none that a psychiatrist could cure.

'It's alright, Shep,' I said as we passed into an untidy little living room, 'this isn't a professional visit.'

'Ah. I'm glad to hear that.' There was a note of relief—or was it regret?—in his voice. 'I thought at the inquest you seemed ... a little upset. Do sit down.'

'Cyril gave me your new address. I didn't know you'd moved.' As I sat down, a puff of dust rose from the couch.

'Moved? Oh yes—that was some time ago. It suits me better here,' he said, as if apologizing for the general shabbiness of the flat. Before, he and his sister Jerry had kept an elegant small house in Gayton Street, and he'd seen his patients in a cheerful sunny room giving on to an impeccably neat garden. I wondered what had made him exchange that bright place for this dusty patch.

In a baggy sweater and worn flannels, he too looked dusty. His heavy, contemplative face was grey—almost as grey as his hair—and marked with lines of insoluble anxiety or fatigue. At Cambridge, as a medical student, he had been a few years older than the rest of us, but now he looked in his sixties. He waited with all the impassivity of his profession, and I guessed that he had long ago forgotten how to manage ordinary friendly intercourse.

'How's Jerry?'

'Why do you ask?'

I smiled. 'Perhaps I really meant, how are you?'

'She is not here.' He glanced round the room, as if to make sure. 'She hasn't been well, I'm afraid.' He made an effort. 'In and out, you know. The death of our father was a destabiliz—a great blow. Unfortunately prognosis becomes less hopeful as middle age progresses. For the moment she is better. She has a fancy dress shop.'

'Well,' I said, remembering her tremendous energy and her sense of fashion, 'I expect she'll make a go of that.'

'Yes.' He took off his glasses and began to polish them with his handkerchief. There was no more to be said.

'Shep, I really came to ask you about Vivian.'

'Vivian?' He stopped polishing. 'I can't talk to you about Vivian—you should know that, Ivor.'

I was taken aback. 'Why on earth ... are you telling me Vivian was a patient?'

'I'm not telling you anything, Ivor.'

'So that's why you were at the inquest.' I had put my foot into unexpectedly murky waters. 'Doesn't confidentiality end with death?'

'Not to you, Ivor. I'm sorry, but you're not a professional, and I don't really understand your interest.'

95

I suppressed my irritation and took out a cigarette and lit it with pedantic calm. 'I'm not interested in Vivian's life—I'm interested in his death. Take a look at this.' I handed him Mr Marsham's card.

He put on his glasses. 'Smith—Soper—Camrose. I see. What have they got to do with Vivian's murder?'

'Maybe nothing at all—nothing directly. It's a long shot. You see, Lady Winter has evolved a theory which—well, which I think is worth looking into.'

'Tell me about it,' he said neutrally, yet I thought I detected a spark of interest behind the protective lenses.

I smoked in silence for a few moments, then launched into my sales talk, trying to make as cogent a case as I could out of what might be no more than Lady Winter's thirst for vengeance. It sounded lame even to my own ears and, when I'd finished, I expected Shep to dissect it pitilessly.

But he surprised me. 'Curious,' he said, then lapsed into reflection. Two minutes, three minutes—I waited patiently. 'So what is it that you want?' he said at last.

'Including these three, I want a list of all prisoners convicted of murder—or manslaughter—and rape who have been released over the last five years. I want to know which of them, if any, have died—or if any of them are missing.'

'I see.' He paused. 'Of course, you must realize how comparatively rare vengeance killings are in our society. You are not talking about a man, let's say, who kills his wife's lover—and perhaps his wife too—in hot blood. The nearest approach I can think of to your idea is the prisoner who feels he has been wrongly convicted or sentenced, who swears to get the judge when he is released, and, in fact, does so. There was one such case not too long ago. But what you are positing is very much more complex.

'The effect of a woman's murder and rape upon her immediate family can be very destructive—in terms of death, suicide, divorce and serious mental disturbance the, as it were, peripheral casualty rate is high indeed, but that is not so much an effect of the tragedy itself as it is a result of the guilt the tragedy induces in the individuals of the family. Now—'

'I'm sure that's all very good textbook stuff, Shep.' I stubbed out my cigarette and lit another. 'But couldn't one just as well put down all these "peripheral" effects simply to grief?'

'That is an old point of dispute between us, isn't it?' He smiled faintly—and I was astonished and perturbed to feel that I had somehow wounded him. 'But I think you would agree that grief does not engender murderous impulses.'

'No,' I said quickly, 'of course not.'

'Let us just say then that in the case of a loved one's death—particularly when that death is sudden or accidental or unexpected—there is an element of guilt in the grief. One blames oneself—if only I had or had not done this, that or the other, he/she would be alive today. And on the unconscious level guilt is far more powerful and merciless than that. Grief is prophylactic and does its work naturally, but guilt is a destroyer and a distorter. That is, if it is not brought out into the open, understood and come to terms with. If it is come to terms with, then the prognosis for a family which has suffered such a tragedy is good—that is to say, there would be no undigested desire for vengeance. If the guilt, on the other hand, goes entirely unresolved, the effects are likely to be fairly quickly and obviously shattering—not conducive to the maintenance of a steady purpose of revenge over a period of years until the murderer is released. But you are positing not only that such a purpose is maintained and acted upon, but, in addition, it is transferred to other released prisoners, who have no personal connection at all with the avenger, and even to a lawyer himself guilty of no crime whatsoever.'

'So, q.e.d., I have no case.'

'I am not saying that, Ivor. I am saying that you have a theory which is full of holes.'

'Well, forget about guilt for a moment—there *are* other motivations in life. Take the case of the father whose daughter has been—'

'Why a father?'

'Oh come on, Shep,' I felt the blood run to my cheeks, 'that's just too easy.'

'Is it? Then let me ask you this: suppose that Henrietta had not died because she fell from the window, but had been killed in a hit-and-run accident in the road. How would you feel about the driver?'

'Shep—what the hell do you think you're doing?'

'Answer the question.'

'It's bloody obvious, but I'd like to—'

'Then tell me, if it's so obvious.'

'—to know why you're—'

'How would you feel about the driver?'

I took a deep breath. 'All right. To be honest, I suppose I would feel a murderous rage, but I don't see what that's—'

'And what would you *do?*'

'I'd go to the ends of the earth to find him and. . . .'

'And kill him?'

'No. Bring him to justice.'

'But of course there is in fact no such individual.'

'No, and I don't see—'

'Unless it is yourself.'

'That's nonsense.' I stood up and went to the window and looked out at the mean street for a moment, then turned back to the room. 'Why are you trying to trap me into admitting what I don't feel?'

'I am not seeking to trap you. But is it not remarkable that you have—with only the thinnest of coincidences to go on—that you have on that basis fixed on Vivian's murder as a crime of revenge, in support have hypothesized one or more other related crimes of vengeance, and have imagined an avenging killer for whose existence there is no evidence and zero probability?'

'I—I admit it's a long shot. It's not my theory—but Vivian *was* murdered. Evidence is what I've come here for. It's a possibility, that's all—such an avenger may exist.'

'If he exists, and when you find him—do you think you will have found your daughter's killer?'

I felt a pain in my chest like a cold knife. The house opposite had a hole in the roof and pigeons flew in and out. I moved slowly to the couch and sat down. I was overwhelmed with a sense of abandonment, of the birdless world, of the bright Channel bereft of vessels.

'What? Oh—oh yes, I'd like a drink very much. Scotch, if you've got it, Shep.'

The tumbler, I noticed, was grubby around the rim, but the whisky strengthened me. 'So the whole thing's impossible—beginning and ending in the disorder of my guilt-ridden brain?'

'No. Analysis of motivation does not necessarily destroy the validity of the goal. All I am saying is that no one will serve you as a scapegoat. But the fact that you are seeking one— other than yourself—is an encouraging sign, and I should not like to see you return to your somewhat depressed and closed-in existence.'

'The patient is improving.'

'You are not my patient,' he said quickly. Then he smiled. 'You are a budding investigator, aren't you? And an investigator must be able to look at the facts objectively—which means he must discount any personal emotional investment which would prejudice the direction or interpretation of his investigation.'

I felt a tremor of resentment at this typical psychoanalytical shilly-shallying. 'Shep, if you don't get off the fence, the ambivalence will enter into your soul. You've just been making a heavy point that there are no facts, so what good is all this magisterial objectivity if there's nothing to decide?'

'Sorry,' he said, but gave me a grin—like most extremely serious men, he took a kind of coy pleasure in being mildly teased. 'But I didn't exactly say that there are no facts to support your hypothesis—only as far as I know, there are none.'

'That's a little different.'

'Yes, but only a little. As a member of the Parole Board, it is highly unlikely that the murder of any murderer-rapist released on licence would have escaped my attention. As it happens, I can go further than that and say definitely that no such murder has occurred—at least in the last five years.'

'How can you be so sure? You keep tabs on them all?'

'Of course. Released life-sentence prisoners are never entirely free men, you know; they are let out on licence which lasts for the rest of their lives—which means they have to report to a probation officer at periodic intervals and may be recalled for a variety of reasons. Some of your men, mainly those convicted of diminished responsibility manslaughter, received lesser sentences—but even there, when they are released they remain on probation for a longish period. I can assure you, Ivor, if anything happens to them, we know.'

'I see.' I finished my whisky and lit another cigarette, and tried to think. I was fairly sure Shep had something up his sleeve—they always do—it was just a matter of asking the right questions. 'Don't I recall that you were off lecturing in the States a year or two ago?'

He nodded. 'Yes, I was at Stanford for five months last year.'

'Then couldn't something have happened while you were away?'

'No. I checked.'

'You checked—why?'

'Because I was asked to.'

'And who asked you?'

He heaved himself to his feet and, taking my glass, moved ponderously to the table by the window. He was in shirtsleeves—the room was oppressively warm and stuffy—and I could see how his stocky frame had run to fat. At Cambridge he had won a blue four years running as a middleweight boxer, but it wouldn't take much of a blow to that protruding belly to fell him now.

'Well, that is the curious thing I mentioned at the beginning—and why I have refrained from dismissing your idea out of hand.' He gave me my whisky and sipped one of his own, but didn't sit down. 'You see, the person who asked me was Vivian Winter.'

He got a reaction then, all right. Half my whisky went into my lap as I jerked my head up. 'For Christ's sake,' I said, 'why the hell didn't you say so in the first place?'

'My dear Ivor,' he frowned, 'I had to find out something of what was in your mind, didn't I?'

Suddenly I laughed. 'Yes—oh yes, I suppose you did. One must never dispense with the formalities. Well, come on—spit it out.'

He nodded. 'Wait here just one moment.' He put his glass down and left the room. He came back almost immediately with two sheets of paper in his hand, one of which he passed to me. It was a simple list of twelve names, as follows:

Aspinall, J.
Marlow, L.W.
Haines, F.D.
Latham, D.
Higgs, H.C.
Ward, J.W.

Billings, G.B.
Grange, J.J.
Petrie, P.
Yates, D.W.F.
Maynard, M.H.
Dalby, T.C.

I was puzzled. 'What is this?'

'That is a copy of what Vivian gave to me when he came to see me about eighteen months ago. All those men had been sentenced for the dual crime of murder and rape some time ago, and all had been released within the previous five years. He got the list from Pulteney at the Home Office; he came to me to find out where they were and what they were doing now. It is a most curious and remarkable coincidence, you must admit.'

I felt a lurch of relief in my stomach. I shook my head. 'It's no coincidence, Shep—it means he was on to something.'

'I doubt that—I don't think it follows.'

'Did he tell you anything—did he say why he wanted the information?'

'No. He only said that it was important and that I would have to take it—to take it on trust.' There seemed to me to be a trace of bitterness in his voice.

'But you did give him the information?'

'Oh yes, I gave it him. But I assure you there was nothing—absolutely nothing—to even faintly justify the suspicion that is in your mind.'

'You mean, all these men are alive and accounted for?'

'No—no, not exactly. One was dead and one was missing—and one died subsequently.'

'Tell me about them, Shep.'

He hesitated. 'Very well,' he glanced down at the page he'd kept; it was covered, I saw, with his minute and indecipherable handwriting. 'To take them in order. Marlow. Marlow was an elderly man who had served nineteen years. He was suffering from inoperable cancer of the bladder and was released on compassionate grounds to his wife. In normal circumstances, he would never have been let out—not if I had had anything to do with it. He was a very dangerous man, guilty of a long succession of violent crimes, of which the last was peculiarly horrible.' Shep looked up at me over the top of his glasses. 'He nevertheless retained the love of women—no less than three wished to take him. He died five weeks after release, heavily sedated, at peace in the arms of his wife.'

'Keith—you're making that up.'

'Ivor,' he said carefully, 'you lead a protected life. Latham. Yes, Latham is the man who disappeared—failed to report, not particularly unusual. But all efforts of the police to trace him have so far proved unsuccessful—that is unusual. Latham was an intelligent man. He was the sort of personable and capable handyman—black economy of course—whom we all know. They're at a bit of a premium. Not a vicious man. His conviction actually was for diminished responsibility man-slaughter.' Shep took off his glasses and rubbed his nose re-flectively. 'He'd gone to do some work for a young couple in a block of flats, if I recall correctly. The husband was at work, and Latham took the opportunity to rape the wife—alone, that would have been very difficult to prove—but she then locked herself in the bathroom and, presumably in a state of terror, climbed out of the bathroom window and fell a couple of storeys and broke her neck. I recommended an early release for Latham—he only served three or four years, I think— partly because in my opinion he would have been acquitted if the woman in question hadn't happened to have been pregnant. One of the shibboleths of our society, Ivor, is that pregnant women do not sexually entice men.' He sighed.

'Well?' I said.

'So be it. Not long after his release, Latham simply upped stakes and disappeared—so far, without trace. Foolish, but they will do it. On balance, I don't think he will do any further harm.'

'He certainly won't if he's dead.'

Shep pushed his glasses back on his nose. 'Very well. Next. Maynard. Well, Maynard committed suicide.' He laid down the paper, as if that was that.

'Did he?' I said. Maynard—a common enough name, but I'd heard or seen it somewhere recently. 'How?'

'How? He drowned himself.'

'Or someone pushed his head down in the bath?'

'He threw himself in the Thames at Putney. There's no doubt it was deliberate—he'd drunk the better part of a bottle of whisky; there was a strong tide and with all that alcohol in his blood, he didn't have a chance.'

'Why did he commit suicide?'

'Does it matter?'

'I'm not sure. Did he have a wife?'

'Oh no.'

'A mother?'

'Yes—yes, he did.'

So that was it—Georgina Deirdre Maynard, 12 Ember Road, Putney, fifteen thousand pounds.

'The mother was part of the problem,' Shep said heavily.

'In what way?'

'Well, I don't see why I shouldn't tell you.'

'In layman's language,' I prompted.

'I've been doing my best. I should tell you that I was more than usually involved with Maynard's case—I gave expert testimony on his behalf at the original trial, testimony which was, I may say, ignored in the verdict which was a straight conviction for murder. The boy—he was not quite twenty-one at the time and emotionally quite under-developed—had indeed raped and killed the girl but to my mind it was clear that he had acted under an overwhelming compulsion and was not, in any true sense of the phrase, responsible for his actions. The father, who had been a post office supervisor or something of the kind, died when Mike was a baby. The mother was left in straitened circumstances, but she was a woman of strong character and immediately set about earning her own living, first as a daily woman, because she had no special skills, later as the manageress of a small second-hand clothing shop. She was sensible, prudent, hard-working, but her attitude to her son was lamentable. Although she was a pretty woman, she didn't marry again and I doubt whether she had any serious relationship with men—the result was that the whole weight of her emotional and sexual life devolved on Mike, to whom she was both prudish and seductive. He was an intelligent boy, did quite well at school, was rather good at sport, and eventually got a job in the selling line at Harrods—to all appearances he was a model son, as so often happens in this kind of case.'

Shep sipped at his whisky, holding his glass awkwardly like the non-drinking man I'd always known him to be.

I said, 'But inside he was a mess?'

'Yes, if you want to put it so. His relationship with his mother was absolutely dominant—outside that he had no emotional, and certainly no sexual attachments of any kind. He was essentially homosexual—but that had to be savagely repressed of course. His rather enfeebled efforts to prove his normality ran up against his mother's total possessiveness— on the two occasions he went so far as to bring a girl home, it was a disaster. They were ruthlessly dissected and dismissed—and in any case could hardly stand comparison with his beautiful, devoted, competent and respectable mother. The double bind was complete—to deny his homosexuality, he had to prove his heterosexuality, but any attempt to do so, though superficially encouraged, resulted in an overwhelming sense of guilt and disloyalty. It was an insoluble conflict that might well have led to suicide or total breakdown—in the event it was rape and murder.'

'Why couldn't he simply have left home and lived the gay life?'

'That would have been the worst betrayal of all. However, you are quite right—it was on the basis of that solution that he was eventually paroled. He had been a model prisoner—he was moved to an open prison in two years and, I think, for the first time in his life was really happy. We found him a job at a big London department store—not Harrods of course—and he was released on condition that he lived in an approved hostel in North London. I had him here to stay with me on the weekend of his release and I must say I was optimistic—I thought he had got the situation relatively straight, the necessity for minimal contact with his mother, for instance. Unfortunately, I overestimated his capacity to resist the pressures his mother brought to bear. After six months in the hostel, he went back to live with her in her flat at Putney—she'd had to sell the family house, incidentally, in order to pay for Mike's defence. There was absolutely nothing I could do about it. Within three weeks he was dead. I gave evidence at the inquest. The mother, of course, saw the devil's hand in it, but there's no question that the verdict of suicide was the correct one.'

'But all the same, you blame yourself?'

'I made a mistake. One has no business being in my profession if one starts blaming oneself.'

104

'In other words, you are miraculously exempt from the inexorable laws of guilt which you've been telling me about?'

'Professionally, yes,' he smiled mildly, 'personally, of course, no.'

'A nice distinction—and a neat trick, if you can do it.' I stood up. I wanted to walk about and cogitate, but the room was too small for stretching either the legs or the imagination. I went to the little table instead. 'May I?'

'Of course—help yourself.'

Outside, it was raining and the pigeons perched on the opposite roof already looked bedraggled—didn't know enough to come in out of the rain. I poured the whisky. Perhaps living in this ghastly place was some complex form of self-punishment.

'So,' I said, turning, 'we are left with the three names on Mr Marsham's list. Smith, Soper and Camrose. Vivian didn't ask you about them?'

'No, he didn't need to. He defended them originally and probably kept in touch—so he'd have known where they were. He was conscientious in that way—very concerned.'

'Yes—Howard League, Prisoners' Aid, etc.'

'Oh, you knew? He usually kept fairly quiet about it. He did a lot of good—persuaded a lot of the larger firms to take on a few prisoners every year as a matter of policy.'

'Did he?' I was faintly surprised, with no very good reason—after all, he had got me my job. I drank some whisky. 'You know, I think we'd better check up on those three clients of Vivian's.'

'Oh I did that at the time—just to see if Vivian's list was complete. Camrose didn't come into it because he was still inside, but I know about him anyway because oddly enough his name recently came up to the Parole Board—he's going to be released in two or three weeks. Smith is alive and well—or was three months ago—working in book-bindery just outside Oxford. Now as for Soley, he was released last July after only—'

'Soley? You mean Soper, don't you?'

'Yes, Soper—he changed his name to Soley after he got out. He—'

'Is he married?' I felt a quick thrust of excitement.

'Why this interest in their matrimonial arrangements, Ivor?' He looked at me over the top of his glasses.

'Well, is he or isn't he?'

'He was, yes.' He paused. 'Soley is dead.'

'Cancer or suicide?'

'There's no need to be sarcastic. He died four or five months after his release, in a car accident or some such thing—I didn't bother to go into the details, but the verdict at the inquest was quite definitely accidental death.'

'Where did this happen?'

'In Bath, I suppose—that's where he'd gone to live.'

'And Vivian got him a job.' And left thirty thousand pounds to his widow, Estelle Jacqueline Soley of 45 Riverside Road, Bathwick, Bath.

'I shouldn't be surprised. It would have been a characteristic thing to have done.'

'Yes.' And characteristic to leave small fortunes to the victims of his professional failure? Were all those legacies the price of some obscure guilt? I shook my head. 'Shep, tell me about Soley's crime.'

'I can't, I'm afraid. I was in the States when his case came up for review, so I didn't see the papers. I have the impression that he was convicted of murder and rape though it might possibly have been manslaughter. You'd have to check on that. Why?'

I rested my glass on the arm of the couch. 'We've got fifteen people—twelve on Vivian's list, three on Cyril's. Marlow was a dying man when he was released, Camrose is still inside. Of the remaining thirteen, Maynard and Soper-Soley are dead and Latham is missing, one might say, presumed dead. Just for the purposes of argument, if those three deaths were not accidental or suicidal but were deliberate murders, then why them rather than the other ten? I can think of a good many possible reasons—simple availability could be one—but it might be something particular that the three original rape-murders had in common, something special which the putative avenger somehow identified with. It might be to do with the nature of the victim or the circumstances of the crime, I don't know. But you see my point, don't you?'

'Yes.' Shep sighed. 'There's a certain logic in what you say—there often is in the realms of pure fantasy.'

'Vivian didn't think it pure fantasy.'

'Vivian, poor fellow, must have been understandably upset by Soley's death.'

'Not just Soley's—Maynard's too.'

'What do you mean—how do you know that?' He asked sharply.

I was hesitant to use up my ammunition, on the other hand it was important to plant a real kernel of doubt in Shep's mind. 'Vivian made a new Will, about a month before he died; among numerous other legacies, he left a large sum to Mrs Soley and to Mrs Maynard.'

'I see.' He stood up slowly and came over to the table and refilled his glass. I watched him looking out at the grey sky and the ruined roof.

'Isn't that suggestive?'

'What? Oh yes.' He too was unprotected. 'Yes. Though not necessarily in the way you think.'

'What does that mean?'

He turned to me with a faint smile. 'Nothing—nothing that can be talked about.'

'Look, was there something wrong with Vivian?'

'There's something wrong with all of us.'

'All right,' I said; I didn't have the heart to push him—not now, but one day soon perhaps. 'Well, let's see if you agree with this. There are two points that strike me as suggestive— one is the fact of the legacies in itself. In the case of Soley, he may well have had a sense of personal responsibility, but that certainly doesn't apply to Mrs Maynard. He had no connection with the Maynards. And it isn't as if Vivian had a generalized elephantiasis of the conscience—otherwise he would have left some compensation to Mrs Marlow, as well. The difference is that Marlow died naturally, and my bet is that Vivian knew that Maynard didn't—and nor did Soley.'

'If he knew that, why didn't he go to the police?'

'Because he couldn't prove it perhaps—or wasn't ready to prove it. By the way, was Latham married?'

'Yes—no. That's to say, he had a common law wife—I seem to remember the prosecution making some play with it, "a man of generally loose morals" and all that hypocritical cant.' He went back towards the couch.

'A different name then?'

107

'Yes, possibly.'

'Could you check?'

'All right. Why? Is there another woman named in the will?'

'Oh, several,' I said blithely.

Shep let himself down onto the couch; sitting there, his eyes magnified by the thick lenses, he reminded me of the rabbit crouched in the woods. Shep—the detached expert, the responsible public figure, the cool professional, the old friend and last person to be scared of anything—gave the impression of a frightened man. 'Well,' he cleared his throat, 'go on—what's your other point of significance?'

'The other point is the date of the Will. He didn't just add a codicil or two—he drafted an entirely new document tidying up all the loose ends, as if he might die at any moment. And a few weeks later he was dead. I think he was aware of danger. I think he knew he might be murdered. I don't think it came as a surprise.'

'No, perhaps it didn't.'

I crossed over to the couch opposite and sat down. 'Shep—did it surprise *you*?'

'No,' he said softly.

'Why *not*?'

He stared at me for a long time without expression. At last he said, 'Ivor, I think you'd better get on with it.'

'Right. Then I shall need your help.'

'How?'

'I want the dossiers of Soper, Maynard and Latham for a start—the whole thing, but particularly transcripts of the trials.'

He began to shake his head. 'I don't think I . . .'

'You'd have done it for Vivian.'

'Vivian wouldn't have needed me for that.'

'But I need you.'

'You understand the documents you're asking for are absolutely confidential. The transcripts you might eventually be able to get hold of, if you could show good cause, which I doubt you could, but the procedure is laborious, to say the least. There is no justification whatsoever for my—'

'Yes there is. I understand what you're saying—betrayal of trust and responsibility and all that. But the fact is that if there's even the shadow of a possibility that I'm on the right track, then there's every justification. Without wishing to be melodramatic, it just might be a matter of life or death—for someone.'

'Yes—it's on that basis I'm going to agree. It's unwise—but after all, I've always been something of a rebel.'

I looked away from his grey conventional visage and masterfully fought down a wild burst of laughter. 'Quite,' I said gravely. I stood up. 'Can I have them tomorrow?'

'Tomorrow? I shouldn't think so—I'll try to get them by the end of the week, but I can't promise.' He rose to his feet. 'Er, exactly how do you propose to proceed?'

'I shall go to the horse's mouth. Mrs Soley might be the best place to start.'

We moved into the corridor.

'I can't say I wish you luck, Ivor—the contrary, really.' He began to unfasten the complicated series of locks on the front door. 'You know what I think. Don't let this become too important to you. There's likely to be an—'

'—an element of danger. If I'm right. Yes, I'm aware of that, but hardly from Mrs Soley.'

'That wasn't quite what I was going to say. No matter.' He had the door open now. 'But just remember that however conscious Vivian might have been of some threat to his life, when it materialized it came from an unexpected quarter and he was caught quite unawares.'

'Vivian was a target,' I said as we shook hands. 'Nobody knows about me.'

He smiled. 'Well, take it easy.'

I left Shep happier than I found him; and, after penetrating the professional defensive system, it had been much easier to extract information than I had feared. It was as if I had somehow relieved him of a secret burden. As I descended in the smooth modern lift, I had that curious feeling of being subliminally manipulated. For a man who had spent so many years sedulously (and ineffectively) cultivating his own back garden, the wide world was suddenly full of discomfiting questions.

15 Wine and Roses

It was the kind of case which would be dealt with in a couple of paragraphs under the heading, 'Dorking Accountant Murders Baby-Sitter,' and which one would turn away from with a shrug of distaste. The bare facts were that Kenneth Frederick Soper, 35, driving Frances Price, 18, home late one winter's night, had stopped the car, raped the girl, then had cold-bloodedly placed her under the back wheels of the vehicle and run her over. He put the body in the boot, went home to his wife and the next day drove to work in the normal way. Interviewed by police officers at his Leatherhead office, he led them down to the car park and showed them the corpse.

Yet it was a different and more complex matter reading the transcript of *Regina v. Soper*. Shep had been better than his word and had managed to get the whole Soper dossier delivered to me at the *Gazette* offices that morning. I had rung Mrs Soley at lunchtime and luckily caught her in; we had made a date for six o'clock at her home. I'd handed in Phyllis's copy (which I hardly had to alter at all), packed up next week's review books, and taken the next train down to Bath. I allowed myself the extravagance of a first-class ticket—after all, I was reasonably well-off now and needed peace and quiet for reading. The file came complete with photos, Soper's prison record, a note of his change of name to Soley, and his death certificate—he had suffered multiple injuries, the chief of which appeared to have been a crushed skull. The verdict had been accidental death, but there was no copy of the inquest proceedings—once dead, he was evidently of no interest to officialdom.

Soper's trial at the Central Criminal Court had been a short one, mainly because the defence had called only one witness, the head of Soper's accounting firm, who testified to the excellence, honesty and probity of the defendant's character. This, I thought, did very little to mitigate the simple and convincing force of the case for the prosecution. Just before twelve one February night Soper had been rung up by Mr Trundle, his next-door neighbour, and asked whether he would mind driving their baby-sitter home, a matter of three or four miles. This was Frances—Fran—Price, who was normally fetched and carried by her elder brother Gerald. Gerald's car, however, was in for repairs and Mr Trundle was unable to start his own car. Soper had agreed but, instead of going by the main road, he had taken a series of small lanes. At a spot he had later pointed out to the police, he had drawn into the side and stopped (it had been a snowy night and the marks of the tyres were still clearly visible the next day). He had then raped the girl, in the course of which action she had scratched him on the wrist and bitten his neck.

According to the prosecution, by this time Fran was unconscious or was immediately rendered unsconscious by Soper, who then deliberately drove the car backwards and forwards over her, probably, in view of the extensive injuries, at least twice. He then wrapped her in a blanket and placed her in the boot (it was barely possible that she was just still alive at that point), intending to dispose of the body the following day. He had been forestalled by the police who had been informed by the parents that Fran was missing. While Soper had not been uncooperative with the police, he steadily refused to either admit or deny his guilt.

The straight facts had not been challenged by the defence, nor had Soper been called to testify on his own behalf. The most Vivian had therefore been able to do was to offer an alternative interpretation of what had happened. This essentially amounted to the suggestion that far from Soper raping Fran, she had seduced *him*—the bites and scratches being such as might easily be inflicted in the throes of the sexual act. The fact that Fran Price had been several weeks pregnant might, Vivian had hinted, instil some doubts as to her inexperience or unwillingness. Because of the banked snow over ice, Soper had been unable to gain sufficient traction to move the car; so he had asked Fran to get out and push. As she was doing so, the wheels caught and he inadvertently reversed, knocking her down and running her over; without realizing what had occurred, he had repeated the process. When he did realise, he

111

had simply panicked, and all his subsequent actions had been attributable to that state of panic.

It was not a very convincing interpretation—and it did not convince the jury (nor the judge, who summed up heavily against Soper)—but it was not impossible. Yet it depended almost entirely on the true character of Soper—and to some extent on the kind of young woman Fran Price had really been. Yet no evidence had been offered about either (beyond the usual encomiums). Soper's prison shots showed a man ten years younger than his true age of thirty-five, good regular features, darkish hair, wide-set eyes, an altogether unremarkable, but not untrustworthy, face, tinged, I thought, with a little sadness. It was the face of an ordinary sensible decent citizen who might equally behave with great valour or like a rabbit in a trap.

The police photos of Fran Price did not bear looking at.

I put the file in my attaché case on top of the week's thrillers—the shoddy tragedy giving the lie to the self-indulgent fantasies of blood. I lit the first cigarette of the day and sat back and stared out of the window.

All in all, the defence of Kenneth Soper had been hardly more than a gesture. I wondered why he had not pleaded guilty. It would have saved a good deal of trouble—and, I guessed, some expense—and added much more weight to Vivian's extenuating explanation. But perhaps Vivian had really believed in Soper's innocence—there were plausible points in his final statement. Would a man so cold-bloodedly sadistic as to grind a young girl to death have then so easily panicked? But of course it wasn't now Soper's guilt or innocence that was important—it was Soper's death.

I arrived at Bath Spa at that awkward time when the pubs are about to close—too late for lunch, too early for tea. I managed to gulp a glass of rather nasty white wine at a wine bar and then, still thirsty and hungry, found my way to the public library. It did not take me long to locate the issue of the *Chronicle* that carried a brief report of the inquest on Kenneth Frederick Soley (there was no mention of his old name or his crime). It ran to five paragraphs, but two of them were devoted to the coroner's strictures on hit-and-run drivers. For Soper, as I read with a queer, distasteful sense of excitement, had not been involved in a motor accident—he had been run down and killed by an unseen and subsequently untraced car. He had died exactly as Fran Price had died.

It was only four when I left the library, and on impulse I took a cab out to the crematorium, stopping at a florist on the way to buy a dozen red roses. As soon as we arrived, I realized it was a mistaken pilgrimage. For one thing, it was raining and the marvellous view was quite obscured. For another, there was no grave or memorial where I could lay the flowers—only a garden of remembrance, where the earth was littered with unconsumed fragments of bone and the rose bushes had been stunted by the bleak prevailing wind. I stood for a few minutes getting wet, but I could feel no proper grief. This was a different occasion and my mind kept sliding round to the question of who killed Soper. I gave up at last and, contenting myself with the notion that I was doing my best for Vivian, got into the waiting cab with my roses and directed the driver to Riverside Road.

Mrs Soley was a surprise; at the back of my mind I had been expecting someone thin and fragile and grief-worn, with lank hair, a prim mouth and reddened knuckles. But this woman was sturdy and well-made, with a deep bosom, a square-cut handsome face, thick dark hair and penetrating brown eyes.

'I'm Ivor Speke—I'm sorry if I'm early.'

'That is quite all right.' She gave my hand a strong shake. 'You are wet. Come in and take off your coat.'

I did so awkwardly, the roses making me clumsy. Finally, I handed them to her and then got rid of my coat. 'Here,' I said, 'these are for you.'

'This is meant to placate me—because you are going to ask me awkward questions?' But she smiled as she said it.

'Not at all. I'm not a journalist,' I said, repeating that idiotic disclaimer with unnecessary loudness.

'Very well, then I will fetch a vase.' I followed her into a long living room filled with large and ugly furniture, but well-kept and scrupulously polished and comfortable in a Victorian fashion. She disappeared into what I took to be the kitchen, and I went down to the far end where a massive dining table with bulbous legs was set in a window that overlooked a small garden, a grassy embankment and then a river.

'I suppose that must be the Avon down there?' I said, as she came back and placed the tall vase of roses in the exact centre

113

of the table.

'Yes, but I am sure you did not come here to talk about rivers.'

'No no....' I stared at her. She wore a plum-coloured knit skirt, part of a suit, I thought, and a high-necked long-sleeved blouse of shantung silk (*Love's Loose Strife* had taught me that much) and gave an oddly mixed impression of brisk efficiency and vibrant life.

'Are you satisfied?'

'I'm sorry,' I said, 'but, you know, your face seems somehow familiar to me.'

'And yours to me. That is understandable. I too was at the funeral. Please sit down.'

'Of course.' And I did vaguely recall that frank gaze amongst all the cast-down eyes—something un-English about it. And it came to me suddenly that she was not English; although her accent was perfect, there was a different pattern to the speech—Polish, French? 'Then perhaps I don't need to explain that I was an old friend of Vivian Winter.'

'I know that or I should not have consented to see you. But what is it you wish to ask me?'

I sat down and took out my cigarettes. 'I wanted to ask you about your husband's death.'

'Why?'

'Well.' I dithered. I had thought I would be sympathetically extracting information from a nervous suburban lady, whom I'd take care not to alarm with traumatic theories of unproven murder. But here I was, on the spot right away—for I could see nothing but the truth would do for Mrs Soley.

'Perhaps I should tell *you*.' She had been eyeing me as I hesitated, and now, as if I had passed the test, she nodded to herself and sat down. 'You think the person who killed Vivian might also have killed my husband. Is that it?'

'Yes, that's it,' I said, my voice shaky with the quick surge of adrenalin. 'How did you know? I mean, what makes you think your husband was murdered—and the link with Vivian if there is one, what was it?'

'That is a lot of questions.' She smiled gravely. 'Very well. I made the connection immediately I heard of Vivian's death— it was very foolish of him to let anyone into his flat alone so late at night. But Vivian was not foolish.'

114

'Far from it.'

'So, he had a very good reason to see this person. A compelling reason. So I ask myself, what such a reason could have been, what was he worried about and had much in his mind lately? And I answer—Kenny's death. Perhaps other things too—but that I am sure of.'

'Excuse me asking,' I said, 'but how did you know that?'

'I knew Vivian quite well,' she said calmly, without nuance—yet that very calmness carried its own nuance of intimacy. 'We talked often about it.'

'And did Vivian think your husband's death was not an accident—that he might have been murdered?'

'Yes—he thought that. Let me ask you, Mr Speke—how much do you know about the crime of which my husband was convicted?'

'I read the transcript of the trial on the way down.'

'Good. Then you are serious.' She laid her hands on the table and looked down at them and sighed. I realised intuitively that it was a sigh of relief. She must have been very much alone—a foreigner, wife of a murderer himself killed, her only confidant also killed, the aura of death about her—alone and very probably afraid. But when she raised her head, she was quite self-possessed. 'The trial, you know, was very far from the whole story.'

'Yes. I guessed that. I was puzzled.'

'And you will have asked yourself, was he guilty or was he innocent. The answer, I think, is both. Guilty because of what he felt—but innocent of what he was supposed to have done. Shall I tell you?'

'Please—if you would.' I lit a cigarette.

What had been left out of the trial was interesting and significant, but Mrs Soley spoke about it with a tranquillity which accepted injustice as a fact of life that should not, however, be allowed to ruin or destroy life.

'Kenny would never talk about it, not even when he came out of prison—and I never alluded to it. This was necessary for his survival. All the same, I am quite sure of what happened that night.'

Frances Price had deliberately set out to seduce Kenny. Earlier in the evening she had rung up from her baby-sitting job next door to say that all the lights had fused and she didn't know how to mend them. Kenny had taken his electrical tool kit and gone round to assist. He had been away precisely twenty minutes.

'Which,' said Mrs Soley, 'is too long to mend fuses, but too short for a seduction. But I think she tried—enough to worry and perhaps arouse Kenny. When he returned he was flustered; he explained that she had caused an overload by plugging in all the electrical apparatus at the same time.'

Later, when Mr Trundle had called to ask Kenny to take Fran home, Mrs Soley had been reluctant to let him go. 'Why, I said, could the girl not get a taxi. But Kenny was too conscientious—a good neighbour. He prided himself on that. But I was uneasy.' And justifiably so. Fran's brother Gerald, who was on vacation from college, was an amateur motor mechanic and often worked part-time at a local garage. It was unlikely that his car would have been out of order or, if it had, that he could not have borrowed another from the garage. Mrs Soley was sure Fran had told him not to pick her up—and also that Fran, who sometimes helped her brother at the garage, had deliberately put Mr Trundle's car out of action, just as she had deliberately fused the lights.

'But why,' I interrupted, 'why should she have wished to seduce your husband?'

'Because she fancied him. You must have noticed how little was said about her at the trial, but I can tell you she was not very nice, that little one. I do not know anything specific against her, but it is a fact that several people we knew in Dorking would not have her as a baby-sitter. The Trundles were different—casual people who did not notice anything very much. It was not just that Fran was irresponsible—she was naughty. You only had to take one look at her face—the eyes too narrow, the pointed little chin, and the calculating mouth—to know that she wished to create trouble. I was for a time secretary to the doctor on whose panel the family were registered, and one hears a lot of gossip, of course. The parents were very conventional nice people—stuffy. The boy Gerald was pretty, very intelligent, but withdrawn, morose. I should explain too that Mr Price, who is a solicitor, would sometimes employ Kenny privately to do the accounting for some of the estates he was administering—and there were occasions when Kenny would go over to the Prices' house to bring some

116

finished work. At once we were invited to dinner, but I think I did not make a good impression.' She smiled—and I could see her silent force troubling the conventional soul of the Prices. 'So you understand, Fran Price had met Kenny. Kenny was—how can I put it?—not marvellously handsome, but very attractive in a quiet, gentle way. And she, I think, excited and frightened him—and she knew it.' She looked at me quizzically. 'You are thinking to yourself, this is a jealous woman talking. But it is not true. I was not jealous of Kenny—*for* Kenny. I did not need to be,' she said sadly.

'I see,' I said. And I did. I could very well imagine the mild-mannered little accountant being overwhelmed by the powerful maternal exoticism of this woman, marrying her, then failing to meet it, becoming more and more conscious of his inadequacy, burying himself in rectitude and columns of figures, while at his side Paris was burning, burning. ... And so the offer—on a plate, as it were—of soft girlish innocence would fire him as nothing else. Poor sweet bastard.

I shook my head. 'But why was none of this brought out at the trial?'

'Because Kenny would not allow it—he refused to let Vivian even try. Because he wished to be punished, Mr Speke. If I were to tell you that his years in prison were the happiest time in his life, would you believe me?'

'Oh yes, I can believe that.' Only too well. I felt a small twinge of envy.

'He was guilty about sex. He was guilty about that stupid little girl's reputation,' she said with a sudden flash of bitterness.

I sighed. Though I had only quickly flipped through the police photos, the images were sharp in my head—Fran's body huddled in the boot of the car, Fran's dead face with the hair plastered to the skull and the mouth open, close-ups of Fran's crushed temple, Fran cleaned up with her mouth shut, Fran's naked body with its pathetic tuft of pubic hair and white arrows marking the wounds to flesh and bone, Fran's thin young thighs spread wide, Fran's sex. ... The 'stupid little girl' had died most horribly. But then—so had Soley.

The smell of the roses seemed to fill the end of the room where we sat, and I was faintly sickened. Why had I chosen red, rather than white—white for Vivian, white for innocence?

'He did not wish to die,' she said.

'What?'

'My husband. He wished to be punished, but he did not wish to die.'

'No.' I put out my cigarette. 'I don't suppose he did.'

'We led a very quiet life here, you know, when Kenny was released. He had a job in the bank, which Vivian got for him, and they were very kind there. It was in the centre of town, where I too have my job, and we would walk to work together, except sometimes in bad weather we would take the bus. We went to the cinema once a week, but otherwise we stayed at home. Kenny's hobby was to make model airplanes and he spent many hours at that. And then there was the dog, Ernest, which I had bought. Ernest was not very fond of me but he adored Kenny. I think Kenny was as happy as he was able to be. It was a harmless existence—he was hurting no one. Yet all the same he was murdered.'

I lit another cigarette. 'What makes you so convinced of that, Mrs Soley? Is it just the coincidence that he was run over, too?'

'Just?' She raised an eyebrow. 'Look, Mr Speke—Kenny sustained multiple injuries. Multiple. That means he was not simply hit accidentally once by a passing car—he was repeatedly run over. It was just at the top of this road—where it runs into Corbett Road and where there is a small public park. These are very quiet roads because they do not lead anywhere—there is no traffic except for the residents and deliveries. It was a winter night, though a mild one, so of course it was dark, but the streets are well lit—and there is an especially large and bright light at the entrance to the park where Kenny was killed. He was not even in the roadway. He had taken Ernest for a walk at nine o'clock as he always did and was just coming out of the park—he must have been very clearly visible. And why did he not see the car? Or hear it? I will tell you. Because the car was waiting a little way up the hill and as soon as Kenny appeared, it started to drift downwards without lights. Then, when it was close enough, the engine was started and it accelerated as fast as possible— unseen, unheard, until the last moment. That was no accident. Kenny had no chance. It was deliberate murder.'

'Yes. Well.' I put a note of dubiety in my voice, but I felt in my bones that she was right—that's how it happened. 'And did you tell the police all this?'

'Yes, I told the police. I told them of how Kenny was supposed to have murdered Fran Price. I told them how easy it would be for anyone to observe that Kenny always took Ernest for a walk at nine. I rubbed their noses in the "coincidence," as you call it. They were kind enough—but who was I? The widow of a murderer, not even English. All Continentals are hysterical, are they not? Besides, I am also at the age of menopause—for men that explains a lot of uncomfortable things. You will not believe this, but they also asked me if I had a lover.' She threw back her head and laughed—a good deep, rich laugh.

'Well, I shouldn't make too much of that.' I smiled. 'The police tend to have sex on the brain, you know.'

'On the brain?'

'I mean, sex does account for a good deal of crime, I imagine—so they tend to think it explains everything. That,' I added, 'and money.'

Smiling, she reached forward and patted my hand. 'I like you. You make jokes at the same things—like Vivian. Wait.' She suddenly stood up and disappeared into the kitchen.

I decided I liked Mrs Soley, too—but I could see why the police might not have taken her seriously. She bore her grief and pain with dignity, with a gravity that marked its depth, yet there were those bursts of pure merriment, the sudden vehemence, the swift mockery, the fine touches of contempt—disconcerting to the official mind.

She came back with a plain unlabelled bottle of wine and two glasses. She pulled the cork, filled the glasses and handed one to me. It was a white wine, almost golden in colour and, as I lifted it, I could smell its richness. I set it down untouched, as she'd made no move to drink hers.

'Mrs Soley, do you mind my asking what you do for a living?'

'Of course not. I sell baby clothes. I have a little boutique here in Bath. I design them, make them or have them made, then sell them.'

'You don't have children.'

'Is it so obvious? No. I would have liked one—a little girl, but. . . .' She shrugged her shoulders. 'This is a good compensation, is that what you think? It's true. A child grows up and goes away—as it should—and then the dream is ended. It may even become a nightmare—is that not so?'

'Perhaps.' But I did not want to be asked questions. 'Do you still have a dream?'

'A small one.' She hesitated, then laughed. 'Why shouldn't I tell you? In France there is a great market for well-designed clothes for babies—here in Britain, we don't care about design so much. Well, you have only to look at the women in the streets. But we can also make clothes more cheaply in this country—at least, I can. English materials are good and they have a certain *cachet* still in France. It only requires someone to listen to what the French wholesalers want and then to give it to them—the design, the *cachet* and the cheapness. It is irresistible.'

'Then why don't you do it?'

'Money—capital. Cash-flow.'

'How much would you need?'

'To make a start? Fifty—sixty thousand, perhaps.'

'What about the banks?'

'They will match what I put up. But it will take me three good years—two with luck—to accumulate enough for that.'

'No, it won't,' I said impulsively—then hesitated. But I had committed myself. And Vivian had clearly known exactly what he was doing, so why shouldn't she know now? 'Vivian left you thirty thousand pounds.'

She stared at me. 'Oh dear. Did he do that?' She turned her head and looked out of the window. The rain had diminished and above the swiftly flowing river the beige stone houses rose in elegant tiers through a dreamy half-mist. I sensed her distress. Under the toughness, there was a delicacy about this woman that would disdain cash on the barrel. Oh yes, by this time, I was sure that she had had an affair with Vivian.

I said, 'It was not payment, you know. It was gratitude— hope.'

'Hope.' She turned back to me. 'Yes of course, you are right.' She raised her glass. 'Thank you.'

We drank. A Chablis maybe—I am not an expert—or one of those Mâcon blancs one used occasionally to find in some small Burgundian auberge, untouched by the sulphuric hand of negociant or shipper. It made the head swirl with summer

120

and delight. When all this is done, I thought, I'd take Vivian's money and go—not to my father's half-baked Côte du Luberon—but to the real wine country.

But it was far from done yet. I said, 'Who would have wanted to kill your husband, do you think—and why?'

She frowned. 'I think—Gerald Price.'

'The brother—the mechanic?'

'No no, that was a hobby only. He became a dentist—he is a dentist now. He still lives in the same house. I hear the Dorking news from Tricia Trundle—she writes to me every year at Christmas. He was a gloomy boy. When Fran died, he had a nervous breakdown. I believe it was quite serious, but he recovered. But perhaps he did not really recover, who knows? He was protective of his sister. One has to guess of course, but suppose she was the only person he really loved—and I'm sure his parents were not very lovable or loving. Her death unbalanced him, but perhaps underneath it made him insane, so that he began to think only death was good enough for the man he thought killed her. One can imagine the obsession growing—he did not marry—growing and growing all the time Kenny was in prison. To kill him with a car would be poetic justice. I don't know. But it is what I think.'

'Ummm.' I emptied my glass. It was a lot of guesswork. 'And what did Vivian think?'

'I am not sure. He listened to me and was very solemn—but he was not the sort of person to commit himself unless he was certain.' She refilled our glasses. 'He came to see me quite often when he was in Bath—I think he was bored up in that big house with all his aunts and his mother—but he did not want to be serious. I was, what you might say—light relief. I was glad to be that for him. He was not a happy man, you see.'

'Wasn't he?' Not happy? I drank some wine. I had always assumed Vivian to be the happiest and sanest of men. Yet I trusted Mrs Soley's instinct. And I reminded myself that he had been Shep's patient.

'Unhappy men are always in danger, Mr Speke.'

I looked at her, then turned away. Outside, the garden was shaggy and unkempt—Kenny had died too soon to get it into shape. She spoke with authority, but I did not want my soul read. I too could have done with some light relief.

'It is no more than a feeling,' she said hesitantly, 'but the

last time he came to see me—the Saturday before his death—
he seemed excited, yet also somehow peaceful in himself. I
cannot explain exactly, but it was as if he had made a decision
or perhaps come to the end of something. I didn't like it. . . .'

I thought about that. The surer I felt that Vivian had been
on to something, the more I cursed him for being so secretive.
What had he found out? What had he been doing—laying a
trap for someone, a trap that snapped shut on himself?

'And you,' she said, 'what do you think? There must be a
connection between Vivian's murder and Kenny's.' She
looked at me anxiously. 'Do you not agree?'

'I think there might be, yes—or I wouldn't be here. But I'm
not sure how direct it is. And there are other—factors.'

'What factors?'

I smiled. 'I rather think, like Vivian, I'd better keep that to
myself.'

'No, Mr Speke, no!' She gripped my arm. 'If you do not tell
me—tell *someone*. Promise me that—you will tell someone.'

She was so close I could smell her—a faint scent of almonds,
mingling with the wine, the roses, heady stuff. . . . 'All right,' I
said mildly.

She released me and leant back. 'And what are you going to
do?'

'Do? Oh,' I said, almost without thinking, 'I think I'll go
and see this chap Price.'

She regarded me gravely for a moment and then—laughed.
'You can tell him you have a bad tooth.' Her laughter flowed
in a rich stream, and I let myself be gathered up by it.

We said nothing further of any seriousness.

She told me a little about her life. She'd been born on a farm,
then gone to Mâcon as a young woman to train as a bilingual
secretary—and had done what she called a *stage* at Kenny's
firm in Leatherhead and met him and, two years later, married
him. Twice a year she visited her parents—and what we were
drinking was a Mâcon blanc from her father's own little patch
of vineyard. I was so pleased to have guessed right that she
opened another, even better bottle—one kept only for
weddings and funerals and christenings. She would never go
back to live there—to be buried perhaps—but not to live.

Listening, I thought how well she had survived the double
disaster that had struck her life and had conquered it and

122

made a place of warmth. No wonder Vivian had liked to come to see her.

She understood that I did not wish to talk about myself and did not ask a single question. A woman of great sensibility.

I embraced her on the doorstep in the French fashion and promised to let her know of any developments. And as I walked down to the main road, I found myself whistling.

16 Ill of the Dead

Phil laughed. 'You sound as though you've fallen in love with the woman.' Settled on the beige couch with cigar and whisky, red in the face this late in the day, his comfortable presence lent cheer to the characterless flat.

'I could do worse,' I said. 'But I haven't time for that sort of thing at the moment. The point is—'

He interrupted me with more laughter. 'I'm sorry, Ivor, but I haven't seen you like this for years. It does the heart good. Go on, go on.' He poured more whisky into his tumbler. 'But I must say it all strikes me as a bit thin.'

'I admit Vivian's death doesn't exactly fit into the pattern. We have to assume he was killed because he was on to Soper's murderer and—'

'What pattern? All you've got is one isolated incident—a chap run over in the dark. Could happen to anyone.'

'No, we've got more than that. We've got Maynard.' I took a photocopy from my wallet and gave it to him. 'It's all I could dig out from the *Gazette* at this time of night, but it'll give you the general idea. Read it.'

Phil made a business of putting on his glasses, then read aloud in his throaty baritone:

Life sentence for salesman
'A former Harrods sales assistant who raped and then drowned an eighteen-year-old woman was sentenced to life

imprisonment at the Central Criminal Court yesterday.

Michael Hugh Maynard, 22, of 17 Peach Place, Putney, who had pleaded not guilty, raped Elizabeth Florence Gray in a punt on the river Thames above Richmond and then forcibly held her under the water until she was dead.

In convicting Maynard of rape and murder, the jury rejected the expert evidence of Dr Shepperton Keith, consulting psychiatrist at the Tavistock Clinic who, in testimony for the defence, described the accused as "a deeply disturbed personality with latent homosexual tendencies."

Mr Justice Blazon, in recommending a minimum of ten years in prison, said that Maynard was a well-educated young man of good background and must accept full responsibility for what he had done.'

'So what's all that about?' He put away his glasses.

'Seven months after he was let out on licence, Maynard was drowned in the Thames at Putney.'

'No great loss to society, I imagine. I suppose your idea is that he was pushed?'

'Yes. I think it's part of the pattern.'

'There must have been an inquest?'

'Yes. Suicide while the balance of the mind was disturbed.'

'Well, that vindicated old Keith all right—he must have been pleased. So what are you on about?'

'One case of a man being killed in the same manner as he committed a murder is bizarre enough. Two must be more than a coincidence. And I have a strong suspicion there is at least one more. I think we're being given a message.'

Phil smiled sweetly. 'Crime doesn't pay? It almost makes one believe in Divine Providence.'

'Yes, in a way you're right. I think someone is trying to play God. You have to admit there is a pattern and patterns aren't accidental.'

'Pattern, pattern! You sound like a demented seamstress.' He stubbed out his cigar and took another from the humidor. 'Look, I don't want to be rude—in one way I'd very much like you to be right about all this—but isn't it becoming a bit of an *idée fixe?*'

'Maybe.' I took a swallow of whisky and watched him carefully cutting and piercing. 'Why would you like me to be right?'

'Get us off the hook, wouldn't it?' He struck a match and began to warm the body of the cigar. 'Have some whisky.' He nodded at the bottle and gave me a quick sidelong glance. 'Police been to see you yet?'

'They interviewed me at Vivian's flat last week. And you?'

'Yes. In the office.' He lit the cigar at last and began to draw on it slowly. 'You know, I never realized before how sinister the phrase "and was asked to account for his whereabouts" is. The problem is I can't—not for the night Vivian was murdered.'

'But I thought you—'

'Yes yes. I *did* come back here—but not until some time after four in the morning, and there's that damn doorman to prove it. Bolton—had to borrow the cab fare from him as a matter of fact. I was cleaned out.' He watched the layer of smoke that floated above the table.

'To tell you the truth, Ivor, I made rather an ass of myself. I was feeling in high spirits after that lunch of ours, so I went off to a little club I know of in Soho. I drank a good deal—and some time in the course of the evening I picked up some girl or other. I don't remember much more, except being bundled into a cab, as I say, at about four in the morning and being driven back here. Of course, I've squared Bolton, but that's only good so long as he goes on thinking it's just some sexual hanky-panky.'

'But surely this woman would give you an alibi?'

'She might if I had the faintest notion who she was or where she lived. The club don't know her, says she wasn't one of their regulars. All I can recall is a blackish girl living in Paddington or Bayswater or somewhere round there. You know how it is when one drinks a bit too much, the mind goes blank—usually a good thing, but in this case it puts me in rather a spot.' He gave a little laugh and inhaled some whisky.

'Oh come on, Phil—what conceivable motive could you have had for murdering Vivian?'

He regarded the red end of his cigar. 'You tell me.'

My heart gave a little lurch, but I kept my face immobile under Phil's sudden hard stare, as I tried to sift through the conflicts of loyalty with doubt, reticence with duty, vague suspicions with hard facts. But there was no real escape from it.

125

'Money,' I said. Eleanor was going to have to fend for herself.

'Oh God—then it's true.' He groaned. 'The superintendent chappie hinted at it—but I'd hoped he was just playing games.' He raised his glass and drank a lot of whisky at one go. 'How much?'

'A hundred thousand, but—'

'A hundred thousand! Why, the little shit!' The colour flooded his face, then slowly receded. He grunted, took a deep breath, then laughed. 'Let me tell you a little story.' He poured some more scotch into his glass.

'I expect you remember that American deal I was so full of last summer when Easton Camber approached me with what was essentially an offer of a joint publishing venture. The deal was to be a straight swap—fifty per cent of Wavelengths, Inc. in exchange for fifty per cent of Prothero Wood. We'd had a couple of lean years and were consistently missing out on some of the best stuff from New York, so naturally I leapt at the proposition. It looked good. But when the accountants got onto it, their boys weren't satisfied with our cash flow position—can't say I blame them. They wanted us to put up another two hundred thousand—pounds, not dollars. Well, the banks weren't going to lend us anything more and Bob Prothero and I could only come up with just on a hundred thousand—and that was stretching us to the limit. So you know what I did?'

'You went to Vivian?'

'Right. He was receptive, as the bankers say. We offered him two and a half per cent above the going rate—he stuck out for three. We went to three, but then he started to hem and haw—said he wanted a piece of the business. That really stuck in my throat, but the American deal was going to be a life saver, so we offered him a five per cent share—more or less over my dead body, I may say. . . .' He paused. 'Unfortunate phrase, that.

'Well, to cut a long story short, at first he said yes, then no, then that he'd have to think about it. And all the time I was sweating blood, because Easton Camber wasn't going to wait forever. He made me crawl, Ivor. It was a beastly, sadistic performance.' He smoked in silent, bitter contemplation.

But I wondered just how true his version was. I'd seen Phil when he was after something he really wanted. All his tact deserted him and he was like a baby with a bludgeon. 'It's a nasty story,' I said slowly, 'but Vivian wasn't the kind of man who—'

'For God's sake, spare me the adulation! I'm sorry, Ivor, but for me he was a mealy-mouthed double-dealing sadistic swine. I hated his guts.'

'On Sunday,' I said evenly, 'you were telling me how devoted you were to him.'

'Was I? Just a manner of speaking.' He laughed.

I lit my last cigarette and drew on it quickly until I could control the surge of anger that filled my head. 'What,' I said, 'happened?'

'Oh—one day I had enough. I ran into him at the Club and I more or less lost my temper—told him to piss or get off the pot. You know what he did? He looked thoughtful for a moment, then smiled and patted me on the shoulder and said in that way of his, "I tell you what, Phil, I'll leave it you in my Will." We were in the bar and there were a lot of people there who must have heard him—one or two of them laughed. I didn't, but of course I assumed it was a joke. I wish to God it had been, now.' He lifted his tumbler, but put it down again without drinking. 'It's about as bad as it can be, isn't it?'

I hesitated, but my reluctance was tempered by my still simmering anger. 'It's rather worse,' I said. 'Vivian didn't leave the money to you—he left it to Eleanor.'

'Did he?' He went white about the gills. 'Did he, by God?'

'Look, Philip, if it's any comfort to you, there were a lot of other women in the Will too.'

'It's no comfort,' he said. 'Who are they?'

'I don't know. Just a string of names—I've no idea who they are.' But I knew I was going to have to find out. 'Look, what's wrong in Vivian making amends for not coming through on the American deal?'

'It would have been a bit belated, wouldn't it? In the normal course of events I'd have been in my grave for thirty years by the time Vivian kicked the bucket. I don't kid myself—the way I abuse my body with all this muck,' he waved his cigar at the whisky bottle, 'I could drop dead at any moment. Have a drink, by the way.'

'But it wasn't the normal course of events, was it? And his Will was not a gesture—it was a well-timed act of generosity.'

127

'A calculated piece of mischief-making, you mean. My God, Ivor—what am I to think about Eleanor?'

'Look, Phil, if there was ever anything between her and Vivian, it was before you even knew her—years ago.'

'Was it?'

'Of course it was. Vivian wasn't the sort of man who'd carry on with somebody else's wife.'

He caught the flicker of uncertainty in my voice and smiled grimly. 'Wasn't he? I don't know.' He struggled to his feet and went over to the chimney piece and knocked his ash into the gas-fired logs. 'That's the damnable part of it. I don't know. And now I never shall.'

'You could always,' I said, 'ask Eleanor.'

He faced me abruptly. 'Don't be a bloody fool, Ivor—that's the last thing on God's earth you ask the woman you love.'

'He's dead, Phil. It's all over now, if ever there was anything.'

'Jealousy doesn't die. And I'm a jealous man. I can't help it. I'd kill anyone who laid a hand on Eleanor. I'd have killed Vivian.' Underneath the plump flesh of the genial publisher, ruthlessness glinted sharp as a cut-throat razor.

'But you didn't.'

'Tell that to the police.' He sighed and came back and sat down.

'If we're talking about motive, Vivian left me money too.'

'Did he, by Jove? How much?'

'Eighty-thousand odd.'

'Aha! So you're in trouble too!' He gave a low grumbling laugh. 'I find that very comforting—very comforting indeed.'

'Why?'

'Ha ha ha!' He really made those sounds and the tears trickled down his cheeks. 'Join the crowd—another puppet of Vivian Winter, QC, Grand Manipulator and Master of Nightmare!'

'As a matter of fact, my motive is stronger than yours.' I said, reining in my anger. 'A hundred thousand isn't going to make any fundamental difference to you—but eighty can entirely alter my life.'

'That may be.' He stared at me unblinkingly, then shook his head. 'But it won't wash. There's that sort of invincible innocence about you, Ivor—you'll never be a real suspect.'

'Sod off, Philip,' I said. Suddenly I knew I was going to get very drunk. Perhaps by tomorrow my mind would have gone blank too.

17 Scars of Love

When I woke up I hadn't the faintest idea where I was. I lay quietly, staring at the ceiling, glancing furtively at the white walls in the hope of recognition.

Then outside I heard a taxi hoot and a dog bark, and suddenly it all came back to me. I'd had a clean sleep, not a trace of the nightmare, but somewhere at the back of my mind the image of a barking dog pranced. What dog? Marigold in the woods yapping at the rabbit? But whatever it was slid away as I tried to recapture it.

It was nine o'clock and Phil had already gone, but not long, for there was still the smell of coffee in the kitchen. I looked vainly for tea, then settled for a glass of orange juice.

I rang Shep Keith and caught him on his way out. He had been about to mail me the files on Michael Hugh Maynard and Derek Latham, but agreed to send them straight down by taxi, instead.

'And, Shep, when can you let me have the others on Vivian's list? By the end of the week?'

'My dear Ivor, I'm very pressed at the moment—I've got a conference in Edinburgh over the weekend and, well, I don't honestly see the urgency.'

'I think I've got something with Soper—I went down and saw his widow Mrs Soley yesterday. I can't tell you about it on the phone, but it might be important.'

There was a pause while he made up his mind. 'Very well then, I'll see what I can do. Let me know of any developments—and, Ivor, take care.'

As I put the phone down, I realised I did have a strong sense of urgency, though I couldn't quite pin down why. The next order of business was Gerald Price. Mrs Soley had said he was still living at the same address, and there was no problem getting his number from the operator.

But getting an appointment was not so easy. He was evidently a popular dentist and nine-thirty on the following Tuesday morning was the earliest he could see me, the secretary said—unless I was in pain. This I hurriedly denied and explained that I was about to move to Dorking and—flash of inspiration—Mr Price had been recommended to me by Mr Trundle. This seemed to be acceptable, but left me feeling frustrated.

I turned on the gas logs and looked up Mrs Maynard in the phone book. There were two numbers, one under Maynard, D.G. and one Maynard, Deirdre, Ltd. I chose the latter. The voice that replied was so clipped and carefully enunciated I assumed it was an answering machine. But it was Mrs Maynard herself and she was not very pleased to hear from me until I spoke the magic words about telling her something to her advantage. She then agreed to see me at four o'clock at her home, it being early closing day in Putney.

As I hung up, the door bell rang. It was the doorman with the package from Shep. Bolton always slightly daunted me and I felt particularly vulnerable in my pyjamas, wondering whether or not to tip him. How much had Phil spent to 'square' him—fifty, a hundred? In the end, I did nothing.

Despite the gas logs, I was cold, the 'luxury accommodation' apparently not running to central heating in the mornings. I put on my raincoat, still damp from the previous evening, and settled down to the files. There was a brief note from Shep in his minute writing: 'The name of Derek Latham's lady was Sheila Wantage, which I couldn't recall the other day. After Latham's failure to report she was interviewed by the probation officer and twice by the police but insisted she had no knowledge of his whereabouts. A dead end, I'm afraid.'

A dead end—I smiled. I fetched Vivian's Will from my case to refresh my memory—yes, Sheila Wantage of 37A Bilberry Street, Eastbourne had been left fifteen thousand. Shep underestimated the efficacy of money in extracting information. Vivian had laid the trail, and it was a fair bet that he'd gone to see both Mrs Maynard and Sheila Wantage. But I put aside the Latham file for the moment, and started on Maynard. As I did so, I felt a twinge in a back tooth, like a premonition.

Two hours later when I finished, I felt the pain—pain and disgust. Shep's expert evidence had been, as these things so often aren't, a model of clarity, but I found myself thinking of old Mr Marsham's *mens rea*. Maynard, according to an eye-witness, had deliberately held Elizabeth Gray's head under water—as though she had been a kitten too many. Despite what Phil called 'my milksop *Gazette* conscience,' I simply could not believe he hadn't known exactly what he was doing. If Shep's evidence meant anything, it simply indicated that Mrs Maynard was implicated too, and my gorge rose in loathing and contempt for her. All the same, I was going to have to go through with it; and I had to remind myself once again that it was the death of the murderer that was my vital concern. It was none of my business to judge on the justice of such deaths.

In the bathroom I took a couple of aspirin I found on the shelf—my head was clear, despite what I'd drunk, but I thought they might calm the spirit. My own medicine cabinet contained no drugs at all, a precaution I had taken years ago when they might have been a real temptation. I cut myself shaving and, as I dabbed at the wound, I found myself examining my own reflection. People had sometimes remarked on the resemblance between Vivian and me—the same colouring, dark eyebrows, grey eyes, a prominent nose, though mine was coarser than his—and abroad we had once or twice been taken for brothers. Was that why Lady Winter had picked me?

Maynard, Soley, Wantage, Wood—I knew, at least, *who* they were now. The unknowns were Ashe, Jasperson, Quinn and Salisbury—and the greatest of these, at a hundred and fifty thousand quid, was Salisbury, Joanna Marigold. And she lived not very far away, in Maida Vale. I made up my mind, found her in the book, and dialled.

On the fifth ring it was answered by a sleepy male voice, 'Yeah?'

'I'd like to speak to Joanna Salisbury, please.'

'You've got the wrong ... who did you say?'

'Joanna Marigold Salisbury,' I said with a brisk precision that would have done credit to Mrs Maynard.

'Oh, yeah, right—hold on. Goldie! Goldie—phone for you.'

Goldie! It clicked—and when she spoke, I immediately

recognized the throaty, languid voice.

'Yes, this is Goldie.' Goldie Grayling—Cyril's wife, or, I rather thought, ex-wife by now. And the bastard hadn't told me—another of 'Vivian's lame dogs,' smirking. 'Hello? Who's speaking?'

'This is Ivor Speke here, I don't know if you remember me, but—'

'Of course I remember you. You're the writer friend of Vivian's. I danced with you at my wedding.'

'Yes, I remember that too.' She was tall, at least two inches taller than me, and I remembered being rather embarrassed by that and by the way this faintly foppish blonde beauty had clung to me.

'I'll bet you do, I was pie-eyed—I expect it was the idea of having to go to bed with that rat Cyril.'

'Oh. Look, I wonder whether I could come along and see you some time, I'd like to—'

'Of course you can. Come and have a drink. Where are you? Well, that'll only take you ten minutes. Come along right now.'

But it was more like forty minutes before I was ringing the bell of her flat in a house just off Sutherland Avenue.

Goldie was a shock, but not as much as I had feared. The facial beauty remained—the high cheekbones, the pleasing contrast of large brown eyes and straw-blond hair which had once plastered her all over the classier women's magazines—but she had grown fat. Even under her loose pink house dress I could see the push of the belly and the rolling bulges of the breasts.

'Have I changed so much?' she asked, catching my glance in the elegant sunny little living room.

I smiled. 'You've lost the bridal look.'

'About time!' She laughed, then gave a little shiver. 'I'll never be a bride again. There's only one man I ought ever to have married, and now he's dead too.'

'Vivian?' I said.

'Vivian. I asked him often enough, but he wouldn't have me. Gin?' she asked, lifting a glass of what looked like pure water from the table. 'That's what I'm having.'

'Fine. Some ice if you have it.'

'All right, darling, I won't be a sec.'

132

I went over to the table and instinctively put my hand on its polished mahogany; her glass had left a damp ring on the surface and as I wiped it clean with my handkerchief, I noticed other more indelible marks.

Close by, a door opened. 'Rex, you fucking pig, haven't you got out of here yet?' But the words were not spoken sharply and her throatiness lent them a kind of caress.

Looking more carefully about the room, I saw other scars and frays. A wing chair with a bright orange loose cover was oddly placed; conscious of my stealth, I moved it—underneath there was an ugly brown wound on the silver beige carpet. I put the chair back and sat on it and lit a cigarette.

'Here—here we are, darling.'

'Oh—oh yes. Thanks.' I took the proffered glass and looked up at her; in the full sunlight her face bore the mark of time's careless way with beauty.

'Yes, it's all a bit tatty nowadays.' She smiled and settled herself on the small, cushion-strewn sofa. 'It's that bastard Cyril's fault. Still, I don't suppose you've come here to listen to all that.'

'Well, yes, in a sense that's just why I have come.' I sipped the neat gin cautiously. 'I'd heard that you and Cyril had split up of course, but I never heard the ins and outs of it. I am not a great friend of his, you know, and even if I had been, I doubt whether he would have confided in me—he's not the most forthcoming of people.' And, I might have added, a damned liar to boot.

'You can say that again. I'm not much of a women's libber—I was a well-known sex object for too long to be able to change my ways, even if I wanted—and then I'm stupid. Oh yes I am,' she said as I started to demur. 'I'm a dumb broad all right. And there's not much for a stupid woman except men. But there are limits—and Cyril was mine. Of course when I married him I thought he was brilliantly intelligent, strong, stable, sensible, just what a featherbrain like me needed. What he was—is—is a total chauvinist pig. Why pig, I don't know— I've always liked pigs. A chauvinist snake, more like it.' She took a heavy swallow of gin.

'How exactly?'

'You really want to know, don't you?' She stared at me with her large brown eyes. 'Well, take money. When we were married, I was making a lot—forty, fifty thousand a year easily, sometimes more. When we bought that house in Regent's Park Terrace, it was with my money, though I found out later—maybe I even knew at the time—it went down in his name. I paid for the furniture, the decoration, all the bills, the ordinary living costs, expensive weekends abroad, holidays in Kenya, Bali, the Seychelles—the lot. I thought nothing of it, it never crossed my mind to ask him what he did with his own loot. He never seemed to have enough money to pay for drinks even, unless there was someone else there to impress. Of course, I had to try to keep off the bottle in those days and I had to watch my diet like a hawk. At first, he didn't seem to mind, he'd smirk a bit as he worked his way through some colossal meal and I picked at a lettuce leaf. The only times he'd get amorous was when he was squiffed and then of course he wasn't much good at it.' There was hardly a trace of anger in her voice, which made it somehow more ghastly. These are not the things one wants to hear about anyone.

I said, 'A nasty picture.'

'It gets nastier. After a bit—two or three years maybe—he began to bait me. "Come on, Goldie," he'd say, "have a drink, you look bloody miserable." I'd always been a good girl and done what I was told, and being miserable is the biggest crime of all in most men's eyes. So I'd have a drink and then another and then the control would go and I'd want to eat—I can see him now shovelling sauté potatoes onto my plate with that sly indulgent look on his face. So I put on weight and began to lose commissions and Barney, my agent, would scream at me, so I got more miserable and drank more and worked less and less, until one day Barney stopped screaming so I knew it was the end. Then Cyril really got pissed off—he started talking about useless mouths to feed. So there I was getting drunker and drunker and fatter and fatter, but I didn't dare leave—I hadn't anywhere to go, no man. Who'd want a fat alcoholic weepy ex-sex object? I'd have never got out of there if it hadn't been for Vivian.'

'Vivian?'

She suddenly slung her feet off the sofa and went into the kitchen, coming back with the gin bottle and a crumpled packet of cigarettes. She settled herself again and filled her glass and lit a cigarette. 'Of course he did it deliberately.'

134

'Who?'

'Cyril. He was jealous of me—jealous because I was pretty and rich and successful and a bit of a celebrity. He hid it for a long time because he liked the money, but then he began to do better, they made him a partner—he didn't need me any more, so he set out to destroy me, and he bloody nearly did. I tried suicide once,' she held up an arm and the sleeve fell back to show a thin white scar across the wrist. 'But of course I made a mess of it. I was at rock bottom when Viv came along and got me out of it. He found me this place here and made me go on the wagon and take a secretarial course, of all things. That didn't take, but I got a job as a tour guide for a bit—languages was the only thing I was ever any good at. I couldn't live off Viv and I didn't have a penny of my own. Cyril had the house and I didn't have anything to show for all those years when I'd paid, and because I'd left him, I couldn't legally screw a sou out of him. Besides, I was frightened.'

'Frightened?'

'Frightened of Cyril. I was afraid he'd come round and beat me up. I used to bolt the doors and windows. I'd *defied* him by leaving, you see, even though he wanted to get rid of me. But to suit him I should have died—"Alcoholic Ex-Model Kills Self." Good solid old Cyril let down by unstable sex symbol. The image really counts for him. You know what he did when we got divorced? He gave me five hundred quid on condition I reverted to my maiden name and gave up any legal right to use his. I hated his fucking name—he could have had it back for nothing if he had but known. It was the only laugh I had out of the whole puking mess.'

My drink was down to the ice. I got up and filled my glass again. 'Goldie,' I said, 'did Cyril ever use any violence towards you?'

'Not really—not within the meaning of the act. I mean his idea of making love was awfully like rape, but that's all right when you're married, isn't it? I was raped once—when I was fourteen—so I know. About rape, I mean.'

I tilted the glass and drank. 'Could you bear to tell me about it?'

'About Cyril, you mean?'

'No, about the rape when you were fourteen.'

'All right, I don't mind.' Yet she frowned slightly. 'You're

135

not the salacious type, are you?'

'No. There's another reason.' I hesitated. 'Did Vivian ever talk to you about rape?'

'Good grief no, we never talked about miserable things. Besides,' she said wistfully, 'I hadn't seen Viv in donkey's years. I expect he'd forgotten all about me.' She looked down at her glass. 'It was when I was out riding one day. I usually went with Percy—that was Miss Percehouse—but it was November and she had 'flu and it was really quite safe in the little lanes where we lived, except for the cars sometimes. This man suddenly came out of a gap in the hedge—a perfectly ordinary man in a brown mack and he started to chat me up a bit and offered Nancy some sugar, which is a nuisance because it's not good for their teeth. Then all at once he took hold of my leg and just yanked me off and dragged me through the hedge into the woods. I don't remember putting up a fight or anything, I expect I was half-stunned. He was strong but he had an awful struggle trying to get my jodhpurs off—he was sort of mauling me and swearing and saying he loved me all at the same time. It hurt—it hurt a lot, but what I most remember was the sort of clammy, prickly feel of the cold leaves on my bare behind. And then he was gone and I just lay there staring up at the branches.'

She stretched her hand out—for a cigarette perhaps, for more gin, for comfort.

'Thanks. I just wanted to die. I knew what had happened, you see. I can understand rapists who kill—like killing a horse that's been injured, it's the humane thing to do, a kindness in a way. At least that's what I thought then and sometimes when I've been feeling really grotty I've wondered whether it wouldn't have been better—I mean, you feel sort of ruined. And if you feel ruined—inside, ruined inside—maybe you go looking for ways to be *really* ruined.

'I think I'd have lain there forever if Nancy hadn't pushed her head through the hedge and whinnied at me softly. I didn't tell Mummy and Daddy.' She looked up at me suddenly, her eyes brilliant with tears. 'It's funny—I never told anyone, not even Viv. You're the first one.' She gave a little hiccoughing laugh and I took her hand and stood there, holding it, staring down at the top of her head.

136

'Is that what you wanted?'

'Thank you,' I said. 'I'm sorry.'

'I feel better,' she said, disentangling her hand and lifting her glass. 'Isn't that amazing? Cheers. You must be doing me good, old Ivor.'

I smiled as I went back to my chair. 'Old?'

'All nice men are old—older. Well—oh, you know what I mean.'

'Yes.' I knew what she meant—affection without sex. I felt a feather touch of jealousy—for Rex, for Cyril, for Vivian?

'What next?' She was girlishly keen for confidences now.

'I wondered what Cyril felt when Vivian came along and "got you out of it"?'

'Oh he was furious! Completely lost his rag. He used to ring me up and shout at me and he wrote me the vilest letters. He wanted to prove I'd run off with Viv, but he couldn't, you see. I mean, I wouldn't have minded, but Viv was careful about that—he rented the flat in my name and only gave me the money for it in cash and for a long time he wouldn't come here—because of private detectives, you see, though I always said Cyril was too mean to spend money on having me watched.'

'But he still kept on as Vivian's solicitor.'

'Did he? I'm not surprised, he certainly knows which side his bread is buttered on; besides he wouldn't have dared take it out on Viv. I'm sure it was all smiles and business as usual. He's terribly sly.'

'Yes, I know.'

'Oh—what's he done to you?'

'He didn't tell me that Joanna Marigold Salisbury was you.'

'Well, he wouldn't, would he? Why did you want to know?'

I laughed. 'It's not quite like that. Let's just say it wasn't entirely honest of him not to. By the way, have you heard from him lately?'

'Funny you should ask that.' She leaned forward to look at me—and it came to me that she was painfully short-sighted. 'Or did you know?'

'No. But I'm glad you have—it greatly relieves my mind. So you....' But of course she didn't know! 'Now, hold on, when did he write to you?'

137

'He didn't write—he phoned. The first time must have been oh a couple of months ago, bloody embarrassing, I was in bed with Rex. Then he rang again, I don't know, a week or two later; then the last time was when Viv died.'

'What did he say?'

'Nothing much, but—but it was creepy.' She ran her finger round the rim of her glass. 'He was actually nice! He said he thought he'd treated me rather badly, couldn't we let bygones be bygones, etc.—all that crap. He can be terribly charming when he wants to, in that heavy-handed way of his, and if you didn't know, you might ... but of course I do know. Then the last time he said he knew what Viv's death must mean to me and what a terrible loss it was to us all. He actually offered to drive me down to the funeral.'

'Is that why you didn't go?'

'Yes. No. I always wanted Viv for myself. I didn't want to share him with all those people. And I didn't have to be reminded of him—there's no way I can ever forget him.'

'Is that all? I mean—Cyril didn't talk to you about anything else?'

'Nooo. Should he have?'

'What he should have told you by now is that Vivian has left you a hundred and fifty thousand pounds.'

'He. . . . Gosh!' She stared at me unblinkingly.

Then she was off the sofa and across the room and on her knees beside my chair, clutching me, her head pressed against my chest, sobbing. 'Oh he loved me—he did love me after all!'

'There there,' I murmured, stroking her smooth hair, 'there there.' It was the first time I'd held a woman in my arms for all these years. Yet her soft warmth pressed against me brought no present comfort nor any touch of desire. Instead, I was transported to a summer's day long gone, a laugh, a golden morning, an innocent embrace. And as at the sound of a distant band or unseen laughter from an open window, I was washed with loss. I seemed to stand at the edge of the bright pool of grief. And hastily I drew back.

'Goldie,' I said matter-of-factly, 'did you ever make a Will?'

'A Will?' She sat back awkwardly on her heels, marvellously ugly with streaked tears of mascara. 'No. I've nothing to leave, except a few petty debts. Oh, wait a minute, yes, I did once—Cyril made me do it just before we got married. He made one too—we left everything to each other.'

'And you haven't changed it?'

'Well no, but it's all out of date now. Isn't it?'

'Not unless you've destroyed it and/or made a new one. Goldie,' I leaned forward and took both her hands in mine—my glass had tumbled to the floor spilling a cold seep of gin on my loins, 'Goldie, you've got to make a new Will right away and tell Cyril you've done it. You've got something to leave now, you're a rich woman.'

'Am I?'

'Richish. And the point is, if something happened to you, as it stands now, Cyril would get the lot.'

'Oh snakes! Would he? Then I'll change it.'

'Yes. Now. Right away. Do you know a solicitor?'

'There's one next door—they're called Festival and Pride, I always notice their little plate. But what's the hurry, nothing's going to. . . .' Her cheeks, rosy with weeping, went suddenly quite white. 'Cyril!'

'Maybe. I don't know what Cyril would do, though I'm beginning to wonder. But let's be on the safe side, let's go and see Mr Festival right now. You make a new Will and have him write to Cyril asking for the old one back.'

'All right.' She nodded and stood up a little unsteadily. 'I'll get dressed.'

'And when we've done that, I'll take you to lunch. There must be a good place round here.'

'Prunelle's, but it's fearfully expensive.'

'What the hell does that matter?'

'That's right. I'm richish. And I expect you've got pots of money.'

'Oh pots.'

My cigarette had burned itself out on the carpet, adding one more to the innumerable scars of love. I lit another—Goldie could afford a hundred carpets now—and poured some more warm gin into my glass. I stood at the window and let the sun warm my face. I had talked coolly enough about Cyril, but I couldn't think of him without the anger coursing round my brain like a mad hare. As I stared down at the peaceful back gardens, my hand shook with the battle to fight off this sudden murderous rage.

When Goldie came back I smiled with relief—and astonishment. She wore a peach-coloured linen suit, with white shoes and a little white bag, and she looked as beautiful as she had on her wedding day.

It was Mr Pride we saw, as it turned out. A nervous little man with damp hands and a bowing and scraping manner, but he got the point at once. A very simple Will just leaving everything absolutely to ... 'to whom, Miss Salisbury?'

Goldie looked at me speculatively.

'No,' I said, 'absolutely not.'

'I know—Mummy! She will get a shock.' She laughed happily. 'She disapproves of me horribly.'

'I think, you know,' said Mr Pride when it came to drafting the letter, his lips a little blue from sucking his ballpoint, 'that if you have reasonable grounds for thinking that you might have expectations under your friend's Will, it would be quite in order for me to enquire. Shall I add a paragraph? Yes? Good. Very well. As I gather it is a matter of some urgency, I shall have everything ready for you to sign this afternoon at—three-fifteen? Excellent.'

It had been a long time since I had taken a beautiful woman—any woman—to lunch. I had forgotten the delicate lift of pride at the hush of waiters, the elaborately decent glances of the diners, one's own sense of restrained panache. Goldie needed champagne, so I ordered a vintage Lanson—rather more than I spent on food in a fortnight. Easy enough to prove I wasn't Cyril, but how could I prove I was not Vivian?

'Ivor,' she said after we had drunk a preliminary glass, 'do you really think I'm in danger?'

'No. Not now. Not after Pride has sent that letter.'

'But all the same I shall bolt the door tonight.'

'It can't do any harm.' I ate an olive.

'Do you think he murdered Viv?'

I carefully spat the stone into my cupped hand. 'No. For the money? But he'd have had to con you into handing it over to him—or kill you too. Nobody could love money that much.'

'I'm not thinking about the money.'

'What then? Jealousy? He must have got over that years ago—even if there was any real cause.'

'Oh, there was real cause all right. And Cyril's patient, you know—look how he worked it with me. But it's not that really—it's that he hated Viv.'

140

'Hated him?' It was a disturbing echo of Phil Wood's words last night.

'Yes. He told me once, when he was bombed out of his skull. I'm sure he didn't remember the next day. You see, Viv had all the things he didn't have—money to start off with, good looks, easy success, friends, women, everything Cyril had to work for and most of which he couldn't ever get. I think what riled him most really was Viv's total confidence in his own charm. It was awful—all that seething jealousy and hate, I mean, which he simply pretended didn't exist. I think that's when I started to be afraid of him.'

'Yes—well, that's just it. From what you say—and from what little I know about Cyril—self-interest is the dominating factor. That's the restraint—that's what would stop him doing anything like that, perhaps what stops any of us doing anything like that.'

'If I wanted to murder someone, it wouldn't stop me.'

For an instant the waiter's hand jerked as he refilled our glasses and a single drop spilled on the cloth. Goldie and I looked at him out of our absorption, looked at each other, and burst out laughing.

We ate lobster and quail and *îles flottantes* and didn't talk of anything serious again.

'And what'll you do with the money?' I asked.

'Oh, spend it, I expect. Don't look disapproving, darling—what should I do with it?'

'Invest it.'

'You sound like Daddy. That's what Daddy would have said—and he went bankrupt, bless his heart.'

'Well then, buy a flat or a house and then put the rest into something you know about—clothes, fashion, I don't know. A model agency?'

'Christ no, not that! I'd only end up giving it to some man. I'm too stupid for business.'

'Goldie, where do you get this idea that you're stupid?'

'I expect I was brought up on it. But I am anyway. There's nothing wrong in being stupid, is there? Most people are, aren't they?'

'Everyone is some of the time, but not everyone is all the time.'

'You don't mind, do you?' She put her fingers on the back of

141

my hand and gave a little caress.

I shook my head. At that moment I was happy as I had not been for years, enthralled but detached, buoyant and sagacious, drunk with all my heart but bright-eyed for truth.

'I know! I'll buy a little house in the country and start a stable and teach riding and jumping. I was really good once—and you don't lose that. I'll shovel out the muck and get fit and stop drinking. And I'll have horses, so I won't need men. Oh Ivor!' She gave me a smile of brilliant glee. 'And Mummy can come and live with me and do the accounts and get cross at my cooking and I'll be a pillar of the village and—'

'You'll be a man, my daughter.'

She threw back her head and laughed so hard that everyone looked round.

'Oh Ivor darling—*you* can always come and stay,' she said, wiping the tears from her eyes with the napkin.

18 Memento Mori

'And what can I do for you, Mr Speke?' She spoke as though I were an obviously dubious customer—the kind of man perhaps who only entered her boutique to purchase a cheap printed scarf for his mistress.

'Mrs Maynard, I have reason to believe—I mean, I rather think that some time ago you had a visit from Vivian Winter?' We sat opposite each other in front of the dead television, on those plump plush-covered little armless chairs that look comfortable and never are.

She said, 'Are you a police officer?'

'No—not at all. I'm just a very old friend of Mr Winter's.' I badly wanted a cigarette, but there was something about the perfect neatness of the place that prevented me.

'Yes?' she said neutrally. In an elegant plain black dress with a double string of jet beads round her neck, she looked exactly the part of a dress-shop manageress or, possibly, a high-class madame. Although she must have been at least fifty, she could have passed for a young forty; she had in a modified form the feline look that I recognized from Maynard's mug shots and which just put her face the wrong side of the beautiful. 'Yes?' she said again with a touch of impatience.

'I am also an old friend of his family. They—that is, his mother Lady Winter—and some of his friends feel that Mr Winter's death might have had something to do with a line of enquiry he'd been making. To be perfectly honest with you, Mrs Maynard, that's not the view of the police. One of the matters he seemed to be taking a special interest in was the case of your son—and of your son's death.'

'What makes you think that?'

'I'm not precisely authorized to tell you this, but Lady Winter has permitted me to look at her son's Will and, under the terms of it, you have been left the sum of fifteen thousand pounds.'

'I see.' She opened her mouth slightly and for a moment the tip of her tongue appeared between her small even white teeth. She stood up. 'Mr Speke, may I offer you tea?'

'Thank you, yes, that would be fine.'

She moved in a rather mincing manner, but she had a perfect figure and beautifully moulded legs. Perhaps I was getting somewhere—at least I had been judged worthy of tea, and tea was exactly what I wanted. After I'd left Goldie I'd had a fearful rush to arrive at Ember Road on time, pushing my old green monster up to a shuddering ninety on Westway. I had risked my licence, being well over the count, and now I desperately needed liquid to absorb the alcohol—and to loosen the taut wire of excitement in my body.

Mrs Maynard placed a silver tray on the table, silver teapot and milk pitcher and hot water jug, bone china teacups, a plate of scones—she must have had it all ready.

She conducted the usual palaver with what I was beginning to see as a characteristic efficiency. Her flat too was neat and efficient, with an unornamented bandbox perfection. Yet it was bleak, as though it as well as the owner had suffered a dreadful loss.

We drank our tea in silence, then she put down her cup. 'Yes,' she said, 'you're quite right. Mr Winter did come to see

143

me. In January.'

'And was it about your son's death?'

She nodded. 'I don't know how much you know about my son, Mr Speke?'

'I am fairly familiar with the original case in which he was convicted, and I know the broad outlines of the evidence and conclusions of the inquest on his death.'

'And what is *your* conclusion?'

'I'm really more interested in what you think, Mrs Maynard. What is your opinion of the verdict of the inquest?'

She had taken a scone and was eating it in a delicate yet curiously ravenous fashion.

'It was utterly wrong. Anyone who knew Michael could tell you how absurd it was. He would never have committed suicide. For one thing he was an exceptionally strong swimmer, before he was sent to prison he had been of county class—if you care to come to his room, I can show you the cups and medals he won, one of them gold.'

'I'll take your word for it.'

She had finished the scone and took a napkin to pat her lips—the upper was narrow, but the lower had a droop of fullness in the centre. 'Michael was perfectly capable of dealing with the river, however fast the tide was running. Then it was said that Michael was drunk at the time—but he never drank. We would occasionally have a glass of sherry in the evening and Michael liked a glass of Guinness with his Sunday dinner, but that is all. A mother knows, Mr Speke.'

She actually said it. 'I'm sure she does,' I murmured.

'He never touched spirits in his life. His father—a civil servant, you know—often drank pink gin. A habit which I strongly disapproved of. He was cut off in his prime.'

No wonder. He must have been a brave man to defy that piercing look of disdain. I cleared my throat. 'But you're not actually disputing the medical findings about the degree of alcohol in your son's blood—or are you?'

'I'm not a fool, Mr Speke. If that was what they found, that is what was there. He was *forced* to drink that whisky.'

'Well, that's an awfully difficult thing to do, you know—to force someone to drink against their will. And you say Michael was strong—presumably well able to take care of himself.'

'You sound like a lawyer. You sound like Mr Winter.'

144

'I'm sorry if I—'

'But *he* came to see my point of view in the end.' Again the tongue tip slid between the gleaming teeth. 'My son was *physically* strong and fit—he did twenty minutes of exercises every morning and his jogging in the evening. But there was a weakness in his nature. I don't deny that and I have never denied that. He was too easily open and affectionate. That is all very well in the home, Mr Speke, but it will not do in the outside world. Perhaps I should have said *persuaded*—he was persuaded to drink whisky.'

'Yeees. But the evidence was that he went into the off-licence by himself and bought the bottle.'

'I have thought about that a great deal. I can see how it happened. Michael was out jogging—it was a cold, windy night, but nothing would prevent him jogging. Sometimes he would go up to Wimbledon Common, sometimes down by the Embankment—this time it was the Embankment. The murderer has his car parked down by the boathouses, probably along towards the end. As Michael jogs by, he leans out of the window; he says perhaps that he isn't well—heart trouble or feels faint—and asks Michael to get him a bottle of whisky, probably gives him the money. As I've said, Michael was always ready to do a good turn—too ready. When he came back, the murderer would ask him into the car—to help with opening the bottle or to pour it. To be friendly, Michael would accept a drink for himself, then another and another, each one easier. He wasn't used to it, Mr. Speke—it wouldn't have taken much to put him out, and he had a lot. Then the murderer pulls him out of the car, drags him to the edge of the embankment and pushes him in and holds his head under the water and then—let's go.'

Her voice hadn't quavered during this recital—she might have been asking me how many lumps I took in my tea. I put down my cup.

'Yes. I see.' And I did—no one went out on a night like that except some physical fitness nut, who'd jog come hell or high water. And the murderer would know that—just as he'd known when Soper walked his dog. He'd watched their movements, studied the terrain, chosen his moment. I could see the boy in that car, with the rain beating on the roof and the river rushing a few yards away, being polite to the stranger who said

145

he was ill, not knowing how to refuse to drink, and soon not knowing anything anymore. . . . Despite the horrible crime he had committed, how could one help but be sorry for the poor blighter with his mania for exercise and his god-awful mother?

Perhaps she detected my sympathy, for she went on: 'There was no reason why Michael would have killed himself, Mr Speke. He had come home at last after almost eleven years away. Whatever other people may have said or thought—and there was a psychiatrist who said the most horrible things about Michael—I never wavered. We had just started a new life together. It was the happiest time in his life—and in mine too.' She put her palm down and slowly stroked the velvet of the chair. 'I loved my son, Mr Speke.'

'Yes. Do you have any idea of who might have wanted to murder Michael?'

'There are always those who hate good, decent, respectable people like us. I have never tried to hide the terrible things we have suffered. I did not run away or change my name. I would not give them that satisfaction. Despite them, I have made a success of my life. I have held my head high. I have refused to accept punishment for a crime of which my son was innocent. They punished him—and now they have killed him. But they shall not punish me.'

I think if I had simply heard her—and not seen the soft little motion of her white hand on the red velvet—I could have accepted the dignity of her words. It wasn't the touch of paranoia that made me feel slightly sick—I wasn't sure what it was. I lit a cigarette, I didn't care whether she minded or not. But to my surprise she got up and fetched an ashtray from the mantelpiece and put it beside me on a small table. As she bent over I smelled her—a whiff of perfume, but under it, a sour sexual scent. And for a moment I couldn't stop myself imagining the white naked body beneath the black dress.

She sat down again without a word, but I was sure that I had been subtly, secretly propositioned. And yet I couldn't believe it; there had been no overt signal of any kind.

I pulled myself together. 'You believe your son to have been innocent of the crime he was convicted of?'

'Michael was innocent.'

'And what about the witness who testified he saw Michael push the girl's head under the water?'

'An old man with a stick. One doesn't have to be very clever to know what he was doing prying and poking about on the river bank on a summer afternoon. Evil-minded people see evil things.'

'That may well be true. But the fact is, Elizabeth Gray did drown and, as you've said, your son was a strong swimmer, so it does seem a bit strange that he didn't manage to save her.' I knew she was incapable of sensing any irony in my words.

Her fingers toyed lightly with the jet beads; as she leaned forward, it seemed to me her lower lip was thicker, heavier. 'If Michael could not save her, she did not deserve to be saved!' She spoke with a soft chilling intimacy.

'Deserved? How is that, Mrs. Maynard?'

'She was a tart, Mr Speke—a whore, a harlot.'

'Oh. Did you—did you know her?'

'I didn't have to. I know her type all too well. I see them every day in the boutique, with their innocent ways and their enticing wiles—and their rottenness inside. I have to nod and smile and be nice to them—these filthy women who destroyed my son.' She leaned back, her hand pressed against her left breast. 'You cannot imagine what a dreadful pain that is to me—a sword under the heart.'

I stubbed out my cigarette and lit another. I couldn't stand much more of this. 'But Elizabeth Gray was from a respectable family and—'

'Respectable? The father was a publican and the mother a barmaid! Do you call that respectable? I know those people, they think of nothing but drinking and gambling and self-indulgence. They're irresponsible scum—and scum spawn scum. Can you imagine a girl brought up in such an atmosphere—fawned on and petted by drunkards and spend-thrifts, fought over, spoilt, corrupted. No wonder she was pro-miscuous, spreading her vileness wherever she went. I only thank God Michael saved himself from her.'

I sat silent, trying to remind myself that she had actually lost her son, that she was to be pitied.

'Mr Speke,' she used her soft voice again, 'Michael would never have killed her, but if she had laid a hand on him—if she had corrupted *him*—I would have killed her.'

And I believed her. Last night Phil had said something similar—*if anyone laid a hand on Eleanor, I'd kill him*. But *that*, I

147

assured myself, was no more than a manner of speaking. *This was the truth.* Mrs Maynard was what killers are made of—it was in the curve of her hand on her breast, the sexual droop of the lip, the sharp dead look of her eyes.

'Well,' I said, injecting a grating note of heartiness into my voice, 'of course we all feel like that at times. But we don't do it, do we? Yet if Michael was murdered, some specific person did do it—have you any idea of who that person might have been?'

'Indeed I do. Isn't it obvious?'

'Not to me, I'm afraid.'

'Do you think it was just a coincidence that Michael was poisoned with alcohol before he was drowned?'

'Oh. You mean Elizabeth's father, Jacob Gray, the publican?'

'Precisely. It needn't actually have been him, you know. People like that know people who will kill for money.'

'Contract killers. I suppose it's a thought.' She spoke as though Mr Gray ran a Mafia speakeasy in the heart of downtown Chicago; in reality he had a pub—or had had—in Richmond, hardly a gangland home.

'Another cup of tea, Mr Speke?'

'No thanks, no—I really must be going.'

'A glass of sherry then?'

'No, really.'

'Oh but I insist.' She got up and went across to a plain white-pine sideboard.

I watched her. Her suggestion about Gray had been no more than half-hearted. She seemed to have lost interest—as though her venom, unlike Amelia's, needed no particular focus. There was a likeness between them which I couldn't quite put my finger on. Amelia's desire for particular vengeance was a cold clear driving force, but for this woman it was like a casual overlay. Why? Had she already had her vengeance? Had Mrs Maynard killed her own son? Vivian couldn't have thought so—or else why would he have left her money? No, if Mrs Maynard killed anyone, it would be another woman. Men she killed in a different way.

'Thank you,' I said, accepting the small glass. Did she think a thimbleful of sweet sherry—for of course it was sweet—was going to set me on my ear? I wanted to pity this woman, but I was not going to console her, in or out of bed. I knew I ought to

148

leave at once, and yet she emanated an extraordinary kind of invisible lasciviousness that fascinated, and frightened, me.

And she watched me. I have never felt more like a mouse hypnotized by a cat.

I gulped the sherry. 'I really must be off.' I stood up.

'Very well. But you must see Michael's trophies before you go.'

There was no way I could refuse. I followed her down the passage and into the boy's room. A green carpet, green velvet curtains, flower prints on the green walls, a desk, a clothes horse, chest of drawers—an unmasculine room. And there was a bed—made up but without a bedspread, and the covers turned down for the night, for sleep, for God-knows-what.

'There,' she said. There was a caress of triumph in her voice. I could smell her closeness to me, the sour heat of her and the clean white smell of the turned-down sheet.

I looked at Michael's memorials on the mantelpiece—two small cups, mounted medals and a bronze statuette of a grotesquely muscled swimmer. But the real horror was behind them, reflected in the mantelpiece mirror—Mrs Maynard and myself staring at our respective doubles. Her hand slid into mine with a dry slither—and every nerve in my body seemed to jump. The odour was thick about me, the bed touching my knee, but I could not take my eyes off that naked reflection of distorted lust. *Evil-minded people see evil things.*

'Very nice,' I muttered and with an immense effort pulled my hand away and turned and fled down the passage with not a remnant of my middle-aged dignity, in sheer terror of that overwhelmingly malignant ritual of incestuous death.

'Goodbye, Mr Speke,' she said at the door, unflustered, untouched. 'It was very nice meeting you.'

I by-passed the lift and ran down the steps into the open air and breathed deeply, like a man saved from drowning in the nick of time.

Then I started to walk slowly down to the river close by.

19 Daughter and the River

I don't know much about dogs. On the whole I don't care for them. When I was a boy they were apt to bite my heels, and I was frightened of them. But I liked this one all right—he was large, beige, with floppy ears and a very warm tongue. He licked my hand, moved away, then came back and licked it again. After a while he put his muzzle in my palm and rested his jaw there contentedly.

The tide was low, exposing the gravelly mud flats. Below me, a child in a red raincoat was throwing stones into the glittering water, watched by its mother with a baby-buggy from above. A single sculler pulled upstream with measured strokes and a man in a wet-suit scudded down to Putney Bridge on a sailboard and promptly fell off. He remounted and came back, skilfully weaving the flat piece of wood on the rippled waters until he was almost level with where I stood. The child clapped. He turned and shot down again to the bridge—and fell off.

It must, I reflected, be a game. He was the child's father, the woman with the buggy his wife. Every spring evening they would come down to the Thames and he would perform for his daughter and his wife. He would mount and skim and fall and remount and skim again, until it was time for them to go home to a supper of scrambled eggs and spinach and mashed potatoes.

The Norman tower of Putney church gleamed almost white in the clear air. The trees on the opposite bank were youthfully green. The sculler was out of sight round the bend of the river. And a little fleet of red buses passed over Putney Bridge.

The movement of the dog's muzzle in my hand comforted me. None of these people—with the exception of Phil Wood— had children. They were either childless or their children were horribly dead. Everywhere innocence was being killed. Hatred and grief had eaten up the amiable days.

I couldn't let it go at this.

I patted the dog's head, dried my hand on the seat of my trousers, and drove the car leisurely up through Richmond Park, across the Terrace and down the hill to the Grape and Bottle in Prince Edward Road.

It was barely opening time and there was no one at or behind the bar. After a while, an enormous woman waddled out from the back parts—she wasn't so much fat as massive, with a huge head and long drooping jowls. She had a pint glass of Guinness in her hand and a half-smoked cigarette stuck grimly in the corner of her mouth. I ordered Guinness too.

'Changed a bit since I was last here,' I said mendaciously, glancing round the big three-sided bar with its fake, log fires and fruit machines and ugly plush furniture.

'Muck,' she said tersely. 'When was that?'

'Oh, years ago—when Jacob Gray was the licensee.'

'Don't remember you.' Her voice was hoarse and seemed to be pumped laboriously from somewhere deep inside her.

'I had a beard in those days,' I said.

'An artist then, are you?' She put my glass in front of me, slopping a little over the brim.

'In a way.'

'Takes all sorts.'

'Will you have one yourself?'

'Thanks,' she said lugubriously.

'What happened to Gray?' I said, watching her slide a shot of gin into the stout. 'Didn't he have a son who was involved in some kind of accident?'

'Daughter,' she was evidently pleased to be able to correct me. 'And it wasn't any accident. Murdered she was— drowned. Right here, just upstream beyond the first lock, in a punt under those willows overhanging the water—raped she was, then shoved in the river and held down.'

'What a fiendish thing.'

'One of these sex maniacs. Cheers.' She lifted her glass, taking the cigarette from her lips at the last moment, and drank.

'Did they catch him?'

'More or less caught him in the act. Sent him up for life. Bugger all that means these days.'

'They wouldn't let him out if he really was a maniac, you know.'

'Huh.' She took a tremendous swig, chuckled. 'Fat lot you know. They *did* let him out. But he got his comeuppance alright. Drowned himself in the river at Putney,' she said with satisfaction.

'Suicide?' It was not surprising she knew—it was a local affair, after all.

'That's right. Remorse. But I tell you,' she leaned across the counter and a piece of ash dropped unnoticed into her glass, 'if he hadn't of done it himself, there'd have been plenty round here who'd have done it for him.'

I smiled dubiously. 'Such as her father?'

'Jake? Jake's dead. It killed him—killed him stone dead. Took the heart right out of him. He only lasted six months.' She let out a sigh so deep that it seemed to diminish her bulk. 'It's never been the same here since.'

So that was that. Death had exonerated Jacob Gray.

'I'm sorry,' I said. And I was. All the potential villains were turning out to be victims. 'What happened to the widow?' I asked idly.

'Maudie? Maudie wanted to carry on here when Jake died, but they wouldn't let her take over the licence—not a woman. Then Jake's brother applied, but they weren't having him neither. Josh was a boatman, but he knew the business okay— used to help out here in the winter. But he'd been caught out in some fiddle when he was hardly more than a kid—a criminal record they called it.'

'A boatman?' I said, alert again.

'Used to hire out the punts and skiffs down at the boat-houses. Big strong bloke, but not one to set the Thames on fire.' She chuckled heavily and finished her drink in one swallow. 'But he did all right.'

'Oh?'

'Went up in the world. Got himself a smart little launch. Does day trips to Hampton Court, Westminster—anywhere you might want to go. Private parties only—very classy.' She lumbered away to serve another customer, but immediately she had done so, gravitated back to me and accepted a second round without fuss. 'Made himself a pretty penny, I wouldn't mind betting. Not that he needs it.'

'Oh?' Monosyllables seemed to make her voluble.

'He married Maudie, see—they waited a year of course—and Jake had left her set up for life. Not rich exactly, but a sight more than comfortable. It was she who bought him the motor launch. The *Liz* he called it—after *her*, you see.'

'And they still live in Richmond?'

'That's right. They got that green painted house on the corner of Seeley Road, just off of the Vineyard. Lovely place it is. She sends me a big fresh turkey every Christmas—she's that thoughtful. Of course, I sell it—what would I do with a turkey?' She laughed. 'An' I always go to the big party they have on Boxing Day—it wouldn't be the same, she says, without Dora.'

'Ah,' I murmured, wondering how I could free myself from her vein of loquacity which seemed about to verge on the sentimental. But I was wrong.

'Of course she never comes in here. Look at that,' and she pointed with vigorous disgust at a large tank of tropical fish along one wall. 'Fish! Swimming about in bloody water! A sodding aquarium—that's all we are nowadays!'

I don't know Richmond well, but I remembered the Vineyard was a turning off the road that led up the hill where the second-hand bookshops were—and I found Seeley Road without any trouble. The corner house was a pale apple green with white window frames and a darker green front door. The windows gleamed in the evening sun and the brasswork shone.

Perhaps because I had been expecting a more human version of Mrs Maynard, I was taken aback—for Maud Gray was an old woman. And yet as she took me back and sat me down in a conservatory that overlooked a well-groomed little garden, I saw a life and alertness in her lined face, the very opposite of Mrs Maynard's dead mask. Small and straight-backed, she wore a mauve dress with a multitude of purple beads; her white hair was cut short with a fringe; she was in no sense beautiful—her features were rather flat, a broad nose, a mobile mouth, and lucid blue eyes that regard me tranquilly as I said my piece.

I gave her the ostensible reason for my visit and somewhat haltingly explained the nature of my book. I felt awkward about it in a way I hadn't with any of the others—for here I was, talking of compassion and high purpose to an old lady

153

into whose house I had come as a spy.

'Well,' she said when I had finished, 'so long as you're not from one of the Sunday rags . . . I like a new face as much as a good gossip—so don't you mind about upsetting me.' She gave me a kindly smile—clearly she had detected my embarrassment. 'I'm an old woman now, but young or old, women are tougher than men. Of course they take things to heart, but they're used to that, and men aren't. It killed my Jake. Where there's life, there's hope, that's what they say, isn't it? When Liz died, Jake lost hope, you see—couldn't find it, didn't want to find it in a way. But a woman doesn't need hope like that, she's too busy picking up the pieces.' She spoke in a rapid, easy tone as though we'd known one another for years.

'I loved Liz, but for him, she was the light of his life. Particularly because she was unexpected. For years we thought we couldn't have any kids. Liz came along late—Jake, he was fifty. They say you love a child more when she comes late in life and I dare say that's true. Oh I don't say I didn't have my moments when I could have given up. When Jake died, I said to myself maybe it would've been better if she'd never have been born. We'd be down there now—Jake and me—at the old Grape and Bottle, having a nice comfortable time of it. But I only said that to myself once, that one time. Because it wouldn't have been true, you see—we wouldn't have had that brightness in our lives for eighteen years, would we? I was brought up a Catholic and I still sometimes pop down to St Elizabeth's, not regular and not for mass or anything like that, but just to sit and be quiet and say I'm grateful for those years we did have of her. Jake didn't see it like that and even when he knew he was dying, he wouldn't let Father Lambert in the house. We all know there's wickedness in the world, but just because it happens to you unexpected, it doesn't make sense to go blaming the people who've been telling you about it all along—now does it?'

'No. No indeed.'

'Here am I chattering away, and I expect you could do with a drink, couldn't you. Whisky?'

'How did you know?'

'Listen, love, I wasn't a barmaid for forty years without being able to spot the difference between a gin drinker and a whisky drinker.'

There was a small bar at the end of the conservatory and she half-filled two cut glass tumblers.

'There you are. Hope you like a malt—Josh got it off one of his customers. Josh is my husband, Jake's brother. I married my brother-in-law. A lot of people disapproved, but he'd always fancied me and he's a good, solid bloke. And he needed someone. Cheers.'

We drank and she was silent for a moment. Then she gave a little sigh. 'He'll be back in a bit. He's not a great talker—not like my old Jake. So I have to do it myself.' She laughed. 'Josh took it very hard too, you see. He fair doted on Liz. In those days he worked down at the boatyard on the river and it was him as hired out that punt to that Maynard who murdered her. He's never got over that—never. He thinks it made him responsible in some way. It's no good me telling him different. Sometimes of an evening we sit here watching the telly, but I know he's not seeing it. What he's seeing is Liz going off that morning for a day out with Nancy, that was her girl friend, in white shorts and a halter and sunhat and sandals—all smiles, they were. And he's seeing that bloke, watching him pole away in the punt, going up the river to kill our Liz.' For a moment her wide mouth was tremulous; she drank some whisky. 'Well now, you'll have me crying before long, after all.'

'Mrs Gray, I don't want to—'

'No no, don't mind me. It's important what you're doing. I see that.'

'Then could you tell me a bit about Liz?'

Maud Gray smiled. 'Oh she was a pretty one, she was—she had her father's looks, not mine, and he was a handsome man. But she had my spirit—lively and jolly, she was. I don't say she wasn't a bit spoilt, how could she help it being an only child like that and everybody loving her right from the word go? She was one for the lads all right—I was myself, but I daresay she went a bit farther than we did in the old days. But she knew what she was doing—had a lot of confidence, maybe too much confidence. There are things no girl can handle. Jake didn't like her going off like that—half-naked, he said. All the girls dress like that nowadays when they get the chance, I told him, it doesn't mean they're tarts. Innocence isn't in what you wear, it's in the heart. Oh yes, I knew it all. He never blamed me. He blamed himself. That was the worst of it, that's what did for him as much as the grief. I still don't think what she wore had anything to do with it. He was a nutter, and if she'd been dressed like Queen Victoria it wouldn't have made any difference. There are a lot of *ifs* that would have though—*if* she hadn't had a tiff with Nancy and jumped out of the boat and gone off on her own, *if* she'd have gone a bit further upstream, *if* she hadn't been hungry enough to accept sharing his picnic lunch, *if* it had been raining. And of course if her boyfriend George hadn't had to work that Saturday she wouldn't have been out on the river at all.'

'George? I haven't heard about him.'

'Oh he was a lovely boy—in the second-hand book trade. Saturday's their big day, see. He read, my goodness how he read—knew everything, he did, but never forced it on you, if you know what I mean. He was quiet and gentle and I sometimes thought Liz was a bit of a handful for him, though he was four year older. Jake wanted to set him up with his own bookshop, but he said no, he didn't know enough yet. He was a *good* man and I didn't have no worries about Liz as long as she was with him. When Jake died he wanted to come and live here in this house, but I wouldn't let him—it's no sort of life living on memories. She's dead and gone, I told him—and you'd be better gone yourself. I gave him a bit of money, and I knew Jake would have wanted that, and he went off to Australia and opened his bookshop. He's married and got a little girl now—he called her Liz. He still writes me regular every Christmas and on my birthday.' She smiled softly.

'It's a funny thing, but I don't miss Liz. Of course, I've always seen to it that I've plenty to do—I run the business side of Josh's launch hire and I've got a fish and chip shop just off the Green with a nice little Paki manager, and good works—blimey, I'm full of 'em. And I was never one to sit and mope. The way I see it, your life's divided into parts, and when one part's over, you got to get on with the next. I'll tell you what I do miss though—and that's something I never had. I miss not having that grandchild. I wake up in the night sometimes and I seem to hear her little voice calling. Silly really, to mourn a life that never was nor will be. I always think—hold on, here's Josh.' She leant forward quickly. 'I'd rather you didn't mention any of this in front of him.'

'No—of course, all right.'

'He's touchy about it, I told you—always will be. We'll say you're from the Star and Garter.'

'The Star and Garter?' Was I to play the part of a publican?

'You know—the old servicemen's home up on top of the hill. You've come to talk about fund-raising. Josh, is that you?'

'Hello, Maudie.' Standing on the threshold of the conservatory, he was a striking figure. Though his shoulders were bent, he must have been all of six foot three, and broad to go with it. His hair and beard were grey, his impenetrable blue eyes were set under thick grey eyebrows, the nose aquiline. He was perfect for the part of Captain Ahab.

'This is Mr Speke from the Star and Garter.'

'How d'you do.' He stepped down into the conservatory and sat on a wickerwork couch that creaked at his weight. His voice was oddly soft and light in so big a man. The hands he put on his knees were huge, the joints thick with rheumatism.

'Mr Speke says we badly need a new batch of walking frames.'

'Er, yes, quite. Amazing how they get worn out.'

'What do you think they do, use them as weapons?'

I laughed—a little too loudly. 'Maybe. Like walking sticks—a symbolic remnant of the military life. Something to do with the hands, to prove you don't have to work with them, I mean.' I realized I was half-drunk and making a hash of it. 'Like the businessman's cigar and the, er, Queen's sceptre.'

Maudie grinned at me. 'And the writer's pen?'

We kept it going for a few minutes, and all the while Joshua Gray sat without movement, like some timeless giant.

At the front door, as I left, she said, 'You know, you remind me of George ever so much.'

'Do I?'

'Yes.' Then she put a hand on my shoulder and, leaning forward, kissed my cheek. 'Good luck, love.'

20 Official Warning

They stood there with the traditional impassivity of their kind, except for the faintest of smiles on Ginger's lips.

I hesitated. I was emotionally exhausted and yet at the same time strung on a high wire of excitement. In no state to drive all the way back to Leeching, I'd been glad of the dispassionate haven of Phil's flat—I wanted no more disturbance. Yet I knew that it was time to let the police in now.

'Come in,' I said and then, when they were settled side by side on the couch, 'can I offer you a drink?'

McQuade shook his head and looked at his watch.

'Well, I shall, if you don't mind.' I poured myself a decent-sized whisky and went over and leant against the mantelpiece; it was (in a sense) my house, so I felt I had the right to stand. 'I expect you remember asking me to let you know of any little thing that occurred to me—however insignificant?'

McQuade nodded and Ginger Roughead took out his notebook.

'I'll try to make it brief,' I said, taking a gulp of my drink, 'but I think I have come across several facts which—taken *together*—are actually of some significance.' At that moment I had a pang of conscience—hadn't there been at least a tacit agreement with Lady Winter and Cyril Grayling that I should *not* go to the police? But I owed nothing to Cyril, that lying hypocrite, and surely not much more to Lady Winter, whose fanatical bent for vengeance overmastered all common dictates of good sense.

'Yes, sir?' I felt McQuade's impatience beneath the neutral tone.

'It began when I came across a curious coincidence....' And as I started to speak, I experienced a sense of relief. I told them how the coincidence of the stab wounds had led to the hypothesis of retributive killings and then to my trip to Hasle-

158

mere and my talks with the Brigadier and Walter Hodder. I felt in good form and laid the foundations well, and soon Ginger was scribbling rapidly. I dealt briefly with Soper and Maynard, mentioned Latham, and by the time I got to my interviews with Mrs Soley and Mrs Maynard, I was beginning to be surprised by the strength of the case I was making. But I was careful not to make too much of it and only touched lightly on Gerald Price and Josh Gray as the sort of men whose grudge might lead them to think of murder. Of course, I said nothing about Goldie Grayling or Eleanor, and some instinct warned me to keep Shep Keith's name out of it for the moment. But I made play with the fact that Vivian in his Will had himself laid the trail of investigation.

I had not expected applause, but nor had I expected a stony silence, made all the stonier by the sudden cessation of Ginger's scribbling.

'Well?' I said at last.

'Well, Mr Speke, I hadn't realized you were so much of a journalist.'

'What does that mean?' I said, my hackles rising.

'The last time we met you didn't seem any too greatly concerned with who might have murdered Mr Winter, now here you are showing a very keen interest indeed—one might almost say an obsessive interest. Clearly you've had access to information not available to ordinary members of the public— don't worry, I'm not going to ask your sources. Then again, last time I saw you, you seemed to consider Mr Winter's Will an irrelevance—but now, not only are you thoroughly familiar with the terms of that Will but you've actually gone out and interviewed, how many—two, three, four?—of the beneficiaries. And you've developed a full-blown theory about the origin of the crime which involves a whole network of other crimes. Altogether you've put in a great deal of time and trouble over this matter. Now why is that, sir?'

It was a long speech for McQuade and I realised that by presenting my case in such a complete and detailed way I'd overdone it—I had, unforgivably, intruded on his area of professional competence. 'You think I'm simply after a story?'

'What else am I to think? Isn't that what you call investigative journalism?'

The sensible softly sardonic Scots accent exasperated me. 'I

159

don't know and I don't care. Look, Chief Superintendent, as a close friend of Vivian Winter—and simply as a good citizen—I want his murder cleared up. Any investigation, as you call it, that I've carried out has been to that end and to that end alone. I've no personal axe to grind.'

'Eighty-three thousand, three hundred and thirty-three pounds?'

'What do you think that is—payment in advance? That's not the way things are done in my profession,' I said sarcastically.

'But it's a powerful motive, isn't it? Powerful enough for you to exercise your very considerable imagination to construct an elaborately unlikely theory to explain a few relatively simple facts.'

'Perhaps I'm doing that merely to amuse myself.'

'I doubt it. You strike me as a serious man. But you may well be putting up a smokescreen. No, listen to me, sir,' he raised a warning hand as I opened my mouth to speak—an extraordinarily dramatic gesture in a man who held himself so still and expressionless. 'I'm just stating the obvious. There are several possible motives for Winter's murder and a number of suspects—and suspects sometimes go to extraordinary lengths to establish their innocence. You may well be propounding your theory in order to protect yourself—or to protect someone else, Mr Wood, for instance—from close scrutiny. It's called laying a red herring across the trail. I have to consider that. I have to consider why you have gone to all this trouble.'

'I've told you why,' I said shortly—his reasonableness annoyed me even more than his irony. 'I feel strongly about it and as a good—'

'—citizen, yes sir. I understand that. But let me ask you this—did you think of this all by yourself or have you been put up to it?'

'Certainly not—it's entirely my own—'

'You've not discussed it with anyone else at all. Not even your editor?'

'No.' I was relieved to make a truthful denial.

'With no one at all?'

'I—well, I may have mentioned it in a casual way to...' Dammit, he wasn't going to let go.

'To whom?'

'Oh—to Lady Winter.' I cursed my inability to lie flatly. I drank some whisky—and cursed Lady Winter too.

'I see. Lady Winter is a very courageous lady—but she has some funny ideas.' As McQuade spoke, a ghost of a smile flickered across Ginger's features.

'I absolutely don't see the relevance of all this. Good God, you talk as though I'd committed some sort of crime, instead of—'

'Interfering with police officers in the course of their investigation is a crime, Mr Speke.'

'Oh come on, Chief Superintendent.' I gave a small half-laugh, but felt far from merry. 'That's ludicrous. What possible harm could I have done to your investigations?'

'You seem to have a fashionably poor opinion of the police. Do you honestly think that we're incapable of doing our own homework? Don't you think we investigate everyone who could remotely be connected with Winter's murder—and that includes not just those people mentioned in the Will but anyone, and I mean *anyone*, involved in Winter's more serious court cases?'

'Well, I....' I was nonplussed—how far had Lady Winter brainwashed me? 'You mean, you've seen all these people?'

'We don't have to *see* people. There are other methods of establishing motive and means and opportunity. We don't regard it as an effective method of investigation to go up to every possible suspect and ask them straight out, "Did you kill Vivian Winter?" If your theory by the remotest chance held any water at all, doesn't it occur to you that you have effectively warned off the suspect and queered our pitch?'

'I—look here, are you telling me you're absolutely satisfied that Soper's death and Maynard's death—in exactly the same manner as that of their victims—is just some laughable coincidence?'

'I don't laugh about death, Mr Speke. There's not a shred of evidence to suggest that they were anything other than what the inquest said—accidental death and suicide. I listened very carefully to what you had to say, but you've offered not one new fact for all your theorizing.'

'I know that. What I'm suggesting is a new way of *looking* at the facts—connecting them up and relating them. And then I

161

think you see some remarkable coincidences.'

'What I see when I look at the facts is three ex-prisoners, one killed in a road accident, one suicide and one failure to report. There must be at least a hundred men convicted of murder and rape and now at liberty—two deaths among that lot isn't even statistically significant.'

I was getting tired. 'Look,' I said as reasonably as I could, 'I may be wrong about this, but there is one thing that seems to me significant, to put it mildly, and that's that Vivian left money to the—well, the relicts, I suppose one'd say—of these three men.'

'Ah yes, sir,' Ginger interposed, 'but Mr Winter was by way of being a philanthropist, wasn't he—particular where ex-prisoners and that were concerned?'

'Yes yes, I suppose he was. I mean, he was.' I sat down in one of the deep armchairs. I badly wanted to call it a day now. 'Listen,' I said, 'if that's all, I think. . . .'

'Well, there is just one other point, Mr Speke,' Ginger said in his cheerful manner. 'What are you doing here in Mr Wood's flat?'

'Eh? Oh,' I smiled, 'Mr Wood is an old friend—he generally puts me up when I'm in town.'

'And that's usually on a Wednesday, I think you said?'

'Yes, that's quite right. I come up on a Wednesday, do my business, dine at the Club and then sleep over here and go back in the morning.'

'But not on Wednesday April the fourteenth—the day of Mr Winter's murder?'

'No no—surely I told you this—I had a heavy-ish lunch, wasn't good for much after that, so decided to drive straight home.'

'And who did you have lunch with?'

'Mr Wood, as a matter of fact.'

'And what precisely did you do after this lunch?'

'I drove—oh, I see, well, I took a taxi back here, picked up the car and then went straight down to Sussex.'

'And Mr Wood?'

'What about Mr Wood?'

'Did he come back here with you?'

I was suddenly horribly alert. Hadn't Phil told me he'd told the police he'd come back here? 'No—I think he was going to,

but I had to stop off at the *Gazette* to pick up some books. . . .'
That was untrue—maybe I was more glib at lying than I
thought—but, Christ, couldn't they check on cab rides? 'So we
went our separate ways.'

'And then you came back here to pick up your car?'

'Yes.'

'Did you call Mr Winter to say that you would not be dining
at the Club?'

'Good heavens, no. It was an entirely informal arrangement. Besides, I rather fancied he'd still be in Bath.'

'Is that why you didn't go to the Club?'

'No, I've told you—I don't care for two large meals a day, so
I—'

'How often, in fact, do you vary your routine and *not* dine at
your Club?'

'Oh well, not that often, but—'

'Did it not occur to you to come back to this flat, rest a bit,
then go to the Club?'

I stared at Ginger's freckled face and wondered how I had
ever considered it open and jolly. 'Perhaps it did,' I said as
slowly as I could, 'but I can't honestly recall. Mr Wood had
been persuading me to write a full-length non-fiction book.
When my head's full of ideas I need peace and quiet to think
them through so—I went home.'

'Varying your invariable routine?'

'Nothing is invariable, Sergeant.'

'So it is pure coincidence—just a curious coincidence—that
the variation occurred on the day that Mr Winter was
murdered?'

'Is that an accusation?'

McQuade stood up. 'We are not of the opinion, Mr Speke,
that curious coincidences have much bearing upon the
possible culpability of anyone.'

The armchair was deep and I had a hard struggle getting to
my feet. 'Well taken, Mr McQuade.'

'Well, I do hope so, sir. And if you'll take something else,
you'll take my advice to leave well enough alone. Go home and
forget all about it. We'll find Mr Winter's murderer in our own
good time and in our own good way.'

'Well, if I could believe that. . . .' And, standing there, more
than a little drunk, I did believe it. Almost.

'And I'll tell you what I'm going to do. I'm going to run a check on all prisoners in your category released over the last ten years. Just to make sure we don't come up with any unexplained deaths. Does that satisfy you?'

'Yes,' I said doubtfully. 'I suppose it does.'

'Then I'll ask you to do something for me.'

'Cease and desist?'

'That's right. Of course I can't order you to do so, but it is my duty to warn you that undesirable consequences may ensue if you don't.'

'I'll have to think about that one,' I said, trying to hang on to the vestige of dignity and stub out my cigarette at the same time. 'But surely the worst I could do would be to make a fool of myself?'

McQuade led the way to the door of the flat. He turned. 'I don't underestimate your capacity for making a nuisance of yourself, Mr Speke. But as a police officer, my concern is that if you get yourself into trouble, we might not be able to get you out of it.'

I opened the door. 'That's very thoughtful of you, Mr McQuade—I appreciate your concern.'

'Don't misunderstand me, sir. I don't give a damn what happens to you personally.' He stepped into the corridor. 'I just don't want another bloody corpse on my hands.'

Ginger gave me a friendly little wave and then they marched off down the hall without looking back.

I was hungry, ravenous, but all I could find in the kitchen was a slice of ham and, tucked away in the back of the freezer, a bag of frozen radishes. I ate the ham and stuffed the radishes down the chute. There was nothing else except two stale water biscuits. I ate those too.

Then I called Phil. It was Eleanor who answered and I immediately apologized for putting my foot in it on Sunday. Listening to her high, clear voice telling me not to be silly, I seemed to detect the tone of what Phil had called 'invincible innocence.' Whatever the evidence, no jury would convict her of even the most heinous crime if she denied it with such silvery serenity. Of course sleeping with Vivian was hardly a crime— in fact I was beginning to think it had been a fairly popular pastime.

'What? Oh yes, I would just like a word with him if he's

about.' And when Phil came on, I could tell at once he was drunk—or as drunk as he ever got. 'Is Eleanor there?' I asked. 'Yes, I know I've just been speaking to her—I mean, is she within earshot? Well, brace yourself. I've just had a visit from the police—or rather, you have. Yes, I'm in the flat. McQuade and his minion—the one you were so rude to in the car park. Obviously they wanted to ask you some questions—I rather think about where you went after that lunch of ours. I said we went our separate ways, but I thought you came back here. They were fairly snotty about it.'

'Damnation, Ivor, you might at least have said you came back with me.' His voice was clotted with whisky and rage. 'Would that have been too much to ask?'

'Yes it would. I'd already told them I went home. How could I possibly suddenly change my story? Particularly when Bolton knows you didn't get back until the early morning.'

'Bolton—oh Christ! Bolton must have spilled the beans. Oh Christ oh Christ oh Christ. What the hell am I going to do?'

'Tell them the truth. They have resources—they can turn up your black woman of the night a lot more easily than you can.'

'The truth, the truth—you make it sound like a bunch of bananas on a stall. What is the truth? I can't remember— there's just a bloody great blank where the truth ought to be.' Then, *sotto voce*, 'And Eleanor's bound to find out if I do, I don't trust the police to keep their mouths shut.'

'If I were you I'd tell her before she finds out some other way.'

'Christ Almighty, man, I can't do that. She'd turn me out— clean me out too, if I know anything about women. I can't start living in a bed-sitter at my age. It'd kill me. I'd rather . . . oh yes, all right,' he said, briskly switching gears from anguish to joviality, so that I guessed Eleanor had come back into the room. 'Nice to hear from you, Ivor. I expect I'll see you next week. Ciao.'

I put the phone down with exasperation mingled with guilt. How could you help the sort of damn fool who froze a bunch of radishes? I was finding out more about my friends than I wanted to know. And that included Vivian—at the head of the list.

I took a cigar from the humidor and lit it without any of

165

Phil's fussification. I drew on it gently, trying to let the odour of simple opulence calm my nerves. I could afford my own cigars now—and decent wine, books, music, a new car to replace my green wreck, long holidays, I could even afford a gardener. All due to Vivian—to Vivian's generous death.

It all came back to Vivian. And I was having to believe things about him which I would have treated as contemptible gossip when he was alive. Silence is the better part of friendship, but now that he was dead, noise was coming up all around me, rank weeds of mischief and wagging tongues.

21 Letting Go

Amelia Winter was dressed in old ladies' lavender, with a cameo brooch and lace at the throat. There was a transparent look about her face and on her ivory white hands the tracery of veins was sharp and clear. In the sunlit, perfect sitting room, she had the air of a delicate porcelain ornament, vulnerable to any careless hand. I wondered whether she had done it deliberately to make my task harder, some instinct having whispered to her my decision.

For I'd woken with my mind made up; the wise jury of sleep had reached its verdict: Not Guilty—or rather, Not Involved. And as I'd walked down to Marble Arch and across the park, I felt as free as a bird, as fresh as the budding trees. I was resigning, sending in my papers, collecting my cards, in short—buggering off.

Nevertheless, I had my duty to do, and I delivered my report with care. I didn't mention Eleanor or Goldie Grayling and I kept well clear of the sexual miasma that hung over Vivian's death like marsh gas. As far as Lady Winter was concerned, this aspect of her son's character had been disposed of once and for all by the destruction of his address book and diary—the dirt under the rug had no connection with the stain on the kitchen linoleum.

Otherwise, I gave a full and faithful account.

When I had done, she was silent for some time; then she said, 'You've done very well. I do congratulate you, Ivor.' She smiled, but it was clearly an effort. She was tired; perhaps she had her own nightmare—but if so, I was no longer willing to share it.

And now was the moment to say so. 'Lady Winter.' I cleared my throat. 'Lady Winter, I want to—'

'One moment, Ivor. I think we could both do with a little fortification. The sherry decanter is on the side, if you'd be so good.'

I got up reluctantly—I'd seen it there when I'd come in and had determined not to have a drink. I did not wish to garnish my betrayal with wine. But the old lady could not be denied.

She indicated that I was to put the glass on the side table, then reached up and took my hand. She looked at me with Vivian's blue penetrating eyes and said softly, 'Thank you, my dear.'

As I sat down, I think I blushed—at any rate my cheeks felt unnaturally warm.

'Now, Ivor, I have something to say to you.' She picked up her sherry, drank a little, and replaced the glass. 'You may think I am a very foolish and ungrateful old woman,' she sighed, smiling gently. I was torn between uneasiness and admiration—whatever she was after, she was playing it up to the hilt. 'I think I have involved you in something very difficult. I did so, not just because I knew you loved Vivian, but because I knew—I felt—that you are a man of great perspicacity and, to use an old-fashioned word, sensibility. But, because of those very qualities, I realise your enquiries have involved you in some considerable—anguish. No—please let me continue,' she said to my movement of protest. 'I see it in your face. You are a man for whom it's a hurt and a harm to dwell upon wickedness. You need to be nourished by the good. So I'm going to ask you not to go on with this. I know it's a great deal to demand, but I do demand it.'

'I—Lady Winter, I don't know what to say.' I looked out of the window at the sunny day, trying to disguise my astonishment at this sudden volte-face. My wish had been granted before I'd even stated it and yet, perversely, I felt the wind had been taken out of my sails. 'I'm afraid you think I have made rather a mess of it.'

'On the contrary, you have done exceptionally well.'

'All I've really succeeded in turning up is two women unable to face up to the way their husband and son died—and looking desperately to any explanation but the most likely one.'

'And I, of course, am a third such woman?' she said, smiling.

'No, not at all. Vivian's death was no accident—nor suicide.' I hesitated, puzzled by the almost playful irony which had replaced her old implacability. 'I know the police don't think much of the notion of vengeance as a motive, but—'

'You have talked to them?'

'I had a visit from McQuade last night.' Again, I felt abashed—I had let her down by spilling the beans to the police.

'And of course he still thinks the murderer is to be found among Vivian's close connections?'

'Well, yes.' I wondered suddenly if she had come round to the same opinion. 'Lady Winter,' I said, curious despite myself, 'you're not going to let it go at that, are you?'

'Oh dear me no.' She sipped her sherry. 'I shall have to ask Hugo to bring a little pressure to bear on the Commissioner. Poor Hugo—he hates to bring pressure. The old boy network is in tatters these days.' She smiled at me with something of her old vitality.

And I smiled back in guilty relief. It was safely out of my hands now. I felt a fleeting pang of pity for Hugo Pulteney— even more of a pompous windbag than Cyril Grayling.

As we sat on, finishing our sherry, chatting desultorily, I sensed an almost physical distancing between Lady Winter and myself. I was redundant and I couldn't blame her for casting me off now my usefulness was at an end—although I would have preferred the dignity of doing the severing myself—and yet I regretted it. The last link with Vivian was being cut. He was truly dead now. I had to resign myself to that.

I wasn't asked to lunch.

The gates of the lift were propped open with a suitcase and there were two more inside. Posey's door was ominously ajar. I made for the stairs but was not quite quick enough.

'Hello, old man. Long time no see. Holding you up, are we? Sorry about that. Won't be two shakes of a bee's knee. Very! Come on, old girl.' He carried two large plastic shopping bags and, stuck ridiculously under one arm, a shrimping net.

'Oh hello, Posey. Where are you off to?'

'Frank, old lad—Frank. Not Paris, eh—not with this lot.' He gave a guffaw. 'A weekend in the country—restore the tissues a bit, get the old kite tuned up. Can't stay at home on a Bank Holiday. I envy you, old man.'

'You do? Why?' I had edged to the top of the stairs, ready for a dash.

'The country, old man—living in the country. Sea air, green grass, warbling birds, nature in the ruddy pink and all that.'

'I thought you didn't care for the country?'

'Depends, old man—depends. Sorry I can't ask you in for a drink, but we've got to press on. Come on, Very! Ivan's here waiting for the lift.'

'Ivor.'

'That's right. How's the old lady?'

'Oh, she's managing.'

'Managing, is she? Good. Still a bit down in the mouth, I expect. You just tell her if there's anything she needs—bit of butter, cup of flour, doesn't matter what—we're always ready to oblige. Disorganized lot, women eh? No sense of time—but that's what we love them for, isn't it, bless 'em? Very!' he shouted, half turning to the door. His jacket flapped open and strapped to his waist was a large pistol in a holster.

I had taken a couple of steps down, but I stopped. 'Do you always take a gun to the country?'

'Eh? Oh that—just my service revolver. Never can tell. Dangerous place the country—bulls and all that.'

'Bulls!' Very appeared behind him. She wore jeans and a grey fisherman's sweater, but looked as lovely as ever. 'Hello, Ivor. Frank wouldn't know a bull if he saw one, would you, darling?'

'Of course I damn well would.' Posey's cheeks took on a ruddier hue.

'He once shot a cow in a field—didn't you?—right through the head.' She smiled and her nose made a little leftward leap.

'It was a damn great bull running at us full tilt.'

'A fat old cow wandering across our path.' The nose gave a

169

violent twitch of amusement. 'It cost us a hundred pounds—
I've never seen a farmer so angry.'

'Well, anyway, it was a spot-on shot,' he said, gallantly
joining in our laughter.

'Well, I'm afraid I've got to run,' I said with, suddenly, a
real reluctance—I should have liked to sit over a glass of gin
watching the sad eyes and the gyrations of the nose. 'I'll leave
the lift to you.'

As I went down the stairs, I could hear their voices magnified perhaps by the lift shaft.

'Why the devil did you want to tell him all that about the
cow?'

'It's funny, isn't it?'

'Makes me look like a bloody fool.'

As I stepped into the street, I thought that I too had been
made to look a fool, like an old retainer summarily dismissed
for some unwitting offence. Perhaps I, like Posey, had been
trespassing on private property, or too industriously inspecting the family closets. Yet I had found no skeleton to speak
of—at least, none that I recognized.

22 A Breach of Confidence

'And what have you been up to, Ivor?' Although he'd not risen
to greet me, Cyril spoke with a fair semblance of geniality.

'I've been on the hop a bit since I last saw you.'

'Really—really? Any joy?'

I lit a cigarette and watched him. He sat with his back to a
window that looked out onto a piece of plain lawn—Lincoln's
Inn Gardens, I suppose. The room itself was large and lofty,
but everything in it—except Cyril himself of course—seemed
slightly tatty: the carpet worn, the curtains dusty with age, the
leather desk top scratched and discoloured. Like the tin
ashtray, these perhaps were deft little tokens of hard work and
honesty, in a profession not unduly noted for either.

'I wanted to talk to you,' I said as Cyril opened his mouth to

170

speak, 'about one or two of the people mentioned in Vivian's Will.'

'Oh. Who?' He was wary.

'We might as well start with Estelle Jacqueline Soley.'

'Soley? Isn't she the one that lives in Bath—in for thirty thousand? What is she, the old nanny or something?'

'Vivian didn't tell you?'

'My dear fellow, Vivian just handed me a list of names. I don't know the woman from Adam—or Eve, as the case may be.' He laughed in his heavy manner.

'She's the widow of Kenneth Frederick Soper—one of the three on Marsham's card. I went to see her. Soper changed his name to Soley when he came out. He was killed last December—run over by a hit-and-run driver close to his home.'

'Was he, by God! Ivor, I never thought you'd ... this is magnificent. Run over, you say?'

'Does that mean anything to you?'

'One in the bag, eh?' He rubbed his hands. 'Or is there more to it?'

I gave him a brief resume of everything I'd learned about the Soper/Soleys.

'That's absolutely fascinating ... fascinating. Old Toby Marsham's no fool, but in all honesty I didn't expect him to strike gold like this first time round.' He glanced at his watch, then pressed the intercom. 'Miss Dishley, bring in a cup for Mr Speke and some extra biscuits when tea's ready, would you?' He leaned back. 'So it looks as though Vivian was really onto something, eh?'

'Yes it does. The Will is obviously some sort of a signpost—and Mrs Soley isn't the only person it points to. There are one or two people even closer to home.'

'Closer to ... what d'you mean?' His body seemed to stiffen slightly. 'Who?'

'Georgina Deirdre Maynard—of Putney. In, as you'd say, for fifteen thousand. Does that name ring a bell?'

'Nope. Tell me. This is intriguing.'

At that moment Miss Dishley entered with a tea tray—as elegant as anything Mrs Maynard had produced. Earl Grey in a decorative porcelain cup, Rich Tea biscuits, a silver Apostle spoon—I was in favour. But it wasn't, I thought grimly, going to last long.

As I told him about Mrs Maynard, he gobbled biscuits and drank tea thirstily.

'Well, I do most heartily congratulate you,' he said at last, brushing crumbs from his lower lip with a silk handkerchief. 'A quite spectacular debut, if I may say so. You've really got your teeth into it, I can see that. Of course, there's a long way to go before—'

'Not for me,' I interrupted, putting my half-empty cup on the desk.

'No? You don't care for Earl Grey?'

'I wasn't talking about the tea. I meant I'm not going on with this—this investigation.'

'Oh dear,' he said with an amused smile. 'Don't tell me you've got an attack of cold feet?'

'Perhaps I have. But the main reason is that Lady Winter has asked me to give it up.'

'Has she?' He raised an eyebrow, but didn't seem unduly surprised. 'Well, you know what women are—always changing their minds.'

'Amelia Winter isn't someone who easily changes her mind, I should have thought. She has a damn good reason.'

'Of course, of course.' He nodded sagely and carefully poured himself more tea; all the biscuits had been devoured. 'Has it occurred to you she might be worried about your safety? Come to think of it,' he said blandly, 'you could be getting into some rather dangerous waters, you know.'

'Dangerous for whom?'

'Er? For you of course, my dear fellow.' He swallowed more tea. 'Yes—on the whole, it might be wise for you to lay off for a bit.'

'You mean before I get to some of the other beneficiaries?' I stubbed out my cigarette in the tin ashtray. 'Such as Joanna Marigold Salisbury, *alias* Goldie Grayling?'

'Oh!' His colour heightened nastily. 'So it was you, was it? I wondered who I had to thank for the letter I received this morning from some damned little suburban solicitor.'

'Mr Pride of Maida Vale? Hardly the suburbs, Cyril—in fact, not very far from your own lair.'

'I thought I specifically instructed you not to inform any of the beneficiaries of the terms of Vivian's will. So you immedi-

172

ately turn round and tell Goldie—that is a quite unforgivable breach of confidence.' Anger had tightened the flaccid skin around the jowls.

'Only confidence breeds confidence. I shouldn't have gone to see Goldie if you hadn't lied to me about her identity.'

'You'd better watch what you say, Speke. I'm not having you poking your nose into what's none of your damned business.' He looked at his tea, put it down and took a deep breath. 'Well—no harm done. Did she give you a nice roll in the hay for your pains?'

'Like Vivian, you mean?' I said quietly.

'Vivian?' He sat back with a poor attempt at a nonchalant grin. 'That was years ago. That's all water under the bridge. Why should I hold that against him particularly? Goldie slept with everyone. To tell you the truth, I was glad he took her off my hands—it's no fun being married to a pea-brained nympho, you know.'

'But no doubt you'd be quite glad to have her back with a hundred and fifty thousand pounds in her pocket.'

'Don't be ridiculous. If you're suggesting that I murdered Vivian on the off-chance of getting money out of Goldie, you must be out of your sordid little mind. What sort of a man do you think I am?'

'Devious. You always were. And unforgiving.'

'You're beginning to annoy me, Ivor. You're meddling in the nastiest kind of gossip. No wonder Amelia's had enough of you. Why don't you go back to your cold comfort farm and attend to your cabbages?'

'How odd that everyone's advising me to go home these days. It's the only thing that makes me feel I might be getting somewhere. I'm beginning to think this whole idea of a madman's vendetta is some kind of elaborate blind you and Lady Winter have thought up between you to keep me off the scent.'

'What *scent*? What the hell are you talking about? Aren't you getting just a wee bit paranoiac?'

'No more than Mr McQuade. He thinks Vivian's murderer is to be found fairly close to home. I'm growing inclined to agree with him.'

'Then you should be a good deal more worried than I am. Vivian's death means nothing to me, but you're eighty

173

thousand to the good, aren't you?'

'No. That's another thing I wanted to tell you. I am refusing Vivian's legacy.'

'You...!' Cyril gaped—then he threw back his head and roared with theatrical laughter. 'You really *do* have cold feet, don't you?' He slapped the leather of his desk. 'Why, you poor fish, do you imagine that's going to make any difference *now*?'

'It will make a difference to me. I don't expect you to understand. But I loved Vivian, and it would give me no sort of pleasure to spend his money, knowing I could only do so because he's dead—because he was most horribly murdered.'

'That kind of mush would make you a fortune with Mills & Boon,' he said tolerantly. Then he leaned forward and his tone hardened. 'But when you've finished shoving your insufferable integrity under my nose, let me give you a bit of advice. You weren't so choosy about accepting favours from Vivian when he was alive, were you? Those cosy little trips abroad, for instance. And he got you into the Club, didn't he? You even owe your wretched little job to Vivian, don't you? People may wonder about the *quid pro quo*. Your wife's warm bed, you may say—well, join the crowd. But people might think there was a bit more to it than that. The police, for example—they have particularly nasty minds. No, Ivor, if I were you, I wouldn't go bragging about how much I loved Vivian Charles Alexander Winter.'

'Are you suggesting I had a homosexual relationship with Vivian?'

'You wouldn't have been the first. We all know he was ambidextrous. And the police do love a bit of sex in their crimes. I expect they're giving poor Alva Norman a *very* rough time.'

'I am not Alva Norman.'

'No, of course not, my dear fellow. You're much too secretive, aren't you? But you might well be in the same queue—or closet. Oh yes indeed.' He had worked himself back to blandness.

'You know, when Goldie told me about you, I took it all with a pinch of salt. You know how women exaggerate.' I smiled. 'No one, I thought to myself, could be quite as nasty as that, certainly not—what is it? An Old Rugbeian?—but,' I said, standing up, 'she didn't tell the half of it.'

'Get out of here, you little shit!' He rose slowly, his hands trembling at his sides. He was a good three inches taller than me, but with all the fleshiness of the self-indulgent. I longed for him to hit me. But as though he had caught my thought, he braced his shoulders and pushed a finger on the intercom button. 'Miss Dishley, Mr Speke is leaving now. Would you be so good as to show him out?'

As if in defiance of her name, Miss Dishley was one of the plainest women I have ever seen, but she had a nice smile.

'Tell me,' I said, 'do you happen to know if Lady Winter is in town this week?'

'Oh yes, sir, I know she is. Mr Grayling rang her this morning twice.'

As I walked down the worn steps of Stone Buildings, I wasn't proud of myself, and the spring verdure gave me no pleasure. I'd done what I came to do, yet I had raised ghosts rather than laying them. I remembered a scene at a Cambridge party after a Union debate—Cyril in white tie and tails, drunk and sweating with self-pity, hiccoughing or sobbing on a couch, clutching Vivian's hand in his.

I didn't really need Miss Dishley to tell me that Lady Winter was in collusion with Cyril. But why did she surround herself with such sly and morally seedy men—Cyril and Alva and Hugo Pulteney? What was she *doing*—protecting Vivian, protecting herself? I didn't want to know. I didn't have to know now.

I stopped and looked up at the narrow strip of sky between the close buildings—the white trail of a plane traced its way disinterestedly across the high clear blue. You're well out of it now, Ivor, I thought. Perhaps I said it aloud, for an approaching woman, disconcerted by my abrupt halt, gave me a disapproving glare and a wide berth.

'Sorry,' I said automatically, 'I really am most terribly sorry.'

It was certainly time to go home.

23 *A Step Back*

'Morning, Jim—you're out early.' It was just after half-past eight on a clear sparkling morning that should have made the heart lift, but Jim clumped in looking unusually surly, even for him.

'Here. Parcel. Registered.' He panted dramatically. 'Ought to put some steps up that driveway of yours, you ought.'

'Have a cup of tea? It's a fresh pot.'

'Can't hang about this morning. Got to get a move on. Taking the missus up to London for the holiday weekend.' He made it sound like a sentence of death. 'Sign here.'

I reached over and signed. 'That should be fun.'

'Fun? You got to be joking.' He dumped the heavy brown parcel on the table. 'Just an excuse for her to spend money, that's all it is.'

'She won't be able to spend much on a Bank Holiday—all the shops will be shut. You'll be at a hotel?'

'Hotel? I'm not made of money. Mortlake—at her brother's place. Five kids, they've got—and with us lot it'll make twelve in a little flat as big as your thumb nail and the walls as thin as paper.'

'Well, you can take them all out on the river—that's cheap enough and it ought to be lovely at this time of year.'

'You got to be kidding.' He gave a rich phlegmy cough and spat into his handkerchief. 'You wouldn't catch me within a mile of the water.'

I got up to shut the door behind him, reflecting that most of his round was within a good deal less than a mile of the water—if the sea counted as water. But this morning I found Jim's sour view of the world unamusing.

As I turned round and saw the parcel from Shep on the table, alongside the teapot and the neat pile of review copies and the files of Derek Latham and Soper and Maynard, I had a heavy sense of *déjà vu*. The only thing missing was *Love's Loose Strife*; last Saturday morning I had put it away—for good, I thought. This Saturday morning I would have to take it out again—for good or ill.

Coming back to the cottage yesterday afternoon, I had looked forward to the balm of my familiar retreat and habitual round. Stepping back into my old world would, I thought, be an easy healing, a liberating simplicity. I'd lit the stove, fetched logs, warmed the house, taken a bath, made my supper, even jotted down a few preliminary notes for next week's review. And yet I'd had a feeling of unease which puzzled me, then irritated me—like the feeling after a bad piece of writing which one's too lazy or disdainful to revise, of loose ends untied and a job not properly done.

The home-made goulash I'd taken from the freezer seemed tasteless and when I'd cleared away, it was still only seven o'clock. I'd not felt like going to the pub—I'd had my surfeit of company lately. So I'd poured myself a large solitary whisky and then, almost guiltily, I'd separated Latham's file from the other two and sat down to read.

Derek Latham had been convicted of the rape and murder of Wendy Duke, a twenty-three-year-old expectant mother, who'd been married just over a year to Ralph Duke, a local government employee. The Dukes lived on the fourth floor of a block of flats in Tufnell Park; and Latham, described as a self-employed builder and decorator, had gone there one Tuesday morning to give an estimate for redecorating the spare room for the baby which was expected in three months. Wendy Duke had been alone in the flat and the prosecution's case was that Latham had attacked her, raped her and then, when she had struggled free and rushed screaming into the bathroom and locked herself in, had broken down the door and pushed her out of the bathroom window. She fell five storeys onto a concrete walkway and had died of multiple skull fracture and a broken neck.

Latham claimed that it was Wendy who had made the sexual overtures and invited him to have intercourse with her—then, in the middle of it, had changed her mind. He admitted to using force at this point to hold her down, 'I thought she was a typical little cock-teaser who wanted it all right but wasn't going to make it easy.' It was probably that remark, I thought, that did for him as far as the jury was concerned; for Wendy, who before her marriage had been an

177

assistant manager at a supermarket, had a reputation of ultra-respectability—the very model of virginal, then marital chastity, who'd never in her short life put a foot wrong. And the wedding photo, somehow slipped in among the shots of her in death, showed a conventionally pretty blonde, but with an undeniable look of primness.

Latham confessed that when she had run into the bathroom and started to scream, he'd panicked. 'Christ, I thought with all that racket she must be slitting her wrists ... I dunno what I thought, I just knew I had to get in there.' When he did get in, he said, she was standing naked on top of the lavatory yelling out of the window; and as soon as she saw him, she started to climb out. 'I tried to grab hold of her, but she was slippery and she had one of those spiky hairbrushes in her hand and she hit me in the face with it as hard as she could, so I sort of let go for a moment—and she was gone.'

When I'd finished I went to the door of the cottage and stood listening to the faint murmur of the unseen sea as the night fell. It brought me none of the usual comfort. Latham weighed on me like an iron clamp. There was a ring of ordinary truth about his statements—but then we could not hear the countervailing voice of Wendy, perhaps equally convincing. Had he pushed her or had he tried to save her? And if the latter, what agonies he must have suffered in prison—and out of prison too. And yet apparently that was not the way it had been. Released after only four years, he'd gone happily back to Miss Sheila Wantage who'd established herself in Eastbourne, worked for a few months and then—vanished. Or had he been pushed?

Maynard, the drowner, drowned; Soper, the crusher, crushed; Bateman, the stabber, escaping a knifing by the skin of his teeth—what more likely than that Latham, the pusher, should himself have been pushed? And the best place in England for such a deed was close at hand—Beachy Head.

What I needed was a sharp, hard tramp over the hills, up to the Head—yet I was seized with an unaccountable distaste for the trepid night—fear of the dark. I closed the door and hooked the shutters and lit my old paraffin lamp. Then I poured another whisky and drank it slowly, warming my hands at the stove.

I went to bed early, but I didn't sleep for a long time and, when I did, I fell directly into nightmare. I was in the marshy valley, running—but running faster than ever I had before, my feet darting from tussock to tussock so that I had a sensation of great speed to match the terrible urgency, and, yet for all that, I hardly seemed to move. The mist drifted about me and I drank it in great lungfuls until it thinned and shredded, creating a clear narrow passage in front of me and as I hastened down the tunnel of clarity thus formed, the house reared up to a new and monstrously extended height so that try as I would I could see no roof or summit—and the gaping windows were not blank eyes, but mouths, open mouths screaming and screaming. . . .

It was my own screams that woke me and brought me shuddering out of the bed. Hardly knowing what I was doing, I hurried across the passage and opened the door of Henrietta's room and switched on the light. It was all there as before, unchanged, untouched—the flowered walls, the cot with its animal-patterned coverlet, the tasselled lampshade, the milking stool I'd bought in a Seaford antique shop, the Harrods teddy bear Phil Wood had got her for her second birthday . . . yet there was a staleness in the room. I opened the window and leant out into the night. Away to my right, the floodlit church tower stuck up above the surrounding screen of trees. Mr Brimbright the vicar had raised quite a lot of money to floodlight the church on what (according to some bizarre calendar in his hare brain) he considered auspicious occasions—and this was evidently one of them. The artificial radiance burnt away all hint of grace or taint of mystery—depressingly symbolic of the pretence of rural life we played at.

Now, as I shut the door after Jim the postman and returned to the table, the depression was still with me. With a sigh, I took out my pocket knife and cut the string binding the large brown parcel. The covering note read:

Dear Ivor,

Herewith photocopies of the main items in our files on the remaining eleven men in your category. Transcripts or précis of the trials are included in each case. All eleven are alive and well. Let me hear from you soon . . .

Yours ever,
Shep.

The eleven were: Aspinall, Smith, Haines, Higgs, Ward, Billings, Johnson, Grange, Petrie, Yates and Dalby.

I sat down and poured myself a third cup of tea.

All shots of the deceased at the scene of the crime or the mortuary had been omitted. I was grateful, for the facts were nasty enough in themselves. I read the accounts with the attentive detachment I gave to a batch of thrillers—'taking the meat out of them' with as much speed and little effort as possible. Now and again in these trials there was a shaft of savage revelation, but for the most part reality was a remote and technical affair: the details of trivial lust and careless brutality gave small hint of the passion of the perpetrators or the agony of the victims. These rapist-murderers seemed flat figures, inadequate to bear the great weight of expert medical testimony and its dehumanizing psychobabble; despite all the laboured efforts at understanding, their motives seemed obscure, their actions pointless; only the consequences were appalling. The men remained inaccessible. The women, of course, were dead.

And there was nothing that I could find to suggest why they survived at liberty, while Soper and Maynard—and very likely, Latham—had been sought out and killed. What punishment did these three merit that the others did not? It was nothing to do with their victims, who ranged in age from fourteen to seventy-three and came from a variety of backgrounds. Nor was it a matter of timing—Johnson, Grange and Petrie had been let out after Latham, and Yates and Dalby after Maynard and Soper. Yet they too, like the other six, were alive and well.

I left the house and, taking the short way through the hedge at the back of the garden, marched swiftly up the hill, fighting against the stiff breeze and my heaviness of spirit. By the time I reached the Head, I was panting with exertion—too much whisky, too many cigarettes in the last few days. I stood too close to the edge to be bothered by the dogs barking and children darting and the fretful parents' occasional shouted warnings. The breeze snatched at my hair and I had to half-close my eyes against the glitter of the Channel. There's an intoxication in the mingling of the wind's chill and the sun's heat on the cheek; sea and sky sway gently and the world falls away and the mind's free, the body delicate.

180

Something hit me on the back and I stumbled forward dizzily and came down on one knee. I was on the very brink, and five hundred feet below the green-grey waves snapped whitely at the cliffs, as a red ball soared out over the edge and plunged downwards, was slapped against the cliff wall by the wind, bounced out again, caught by a whirl of air and tossed in dancing descent till too small for my eye to see.

I got up and stepped back and turned round.

'Ian, oh you naughty boy, come here at once!'

But Ian paid no attention; he stood a few yards away staring at me with that concentrated solemnity of a six- or seven-year-old.

'You nearly fell over the cliff,' he said.

'Yes. And you've lost your ball.'

'I've got plenty more at home.'

'But I've only got one life.'

He pondered this, the wind whipping and tangling his hair. 'Cats have nine lives.'

'Ian! Say you're sorry to the gentleman!'

'Yes,' I said, 'that's why people have to be more careful than cats.'

'I expect you wish you were a cat. Cats can see in the dark.'

'*Ian!*'

'That's certainly an advantage.'

'Cats don't have to wear clothes,' he said, adding a point.

'Perfectly true.'

He waited a moment courteously, in case I wished to throw in some other feline virtue. Then, 'Cats are better than people,' he said, nailing the argument.

'Ian—*will* you come here!'

'In many ways,' I said, 'you're right.'

He gave me an approving nod and began to turn away—then he glanced back over his shoulder. 'My Mum hates cats.'

And as he ran—in little intricate loops—back to his mother, I threw back my head and laughed.

Then, swinging my stick and still benign with merriment, I set out for Eastbourne.

24 A Step Forward

No sane person goes to Eastbourne on a fine Bank Holiday weekend, but I thought I had a fair chance of finding Sheila Wantage at home for lunch. Natives of seaside towns don't usually spend much time on the Front, just as they seem to eat less fish than the inland city dwellers. Familiarity induces a peculiar disdain for local advantages—how many true Londoners actually go to the theatre? New Yorkers dream of Paris and Parisians long for New York, the Swiss fear the Alps and the Dutch detest the flatlands and rush to buy up France. Everybody's heart is in the wrong place.

Bilberry Street was in the back parts of Eastbourne, but Sheila Wantage was not at home. As I was turning away half-thankfully, a head crowned with a mass of pale blue curlers poked out of an upper window.

'You looking for Sheila?'

'Yes.'

'She'll be round at the pub—they're always glad of an extra pair of hands on the weekend.'

'She works there?'

'On the weekend, and evenings now and again,' she said. 'The Bilberry Tree, the one on the corner, you can't miss it.'

It was a pub for locals, not for trippers, but was fairly crowded. I had no trouble spotting Sheila—she was much in demand. I ordered a large Bell's and a ploughman's lunch and decided to wait until things had thinned out a bit. She was a large fattish woman, with glasses, straight black hair and the pasty complexion of a barmaid uninvigorated by sea air. Yet she was not unattractive and had an agreeable laugh and an easy soft manner.

As I ordered a second whisky, I asked her if I could have a word later on, about a private matter.

'What private matter?'

'About your—about Derek Latham.'

'Oh. I don't know.' She looked at me closely, still for a moment amongst the bustle. 'Are you a policeman?'

'No.'

'Probation officer?'

'Do I look like it?' I smiled.

'I don't know—some of them look pretty funny these days.' Then she laughed. 'No, all right—but you're not a friend of Derek's, are you?'

'No. I'm a friend of Vivian Winter.'

'Oh. I see. Can you wait?'

'Yes, of course.'

'All right. We close in half an hour.'

After that, she kept an eye on me, refilled my glass as soon as it was empty—she was measuring me as carefully as she measured the Scotch.

It was more like three-quarters of an hour before the last of the customers left, the glasses washed and polished, and the landlord and his wife gone upstairs.

Without the rattle of the fruit machine and the perpetual Muzak, the pub regained something of its Victorian sobriety. The sun shone through the decorated window in a variegated pattern on the worn ox-blood carpet.

We sat in a corner with an unmarked bottle—'Billie's private malt'—and a flagon of water on the table between us. Leaning forward so that the curve of her white breasts rose above the line of her black blouse, Sheila listened to me attentively.

'It's funny, you know,' she said, 'he was after the same thing, Vivian was. And I wanted to help him—not like those bloody probation officers all wax and warnings, poking about the flat. "Are you sure you have received no communication at all from Latham, Miss Wantage?" Well, I wouldn't of told them even if I had—and I had. About a month after he'd gone missing he sent me a postcard—it was from Oxford or maybe it was Cambridge, that's all I could remember. When your friend came down here—twice he came—he was so keen, I had a real old hunt for it. I don't usually throw postcards away, but I couldn't find this one. He was very disappointed. "Ring me up right away if you find it," he said. But when I did, it was too late. He was dead. It gave me the shock of my life, I can tell

183

you.'

'You found the postcard?'

She got up and went behind the counter and plucked a card from the side of the mirror.

She handed me the card picture-side up and I recognized it immediately—St Peter's Church, Cambridge, at the bottom of the street where I'd had my third-year digs.

'May I read it?'

'Sure, go ahead.'

I turned it over. There was no date, but the church was noted at the bottom and there was a Cambridge postmark with a date too faint to be readable.

> Hello love—How are you?
> I'm fine—plenty of work
> here and lots of gigs.
> Throw this away just in
> case—OK? Love
> Jeshni

'I didn't throw it away, but I put it at the back of the till under the cash drawer—out of harm's way—and then forgot about it. Only found it a fortnight ago when Billie had the new till put in. I didn't know what to do with it. You don't think it had anything to do with your friend being murdered?'

I looked up at her—she had taken off her glasses; her eyes were fine and large, of a greenish tint, with long dark lashes. In the placid light of the empty pub, she was almost beautiful. And she was distressed.

'I'm quite sure not,' I said firmly.

'Thank goodness for that. I'm glad I couldn't find it for that copper—he'd already wheedled enough out of me about Derek, him playing the guitar and doing gigs in pubs and joining those cherry-coloured people.'

'Cherry-coloured people?'

'Yes, you know, they wear these sort of pink and orange clothes with a picture of their big chief round their necks—got a name like Bagwash. They live in communes and call themselves San something or other.'

'Sannyasin. Yes, I've heard of them. And Derek was one of them?'

184

'Was?'

'Is, then.'

'You think he's dead, don't you?'

'I don't know. I believe it's possible.'

'I think that's what your friend thought.' She poured us each some more malt. 'I expect you'll think it's silly ... but I had this feeling one night, two or three months ago it must have been. A Monday night it was and I was serving right in this bar. I was standing there with a pint of Guinness in my head and suddenly I had this feeling like I was going down in a runaway lift. It's true what they say—my heart went into my boots and I dropped the glass and everything went dark for a second. "Whatever's the matter?" they said. "He's dead," I said. "Who's dead?" "Nothing—a goose," I said, "a goose must've walked over my grave." We had a good laugh about it—and some of them still ask me how my goose is doing. But I didn't get over the shock for days. And then when I read how your friend had been killed, I had it again. And I got the feeling as if—as if I'd brought some sort of curse down on him. And Derek too. And I....'

I reached over and took her hands in mine. Her head was lowered and she was trembling.

'You've no reason to feel that,' I said. 'If Derek is dead— and even more, if he was murdered, then it's part of a pattern. That pattern includes at least two other men in similar circumstances to Derek, who have died after release from prison in a rather suspicious way, who were perhaps murdered. We don't know for sure—and we don't know why. Perhaps Vivian did know—or at least suspected—and maybe that's ... well, that's exactly what I want to find out. But if it's true, you must see that it's got nothing to do with you—it must be part of some complicated mad vendetta. And if all that's just my imagination—well, then Derek is probably alive.'

She looked at me, her eyes shiny with tears. 'Oh God, I wish I knew.'

'Yes, so do I.' I released my grip and gently put the glass into her hand. 'You'd better tell me a bit about Derek—or what is it, Jeshni? Is that part of the Sannyasin thing?'

'That's right.' She drank some whisky, then wiped her eye with a knuckle. She smiled. 'He was a lovely guy—full of fun and life and good-looking, oh yes he was handsome all right.

Of course he had an eye—well, that's natural, I've got one myself, and it never came between us. He's a kind man too—which made it so silly what they said he did to that Duke woman. Not that I'm not sorry for her, being dead. But Derek never had any need to go *forcing* a girl—it was nearly always the other way round. It upset him—he just couldn't understand it. When he came out, he was quieter—not quiet, but quieter. Of course he kept on with his guitar and that, and he played beautifully and sung too. But sometimes I'd catch him just sitting and looking. "What's up, love?" I'd say. And once he said, "She just came at me, Shiel—that bird flew right at me, practically stark naked. What was I supposed to do?"

'It affected him, see. He wasn't as easy with women any more. I think that's what attracted him to these Sanny people—they were serious and believed in something, but they weren't puritanical and they weren't prejudiced against him—and a lot of people were. He felt he could trust them, and then there was one, I forget her name, but he liked her a lot. I could feel him slipping away, so it didn't surprise me one day when he comes in in his pink clothes and says, "We're off, old lady. I won't tell you where," he says, "because they'll be after me, so it's better you don't know." He gave me three hundred pounds—he was always generous and made good money; he could do anything in the building line. When he had it, that is—he was always in and out of the betting shop, so we never saved. Except when he was in prison—I put by a bit then. I moved down here and got this packing job in the week, and what with the bar here nights and weekends, I got a mortgage and bought a little flat up the road. I had to have a steady job and a nice place, if they was to let him come to me instead of one of those hostels. But like I say, you see, he'd changed—he wasn't really that happy with it any more....'

Feckless Derek—compulsive gambler and womanizer with a chip on his shoulder, who'd left Sheila in the lurch from one day to the next. I lit a cigarette to cover my anger; I'd read enough of *Regina v. Latham* to know that he was probably responsible for Wendy Duke's death, whether he actually pushed her or no. I said, 'You must have a bit of a hard time of it financially.'

'Oh I manage. I'm not complaining. I'll have the mortgage

paid off in sixteen years—I'll take a holiday then.' She laughed.

'You haven't had a letter from a man called Grayling—a solicitor?'

'No. A lawyer? Oh dear—what about?'

I told her briefly about the legacy—fifteen thousand would be enough to buy the whole house, at a guess, and to pay for a very decent holiday.

'Vivian did that?' It was the first time she'd used his name unadorned. 'He didn't have to do that.' She blushed. 'You don't think he meant it as. . . .' She stopped, confused.

'As some sort of compensation for Derek?'

'Oh. Oh yes. Only I wasn't—yes, I expect that's it, isn't it? He came home with me, you know—both times he was here.'

'Well, that's perfectly natural, isn't it?'

'Is it? A lot of people wouldn't think so. He was a lovely man.' She gave a kind of smiling sigh. 'You're a lot like him, aren't you?'

'Am I?' I said awkwardly. Suddenly I was as conscious of her young white faintly pregnant-looking body as though she had been sitting opposite me entirely naked. And she was young—much younger than I had expected, in her late twenties, if that; she must have been no more than a girl when she'd first lived with Latham. The idea of her youth, the vital presence of it, filled my head with quick, unscrupulous fire.

'It doesn't matter,' she said softly, as if instinctively aware of the spurt of desire that made my hand shake.

Yet it did. I could easily bring myself to believe that the lively action of lust could revoke the curse of death which hung about us both like a contamination. 'It's not that,' I said.

'You're not—not afraid of me—of what I might ... are you?'

'No—I—on the contrary. It's just that I'm not like Vivian.' And I'm not like Derek Latham either— or Maynard or Soper, or Aspinall or Dalby. That unspoken affirmation seemed to sound in my ears like a sort of blasphemy, and I snatched at my glass and drank off the whisky and poured some more. 'Sheila,' I said.

'It's all right, love.'

'No-no it's not. It's just that I've got to finish this first.'

What in God's name was I committing myself to? 'Believe me, it's not that I....'

'You mean, find out about Derek—and Vivian?'

I turned my head away and stared at the patterned sunlight on the floor, the soft blotches of spilled whisky and slopped beer. And I thought of the scars of love on Goldie's carpet—and the stain of blood on the Winter linoleum.

'What?'

'Do you mind if I call you Ivor?'

'No, of course not.'

'Ivor—can't you give it up?'

'Give it up? Do you know— I thought I had.' I smiled, but she, unsmiling, took my hand.

'You think perhaps Vivian was killed because he knew too much—oh, I know you haven't said it, but it's what you think. So it's dangerous, isn't it? Dangerous for you, I mean.'

'I don't think so,' I said. 'You see, if Vivian's murder *was* part of a series, he must somehow have tipped his hand. But nobody knows that I'm—well, following in his footsteps—at least nobody who could possibly be the murderer.' But then I thought suddenly of Maudie Gray in her sun porch and Josh Gray, with his massive head and huge hands, sitting there wordlessly—he who 'had fair doted on Liz'—watching the telly, watching his niece go off in the bright morning to her death, watching me.

'But you can't be sure, can you?'

'Ninety-nine per cent sure,' I said with a smile.

'Ivor,' she tightened her grip on my hand, 'you don't want to die, do you?'

And abruptly it was my turn to tremble—it came in a quick convulsive fit that shook my whole body like an ancient ague, like a St Vitus's Dance, like a thousand geese walking over a thousand graves. It lasted perhaps thirty seconds, and then it was gone. I explained to Sheila that it was a delayed reaction to my near-accident on the clifftop and I even made her smile with my account of the little boy and his red ball. But I knew she was only half-convinced that it was not a premonition—and it was a long time before she would let go of me.

I would have been a wiser man to take it as a warning too, but, as it was, I only saw it as a confirmation of the decision I realised I had already come to. It was no good withdrawing to my own back garden. My back garden was full of weeds.

I took Sheila home and kissed her on the doorstep and promised I would let her know if I found Derek.

25 A Final Push

Cambridge was all beige and gold in the late afternoon sun. I arrived just as the pubs were opening, after a quick and painless drive. Normally the beer and whisky I'd drunk at lunch would have put paid to the rest of the day, but on the contrary I felt exhilarated and purposeful as I wove my way among the bicycles in the town centre and past Magdalene to my old lodgings in St Peter's Street.

I was faintly outraged to find half of the street had been torn down for a playground, but Mrs Hepplewhite's house was still intact. And so was Mrs Hepplewhite—rosy-cheeked, smiling, and only a little whiter.

'It's Mr Speke,' she said with real pleasure, then raising her voice, 'Henry—it's Mr Speke come back to see us!' Her husband Henry suffered from some incurable disease (or perhaps just an excess of natural moroseness) and it was no surprise to find him still fixed and silent at the kitchen table. He probably hadn't moved since I'd left.

'Henry,' she said with marvellous optimism, 'will be pleased.'

The back room was available—in the old days it had been kept mainly for undergraduates' girlfriends up for what we used to call so oddly 'dirty weekends.' Nowadays there were so many women students, she told me over a cup of tea, that sort of thing wasn't much in demand, so they'd turned to the tourist trade.

'Ever such a lot of Americans we get—*very* clever gentlemen, and their wives so polite. Of course they always seem to have a baby, so we had to put in a cot—I hope you don't mind, Mr Speke?'

'Not so long as I don't have to sleep in it,' I said.

Henry said something under his breath which sounded remarkably like 'fuck'.

'And how is that nice young wife of yours?' she said.

'Oh—she's very well. Not so young now, you know. Perhaps I could go up and have a wash,' I said quickly to forestall enquiries about children. I remembered almost with fright Mrs Hepplewhite once telling me how her two-year-old son had died in an epidemic of diphtheria, 'ever such a bright lad, he was,' she said, 'just like his father.' Perhaps it was that which had finally crushed Henry, though Mrs Hepplewhite's sprightly good spirits had survived unsullied. I was not willing to accept any kind of kinship with Henry.

As I unpacked my bag and stuck my toothbrush in the mug above the basin and covered the child's cot with the spare blanket, I suddenly thought about Marion, not the Marion who (by Eleanor's account) was happy and prospering and about to be married, but as she had been long ago when we'd come up to Cambridge for a night or two and spent slow, loving nights in this room, on this bed.

I had filled my old briefcase with all the documents, even including Vivian's Will—they would be my bedside reading, for somewhere among them was the key, if there was a key. But I didn't need them at the moment. I had two clues to follow up in finding Latham—or Jeshni. First there was the postcard of St Peter's, which might be available in the church porch or possibly sold at the stationer's at the corner of Magdalene street. Second was the fact that Jeshni played his guitar in pub gigs, which would mean a good deal of various drinking.

But in the event it turned out to be much simpler than that. On the way out I asked Mrs Hepplewhite if she had seen any of the Sannyasin about—the pink and orange people.

'Oh yes, them,' she said. 'They've got a house in Alpha Road—I can't remember the number, but it's all very neat and spruce-looking. Some people don't care for them, being strange-looking, you see—but Henry and me think they're very polite and helpful. One of them repaired our old cistern for us last winter and it works better than it ever did now and he hardly charged anything at all. Of course, there's their goings-on, but as I say to Henry that's none of our concern.'

I told her I wouldn't be in late, but she insisted on giving me the key and promised me some nice kidneys for my breakfast.

In Alpha Road, I was lucky on my third try. I rang the bell and waited—maybe I was interrupting some religious ceremony, I thought. But when the door was opened at last it was evident I had disturbed another sort of rite.

Naked to the waist and smelling of sweat, the tousled young man was busy buckling the belt of his red trousers.

'What is it then?' He asked with surly disinterest.

'I'm looking for Jeshni,' I said.

His hands stilled and his eyes were suddenly alert. 'No one of that name here.' He started to close the door.

'Maybe not—but in that case I'd like to know where he is.'

He made a little grimace. 'Who are you, may I ask?'

'I'm a friend of a friend of his.'

'What friend?'

'Sheila—Sheila Wantage, Bilberry Street, Eastbourne.'

'You the police?'

'Do I look like it?'

He grunted—it seemed to be a convincing line.

'You better come in. Hold on—you can wait in here.' He showed me into the front room, bare boards and peeling wall paper, a geriatric couch, stacks of packing cases against one wall, and a cracked and dismantled sink under the window— so much for neatness and spruceness.

'I'm Anila—what is it you wanted exactly?'

'My name's Ivor Speke. I'm trying to locate Jeshni—Derek Latham. I'm a friend of Sheila Wantage—she and Jeshni used to live together. He sent her a card from here not long after he left, but she hasn't heard anything since. Since I'm often up in Cambridge, I said I'd look him up if I could. Just to reassure her, you understand.'

She considered me carefully. She was a fine-looking woman—thick brown hair brushed back over her ears and a strong intelligent face with a high forehead and emphatic nose. She was too formidable to be pretty; she exuded a sense of power and I could immediately see if she'd said 'come here' or 'go there' a weakling like Latham would have come and gone. The Sheilas of this world didn't stand a chance against her.

'That's all over,' she said.

'She knows that. But you can't just cut feelings off. She's

worried about him because she's still fond of him. Can you tell me where he is—or not?'

'Give me one of your cigarettes?'

I gave her one and lit it and we sat down on the old couch which gave out a little gout of dust. Perhaps she was pretty after all, sitting there silently, dressed in the obligatory pink jeans and orange shirt and wooden beads bearing a photo of the bearded guru.

I said, 'He's dead, isn't he?'

'What makes you think that?'

'Sheila had a feeling about it. More than a feeling—a kind of psychic experience, I suppose you'd call it. One night not long ago she suddenly felt she was going down in a runaway lift and everything went dark for a moment. She thought it must have something to do with Der—with Jeshni.'

'That's fascinating.' She hesitated—I was almost in. 'You're sure you're nothing official?'

'Yes. I know you might be vulnerable for harbouring a fugitive or whatever it might be, but I'm not interested in that and nor is Sheila.'

'All right then.' She nodded decisively. 'Yes, he's dead. Eleven weeks next Monday it happened.'

'A Monday—you're sure?'

'It's not something you forget easily. Besides, him and me were together. I expect you think just because we live in a commune, we have sex all over the place, but—'

'I'm afraid I'm completely ignorant about your beliefs and practices.'

'—but it's not like that at all.' She wasn't interested in my ignorance. 'And I expect you think I'm a rat for snatching Jeshni away from that woman—but he was lost and getting more lost every day with her. He needed a firm hand, he needed to believe and be part of something. We all do—but him particularly. Do you believe in anything?'

'Me? Well...' I was unprepared for such a challenge on a Bank Holiday Saturday evening and I looked away from her dark brown, judgmental eyes. 'Probably not—not in your sense of the word *believe*. I do believe in the rational ordering of human affairs—in elementary justice and human compassion. That sort of thing,' I said tamely. Then I shook myself out of this silliness. 'Look—I'm not judging you. Couldn't you just tell me how he died?'

She dropped her cigarette on the floor and trod it out. When she spoke, the undercurrent of hostility had dispersed. 'Most of us in this lot work in the building trade—not the official one. We're all black economy. So we don't mind how much or how long we work. No union nonsense. I'm a carpenter—I trained as a cabinet maker for a couple of years. Jeshni—he could do anything, he was even a fair hand as an architect, and I can tell you we've got in some fucking messes since he's been gone. Well, this winter we had this house to do up the hill—gutting it, rewiring, replumbing, central-heating, the lot. It was one of these four-storey terrace houses and we were putting in a big dormer at the back with a little iron balcony overlooking the garden—a heap of rubble it was then. The night it happened we were all working late up there—the three of us knocked off, but Jeshni wanted to stay on for half an hour to finish tiling the sides of the dormer. I didn't think anything of it when he didn't come home—he often went and had a few pints. But by midnight I began to get worried. So I went up there. I found him on the rubble in the back. He must have slid clean off the roof. He wasn't dead, not quite. Multiple fracture of the skull. They put him in intensive care and all that, but he died the same night. He never regained consciousness.' She held out her hand for another cigarette.

'Was there an inquest—there must have been of course—what was the verdict?'

She bent her head to the match. 'Accidental death—but I can tell you they made a bloody great fuss about it. We weren't covered, weren't insured, working illegally. We had the police in here for days. I thought we'd all wind up in the slammer, but all we got in the end was some fines.'

'When you went up there that night—was it easy to get into the house? The front door wasn't locked or anything?'

'No. I could have got in anywhere. It was only a shell still.'

'Anyone could have got in?'

'Yes. Why—'

'What was Jeshni like—as a workman, I mean—careless? Apt to skimp ordinary precautions?'

'No. The opposite. Oh, he was careless about money and time—a bloody idiot in some ways. But not about work—he was dead careful. It used to piss some of the lads off, but I told them he knew best. And he did.'

'You wouldn't have expected him to fall off a roof?'

'No. One or two of the others. Not him—no.'

'You do know what Jeshni had been in prison for?'

'Of course—for raping this chick and pushing her out of the window. I don't believe it.'

'But somebody might have done—have believed it. The manner of the two deaths was the same—falling.'

'That's right.' She stood up abruptly and left the room. Falling, I thought, not off Beachy Head, but out of a window, if an unglazed dormer is a window. Falling for falling.

Anila came back with two white mugs and a gallon jug of white wine. I held the mugs as she poured.

'Of course I've figured that one out. Someone pushed him. Maybe. But who? And why? And how? No one knew who he was—and anybody who did know wouldn't have known *where* he was. They couldn't even identify him at the inquest—Jeshni, that's what he was.'

'You didn't tell them?' But of course she hadn't—as far as the records went, he was still missing.

'Not me—and I was the only one who knew his old name. We've got enough trouble with the police, we didn't need that too.'

I tasted the wine—it was a bit thin, but not undrinkable. 'What sort of trouble?'

'Oh the usual. They're always on at us a bit because we're different. It doesn't bother us much.'

We drank in silence for a while. Watching her, I wondered what she had seen in Derek Latham. Sheila Wantage had liked the easy-going amiability, but that wouldn't have been enough for Anila. Sex perhaps. Whatever it was, she was in one respect like all the others—Sheila and Estelle Soley and Mrs Maynard; none of them could accept their man as a murderer. And it was true that the more I heard of the human side of these people, the more doubt I had about their guilt. Perhaps if—instead of reading the transcripts' cold recital of the brutal facts—I were to listen to other mothers, wives, lovers and sisters, daughters and great-aunts, I would come to doubt the guilt of the Marlows and Dalbys and Aspinalls. And that would be a specially insidious craziness—the sympathetic fallacy: because they are as human as I, they could not have performed such inhuman acts. Yet they had. Anything else would entail an inconceivable sequence of miscarriages of justice. And yet ... and yet ... I felt I was on the edge of some important truth, which just eluded me.

I didn't wish to hear any more about Jeshni. I would finish my wine and go. But it wasn't to be so easy.

As if divining my intention, Anila put her hand on my knee. 'You're not just here because of that Sheila, are you?'

'What makes you say that?'

'You wouldn't be asking all these questions if it was just her. There's more to it, isn't there?'

I felt her dark stare absorbing me. 'I—I'm not sure,' I said.

I stood up and went to the window and looked out. The small street was the same as a million others. Beneath the placid façades and ordinary boredom the killer dwelt in a million hearts—leapt out in lethal lust and vengeful rage and secret homicide. But who killed the killer?

'I think you ought to tell me. I loved him.'

I turned and slowly went back. I sat down and held out my mug and she refilled it. 'All right,' I said. 'It's like this...'

26 Life Fright

The hypothesis had passed the severest test of truth; it had been used to predict the death of Derek Latham and dead he was—in exactly the predicted manner. There was no shadow of a doubt now that the retributive killer existed. Anila had been convinced at once and had not unnaturally leapt to the conclusion that it was Ralph Quintin Duke, Wendy's husband. With the decisive energy I saw as typical of her, she had picked up the phone, found Duke's London number and rung through to him without paying the slightest attention to my protests. With a smoothness that amused at the same time as irritating me, she arranged for me to meet him at six-thirty the following day at the MacDonald's in Kentish Town,

195

having blandly hinted that, if he didn't agree, a forthcoming series on old murder trials might have some unfortunately inaccurate things to say about Wendy's character.

'For God's sake, Anila—you must have frightened the life out of the poor guy. And why MacDonald's?'

'Because he wants to keep you away from his new wife. He sounded frightened anyway—and sly. Watch your step, Ivor Speke.'

'What's he going to do, shove arsenic into my Big Mac?' And that had immediately made me think of McQuade. I explained that sooner or later I was going to have to tell the police about Derek–Jeshni, which would certainly get Anila and her chums into trouble for having concealed evidence as to his identity.

'Sod that,' she'd said coolly. 'We'll survive. As long as they catch the mother-raper.'

And she was right—the weight had shifted from the *why* to the *who*. As I ate my kidneys and bacon in Mrs Hepplewhite's small upstairs drawing room, I considered this. I was reluctant, after my last experience, to approach McQuade until I had some more cogent clue. He could be right that my investigation might queer the pitch, yet I was beginning to share Lady Winter's doubts about the competence of the police, if not their motivation—it was my initiative, not theirs, which had discovered Latham and connected up Soper and Maynard. I had done so simply by following Vivian's leads— and there were still some I had not checked up on; three to be exact: Veronica Ashe, Geraldine Jasperson and Cicely Quinn.

I stood up and went over to the window. 'Wet and warm,' Mrs Hepplewhite had described the day, and the drizzle was falling in a fine mist over Cambridge. I had time to spare, but the prospect of a nostalgic tour left me cold— nostalgia no longer held any attraction, or danger.

Ashe, Jasperson, Quinn most probably had had some personal connection with Vivian, like Eleanor and Goldie, but there was a chance at least that one of them might be part of the 'pattern.' A mother or wife or daughter of another executed rapist-murderer—not one on Shep's list of course, but that only went back five years. But McQuade's ten-year sweep might disclose other victims, other connections. And I wanted to get to them first.

I turned back from the window, wryly amused at this absurd surge of the competitive instinct—or was it, I thought, less amused, the sadistic impulse of the hunter (a nasty notion for a fully paid-up member of the Anti-Blood Sports League)? I picked up my cup and rapidly drank off the remains of the tepid tea. I made up my mind. Ashe lived on the Norfolk coast—Lissom Cottage, Near Blakeney, I verified from the Will. The sort of place by the sea an old nanny might easily retire to—and not much more than an hour's drive from Cambridge.

I said goodbye to Mrs Hepplewhite and, as I drove through the dull drizzle, I pictured an innocent old lady sitting in a whitewashed cottage, placidly crocheting and serving tea on a good Worcester service.

I was right about the cottage, but wrong about the rest.

Lissom Cottage was a little way out of the town, about two hundred yards from the nearest house and fifty yards from the sea—or where the sea would have been at high tide. But the tide was so far out now on the flat sandy banks that the water was invisible behind the mist of straggling rain. Compared to this bleakness, the cottage looked agreeably cosy, with a pink front door, climbing roses on the wall and smoke curling from the single chimney. There was no bell, so I used the cast-iron door-knocker in the shape of a mermaid.

The door opened . . . and we stared in mutual amazement. Then the nose twitched.

'Ivor—what on earth are you doing here?'

'Very!' I grinned with pleasure. 'Veronica Jane Ashe, I presume?'

'Yes.' She poked her head out of the door and looked down the road. 'What do you want?'

'It's all right—I'm all by myself.'

She shook her head doubtfully. 'Frank's not here.'

'Well, that's fine. I don't want to talk to Frank, I want to talk to you.'

'He's just gone to the pub.' She hesitated, and her nose twitched to the right as though pointing the direction. 'I suppose you couldn't go away?'

'But why? I've only just arrived.'

'Oh, you'd better come in then,' and she stood aside to let me pass.

As I brushed by her, I caught the oily odour of her heavy sweater and a fresher smell, of newly washed hair maybe. I was intrigued by her ungraciousness—and by the room into which I stepped. It was quite bare—highly polished oak boards, unstained, with a single oatmeal coloured rug, two tubular steel chairs in front of the fireplace which had an anodized aluminium hood, a steel and glass table with a vase of irises in the centre. I was wrong again—it had a Scandinavian elegance, but even with the happily burning fire, it was not cosy. It was in perfect contrast to the flat in Alderney Court—but this of course was Very's taste.

I turned to find her still on the threshold looking out.

'Look,' I said, 'if you really want me to go, I will.'

She drew back quickly and shut the door behind her. 'I'm sorry. Won't you sit down? Would you like some coffee or perhaps you'd prefer a drink?' She said it all in a gabbling whisper without inflection.

'No, nothing thanks,' though I could certainly have done with a drink, 'but I'll sit down. This is a bit of a surprise, isn't it?'

'How did you find me?' She took the only other chair—the Poseys obviously had few guests—and sat with her hands clasped on her knees.

'Through Vivian,' I said, 'although of course I didn't realize it was you.'

She glanced round the room as if searching for the source of my voice. 'Vivian?'

'From his Will, to be exact. He left thirty thousand pounds to Veronica Jane Ashe of Lissom Cottage, Near Blakeney.'

She said nothing, but I thought she went paler.

'Very, are you all right?'

She shook her head and the small movement sent two tears down her cheeks. I was on my feet and had her hand in mine before I thought what I was doing.

'He. . . .' She turned her head up to me and her tears glittered in the firelight.

'Yes of course,' I said, 'of course he did.'

And then she smiled at me. Slowly she rose and kissed me on the mouth, and she held herself against me; the fire flickered and danced and in that moment I, the surrogate lover, was content. Perhaps it was safer this way—for might it not have

198

been love that proved fatal to Vivian?

But suddenly her body was rigid. 'Ivor!'

'What? What is it?'

'Can't you hear? He's coming. The car. What are we going to tell him?' She drew back from me and her nose gave a rapid flicker.

'Why can't we just tell him the—oh, yes, I see.' How could she explain away a legacy from Vivian? Even thirty thousand might not be sufficient compensation for cuckoldery

'Quick, quick! How did you find us, why did you come?'

I heard the car then myself, and I slid easily into Very's fear.

'Right. That time you gave me coffee and Frank went out— you told me you had a cottage by the sea at Blakeney. I've been up visiting a senile great aunt in a home at Hunstanton, thought I'd drop in and see you. Asked at the village shop. Can you manage that?'

The colour came back into her cheeks. 'I ought to be able to,' she smiled, 'I used to be an actress.'

The car door slammed and we took our seats on either side of the fire as though at a pre-arranged signal.

'I didn't know that,' I said conversationally, 'why did you give it up?'

'Because of this,' she touched her nose with one finger. 'You must have noticed?'

'Yes. You mean it happened on stage?'

'It was my first decent part—Cordelia. I suppose it was a sort of stage fright. People laughed, and I didn't know why— I'm not conscious of it, you see. I often thought it would have been all right if they'd cast me as Regan. Of course I tried all sorts of—'

The door burst open and Posey stood there, filling the doorway.

'Well well well. Hello hello hello. This is a surprise.' He banged the door behind him and came into the room. He wore a suit and his RAF tie and, presumably as a concession to the seaside, a pair of open sandals with bright red socks.

'Hello, Frank.' I stood up and held out my hand. 'Hope you don't mind, but I was in the neighbourhood and thought I'd just drop in.'

'Delighted delighted.' He disentangled a basket from his arm and shook hands vigorously. 'In the neighbourhood, eh?'

'My great-aunt Myra's in a home over at Hunstanton. I pop up and see her two or three times a year.'

'Hunston we call it in these parts, old man. Don't we, Very? Hunston.' He started to unpack the basket on the table—two large bottles of tonic, a bottle of gin and some tins of baked beans; twelve tins of baked beans, to be exact. 'You haven't got a drink. Hasn't Very offered you a drink? How about a drink? Pink gin suit you?'

'Yes, that would be fine, thanks.' I sat down, staring at the beans.

Posey had opened a cupboard in the wall and was busy dashing bitters into three glasses. 'You'll stay to lunch of course, old man?'

'Well, I don't really want to—'

'Of course you will. Not often we have company, is it, my dear?'

Very's nose moved, but she managed a little laugh. 'It's all right, it won't be baked beans.'

'Baked beans?' He laughed heartily as he passed us our glasses. 'I should damn well think not. Had enough of that bloody muck in the war, eh, Ivor?'

'I wasn't in the war.'

'No of course not. Much too young. Bad luck.' He was standing with his back to the fire; he gave a quick upward brush to his moustache which was sagging slightly from the damp day. 'Well, here's how!'

'Cheers,' I said. Very said nothing.

We drank.

'Clever of you to find us.'

'Oh, I mentioned about the cottage when Ivor had coffee with us that time.'

The Squadron Leader seldom met one's eye, but now he was staring at me hard. 'I don't remember that.'

'You went out to get the paper.' She said it naturally, but her nose was positively wriggling.

'Did I? Perhaps I did.' He was quite motionless, staring. 'Stopped at the first house you came to, eh?'

I smiled. 'As a matter of fact I asked at the village shop.' And I had too. I felt smug until I saw Very's face. It wasn't part of the script—but what had I done wrong?

'You did, did you?'

Of course—I had naturally asked for Miss Ashe and been corrected: *Mrs* Ashe. Which meant that they weren't known as the Poseys—perhaps the bloody man was a spy, after all—and I, of course, couldn't have known the name Ashe.

'They hadn't heard of the Poseys at first—until I asked for the squadron leader.' I gave a genial laugh. 'They've got you typed all right, Frank.'

'Ah!' He gave a quick glance to Very and back to me, but the tension had gone out of him. 'Ha ha! Yes, I fancy I'm pretty well known about these parts.' He drank rapidly. 'How about another? No, not just yet? Well, I think I will, old man. Very, we'll need another chair.'

She was on her feet immediately.

'No no, my dear, I'll get it—those stairs can be a bit tricky.' He vanished through the door and a moment later I could hear him on the staircase.

Very leaned forward. 'You were marvellous,' she whispered.

'Was I? Look, Very, what on earth are you so worried about?'

'He'd kill me if he found out about Vivian.'

'Oh come—that's all over. Besides, you're not married—you could always leave, if you were really worried.'

'Leave him? How could I? He'd never let me go. Hush, he's coming,' she said stagily.

Our whispers had leant an urgency to the exchange that left me uneasy. But it wasn't stage fright that Very suffered from, I decided—it was life fright.

And Posey wasn't such a bad sort.

'Here we are,' he said, 'one chair. Hello, you're looking very serious. Ready for the other half now, Ivor?'

'Yes thanks, I think I will. Frank,' I said as he started on the drinks, 'I was about to ask Very—if you don't like baked beans, why do you buy so much of them?'

'Oh well, you see, Frank uses them for—'

'Now now, old girl—that's my little secret, isn't it?'

'Oh I'm sorry, I thought—'

'Not too much in the thinking department, eh? I thought perhaps after lunch I'd—well, we'll see. Here you are, old man.' He gave me my glass. 'And talking about lunch. . . .'

Lunch was surprisingly good—a home-made minestrone,

cold chicken with potato salad and a cucumber salad made in the Welsh fashion and a fine mature cheddar—and yet it was an awkward business. Posey was not a good trencherman but he drank—well, like a fish. Perhaps that was the symbolism of the mermaid door-knocker. He drank pink gins steadily—and I less steadily—so by the end of the meal we'd finished the bottle. We talked interminably about the war—about how long one had to be in the theatre of operations to get the campaign medal (an hour for the Italy Star), about the bonuses one got for picking up the human pieces after a plane crash, about the available brands of cigarettes and whisky, about the comparative complaisance of WRNS, WAAFS and ATS (the Wrens won). I learned more about the trivia of war than I would have believed it possible to know.

'Frank,' I said, as one does when there's nothing left to say, 'you ought to write a book.'

'Haven't got the knack, old man.' He shook his head, but he was flattered. 'Got to have the knack or else it's no bloody good. How did you pick it up?'

Very said, 'You make it sound like something you find lying about in the garden.'

'A windfall, eh? Yeees. Of course you must be pretty well-off, old man?'

I wondered what garden Very was referring to—Eden, perhaps.

'Bruised apples don't fetch much of a price on the market, old man,' I said.

He laughed. I made him laugh a good deal and gradually the wan look faded from Very's face, and the nose rested.

I had really drunk too much to drive, but I knew I must leave soon, before my tongue became slippery.

'Well, if you must, you must,' Posey said. 'But I'd like to show you one little thing before you go.'

He disappeared into the kitchen and before I'd had a chance to exchange a smile with Very, he came back with the basket on his arm. 'Come on, old man. I expect you'll want to clear up, my dear.' It was not a question, but an order. 'Better say goodbye to Very.'

We shook hands, and then I was following Posey out of the door and along the beach. The drizzle had ceased, but the air was humid.

'Come along then—not far to go.' His step was quick and springy for so bulky a man. 'Here we are.' He halted at a small fragment of wall about three foot high.

'What—' I began.

'You'll soon see.' He delved in the basket and brought out the baked beans—six tins of them. With great care he ranged them on the wall about six inches apart. 'Come on.' He was walking with measured paces away from the wall. I followed dutifully. I knew what was coming now.

'Twenty-five yards—about right, I think?' He turned round to face the wall, the sea, the world, the baked beans. He brushed his moustache, straightened his shoulders, pushed back the right flap of his jacket and slightly bent his knees. 'Look at the wall,' he commanded as his hand went down to the gun at his hip. The first shot must have only grazed a tin which did a little dance then fell forward onto the sand; but his second shot hit one square and it burst with a plopping noise and flung out a spray of juice and beans. He hit all the remaining tins and they seemed to explode from within—perhaps there was a charge in the bullets themselves.

'Not bad shooting, eh?'

The wall dripped slowly with red sauce and pink beans like remnants of flesh. In the silence after the shots, the soft murmur of the sea could be heard across the sands. The tide was coming in.

Posey had put away his gun and was buttoning his jacket. 'Bad show missing that first tin, though.' He gave his moustache a contemplative caress. 'Well, have to get a bucket and clean this little lot up. We're very keen against littering in these parts, you know, ha ha!'

'Do they give you a bonus for that?'

'A bonus? What do you—oh, yes, very good, ha ha! Witty chaps, you writers. I say, old man, you're looking a bit pale—too much on the gory side for you?' He laughed merrily and, strolling over to the wall, picked up the unpunctured tin. 'Fond of baked beans, are you?'

'So-so,' I said with a shaky smile.

'Well, here you are then—a little souvenir,' and he tossed the tin at me.

I caught it—just. 'Thanks,' I said evenly.

'That's all right, old man—plenty more where that came

from,' he gave me a hearty clap on the shoulder, 'won't miss next time.'
'I must be off.' I moved towards the car.
'Really? Sure you won't have one for the road?'
'No thanks.'
'Steady the old nerves and all that?'
'I've had enough, thanks,' I said, opening the car door. 'Thank Very for the lunch for me, won't you?'
I started the motor, half-expecting it to be wired to a bomb.
Posey waved vigorously as I drove away from the idyllic little cottage. Having avenged himself against the countryside, he was in fine fettle.
Very wisely kept indoors.

27 Duke's Solace

I arrived with ten minutes in hand, so I sat or, rather, perched—for there were no seats, only sloping ledges designed to prevent any possible illusion of comfort—and drank a cup of coffee and looked out of the window at the rain. There can be few places on the face of the earth more utterly depressing than the Kentish Town Road on a rainy Sunday evening just before opening time. And I didn't suppose opening time was going to make much difference, either. Like the street outside, Mac-Donald's was deserted.

But however full it had been, I should have had no difficulty in recognizing Ralph Duke. He came in at six-thirty precisely. I recognized the grey-faced, thin-haired humourless look at once. In an earlier age, with his neat suit and pursed mouth, he would have been marked down as a chapel-goer, but nowadays his Gods more probably dwelt in Camden Town Hall.

'Mr Duke?'
'Oh. Er, Mr...'
'Speke. Ivor Speke.' I held out my hand.

'I haven't got long.' The hand he gave me trembled noticeably. 'It's the hamburgers—they don't keep warm long,' he said, leading me over to the counter.

'I'll drive you back, that'll save time and we can put the hamburgers over the heater.'

He looked at me suspiciously—as though I'd made some obscure joke at his expense.

'Unless you've brought your own car, that is,' I said.

'I don't have a car. Two quarter-pounders, please, Miss, and one order of french fries to take away.'

'Large or small?'

He hesitated. 'Large,' he managed—it was, after all, a Bank Holiday weekend.

'But you *can* drive of course?'

'No, I can't—and what's more I wouldn't want to,' he said, as though driving were an anti-social activity akin to littering or allowing one's dog to foul the footpath. 'Listen here, I thought you wanted to talk about—'

'About Wendy. Yes. Yes, I did. Do.' But there was no need now. A Ralph Duke who didn't drive could not have run over Kenneth Soper. And as I watched him fumble with his change purse, I realised his trembling was due to some definite physical disability rather than to timidity; and Latham had not been pushed nor Vivian stabbed by a man with a shaking hand.

'It's rude to stare,' he said abruptly. He was having trouble getting the plastic containers into his cloth shopping bag.

'I'm sorry—can I give you a hand?'

'I can manage.'

Outside he put up an umbrella although it was only a yard or two to the car.

'Where to?' I said, moving the dented tin of baked beans from the front seat so that he could sit down.

'Nineteen Solace Road. I'll direct you.'

'Look,' I said, 'I'm sorry—I seem to have got off on the wrong foot a bit.'

He said nothing, only waved his hand to brush away the smoke as I lit a cigarette.

I said, 'Mr Duke, did you know that your wife's murderer was dead?'

He looked at me then and for a moment the surprise in his

eyes was vivid. 'Latham?'

'I have reason to think he was murdered.'

'Murdered.' His eyes dulled and he turned his head to stare at the rain-dimmed windscreen. 'Is that what the police say?'

'As far as they know, Latham just disappeared. I only discovered he was dead myself yesterday. He fell out of the window of a house he was working on—or was pushed.'

He looked at me with a steady lack of expression. 'And why should you care, Mr Speke?'

'Because a friend of mine was murdered not long ago. A lawyer. And I think there's a possible connection between his death and Latham's. If you've got a few moments, I'd like to tell you about it.'

'All right,' he nodded. He didn't take his eyes off me as I gave him a rapid précis of facts and theory.

'And you thought,' he said when I'd done, 'that I might be the murderer?' A small, surprising smile.

'Yes. That was a possibility.'

'But not now.'

'No, not now.'

He looked down at his hands which rested quietly on the bag of hamburgers. 'I'm not a believer in retribution.' He gave a little sigh. 'But it wouldn't be honest to say I'm not relieved.'

I opened my mouth to speak, then shut it. There was more coming.

'You might think having a handicap like mine makes you vindictive, but it doesn't you know. You have to spend too much time getting over it for anything like that. It was sort of the same thing with Wendy, you see—when she died. My wife doesn't like to talk about it. Well, that's understandable, isn't it? I've made a new life. I've made up for what I lost—I've got a wife and I've got a baby. A little girl. And Wendy, well, she was a bit of a handful for me, in a way. She was a decent, good girl—but underneath, she was ... lively, if you know what I mean. Maybe having a family would've quieted her down. I don't know. People say—oh they don't say it, but I know they think it—they think I'm better off with Yvonne. And perhaps I am. I try not to think of it—think of *her*. But I dream about her—oh yes, I dream about her all right. Some people would call them nightmares, those dreams.'

He gazed at the melancholy drops trickling down the windscreen. 'Maybe—maybe they'll stop now,' he said. 'What do you think?'

'I should think they very well might, yes.'

'Do you? Yes, that's what I thought.' He looked at me. 'Perhaps I shan't be sorry.' And he turned away, but not before I'd caught the glimmer of tears.

'I'll drive you home,' I said.

Number 19 Solace Road was a large Victorian house split up. He had wisely eschewed a block of flats.

He got out without offering to shake hands. He leant back into the car. 'You won't ring again, will you?'

'No, don't worry—I won't. Goodbye.'

'Goodbye then.'

I watched him for a few moments as he stood in the doorway awkwardly manipulating the key, and then I drove off in the mild steady rain.

I had not asked Duke the nature of his dreams, but I could guess.

28 Second Sight

I don't like Holidays, and this one had started badly. I dressed carefully, putting on my second best suit and a sober tie; I made the tea and ate two slices of toast. I put the tea cosy over the phone and had settled down to an hour's steady reading, when I became aware of an intermittent dripping sound. It was coming from the kitchen ceiling. I stared at it for a few moments—it was the other end of the house from the bathroom—and then I was bolting up the stairs.

I'd forgotten to shut the window in Henrietta's bedroom, and it had been open to all of Sunday's long drizzle. The soggy carpet made a sucking noise as I trod on it. I went to work with a sponge and cloths and a bucket, and at the end of half an hour it was only damp. I knew I should have ripped the whole lot out and hung it to dry on the line in the back garden, but

207

somehow my heart failed me. Whatever I did, nothing would eradicate the tidemark stain on the pink wool. The room was blemished beyond cure.

And my trousers were soaked. I changed into my best suit and drove into Eastbourne. As I parked in Bilberry Street, it seemed to me that half the day had already gone by. In fact, it was only just after ten o'clock and when Sheila Wantage answered my ring, I'd obviously got her out of bed.

'Ivor,' she said sleepily, and then—perhaps warned by my dark suit—she knew. 'He's dead, isn't he?'

'Yes,' I said, 'he's dead.'

She made coffee and, sitting in her small flat—all cushions and chintzes and cosiness—I told her about Jeshni's death. She wept a little—not much, but a little. I suppose she'd already done her mourning for Derek. She was only passingly interested in who might have killed him, but she was curious about Anila and the Sannyasin and the way they lived—'perhaps I'll write to her,' she said.

'Sheila—the premonition you had on that Monday night, the feeling of falling, can you remember the date?'

'The date? My Lord, I don't pay much attention to dates. Wait a minute, though. . . .' She concentrated, and I was reminded of the solemnity of the little boy on the clifftop. 'Yes I can,' she broke into a pleased smile, 'it was the day after Valentine's, I remember because. . . .'

'Yes? Because what?'

'Well, it was a Sunday this year, wasn't it? And I got sent a dozen white roses, delivered at the door they were and I thought how clever to get anyone to do that on a Sunday. There was no note or anything, but of course I wondered. . . .' She hesitated.

'You wondered who'd sent them? Derek?'

'Not Derek!' She laughed, then blushed. 'I thought it might have been your friend.'

'Yes, very likely—he was fond of white roses.' I stared at her, something was puzzling me. 'You mean . . . you mean Vivian came to see you before that night—the night Derek died?'

'Oh yes—two or three weeks before, it must have been. Twice he came,' she said with ingenuous pride. 'Is it important?'

'I don't know.' I raised my cup and drank—the coffee was cold.

'Ivor—then it was the night, wasn't it? I mean, when I felt it, he was....'

'Falling. Yes, probably. The dates fit. So it wasn't premonition—intuition, I suppose you'd call it.'

She gave a little shiver and clasped her arms over her breasts. 'It makes me scared. Do you think I'm some kind of a witch? They've got second sight, so they say.'

'Of course not—witches don't exist,' I laughed and immediately regretted it—for she was really upset. I comforted her as best I could, but my mind was on other things.

And, as I drove home through the heavy Spring holiday traffic on the coast road, I was nagged by what Sheila had said. One of the problems about Latham's murder was—how had the murderer found him? Anyone who knew that Latham had joined the Sannyasin might eventually have been able to trace him, by putting in a lot of hard work. Clearly, the murderer did so—but had Vivian done so also? If not, why not? If so, why hadn't he warned Latham? Perhaps he had tried and been brushed off—or perhaps he had been too late. He would not have left Sheila money unless he'd known Latham was dead, of that I was sure.

An old man in a scarlet car drove blindly out of a side road directly into my path. I swerved into the oncoming traffic, missed an ancient shooting-brake laden with children by a hair's breadth, accelerated desperately and whipped by the old man and back into my own lane. As the whining hoot dwindled behind me, it wasn't the face of the driver of the brake—agape and wide with terror—that I saw, but Vivian's face. Vivian in La Rotonde that bitter winter morning as he read about Bateman's second murder. Too late for Bateman—too late for Soper. And then—too late for Latham.

I drove on with exaggerated calm, but I knew now just how vitally urgent it was to find Jasperson and Quinn—and, of course, to brave Gerald Price. Danger didn't lurk only on the highways. Sheila Wantage might have second sight, but I didn't, and I didn't intend to be too late for the kill.

29 The Connection

'My editor was awfully pleased with your last effort,' I said. 'Are you sure it's not too much to ask you to do it again this week?'

Phyllis Pleach blushed faintly. 'Of course not—you know how much I enjoy it. And I've nothing to do over the Holiday. Dad's off staying with my sister in Seaford—so I'm free as a bird.'

I had asked her up for a scratch of lunch and had already fished out two of my bachelor packets of veal ragout and put them to thaw in tepid water.

'I've brought you a cos lettuce from the garden,' she said, producing it from a large straw bag. She was out of breath from the climb up from the village, but smiling and eager. 'What can I do?'

'That's marvellous, I was wondering what to do about salad. Well, you could start by scraping the carrots—and then clear everything off the table.'

For twenty minutes we worked happily together, hardly talking, and when we were done, the ragout was warming, the rice steaming, the carrots bubbling, the salad washed and the vinaigrette made. The kitchen was neat as a new pin and filled with the smell of cooking and the scent of sea air and sun-warmed broom wafting down the hillside through the open windows.

'How about a glass of sherry?'

'All right, but a small one.'

'You look very summery,' I said as I handed her the glass. 'I like that outfit.' She wore a long printed dress of vaguely oriental pattern and what I think are called Mexican beads and a wide-brimmed rafia hat.

'Do you?' We both laughed at the word 'outfit' which had given me such anguish and her such pleasure in *Strife*.

Looking at her, I thought what a perfect heroine she'd make for one of those ghastly contemporary romances—*independent, high-spirited and not too subservient ... naturally when she dresses up she is stunning....* And she was in high Spring spirits—I'd never seen her so smiling and rosy. And, all dressed up, she was, I realized, stunning.

'Well—what about the work?'

'The work?' I laughed. 'Oh yes, the work.'

I gave her a quick rundown of the books and, as we bent over my notes, a loose strand of her hair tickled my cheek and I seemed to smell her youth and softness. And I deeply regretted all those lost years when we had worked side by side without in any significant way touching. Waste—an awful bloody waste. Perhaps I could do better in future—when all this was over and done with.

She shut the last book and regarded me with those large grey tranquil eyes, 'You look thinner, Ivor.'

'You mean older.' I smiled awkwardly.

'Perhaps that too.' She put the tips of her fingers on my forearm. 'Are you all right? Are you worried?'

'Well...' I began, and then, in the country stillness, came the sound of a car mounting the drive. 'Damn. Who in God's name could that be?'

Phyllis's hand dropped from my sleeve.

'Hold on a minute.' I put my glass down and stepped outside just as Eleanor Wood rounded the corner of the cottage.

'Oh hello, Ivor,' she said brightly as if we had bumped into each other on the Underground.

'This is a surprise.'

'Isn't it?' She gave me a brisk kiss. 'Phil's off to the races with Isabelle, so I thought I'd just pop over and—'

'The races?' I said. 'Phil?'

'The horses, ducky. The firm sponsors a race at Lingfield every year—champagne, lobster, cigars, a big blowout for the authors, you know the sort of thing.'

'My blasted publisher hasn't even stood me a drink in five years,' I said feelingly. 'Why didn't you go—I thought you were fond of horses?'

'Love horses, hate authors,' she said, putting her arm through mine. 'What a hell-hole you live in. I had to ask my way three times.'

'Well,' I said shortly, 'you'd better come in and meet my aide and assistant.'

'Hello,' Eleanor said warily as I introduced them—she disliked new people on principle.

'How do you do?' Phyllis had the books in the crook of her arm and her straw bag slung over her shoulder.

'You're not *going?*' I said crossly.

'I think I'd better, Ivor. It's an awful lot to do—and I haven't got all that much time. I'll have it ready for you on Tuesday evening or early Wednesday morning.'

'But ... oh, very well. Yes,' I said, mastering my irritation, 'that will be fine.'

'Pretty little thing,' Eleanor said in her carrying tones as Phyllis had barely passed through the door.

'She's very useful to me. Have some sherry?'

'Yes please. Is that lunch I smell? What a cosy nest you've got here—decent and clean at any rate. I expect your little Phyllis livens it up no end.'

'Oh for Christ's sake, Eleanor.' I handed her a glass.

'Although I must say, she dresses in rather a peculiar fashion—like a bride.' She smiled at me. 'Of course, I know you could do with a woman, but she is just a teeny-weeny bit on the common side, isn't she?'

My annoyance vanished and I burst out laughing.

'Oh I'm so glad—you looked so grim when I came in, I thought you must be cross with me.'

'No not really.' I poured myself some more sherry.

'Well, that's good—because I'm cross with you.'

'Why? What have I done now?'

'I've got a pretty hefty bone to pick with you.'

'Then sit down and spit it out,' I said wearily.

'I don't *want* to sit down!' Her high colour clashed unbecomingly with her bright orange skirt and sleeveless yellow blouse. 'Don't pretend you don't know why I'm here.'

'I don't have to pretend—I *don't* know.'

'My God, how you men stick together—it's sickening.' She made a petulant *moue* of disgust. 'Do you know what Phil did after you rang up on Thursday night?'

'What did he do?'

'He got swinishly, piggishly drunk.'

212

'We all do that at times, Eleanor.'

'Not Phil. Oh he gets—high. But he's always articulate—too articulate. This time he was utterly incoherent. I had to get old Mr Winchelsea from next door to help me put him to bed. It was utterly revolting. At least Isabelle was asleep, thank God.'

'Don't you remember what you told him?'

'I simply told him that—'

'I *know* what you told him!' She stood rigid with anger by the table, glaring at me. 'I had to *pry* it out of him.'

'I'm afraid I'm still in the dark.'

'About the money!' she shouted at me. 'About the money Vivian left me—he left it to me me me, but you had to go and tell Phil. Why didn't you tell me?'

'Well, I'm sorry, I—'

'A fine friend you are!'

I sat down slowly. 'I'm sorry, Eleanor. I am at fault about that. I was going to tell you last Sunday when I came down to lunch, but—'

'But, instead, you chose to make your sordid little insinuations.' My God, she really was angry. 'Didn't it occur to you what Vivian's money might have meant to me?'

'I suppose I—'

'Are all "sensitive writers" just a set of gossiping old women?'

'Surely I'm not as bad as that?'

'Oh yes you are. It didn't even cross your mind that it was proof that Vivian loved me—as I loved him.'

'I see,' I said—but I had heard this before. 'It's not so much the money as the—'

'Of course it's the money. It's freedom—I can take Isabelle away from that pig and that bloody great rambling pigsty and—'

'You're not thinking of *leaving* Phil?' I was aghast.

'Of course I am—and I have every reason to leave him. Every reason. Any court would be on my side, wouldn't they?' She looked at me tauntingly. 'Wouldn't they?'

'I don't think I can answer that one.'

'Typical. Keep the ranks closed at all costs. But I *know* you know. He bares his shoddy little soul to you at the drop of a

213

hat—but I had to wrench it out of him. A black Soho prostitute—what do you think I owe him after that?'

'I don't know. Forgiveness perhaps?'

'I'll never forgive him.' Several times, as she'd been talking, she had emptied and refilled her glass; she did so again now. 'And not just an adulterer, but a fool. What a fool, lying to the police. Do you know what I did? I made him go straight off to them and make a clean breast of the whole thing.'

'That's sensible, at any rate.'

'I'll stand by him until it's cleared up—until they find Vivian's murderer. I'll do that.'

'And then?'

'And then we'll see.' She gave a curious little smile.

'And what if it was Phil who killed Vivian?'

'Don't be ridiculous. He hasn't got the—the guts,' she said contemptuously. 'Besides, why should he?'

'Maybe he knew about your affair with Vivian.'

'What a foul word.'

'Well, did he know?'

'I don't care—I don't care whether he knew or not! Phil's alive and smug and drunk and—and Vivian's ... dead!' She sat down with a soft animal moan and, as she began to weep, all the sharpness in her face was blunted.

I made no effort to comfort her, and after a while her grief dwindled naturally and she took out a handkerchief and dried her eyes.

I stood up, suddenly weary of all this. 'How about some lunch?'

'Thank goodness. I thought you'd never ask. I'm starved.'

And she ate as though she was starved. And, although she was already more than a little drunk, she drank the better part of the bottle of white wine I put out.

'You know,' she said apropos of nothing, 'just because I loved Vivian doesn't mean that I approved of him. Anyone who plays with fire can't complain if they get burned.'

'But as it is,' I said, 'it was you and Phil who got burned.'

'Do you think so? I don't know. We've got the money, haven't we?'

I stared at her. She was a little flushed with wine, but, otherwise, her face was quite bland and untroubled. I turned away and looked out of the window. Up the hill half a dozen gulls

214

made swift screeching darts at some dead or discarded tidbit. *We've got the money*—was this how they all felt, Mrs Soley and Sheila Wantage and Mrs Maynard? Is this how Vivian had planned it—due compensation for lost loved ones, and for his own death?

'What?' I asked—she'd said something I'd missed.

'I'm going to have a baby.'

'You're *what*?' I took a gulp of wine. 'When?'

'It's too early to tell yet.' She gave a shy smirk. 'I've always wanted another child, but Phil objected. Still, I think that's the least he owes me now, don't you?'

'I wouldn't ... I don't....'

'Don't sound so appalled—I shan't ask you to oblige. Phil's still capable of *that*, anyway.' She sighed. 'Babies are so marvellous, and it's such a lovely feeling being pregnant—like a cow, placid and calm and every now and again a little bit frisky....'

I thought, so some life is coming out of it, after all. Later, we kissed goodbye as though no storm had torn us, and, as she climbed into the car and drove away, I tried to picture Eleanor pregnant, heavy with child, and Phil with a baby in his arms. Pregnant. I went into the house to clear up, but instead, I found myself staring at the stack of Shep's files beside the phone, and suddenly my thoughts were like the gulls above the hills—soaring and screeching and darting down.

It took me two and a half hours, with growing excitement, to go through them all again. When I'd finished, I had it. At least, I had something. I felt a white surge of triumph. I poured myself some whisky and drank it slowly. Vivian had seen it—must have seen it—but too late for any good that it could do. And what good was it going to do me?

And then I noticed old Mr Marsham's card that I'd pinned to the outside of the Will: Horace Smith ... Kenneth Frederick Soper ... George Leonard Camrose.

I picked up the phone and dialled.

'Professor Keith speaking.'

'Shep, Ivor here. Shep, there's been a development. Latham is dead. Definitely. He fell or was pushed out of an upper storey window. Yes, I know, it fits the eye-for-an-eye theory perfectly. Yes of course I'm taking it to the police, but I'd like to come and see you first. Can we get together tomorrow?

Wednesday then—three o'clock at your place. Right. Shep, just one other thing. You remember that chap Camrose—George Leonard Camrose? He's due out when—two weeks? Well, look, I want you to do something for me—find out whether the girl he murdered and raped, yes, Anne Rourke, find out whether she was by any chance pregnant. No, that's all. I'm not sure—only that he may be in trouble if she was. I'll tell you when I see you. I haven't the faintest idea what it means. Goodbye.'

And I didn't know what it meant; but I'd found the connection all right between Latham and Soper and Maynard—out of the original fifteen, they were the only three whose victims had been with child. Wendy Duke, Fran Price and Liz Gray had all been pregnant—and so, for what it was worth, had been Maddy Hodder. It was not just the murdered women our killer had avenged, but the death of the unborn children.

On the kitchen ceiling the blemish from the room above had dried with a brownish stain. The nightmare had entered my living space.

30 The Lovehouse

'Sit down for a moment, Mr Speke, while I take your details,' said Mr Gerald Price in his soft voice. He glanced down at a large file card, blank except for my name. 'Your address?'

'Thirty-four Bilberry Road, Eastbourne.'

'Eastbourne?' He looked up. He had large dark eyes, with heavy, black eyebrows, but his prematurely grey hair and something about the set of the narrow mouth made him appear much older than he could possibly be. His expression, like his voice, was absolutely neutral; there was no resemblance to the police shots of his dead sister, and yet I had an impression of some—some inner darkness. I had come armed with lies, and it was this feeling that decided me to use them.

'I expect to be living in Dorking shortly—I've made an offer already, as a matter of fact. I thought I might as well fix myself up with a dentist while I was about it.'

'I see. You have no present problems then?'

'I've been having a twinge or two in the back—a wisdom tooth, I think.' This would stand up to inspection, for my Seaford dentist had told me that both my wisdom teeth ought to come out before long, but I decided to wait for actual pain.

'And who is your dental man in Eastbourne?'

'Actually, I haven't got one.' I gave a little laugh. 'I've only lived there a few months. My last dentist was in Bath.'

'Then he would have your records?'

'Yes, I expect so—I mean, naturally.'

'You'd better let me have his address and I'll get him to send them along. You're on the National Health, I imagine.'

'Yes. It's Soley—K. Soley, 45 Riverside Road, Bathwick.'

There was not the faintest flicker of recognition or tremor of the hand as he wrote it down. But then, the retributive killer would probably have had just such imperturbable coolness. Josh Gray had had the same kind of stillness, which might equally well mask murderous purpose or maimed innocence.

'Good. Now I think we'd better take a look at you. How long since you were last examined?'

'Good Lord, I can't remember—two or three years ago, I'm afraid.' That, at least, was the truth.

'In that case—Mary, we'll take some X-rays.'

'Yes, Mr Gerald.' The white-coated dental assistant who had been no more than a comforting background presence—however cool Price might be, he was not going to murder me in front of a witness—came forward briskly. She was very young, red-headed, and quite startlingly beautiful.

'Come along, Mr Speke,' she said and led me to the chair. An unfortunate expression. I didn't seriously anticipate death but, on the other hand, I hadn't even anticipated the rigours of an ordinary examination, let alone X-rays. Having dentists messing about inside my mouth always makes me feel slightly sick. In addition, I'd had no breakfast; and the reclining chair was full in the sun from open French windows.

Outside, a perfectly mown lawn between brilliant herbaceous borders stretched down to an old beech tree and a high wall and one of those old windowed summer houses that can be revolved to catch the sun. But neither the placidity of

217

the scene nor the beauty of Mary made up for the discomfort I was suffering. Within two minutes I was sweating and twice I almost choked over the sharp pieces of cardboard thrust against my gums.

'You have a very sensitive gag reaction, Mr Speke.'

'Do I?' I murmured, digging my nails into the inside of my thumb.

'Nearly done now,' said Mary, and I managed a small smile. 'There we are—last one.'

'Put these in the developer, Mary, would you? Now,' he said, taking up a metal instrument, 'open, please.'

I closed my eyes, breathed deeply and opened my mouth. I was conscious of his finger on my lip, his breath on my cheek, the scrape of metal against bone—and then suddenly an agonizing pain lanced through my jaw and into my brain.

'Jesus!' I heard my own voice cry, was conscious of the chair coming upright, then swaying, tilting, sliding. My last thought against the blackness was that Mary had left the surgery.

'Come on—come on.' I heard the words from faraway as my head rocked from side to side, left right, come on, left right. . . . I opened my eyes and found my head was rocking because I was being softly slapped on the cheek.

'What?' I said.

'Mr Speke, can you hear me?'

'Yes.' I could see him too—his face frowning, severe and dangerous as a High Court Judge's. 'I'm all right,' I murmured. My own body was sprawled on the floor; my head against the hardness of the footrest.

'Why didn't you tell me you were going to faint?'

'Uh?'

'Come on then.' He put his hands under my armpits and lifted me easily. He was strong, far stronger than me, though we were much the same size.

'What the hell was that?' I asked as I sank back and the chair reclined.

'That was your wisdom tooth. Let me ask you—are you often subject to fainting spells?'

'No. As far as I can recall, it's never happened before.'

'Do you have any history of heart trouble?'

'Absolutely not.'

'Are your parents alive?'

218

'My father is. My mother died some years ago. Cancer. Look, I know what you're getting at, but physically I'm as sound as a bell.'

He still frowned—but it was a frown of scientific interest rather than human concern. 'Mr Speke, are you afraid of dentists?'

'I'm afraid of pain.'

'Yes. Well, I'm not surprised that wisdom tooth caused you some discomfort. It's beginning to abscess. The best thing to do in the circumstances is simply to extract the tooth.'

'Take it out? Now?'

'Yes. In a few days you really would be in pain.'

I looked down at the garden; on the stone sundial, a thrush was perched. Outside, peace; inside, dentistry—no danger here, merely discomfort.

'All right,' I said. 'Go ahead.'

'Good. Ah, Mary. Mr Speke has a troublesome wisdom tooth. I'm going to extract it.'

I flinched when he came at me with the long needle of the hypodermic, but I opened my mouth and closed my eyes obediently. There is a certain pleasure in the passive submission that dental science demands of its patients—for these few moments in the adult life, guilt and responsibility are placed squarely in the hands of the manipulator. Every man is a child in the dentist's chair.

'That will begin to go numb very soon. We should be ready in about ten minutes.'

I was left alone. What do dentists do in these ten-minute intervals? Ring their bookmaker, take a few swigs of medicinal moonshine, screw their Marys in the waiting room? Not Mr Price. Despite the strength of his features—and of his physique—all joy of personality had been pressed out of him. I recognized the signs of trauma. Shock is not a one-off occurrence, it's a continuing process.

Whatever he was as a human being, Price was a good dentist. The tooth came out in one quick bone-grating wrench, and there was no pain.

'Mary,' he said, when he'd finished cleaning me up, 'I think you could take your elevenses now. Mrs Blessington cancelled.' He took off my bib, and I sat up. 'It will be a little sore for a day or two, but I think the infection will clear up by itself.

If you have any discomfort, ring me at once. All right?'

'Right.' I got up and we stood facing each other. I felt slightly weak, but I was alive.

I had a curious fellow feeling with this man. 'Goodbye,' I said and, on impulse, held out my hand.

He ignored it. 'My receptionist tells me you were recommended to me by Mr Trundle.'

'Yes. That's right.'

'Mr Trundle died of a stroke two years ago.' He looked at me steadily. 'And there is no dentist by the name of Soley in Bath.'

I said nothing.

'Why did you come to see me, Mr Speke—is Speke your name?'

'Oh yes, that's my name.' I sighed. The numbness from the novocaine made it hard to enunciate clearly. 'I came looking for a possible murderer.'

He stiffened and frowned. 'I don't understand.'

'About a month ago, an old friend of mine was murdered. He was a barrister. His name was Vivian Winter.'

'I read about it.'

'He was defending counsel for Kenneth Frederick Soper who was convicted of killing your sister Frances.'

'I'm aware of that.'

'Not very long ago Soper himself died.'

'I see.' He turned and looked out of the window at the garden. 'In prison?' he asked so quietly that I hardly heard him.

'No. He'd been released some time previously. He got a job at a bank in Bath and changed his name to Soley.'

He glanced at me sharply.

'I'm sorry,' I said, 'but I had to see whether it rang a bell with you.'

'You thought I might have some connection with his death?'

'Soper was run over and killed by a hit-and-run driver who was never found.'

'So you naturally suspected me.' He nodded. 'Are you a policeman, Mr Speke?'

'No. I'm a writer. My concern is with Vivian Winter's death. You see, Winter took an interest in Soper—he was partly responsible for getting him a job and all that sort of thing. And when Soper was killed—well, Winter thought it might have been deliberate. And it wasn't just Soper—there were a couple of other very similar things that occurred. Frankly, it was a little far-fetched, but all the same, not long after he'd started making enquiries, he was killed himself.'

'And you've taken up the torch.' He raised his hand and unbuttoned his high-necked white jacket. 'Weren't you taking a bit of a risk in coming to see me?'

'Not really. I've told people where I was going,' I said mendaciously—but why the devil hadn't I? 'Besides, I didn't think you'd make away with me in your own surgery.'

He gave me a small smile. He took off his jacket and hung it on a chair. 'Shall we take a stroll in the garden?'

As we stepped onto the lawn, he half-closed his eyes and raised his face to the sun. In his short-sleeved blue shirt, his arms white, his neck lifted, he looked very vulnerable. We walked slowly to the sundial and then he turned and indicated the house.

'This was where I was born and brought up, you know. When Fran died, my parents wanted very much to move. But they hung on until I'd finished my training, then they went up North—my mother's people were Tynesiders. My mother was a great gardener, but I was of a mechanical turn of mind, so I've had to learn all this from scratch. I turned the living room into my surgery—because that's where I do most of my living. From there it was easy for my mother to keep an eye on us when we were children playing in the garden. The only place we were invisible was here.' He took me by the arm and led me to the summerhouse. 'Get in.'

Doors and windows on three sides were open and it was not uncomfortably hot inside. Gerald Price put his hand against one side and gently pushed so that the summerhouse revolved until its windowless back was towards the house.

'And we could let down the blinds for extra privacy. You know, even in winter this place was remarkably cosy. Do sit down.'

The wickerwork chairs creaked, just as they had on Maudie Gray's sun-porch. We faced the shade of the beech tree and the brick wall; set in a niche there was a small stone goddess.

'Aphrodite?' I said.

'Yes. My father was a great one for collecting statuettes and busts. He wasn't particularly discriminating. I had Caligula in my room and Fran had Tiberius.'

'Do you mind if I smoke?'

'No. There's an ashtray somewhere—here we are. I expect you—you're familiar with the whole business?'

'Pretty much. I've read the transcript of the trial. And I've talked with Mrs Soper—Soley as she now is.'

'I'm sorry about Soper—it wasn't his fault.'

I blew out the match. 'You mean he didn't do it?'

'No. No, he did it all right. But he was—well, he was tempted, Mr Speke. And he fell—and then he panicked. I'm not sure with what degree of deliberation he killed Fran, but he didn't try to blame it on anyone else—he didn't denigrate Fran. Or perhaps that was your friend Winter's decision?'

'No. It was Soper's idea. His wife says that he wanted to be punished.'

'He was lucky.'

'Lucky?'

'He *was* punished, wasn't he?'

'Yes.' I inhaled and blew out a ragged plume of smoke, my lip still swollen. 'When you say he was tempted—do you mean your sister deliberately tried to seduce him?'

'The only other explanation is that she was almost incredibly silly—and Fran was never silly. Never. As soon as she told me not to come to the Trundles that night, I knew she was up to something. She wouldn't tell me what—she knew very well I'd have disapproved. I'd have stopped her. But she—she wanted to protect me, you see.'

'No—no, I don't quite think I do see. Protect *you*?'

'You're not a Catholic by any chance?'

'No.'

'My mother was—and so us children. But not my father. So along with my Caligula, I had Our Lady—and Fran had the Sacred Heart above the head of Tiberius.' He looked at me steadily, and I knew there was some message I was missing.

'A rather confusing mixture of the sacred and the profane,' I said tentatively.

'I wonder. I don't think it confused us. We were very *good* children. We did everything together, went everywhere together. People used to call us the "ideal couple." Although I was the elder by a year, it was Fran who was protective of me,

222

rather than the other way round. She was more worldly-wise than me—more sensible.'

'Look, Mr Price, I don't want to be brutal, but I do know that Fran had a reputation for promiscuity. Also that she was pregnant. Are you saying she seduced Soper so that she could later claim rape—or at any rate that he'd taken advantage of her—and so explain her pregnancy?'

'I'm sure she would not have claimed rape. But, yes, I think that was the plan. The paternity had to be explained.'

'But why? And, for that matter, why couldn't she simply have had an abortion?'

'We are Catholics.'

'I see—so that had ruled out the use of contraceptives, as well?'

'In theory, yes—prevention of life is as grave a sin as the taking of life. But that's not the way it works emotionally, I'm afraid. One can't murder something that doesn't yet exist. So contraception doesn't seem such a terrible crime. Of course it did to the older generation.' He paused, slowly rubbing an eyebrow with his finger. 'It wasn't in the least sordid, you know.'

'You mean she was in love?' I said with a hint of sarcasm.

'Oh very much so.' He seemed surprised I'd asked.

'In that case, if paternity was so important, why didn't the real father come forward?'

'That was impossible. You see,' he said in his slow soft voice, 'I was the father.'

He stood up and for a moment I thought he was going to run away, but he simply went to the door and, putting one foot to the ground, gave the summerhouse a push so that it revolved until we were facing the garden and the house.

'Perhaps you are shocked,' he said, but when I mutely shook my head, he went on, 'No—it's not so very shocking, is it, not compared to murder, for instance? I've read it up a good deal since, and it's much more common in families than one would imagine, although it goes largely unreported.' He came and sat down again. 'It was harder for my parents to accept that Fran had been pregnant than to accept her death. If they'd known that I was the father, I don't think they would ever have recovered. My mother certainly wouldn't. For the religious, shame is harder to bear than loss. And my mother was—*is* a true believer. My father told me that after the birth of Fran, she decided she didn't want any more children; my father accepted the decision, so they never had sexual relations again.

'Incest. It's loaded with taboo and horror and guilt. But to us it was the most natural thing in the world. It was just the perfectly normal expression of our love. We'd always made love, ever since I could remember. Of course we were careful and discreet, but that only bound us more closely together in our own world. When Fran started baby-sitting, it was easy— and safer—for me to turn up when the children were in bed, and leave and come back when the parents had returned. If we got careless—and of course we did get careless—then it would be thought Fran had had some boyfriend in. What we should have done is to have got Fran on the pill, but the French letters had always worked all right until. . . . Well, we'd had a couple of frights before, and nothing had happened, so the third time, we didn't think much of it.'

He fell silent, and we sat looking out together at the graceful early Georgian house of Sannyasin-coloured brick and at the prettily tamed and obedient garden. The thrush had returned to the sundial. If the human race began with Adam and Eve, it could only have continued by incest. We are all sprung from those incestuous loins, lifted from that incestuous womb. Father and daughter, mother and son, brother and sister— why should the carnal apple be withheld from them?

'We used to call this the lovehouse.'

'The lovehouse.' I looked at him. He held himself less rigidly and his mouth had softened—he had come alive with memories. I was reluctant to speak, yet I wanted to know. 'And when you found out that Fran was pregnant—what then?'

'We weren't sure at first. It was only when she was late with her second period that we knew. We both wanted the child. I've never wanted anything so much in my life. Our parents wouldn't have countenanced abortion either, so that was all right—although I'm sure my father at any rate would have tried to insist on adoption. No, the problem was that Fran couldn't have stood up to my father's questioning about who was responsible. He's a solicitor, you know, and very persistent—never satisfied till he's got to the bottom of something. And Fran has—had, Fran wasn't afraid of him, but she had a short fuse. Not like me, I'm afraid. I think somewhere along the line she would have become defiant and thrown the truth in his face. I couldn't risk that—I couldn't risk what it would have done to my mother.

'No, my plan was that we'd wait a few weeks and then just go away. I had my car and some savings—I earned reasonable money as a mechanic during the vacations. I thought we could go to the West Country, rent a cottage and wait for the baby. I could have got a job in a garage. I had it all worked out—too worked out. In my enthusiasm I just took Fran's silence for agreement. I should have known—I did know—that when she's quiet, she's plotting. Maybe I didn't want to notice. But I was uneasy that night when she told me not to come to the Trundles, not to pick her up—I always did that, you see. Yet it didn't cross my mind that she had her own solution, and I wasn't seriously worried.'

'But didn't you worry that night when she didn't come home?'

'I fell asleep in the sitting room waiting for her. Mother found me in the morning. While Fran was dying, I was asleep.' He stood up and stepped out of the lovehouse onto the lawn.

'I don't want to be impertinent,' I said, following him, 'but what would you have done if she had been successful?'

He smiled. 'I expect I would have forgiven her.'

'And what would you have done about Soper?'

'I don't know. I've often thought about that. I don't know. But you can see why I am sorry for Soper.'

'Yes,' I said. The thrush flew away from the sundial.

'When I came out of the clinic, I thought perhaps I'd become a monk, but they weren't very anxious to have me. So I decided to do something useful in the world—and became a dentist.'

'And a very good one too.'

He looked at me, and then, for the first time, he laughed. 'And how is the tooth?'

225

31 A Missed Rendezvous

'Morning, Ivor.'

'Oh hello, Alva.' I was standing in the lobby with my back to the fireplace so that I could keep an eye on the porter's lodge.

'Are you lunching today?'

'Yes. I have a guest.' Despite the sudden frosty turn to the weather, the fire remained unlit, and I was chilly.

'An important bloke? You look worried—late is he?'

'She,' I said reluctantly. 'Only ten minutes.'

Alva raised his eyebrows and gave an imitation leer. 'I should have thought you were the last person to import sex into these precincts. Oh by the way, Helen showed me the piece you brought in this morning—first-class, almost as good as last week's. I do believe you're developing a sense of humour, Ivor.'

'Yes, I want to talk to you about that some time.'

'Well, don't look so damn serious—there's nothing wrong with a sense of humour. Give me a ring then.' He patted my arm—he was a great patter—and ran boyishly up the stairs two at a time.

It was twelve minutes past one. I sipped my sherry slowly. Where was Very?

Yesterday, when I had got back from Dorking, my tooth had been hurting badly. I'd found half a bottle of Armagnac left over from my last visit to my father and I'd drunk it quickly, swilling it against the wound in my gum, as I went through my mail. There were three pieces of junk, the new *London Review of Books*, my monthly cheque from the *Gazette*— some of which I'd have to give to Phyllis—and a letter from Cyril Grayling:

Dear Ivor,

Pursuant to our conversation of this afternoon, it is my understanding that you do not wish to accept the legacy of

£83,333.00 left to you under the will of the late Vivian Winter. If this is still your intention, you should sign the enclosed Waiver before a Commissioner of Oaths and return it to me promptly.

        Yours sincerely ...

I remember looking up the hill and thinking what a beautiful day it was and how much I needed a walk. But I had been too tired to move. I'd cushioned my head on my arms and shut my eyes. *Pursuant ... promptly*—who but Cyril could manage to be both archaic and arrogant in a two sentence letter? And then I was asleep.

The phone had awakened me and, staggering up blindly, I'd got it on about the tenth ring.

'Hello. Speke here.'

'Ivor, it's Very.'

'Very what? Oh—Very! Very, how are you?' My mouth tasted of blood and brandy.

'Ivor, I can't talk long—but I want to talk to you. Can I—could we meet tomorrow?' She talked so quietly, I could hardly catch the words.

'Tomorrow? Yes—yes, I don't see why not.' Tomorrow—what was tomorrow? Was I going to be taken on in Vivian's place? Pins and needles were stabbing into my leg—I put my full weight on it. Tomorrow was Wednesday. 'Listen, why don't you meet me for lunch? At my club—at one. You know where it is? Just off St Martin's Lane. Is that okay?'

'Yes, I think so. I think I can make it. I can say I'm going shopping, can't I?'

'Very—is there something up?'

'I don't know. I—'

Suddenly my mind began working. 'Very—did you by any chance get a solicitor's letter this morning?'

'A solicitor's letter? No. What about?'

'About Vivian's legacy. At Blakeney. When did you leave Blakeney?'

'This afternoon—we've just got in. Frank's gone round to buy some gin. Why?'

'Did he go to the post office this morning?'

'I'm not sure. Yes, I think so—he usually does.'

'Very, do you think you could leave the flat. Now. Just

227

as you are. Get out. Take the stairs down. Take the next train to Eastbourne—ring me from there and I'll meet you. Very?'

'I can't do that, Ivor. That wouldn't be fair to Frank. Anyway, it's too late. I can hear the lift—he's coming back. I'll see you tomorrow.'

'Very!'

'Don't worry, darling. Goodbye.'

I went to the table and read Cyril's letter again. It had quite evidently been dictated in a mood of particular spite after I'd left him on Friday afternoon. There was no reason to suppose he'd written to all the legatees that same day; it was not likely. I had surely got myself in an unnecessary flap—frightened by Very's fright. 'He'd kill me if he knew.' Slowly I tore up the letter and stuffed the pieces in the stove. I was not waiving anything now—neither rights nor duties.

Yet later, standing at the door and breathing in the sea-scented air, I saw again the exploding cans of baked beans scattering their flesh and gore, and Posey's ridiculous face red with childish triumph. Children in men's bodies are dangerous. And I remembered how, when John Kennedy was shot, his wife had crawled out on the back of the car to retrieve a morsel of shattered cranium. When Latham fell, so Anila had told me, his face had been so bloodily smashed as to be unrecognizable. Vivian had died in blood. And when my Henrietta had lain on the concrete, she had jerked once, feebly, and a small trickle of blood had issued from her nostrils. That was how I knew she was dead.

'Harry,' I said, 'I think I'll have another sherry.'

'Very good, Mr Ivor.'

Mr Ivor. My father had resigned seven years ago, but he'd probably have to die before I was promoted to 'Mr Speke.' The past possessed the club, like pestilence the slums of Calcutta.

I pushed through the doors and went down to the glassed-in phone booth. I let the phone ring twenty times at the Posey flat, but there was no answer. It was nearly half-past one now, but I fought down my uneasiness.

'Look,' I said to the hall porter, 'if my guest comes will you show her into the West Dining Room?'

'Your guest, sir—that will be Mrs Posey.'

228

'Yes—or possibly Miss Ashe.'

'Mrs Posey or Miss Ashe. Very good, sir.'

I got back to the lobby just as Harry brought my second sherry. I took it, but I didn't want it now. I didn't want to lunch. I wanted to just walk out of the club and never.....

'Ivor—you still here? Been stood up?'

'I don't know.' But I did—for whatever reason, Very wasn't coming. 'Come and eat with me, Alva. I've got a table in the West room.'

He made a *moue*. 'Rather depressing, isn't it?'

'I'll stand you the lunch then.'

'Ah—that's not depressing at all.'

'Alva,' I said, having finished ordering a Chablis for the smoked salmon and a Mercurey for the steak and kidney pie, 'I'm thinking of turning in my cards.'

'What? But why? You're excelling yourself at the moment.' He was genuinely nonplussed.

I hesitated—I was about to burn my boats, as I'd burned Cyril's waiver. But, as I watched the door for Very's arrival which wasn't going to happen now, I knew I was right. I had lived the wrong life for too long a time.

'Those last two pieces weren't mine, Alva. I farmed them out. I realize they're much better than anything I can do. It's time for me to go.'

'Ivor, you astonish me. Whence this sudden access of humility? Who did write them? This gal who's just stood you up?'

'No no. A local woman—down my way. As a matter of fact, I'd like you to take her on.'

'Why? Are you in love with her?'

'No. But she's good. You can see for yourself. Her name's Pleach—Phyllis Pleach. She was a teacher for a while, but now she looks after her old father—one of the last slaters.'

'Really. Really?' He watched me sniff the Chablis. 'That *is* interesting. Frankly there are half a dozen people I can think of who'd leap at the job. But, yes, well—why not? There's certainly a sparkle there. Only on a trial basis, mind you. Daughter of a slater? Married—or liberated?'

'Well—neither really. I mean, sort of normal.'

'How I envy you your vivid touch with words.' He took a draught of wine. He was enjoying himself. 'All right—that's settled then. But tell me, my dear—what about your bread and butter, if it isn't a rude question? Or have you come into money?'

'Vivien left me eighty thousand pounds.'

'Eighty thous...' He put his glass down unsteadily, and his lip trembled as he smiled. 'I congratulate you—he mm-must have loved you very much.'

'We were friends. Yes, he loved me. I did love him.'

'Did?'

'Cyril Grayling suggests that you were in love with Vivian.'

'Cyril...' He hissed the name with bright-eyed venom. 'Cyril hates me—he hated Vivian.' He sat up straighter and drank some Chablis to pull himself together. 'I'm sure your pure soul is not interested in gossip—but if you really want to know, there was a time when I supplanted Cyril in Vivian's affections.'

'But it didn't last?'

'Lady Winter and I became very fond of each other,' he said with fragile dignity.

'But Vivian didn't leave *you* any money.'

'Did—did he leave Cyril money?'

'He left Cyril's ex-wife a hundred and fifty thousand pounds.'

'Goldie? He did? That's good. That's very good indeed.' He grinned. 'How Cyril must be writhing! Vivian always was wicked—oh what a wicked man he could be.'

'You were married once, weren't you, Alva? Was your wife's name Geraldine by any chance—Geraldine Jasperson?'

'No of course not, that was—'

'Cicely then—Cicely Quinn?'

'Sissy. She married Freddy Quinn afterwards ... Ivor, you're not telling me he left *Sissy* money?'

'Not as much as Goldie Grayling—thirty thousand.'

He looked slowly round the room—at the confident, theatrically bad portraits in their gilt frames—turned to me, grey-faced. 'Oh the bitch,' he murmured, 'the sweet bloody bitch.' And he wept; the tears flowed freely and dripped from his chin unhindered onto the sliced smoked salmon on the plate.

'I think,' I said gently, but feeling the heaviness of the words, 'that it happened to us all.'

230

'Oh?'

'I mean, that he seduced all our—our loved ones.'

He nodded. 'Very likely.'

'Why, Alva—why?'

He took the scarlet silk handkerchief from his breast pocket and dried his eyes, ostentatious even in grief. He drank a little Chablis. 'I should have thought that was staggeringly obvious, even to you.'

'I can't credit Vivian with a real desire to wound.'

'Why not? He was only human, you know. But, actually, I think you're right. Because he loved us, anyone we loved automatically became lovable. I'm sure he didn't think of it as taking away something from us—just as a sort of general all-round increase of love.'

'That's a rather remarkable bit of special pleading, even for a lawyer.'

'Lawyers are more easily convinced by their own arguments than anyone else. Haven't you noticed what suckers—no innuendo intended—what suckers they are for their own false logic? But I don't suppose Vivian attempted to justify it. He was just one of those deprived children whom all the love in the world will never satisfy. Everyone had to be induced to love him—sexually, if possible, and it usually was.'

'Not with me.'

'No? Well, I believe you,' he said with a faintly pitying air. 'But you were rather a special case, weren't you?'

'How so?'

'Think it out.'

'No, you tell me.'

'Well—you only really became friendly with Vivian in the last few years, didn't you? After you'd separated from Marion and buried yourself down by the sea. He didn't have to push it with you because he was alone in the field. It must have been a tremendous relief for him.'

'You mean he didn't have to try much to win me?'

'Well, did he? I don't want to hurt you, my dear, but you were rather easy game. There were no competitive attachments—the only person you loved more than him was dead.'

At his words I felt the old pain as sharp as ever. I lowered my head and stared down at the transparent flesh of the dead fish. I too wanted to weep—but, unlike Alva, I couldn't do it. One doesn't make a fuss in the Club.

'By the way,' said Alva, tactfully cheerful, 'what you were saying about old Shep Keith's sister—has she come in for some of the boodle too?'

'Shep's sister?'

'The dotty one—Geraldine Jasperson—Jerry Keith when we knew her.'

'Oh. My God, yes, of course.' I coughed and quickly drank some Chablis. 'I mean, yes, Vivian did leave her some money.'

'Don't tell me you've forgotten the Jasperson saga?'

'He was Swiss, wasn't he? A bootmaker or something.'

'Yes, but rather a posh one. Gustaf he was called—she brought him up to a May Ball one year, an oldish little bloke.'

'He couldn't dance at all and his bow tie kept coming undone.'

'I expect that's him. She married him a few weeks later. Then on their way across the Channel he fell off the boat—or so it was assumed. At any rate he disappeared and never turned up again. Some nasty-minded people wondered whether Jerry hadn't pushed him.' He smiled amicably. 'History has it that she spent the honeymoon in a French loony bin.'

After our lunch, I phoned Very, but again there was no answer. On my way out I caught the eye of an overcoated member standing in the lobby. There was an uneasiness about his stance as he leaned on his umbrella, as though he wasn't quite sure he was in the right club or why he was there or who he was waiting for. There was an unspoken fellow feeling in our awkward exchange of nods—not of greeting, but of farewell.

I was glad to leave. I had been there too long for any good I had been doing.

232

32 The Monster

'Yes. Yes, she was. Three months gone.' Shep took off his glasses, looked at them as though verifying their accuracy, then put them on again.

'With Camrose's child?'

'No, definitely not.'

We stood facing each other in the small living room, Shep, his shaggy grey hair recently cut, in a dark chalk-striped suit, I in my worn club tweeds. There was an air of formality between us—not that of therapist and patient, but somehow suggestive of the courtroom. And although it still retained its claustrophobic atmosphere of long dead secrets and exhausted souls, the room had been tidied and swept as if in preparation for a ceremony—an avowal, perhaps, or the delivery of judgment.

'Tell me about it,' I said as we sat down.

Shep cleared his throat. 'George Leonard Camrose was convicted of the manslaughter and rape of Anne Rourke seven years ago...'

Camrose, twenty-one at the time, was a builder's labourer. He was an only child and lived with his parents; he'd never done well at school but, at around 110, his IQ was rather higher than might have been expected. He had no special friends and was inclined to be solitary and shy, particularly with women. The only woman he'd ever been out with was Anne Rourke—just twice, about a year before the murder. His hobby was gardening and he spent most of his time working his father's small allotment. It was there that he'd taken Anne Rourke on the afternoon of her death.

Anne was a year older than Camrose; an attractive and intelligent young woman, she worked as a part-time telephonist. The rest of the time she looked after her widowed mother who suffered from multiple sclerosis. She was engaged to a young research chemist named Pleasance, and they were to

233

have been married in two or three weeks, the plan being for him then to move into the Rourkes' council house.

I said, 'If Anne was engaged to this chap, why did she agree to go with Camrose to his allotment?'

'According to Camrose, because he offered her some fresh vegetables. That might be true—the Rourkes were hard up and she'd have no reason to be afraid of him in broad daylight, although according to her mother, Anne described him as "creepy." Anyway, consent she did—and he drove her to the allotment on the pillion of his motorcycle.'

'What does he look like?'

'Look like?' Shep blinked at me. 'Oh, I see. Well, a rather typical schizoid type—inarticulate, quite unable to make eye-to-eye contact—a narrow face, protruding teeth—and he lost an ear lobe in an accident on a building site.'

'Not pretty.'

'Quite.' Shep gave a rare little smile. 'Which made it all the harder to believe his statement that Anne Rourke offered herself to him as a quid pro quo for the vegetables. According to him, they went into the small shed and made love on a piece of sacking. He then left her in the shed while he went to gather the vegetables.'

What happened next was that the shed simply ignited. A witness in a neighbouring allotment said it just suddenly went up in flames—no smoke, no warning, a single quick whoosh. When he ran over, Camrose was just standing looking at it; all he said was, 'She's in there.' The neighbour pushed the door open and dragged Anne out with the aid of a rake. She was taken to hospital and died some hours later.

'She was burned to death? Christ.'

'Technically she died of shock. But she was almost certainly unconscious when the shed exploded—contusions on the frontal bone suggested that she'd been hit or had fallen quite hard.'

'But, Shep, if he hit her . . . before or after intercourse?'

'No way of knowing. But the defence had an explanation for that. Camrose's version—Vivian's version, I imagine—was that after they'd had intercourse and he'd left the shed, Anne had got up to light a cigarette, stepped on a rake which hit her in the face, dropped the lighted match which ignited some petrol spilling from a two-gallon can with a loose-fitting cap, and that the can had then exploded.'

'Did Anne Rourke smoke?'

Shep sighed. 'You should have been a lawyer, Ivor. No, not in the ordinary way, but there was one exception—she liked to have a cigarette after making love. Pleasance admitted that under Vivian's cross-examination—one can imagine what the admission cost him. But for that, Camrose would surely have been convicted of murder—it just put that one little bit of doubt in the jury's mind, you see.'

'It wouldn't in my mind.' I lit a cigarette. 'He deliberately burned her to death.'

'Perhaps.'

'Why? Why that, in God's name?'

'You may have put your finger on it—because that's what one does to heretics.'

'Heretics?'

'He was fixated on Anne Rourke—worshipped her, if you like. He wrote to her two or three times a week—letters which in the end she was throwing away without reading. Only one survived—it arrived the day after her death. It was mawkish and adoring and largely illiterate, but there was no mistaking the strength—or tenacity—of feeling. Of course it had nothing to do with the actual Anne Rourke. On one of their two dates he'd also taken several photos of her—against her inclination—and he'd literally hundreds of these blown up and stuck on the wall of his room. The prosecution postulated that on the afternoon when he took her to the allotment, she mentioned that she was going to be married—and possibly, who knows? that she was pregnant too—perhaps with the idea that he would then stop pursuing her. If that was the idea, it was a fatal miscalculation.'

I stubbed out my cigarette. 'She killed his ideal, so he killed her?'

'It's not psychologically improbable. Camrose, I may say, has been a model prisoner.'

'So you're going to let him out?'

'I gather you disapprove?'

'What guarantee is there he won't do it again?'

'You know better than that, Ivor. Of course there's no guarantee. But being a model prisoner doesn't just mean never breaking the rules and kow-towing to the prison officers. For a timid, sheltered boy like Camrose who'd never lived away from home, always been able to retreat to his allotment when things got tough, the prison alternatives were growing up or giving up. The Board is satisfied that he's grown up. The percentage of recidivism among men convicted of murder or manslaughter is—'

'All right, all right—so Camrose has turned into a model citizen and a worthy fellow. I'm all for rehabilitation. I don't disapprove of your releasing him—I'm frightened by it.'

'Well, I don't really think you—'

'Shep! If the pattern is anything to go buy, Camrose is due for burning.'

'I ... would you care for a drink?'

I raised an eyebrow, but nodded.

'Whisky? I know it's early, but frankly my Edinburgh conference was quite exhausting—a great mistake to have it on the Holiday weekend,' he said, busying himself with bottle and glasses, 'the best people have something better to do, only the painfully dull turn up—absolutely no stimulation. None.' He handed me a very stiff Scotch and then just stood there. 'Ivor,' he said abruptly, 'I owe you an apology. Your instinct was right and my expertise was wrong.'

'You really don't need to say that, Shep,' I said, touched by the effort of humanity it had cost him. 'Even now it seems to me a fantastic idea that someone is going round specifically bumping off people who've killed and raped pregnant women.'

'Yes, but I ought to be capable of distinguishing fact from fantasy.' He went back and sat down. 'By the way, have you informed the police about Latham's death?'

'I rather wanted to have a word with you first,' I smiled. 'Just to reassure myself that I'm not hopelessly paranoid.'

'Would you like me to get in touch with the Assistant Commissioner? It's going to cause quite a flap, you know.'

'No thanks—I'm rather looking forward to telling Mr McQuade myself.'

'Well, you've earned it.' He took off his glasses and absently polished them on the sleeve of his jacket. 'I'm very seriously worried about all this.' Yet, without his glasses, he didn't look worried—puzzled and vulnerable, but not worried.

I said, 'Isn't the really worrying thing that we're no nearer identifying our retributive killer?'

'Oh, I don't know. No, I wouldn't say that. I'd say we'd got a definite pointer. For one thing, our man—let's call him Jones for convenience—now I wouldn't be surprised if our Jones didn't have some doctrinal justification for these killings. For instance, I think I'm right in saying that Catholics place a higher value on the life of the unborn child than on that of the mother.'

'Well, maybe,' I said, thinking uneasily of Gerald Price and his lost, gentle wisdom, 'but one can't go around suspecting all Catholics just because—'

'No no—I'm merely talking about justification. The imprimatur of religion can add a great deal of moral force to serious distortions of the psyche. But the underlying impetus itself would almost certainly derive from a profound early trauma. This might have been provided by Jones's mother dying in childbirth, say—and the child too in all probability. Naturally the perpetrator would be the father—his sexual aggression has murdered the mother. The infant nightmare fear made real.'

'Oedipus Jones then?'

'Oedipus Jones.' He nodded. 'And no longer an infant, but an adult whose primary rage has been both controlled and re-inforced by religion. A lucid, intelligent, controlled man who has found a way of repeatedly killing his guilty father with full moral justification.'

'Yes, but look here...' I took out another cigarette and lit it. 'If this traumatic event occurred in infancy—'

'Or early childhood.'

'—or early childhood, then the actual murder-rapes committed by Latham and Soper and Maynard were merely triggers.'

'Yes?'

'Well—I've all along been assuming that our retributive killer—Oedipus Jones—was to be found somewhere among the connections of one of the murdered women, the Hodders, the Prices, the Grays and so on. But if that were so, they would have to have had in addition just some such traumatic event as you describe in their background.' I blew a plume of smoke—it curled, slowed, finally settled in the static air.

'Quite. The basic predisposition relating to the early trauma plus the triggering event of the murder of their loved one.'

237

'But the odds against that happening to one and the same person must be, well, a million to one.'

'I agree. It would be extremely unlikely that anyone with a personal connection also had the predisposition. It is the predisposition that's the determining factor—the murder of the pregnant women which triggered the revenge syndrome is, after all, public knowledge. The personal connection is not just unlikely—it's unnecessary and irrelevant.'

'Which eliminates Price and Gray ... so I've been barking up the wrong tree. So—Good Lord—Oedipus Jones could be anyone!'

'Anyone who had the trauma-induced predisposition combined with a strong sense of moral justification. Yes. And one would have to add—intelligence, ruthless determination and physical strength. There can't be a great many people like that in our society—or we would have no society.'

'No, well...' I looked out of the window—there was scaffolding on the house opposite and two workmen were repairing the ruined roof. 'You know,' I said slowly, looking back at Shep, 'it makes sense. I've had doubts about Josh Gray, but on the whole the surviving victims I saw weren't surviving on rage ... they weren't out for blood...'

'You're relieved?'

'Yes. The idea that murder is likely to turn ordinary people into avenging killers is...' I paused—there was something in Shep's voice, I'd heard it on the phone too without giving it much thought. But now I had a flash of intuition. 'You're relieved too—aren't you?'

'What gives you that idea?' But he didn't deny it.

'Jerry—your sister.' I waited, but he said nothing. 'Vivian left her fifty thousand pounds. We know what that means.'

He made a throaty noise—half-grunt, half-groan. 'Oh dear, after all that—what a very mischievous thing to do.'

'They did have an affair then?'

'Yes,' he said. 'Yes.'

He took off his glasses and perched them on his knee and rubbed his eyes with his hands. 'It must have started right away, when Vivian first came to me for treatment. Of course I observed that Jerry was beginning to go into one of her euphoric cycles—but it never occurred to me to connect it to Vivian. It wasn't just a simple affair—although I didn't find that out till later. She forged my signature on prescriptions for him—she was always very dexterous and quite conversant with drugs, of course.'

'What sort of drugs?'

'In his case, a mixture of tranquillizers and amphetamines. Later—later she began to do it for other people, for money. That was after she went off with Vivian. She was caught of course, eventually. She blames me for that. The police agreed not to prosecute on condition she was committed—which was necessary by that time.'

'And Vivian?'

'He was out of the picture by then.'

'You mean, he let her down?'

'Yes. Flat.'

'So when he was murdered, it occurred to you that Jerry might have been responsible?'

'She's physically quite capable of it—and she's an extremely vindictive woman.'

'So you were worried.' I drank some of my whisky. 'You know, at the time, there was a rumour that Jerry pushed her husband off that Channel boat—what was his name, Gustaf?'

'Carl. Carl Jasperson. I don't know, Ivor—in those early days, it was unthinkable.' He shrugged.

'Shep, when I came to you suggesting that Vivian's murder might have been part of a pattern of killings, why weren't you more encouraging?'

'You didn't need any encouragement from me. You had the bit between your teeth. Besides, it did seem most unlikely.'

'Almost too much to hope?'

'Perhaps ... yes.' He gave a small sad smile. 'I must say I am—much relieved now.'

Because I was sorry for him, I felt an awkwardness about what I was going to say. I drank up my Scotch, put out my cigarette and lit another. 'But are we sure that Vivian's murder *did* have anything to do with the others? After all, Vivian himself doesn't strictly fit into the pattern.'

Shep put on his glasses. 'Strictly speaking, that's so—in the sense that he hadn't raped and murdered any pregnant women—but surely the connection is very clear and cogent. Oedipus Jones has a strong sense of personal preservation—to put it mildly, he's not after personal publicity. He killed

Vivian because Vivian knew too much.'

'Yes, that's possible. On the other hand, he may still have been murdered for personal reasons.'

'That would have required a most extraordinary coincidence. And unbelievable luck for Jones.'

'Luck for him, yes. But coincidence, no—or not necessarily. Vivian's murder has always struck me as an odd mixture of the sexual and the domestic, an aspect I ignored once I discovered the nature and number of the stab wounds, which seemed so very obviously to establish a definite link with the pattern murders. But, when you come to think of it, it is the *only* link— and one that could have very easily been forged, as it were, by anyone. All the murderer would have had to have known would have been the facts of the two Bateman cases—he or she didn't need to know anything about Soper or Maynard. The sixteen stabs were a false clue—a blind—and an effective one, far more effective perhaps than anyone could have expected.'

'Effective? I'd hardly say that—it led you to the discovery of the pattern killings.'

'Yes, but don't you see, Vivian's murderer wouldn't care a damn about the murders of Soper and Maynard and Latham, even if he knew about them. What he succeeded in doing was to send me trotting off in the wrong direction—the more I found out about the others, the more attention was diverted from Vivian's murder.'

'I see. And who do you have in mind?'

'When I said earlier that the people I've seen—the surviving victims—weren't out for blood, there was one clear exception. And that's Lady Winter. And I ask myself who was instrumental in sending me off in the wrong direction? And the answer to that too is Lady Winter. She knew about Bateman and, almost certainly about Soper—remember she lives in Bath and she would probably have read a report of the inquest in the *Chronicle*.'

'Lady Winter murdered her son?' He paused. 'Why?'

'My guess is because she found out that he was thinking of getting married.'

'Was he?'

'I don't know. It's a guess, but I've been thinking about it and I rather have the feeling he had his eye on Mrs Soley—

240

Soper's widow. He spent quite a lot of time with her in Bath, and Lady Winter might quite well have found out about it—and if she had, she would have worried about it much more than usual.'

'Why?'

'Because, for Vivian, it was an unusually domestic arrangement—and because she had no way of monitoring it as she did with the others.'

'You think she monitored Vivian's relations with women?'

'Oh yes. I don't mean that she interfered—on the contrary. Ostensibly she respected the limits—he never introduced his women and she never enquired about them. But I have an idea she knew pretty much what was going on—letters, phone calls, address books. They lived together a good deal, shared a social life in which she was the hostess, he the host. She kept on good terms with his homosexual friends—too good possibly, Vivian wasn't awfully keen on that. But she didn't make the same mistake with the women—she very carefully respected the limits of his privacy there. And the more women he had, the better—so long as nothing got serious. For what she feared was a permanent relationship that would have displaced her—marriage.'

'Yes, I see.' He stood up and fetched the bottle and refilled my glass. 'On the face of it, that seems a rather slight motive for the murder of one's son.'

'I'm not talking about the face of it. You're the one to tell me whether I've got my psychology all to cock or not. But my impression is that her relationship with Vivian was very highly charged—sexually charged—and extremely possessive. I think she was probably a very jealous woman indeed—a jealousy that could be controlled and contained so long as there was no menace to her relationship with Vivian, but as soon as there *was* a serious menace to it, the jealousy flared up into decisive action. If she couldn't possess him, then no one else was going to.'

'So she killed him?' He hesitated, then filled his own glass. 'I see a good many difficulties in the way of that—not the least, some practical ones. She struck me as rather a frail old lady, and surely it would not have been easy to come up from Bath and then get back again late at night without being observed?'

'I agree with you, but none of that matters. I'm not saying

she killed Vivian with her own hands.'

'What's that?' I'd felt his attention beginning to wander, but now I had it all.

'One of the things that's struck me in my—my investigations, is how many people had plausible motives for killing Vivian. Nothing to do with the retributive murders or Vivian's investigation of them. Sexual motives, money motives—motives of past damage or future profit or both.' I had the uneasy feeling that I was beginning to sound like McQuade. 'Well, I think Lady Winter knew a good deal about the sexual havoc Vivian had caused, and she almost certainly knew the terms of his Will—i.e., who was due to get what. What could have been easier than to tip the wink to ... well, I shan't mention any names, to someone of the more ruthless of the beneficiaries or the most desperate of the jealous? She knew when Vivian would be in the flat alone, she could even have handed over the keys; she could have suggested the method, so that the death could be linked to the Bateman cases. She would run no risk and the murderer very little—and she would be on the scene before anyone else to make sure any little clues were eliminated and to get rid of the address book and diary. Then all she had to do was to get hold of some poor fool to discover the clue of the stab wounds and go charging off in the wrong direction and provide her and the murderer with a cover story.' I paused. 'I, of course, was the poor fool.'

I took a large swallow of whisky. 'For a time all went well—I did even better than expectations. But then I began getting a little too close to home—and so very nicely, but immediately, she asked me to give the whole thing up.'

'But you didn't give it up.'

'Oh I did. I was going to. I was persuaded, and if I hadn't ben infuriated by Cyril Grayling and if I hadn't glanced at Derek Latham's dossier, I would have given it up. I'm fairly easily manipulated, you know—and manipulated I bloody well was!' I felt the full force of bitter resentment—my God, how I had been hoodwinked!

Shep shook his head slowly. 'I don't think so. I don't think you're easily manipulated at all. We must look at the end result. If you're right about Lady Winter's efforts to manipulate you—well, she was unsuccessful, wasn't she?'

'So I'm making a mistake?'

'No—I have no great fault to find with your psychological analysis, and she might well be capable of having done what you suggest she did do. But I don't think she did. Oddly enough, it seems to me you're leaving Vivian out of the equation. Vivian was, after all, an extremely clever and subtle man. I have a strong feeling that he did know the identity of the killer—and deliberately invited him to the flat. I—'

'Knowing how dangerous he was? That would be extraordinarily foolhardy, wouldn't it?'

'Vivian was foolhardy. He led a dangerous life—he invited risk. He was like an ageing boxer who won't retire from the ring—even though he knows he's no longer invincible and knows that the damage done is past repair and gets much worse with every punch. But he doesn't know what else to do. To hurt and be hurt is his profession/obsession—he has no other. To continue to fight is to invite disaster, but to cease fighting is to become possessed by one's nightmares.'

'You think then that Vivian wanted to die?'

'Death is the solution of all problems. That is seductive to a tortured man.' He paused. 'And Vivian was a tortured man, you know.'

Tortured? Oh, I knew by now that my picture of Vivian— smooth as silk, touched with every blessing, graceful of form, movement, wit, incomparably charming, clever, sensible, tactful, sympathetic—well, I knew that wasn't the full portrait. But despite his air of invulnerability, his secretiveness and what I had come to see as his insouciant sadism, I still thought of him as fundamentally serene.

'Shep, I think you'll have to explain a bit. I've discovered things I don't care for too much—the way he used money, his promiscuity and a certain, well, callousness about the consequences—but I can't fit them in to the Vivian I knew.'

'The Vivian you knew!' he said harshly. He finished his whisky in a gulp and plunked the tumbler down on the table. He sighed, then picked up his glasses and very carefully put them back on. 'Give me one of your cigarettes, Ivor. Thank you, thank you.' He puffed slowly, as though the cigarette had been an expensive cigar. 'Sorry about that. All right.

'Broadly speaking, you are right about Vivian's relationship with his mother. It was intensely—cripplingly—possessive. For the first ten years or so of his life he hardly saw his father—

243

much of it was during the war and Winter held some diplomatic post abroad. Vivian lived with his mother and his aunts—a totally female entourage—and was tutored by them so he didn't even leave home to go to school. A few years after the war ended, the mother went to join her husband somewhere in the Far East, I believe, and Vivian—eleven or twelve by that time—was packed off to prep school at a moment's notice. His mother came back to England regularly every summer, the rest of the vacations he spent with the aunts. He only once or twice went abroad to his parents.' Shep tapped some ash into a teacup.

'A common enough story in the days of the Empire.'

'Maybe. But Vivian was an only child, and far from being neglected, he was the exclusive object of his mother's attention as infant, child and adolescent.·When he was at school he used to write to his mother every day.'

'The poor kid.' Then, as Shep looked at me without comment, I said defensively, 'He must have been pretty miserable, musn't he?'

'Perhaps. But the net result was far more miserable. Vivian never emerged from the latency period. He never had to confront his father, because his father wasn't there. And there was no opposition to his possessing his mother—or to she possessing him. But such a possession of course carries its own nightmare—of being devoured, consumed, totally annihilated. With no chance of breaking free from this smothering love, he devised a strategy—unconsciously of course—of, as it were, arming himself with a multitude of other loves. It was entirely reactive. He could no more permit himself to be found in the love of others than he could allow himself to be lost in his mother's love. His promiscuity was a way of escape, perpetually unsatisfactory because always cut off before the depth of involvement became, in its turn, dangerous. Not only was any deep emotional involvement dangerous, but it would also have been a betrayal of mother and therefore was not permitted. In fact, it was impossible. Vivian's affective life, though omnivorously wide, was superficial and impoverished. To avoid being absolutely mother's boy, he had to be all things to all women—and men. As a result, he was nothing very much to anyone.'

'But that's not so, Shep—a great many people were devoted to Vivian.'

244

'Of course.' Shep frowned impatiently. 'That was the whole point of the exercise—he had to be loved to reassure himself that he existed. He could make people love him, but he could not make himself love them. He was essentially elusive to all his lovers because he was elusive to himself. He was driven to search, doomed to inevitable failure and then, careless of the consequences of the love he had incurred, driven again—to somebody new, a fresh bed, another chance.'

'You make him sound—monstrous.' There was a tremor in my voice.

'He was monstrous.' Shep looked at me and his tone softened. 'In his heart of hearts he was an infant—a desperately threatened infant fighting ruthlessly for survival. Babies have no superegos—they don't know the rules. In the outside world he was a facsimile of a responsible adult—he even chose a profession where emotional maturity is not a requisite and is unlikely to be tested. To put on a wig, make a case, prove a point—and then move on to another brief, another mask, another act—that suited him perfectly. Confrontations confined to the courtroom carry no risk of personal involvement and could therefore be ruthless without danger. In the real world, charm and smooth words ensured there would be no confrontation. Between the ruthless child and the accomplished actor was a great gap—and into that gap vanished the reality of everything he might have been as a man. He was a grown man physically, but with the heart of an infant, which is to say—a monster.'

'No, Shep—no, I don't accept that.' I stood up abruptly, without purpose. 'Oh, I accept some of it—but, dammit, he had feelings! He was—he was decent, kindly.'

'Feeling for Vivian was rather like a landscape he'd often flown over in a plane—he knew it well, studied it, mapped it. But he'd never walked down there—smelt the summer grass, scuffed the autumn leaves, thrown snowballs.'

I went over to the table by the window and refilled my glass. 'He was a good friend to me.' Good God—could I think of nothing better than that to say?

'Yes,' he answered gently.

And I knew precisely what that tone of voice meant—I had been, as Alva said, 'easy game' for Vivian, requiring little, demanding little, giving little—because I had little to give. I must have provided him with an ideal rest cure. A 'good friend'—all I was saying was that he had not done me, at least, any harm. Or hadn't he? What about Marion. . . .

I gulped some whisky and shivered at the bite of the alcohol. It was my day for home truths.

'Why did he come to you?' I asked, moving back to my chair.

He hesitated, then braced his shoulders. 'He was suffering from periodic bouts of impotence.'

I laughed. I threw back my head and laughed as I hadn't done for years—the whisky slopped over the rim of my glass and my eyes were wet with mirth.

'Yes.' Shep gave a thin smile. 'But it was not really funny. Poetic justice isn't. He was frightened.'

I wiped away my tears. 'Yes, I bet he was. It must have seemed like the end of the world to him. Did you cure him?'

'When the more distressing symptoms are ameliorated, the patient often assumes the problem is solved. In fact it almost invariably means that the hard work has only just begun. That was so with Vivian. We had made some good progress, though we had only begun to touch the fringes. But at least he was no longer suicidal. And then—'

'Vivian? Suicidal?'

'Of course; he had very little psychic strength. One day he simply broke off the treatment, although I had warned him that we needed years rather than months. But then, as I said, we had begun to move into dangerous areas.'

'And of course by that time he was getting a little help from Jerry and her forged prescriptions?'

'That too. You know, when he came to ask my help with his list of released prisoners, he didn't mention Jerry; I had to explain to him exactly what he had done. At first I could see he wondered what all the fuss was about—and then a minute later he was effusive with horror and regret. It just took him a few moments to find the right mask, that's all.'

'But if that's so—if he had no conscience, no sense of justice—why did he bother with the Maynards and Lathams and Sopers?'

'Well, that takes us into a rather nebulous area. At first perhaps it was a game, a fascination—and then something of an obsession. Looking at it one way, Vivian had something in

246

common with those men—oh, he didn't rape and he didn't murder. His seductions didn't require force, but were as conscience-less and careless of consequence as any rape. And the damage he did to people's lives wasn't physical, but in some cases it was, psychologically speaking, murderous.'

'Are you saying that he was fascinated by what happened to them because they were punished by death? He in some fashion identified with them and wanted, courted the same punishment for himself?'

'That's putting it into the moral sphere where Vivian did not exist. He was as incapable of feeling guilt as a humming-bird that swallows a gnat. No, I think it presented him with the possibility of a solution—a neat, subtle, symmetrical solution. His life had been for years—always been—one of very severe tension. It's true what I said—he *was* tortured. He had to exert every nerve and fibre to balance nightmare against nightmare, so that neither one could take possession. The impotency was the expression of his failing capacity to maintain the balance—the whole delicate act was falling apart. The solution I offered—the professional solution—was unthinkable. The only other solution was suicide. In this case, suicide by proxy.'

'He planned it all—he invited the murderer to murder him?'

'I think it very likely. It would have appealed to him. By manipulating it that way—contriving to have someone else's hand do the actual deed—death would have been transformed from defeat into victory. Not a pitiable failure, but an organized triumph.'

'And the Will,' I said slowly, 'so the Will was a calculated manoeuvre too. Dissension and suspicion and distrust. False clues, false gratitude, false...'

'Vivian was not capable of love, Ivor. You must understand that the man you loved did not exist.'

'I find it very—hard.'

'Of course. Of course you do.'

'But he was a human being. He was murdered.'

'Indeed so. And the murderer must be found.'

'If it was Lady Winter...'

'No, I don't think it was his mother. That would have been her triumph, not his. His death was a final act of defiance against his mother—his only act of defiance. All she possessed

247

then was his dead body.'

And my thoughts went back to the funeral—to the crematorium on the Bath hillside and the racing wind stirring the flesh of the grass across the meadows, and the sun and the lofty clouds and the tears. And the body smoking up to the sky.

'In any event,' I said, 'the killer is alive and well. So now we have to start worrying about Camrose. In view of what happened to Latham, will you still let him out?'

'Probably. It's a situation that's never arisen to my knowledge. The police will have to be consulted of course.'

'A lot of good that'll do—the police aren't going to give him round-the-clock protection. Where is he going to live?'

'The normal procedure would be for him to spend six months or so in a hostel and then—'

'Jones won't have any problem finding him in a hostel—you might as well exhibit him at Madame Tussaud. Look, Shep—he's a keen gardener, you said?'

'That was his hobby, yes.'

'Well, in my part of the country gardeners are at a premium—in fact can't be had for love nor money. If he came down and lived with me, I could find him plenty of jobs.'

'Oh, I couldn't countenance that.'

'Why not? I'm a responsible citizen, aren't I? And with you to vouch for me. Upper Leeching is the last place on God's earth Jones would think of looking for him.'

'I don't think you quite understand what you're proposing. You've had no experience of prisoners—there is always a problem of adjustment after a long term in prison. There has to be a certain amount of supervision—you'd be giving up a good deal of freedom. In a small community there is sometimes opposition to the idea of—'

'I think I could deal with that—I wouldn't be worth much if I couldn't. I don't expect a fascinating companion. He'll probably be boring as hell. Come on, Shep, you could fix it.'

'I probably could.' He removed his glasses again and rubbed his eyes. 'But why, Ivor? Do you want to do this?'

'Yes, I want to. We can't have any more of this destruction. I'm not being guilt-ridden or sentimental. Something has to be salvaged—something of Vivian perhaps, something of what he might have been. And if we don't do it—if *I* don't do it—we won't breathe freely again. For the rest of our lives we'd be dogged by fear.'

'Fear. Yes.' He smiled. 'I'll, er, take it under advisement, as we say. I can't promise anything but...'

I glanced at my watch—six-twenty. My anxiety for Very had been stifled for hours, but now it swept back and left me breathless.

'... of time, but...'

I stood up. 'Shep, can I use your phone?'

'By all means—it's in the corner there.'

I lifted the receiver—I had the number by heart now. 'Of course, there is one other possibility, Shep—about the identity of Oedipus Jones, I mean.' I finished dialling and looked up at him. 'It's pretty far out, but it's worth consid... Hello? Frank, is that you? Who is this? *Who?*'

33 *Too Late for the Kill*

'Something up, by the looks of it,' said the cab driver as I paid him off.

The evening was warm and sultry with unbroken storms; the sweat prickled my skin, yet inside I had a sensation of utter coldness.

In front of Alderney Court, an ambulance and three police cars were parked raggedly at the curb, and there was a policeman at the door.

'Excuse me, sir, but may I ask if you are a resident?'

'No—no, but I've come to see Chief Superintendent McQuade.'

'Ah—you must be Mr Speke then?'

'Yes.'

'That's all right, sir,' he said, stepping aside. 'Just take the lift up to the third floor—and the flat you'll be wanting is on your—'

'I know the way.'

The porter stared at me with dull fascination as I waited for the lift. The policeman murmured into his walkie-talkie. The ancient cage rose groaning.

The gate was opened by Sergeant Roughead. 'Good evening, sir, would you come—'

'Ginger!' I gripped his arm. 'What in God's name's happened. Is she dead?'

Three ambulance men smoking listlessly against the wall of the corridor eyed me with momentary interest.

'Come along now, Mr Speke. The Super wants a word with you.' He removed my hand from his sleeve and gently pushed me ahead of him.

In the flat I moved left to the living room.

'No, not in there. Straight on, sir, if you don't mind.'

As I passed the half-open door there was a sudden flash and I caught a glimpse of moving figures.

'Super? He's here.'

'Come in please, Mr Speke.'

It was the bedroom—pale rose carpeting, pink-flowered walls, pink coverlet, an overall impression of delicate restrained fleshiness. Vivian had liked it, she'd said.

'Please sit down, Mr Speke. McQuade indicated the tapestried bedroom chair on the other side of the bridge table at which he sat.

'Is she dead?' I asked again unnecessarily—the presence of this quiet messenger of death told me the answer I already knew.

'Mrs Posey? Yes, she's dead.' The voice as impassive as the hard dark eyes.

I took a very slow step and my knee touched the bed. A pulse thumped in my head. The room was black and white, grainy as a bad print of a silent movie. I spread my hands and sat down with extreme care—and sighed and closed my eyes and sank backwards into the bed's receiving numbness.

'Speke—Speke!'

The world settled. Slowly I looked up into McQuade's brusque, unforgiving stare. 'I—I have nothing to say.'

'Blast. Give it here, Ginger.'

'I'll do it, Super.' An arm round my shoulder lifted me into a sitting position. 'Come on, sir—have a sip of this.'

The glass scraped against my teeth. I gulped. 'Christ—what was that?'

250

'Gin. You looked as though you needed it.' Sergeant Roughead grinned down at me.

'All right, Ginger, that'll do.'

Posey's gin. I was alert now. I stood up and automatically smoothed out the impression of my body on the bed.

'I gather from your reaction that you were well-acquainted with Mrs Posey?'

McQuade was back at the table and I took the chair opposite him.

'Yes,' I said, 'in an odd way I suppose I was. Look, before I answer your questions, could you tell me what happened— how she was ... how she died?'

He hesitated for a moment, then nodded. 'She was shot through the heart at close range with a .45-calibre revolver. Her husband then turned the gun on himself and blew out his brains.'

'He wasn't her husband. When? What time?'

'Six or seven hours ago—probably about lunchtime.' He glanced down at a sheet of paper on the table. 'You say they were not married—how do you know that?'

'She told me.' There was a faraway mutter of thunder. 'Is that the letter—from Cyril Grayling, about Vivian's legacy?'

'How did you know about that?'

'I didn't—not for sure. But I had one myself from Grayling, so I guessed Very—Miss Ashe—might have got one too. Then when she rang me yesterday and said she hadn't, I was worried that Posey had intercepted it—he always collected the post at Blakeney, you see. I was up there at the weekend. I knew he was jealous. He was shooting up tins of baked beans with that gun of his. Of course I saw he was a bit off his rocker but I told myself it was harmless. Until Very rang. She was— frightened, worried. I told her to come away, come down to Eastbourne—I think I almost persuaded her. I think if I'd been stronger about it, if I'd.... Well, she wouldn't. We agreed to have lunch today instead. She didn't turn up and I rang—I rang several times, before this evening, I mean. I should have checked with Grayling yesterday. I should have come up myself and taken her away. She told me he was dangerous, she told me he'd kill her if he found out. God, what was I thinking of? She said it wouldn't be fair to Frank to leave—wouldn't be *fair!*' I caught a sharp breath to prevent a surge of inane giggles. 'I'm sorry. I'm afraid I'm being rather incoherent.' I lit a cigarette with tremulous fingers.

McQuade got up and fetched a little painted saucer from the dressing table and placed it in front of me.

'You say Posey was jealous. Jealous of whom? Of you?'

'Of me? Good God no. Of Vivian of course—Vivian Winter.'

'I see. You obviously know a good deal about this. I shall be asking you to make a statement later on—but for now perhaps you'd just tell me what you know in your own words. Take your time, Mr Speke, there's no hurry.'

'No—no, there isn't, is there? All right. I shall be all right now. I....' The thunder sounded closer, a shudder on the air. I looked out at the fading daylight, the darkening skies. Had Very shuddered as the bullet entered her body—had the nose given one last twitch? Had she cried out? Had....

'Winter and Miss Ashe were having an affair, is that right?' He coached me calmly, almost gently.

'Yes. When she first told me about it—casually—well, I thought she was just a rather imaginative young woman, it seemed so unlikely. But that was before I knew about Vivian of course.' I tapped some ash into the saucer. Not really a saucer—a bonbon dish, with an iris delicately painted on the china. It seemed a bit of a desecration to use it as an ashtray, but there was nothing else.

'I first met Very when Posey buttonholed me one day as I was coming out of Lady Winter's flat. It was a Sunday, the Sunday before last, and....'

As I talked, McQuade rose and went to the window and stared out, whether from an unusual stirring of restlessness or some instinct of tact, I don't know. But without his eyes on me, I was gradually able to recover my coherence.

I came back at last to the same place. 'If it hadn't been for that letter of Grayling's. I should have warned her—it was bound to come some time. I knew Posey was suspicious.'

'Suspicious?'

'A suspicious man. Under that bluff heartiness of his, he was always on the alert.'

McQuade turned, but in the dimness of the room I couldn't make out his features. 'You did the best you could. It's more complicated than you think, maybe.'

I gave an astonished half-laugh at his mildness. 'It seems to me the simplest part of the whole business. Oh, I suppose you could say if Vivian hadn't left her any money—'

'Quite.'

'—or if they hadn't had an affair in the first place.' Despite all his woundings, this was the first actual blood on Vivian's hands. How much more was there going to be?

'That's as may be. But we're not interested in the ifs and buts, we're concerned with the hows and, to a lesser extent, the whys.'

There was a rip of lightning and, a few seconds later, a long tearing crash of thunder. In the silence, I realized that the noises in the next room had ceased some while ago.

'How were they discovered, Superintendent?'

'Lady Winter smelled gas on the landing some time this afternoon. She got hold of Trubshaw and made him open the flat—he has spare keys to all the flats. A kettle on a low light had boiled over and put out the flame. The kitchen window was open, so the accumulation wasn't too bad. Evidently they had been about to make coffee. Lady Winter rang us immediately.'

Very's eternal coffee. 'No note? No letter?'

'Just the letter from Mr Grayling—in Posey's pocket.' He moved and switched on a bedside lamp, then took his place at the table. 'I'm going to call on Lady Winter in a few minutes. I'd like you to accompany me.'

'Me?' I was filled with instinctive revulsion—I did not want to see her. 'Why?'

'I'd rather wait on that, if you don't mind, sir. I have my reasons—good reasons.' The pinkish light seemed to have softened his features, dissolving the harshness of his habitual inscrutability.

'In that case. Very well.'

'Good.' He nodded. 'Now, sir. As you took the trouble of going all the way to Norfolk to see Miss Ashe, it's evident you didn't pay much heed to my warning last week to keep out of this investigation.'

'No.'

'Well, I'm not so very astonished.' And he smiled. I wished he hadn't. The sudden appearance of small, even white teeth were disconcerting, not comforting. A crack of thunder

253

overhead made my heart leap. 'I'd like to know what else you've been up to.'

I looked at my watch—eight-thirty. 'Yes. I was going to ring you this evening for an appointment, anyway. But it's going to take some time.'

'Very well....' He went to the door and called out to Ginger, then came back.

I took a few moments to organize my thoughts. None of it seemed to matter much now—but I knew that was merely the initial numbness of grief, of guilt. It did matter; there were people to protect—Sheila Wantage and Anila who'd withheld information from the police, the private disasters of Shepperton Keith and Jerry, of Alva Norman and Ralph Duke and Gerald Price, Eleanor Wood's secret injuries, Cyril Grayling's injured pride, and Vivian—God help us, I still had to spare Vivian.

So it was an edited version I gave McQuade—none of the despised *ifs* and *buts*, only the *whats* and *hows*. The psychology of it he could get from Shep. He took occasional notes in rapid hieroglyphics—asked few questions. Only when I made the final connection—three men killed in the manner of their own murders, whose three victims had all been with child—only then did he look up, his pencil still.

'Are you sure of this—of these facts?'

'Yes. Absolutely sure. And so is Professor Keith.'

'Aye. Professor Keith.'

I hesitated. 'There is a further problem—I mean, if we're right about this.'

'And what's that, sir?'

I explained about Camrose and his impending release. 'I imagine the Parole Board will be getting in touch with you officially about him before long. But I thought you should know as soon as possible.'

'Quite right.' He tapped his pencil thoughtfully against the open pad.

'Mr McQuade—you're bound to take it seriously now, aren't you?'

'I've always taken it seriously.'

'You have? But you were very dismissive.'

'The police don't take kindly to private individuals taking matters into their own hands. But I brought no formal pressure upon you to desist—as I might have done.'

'Are you saying that you—that you deliberately let me have my head?'

'I formed the impression early on that you had certain advantages of access, acquaintance, denied the police. In a complex case such as this, that can be very useful.' He gave me his macabre little grin. 'And I'm bound to say you've done very well.'

I blushed with a kind of foolish gratitude—blushed again with anger. 'Done very well? I've handed you the solution on a platter!'

'I wouldn't go as far as to say that. You've provided some useful information but—' There was a ring at the front door. McQuade lifted his head.

'But what? You know *how* Vivian was killed—now you know *why*.'

Ginger put his head round the door. 'She's here, Super.'

'Right. Coming.' He stood up and looked down at me. 'Maybe—maybe we know that.'

'All you've got to do now is find out *who*.'

'Maybe,' he said carefully, 'Maybe we know that too.' He picked up a long narrow packet wrapped in newspaper. 'You'll have to excuse me for a few moments, Mr Speke. I'll be back shortly.'

I got up and ambled idly round the room, touching things here and there. I stopped at the window. The thunder still rumbled, but further away now, and I realized the storm had passed us by. Lightning, like the photographer's flash, intermittently transfixed the world, catching it in death. But there was no rain—at least, not here.

And what was I doing here? I, who was always too late for the kill. I wanted desperately to be back at home, where the garden grew and the sun shone and the sea perpetually drew and withdrew with neither pain nor grief.

'Oh Very,' I said out to the outer darkness, 'my poor dear Very.' But tears, like the rains, withheld themselves.

'Sir, we're ready now—if you'd just come along.'

I turned slowly. He was standing in the doorway—and there was something about him, a tenseness, a vibrancy. 'Do I really have to?'

'If you wouldn't mind. I think you'll find it instructive.' The

255

Scottish accent was more marked, but there was something else too in the voice, soft but unmistakable—a note of triumph.

34 Blood for Blood

'Hello, Cyril.'

'Ivor! What the hell are you doing here?'

'Mr Speke is here at my request, Mr Grayling,' said McQuade.

'At *your* request?' He looked crossly from one to other of us. 'Well, I suppose you'd better come in, although I can't see why it's necessary—I thought you'd already questioned Lady Winter.'

'Just one or two further points, sir—nothing for you to be worried about.'

'*I'm* not worried—what concerns me is your worrying Lady Winter.' But he held open the door and we trooped in—McQuade, then me, then Ginger.

'Talk about bad pennies,' Cyril muttered as I passed him.

Amelia Winter showed no surprise at my presence. 'Good evening, Ivor,' she said coolly, as though I were expected for cocktails. But, although the whisky decanter was on the side, I knew we were not going to be offered drinks.

As I took the armchair opposite her, the room seemed to me to have lost its former elegance. The yellow velvet curtains, closed against the night, were garish, and there was a starkness about the greys of wall and carpet—a decorator's room, brittle with impersonality.

McQuade and Ginger seated themselves on the couch. Cyril remained standing, one hand resting protectively on Lady Winter's chair. Yet, sitting upright in her black dress with a single mourning brooch at the neck, her dark eyebrows drawn in judgment, she was clearly in need of anything but protec-

256

tion. Medea might have looked like this in her old age.

'There are just a couple of things I should like to get quite clear in my mind, Lady Winter.' He glanced down at the notebook Ginger handed him. 'When you heard the shots shortly before one o'clock, did you take any steps to investigate their source?'

'No.'

'May I ask why not?'

'I assumed they came from some neighbouring television set.'

'I see. Now, when you left the flat at four-thirty, you detected an odour of gas and immediately fetched the porter to open the Poseys' door?'

'Not immediately. Trubshaw had slipped out—to the betting shop, no doubt—and I had to wait fully ten minutes before he returned.'

'Very well. You accompanied Trubshaw to the Poseys' front door, which he proceeded to open. Could you describe to me exactly what occurred then?'

'I have already told all that to your constable here.'

'If it wouldn't be too much trouble, my lady, I'd like to hear it for myself.' McQuade was suave and it made me uneasy.

'The smell of gas was very strong. I entered the flat, went straight to the kitchen, turned off the gas. I opened the bottom of the kitchen window—the top was already open. I then opened the bedroom windows and went into the sitting room. I—'

'One moment. Was the living room door open?'

'It was shut. I went in and found the bodies. I then came back to this flat and telephoned the police.'

'What was Trubshaw doing all this time?'

'Gawking outside the front door.'

'When you went into the living room, did you touch anything?'

'No.'

'Not even to verify whether they were dead?'

'I know a corpse when I see one, Inspector.'

'You left Trubshaw on guard while you went to telephone. What did you do when you had finished phoning?'

'I locked up the flat and sent Trubshaw down to await the arrival of the police.'

'You didn't by any chance yourself re-enter the flat?'

'Only to open the bathroom and lavatory windows.'

'You did not re-enter the living room?'

'No.'

McQuade passed the notebook back to Ginger. 'How well did you know the Poseys?'

'I did not *know* them at all. I occasionally passed the time of day with one or other of them in the lift.'

'You never went to their flat?'

'No.'

'Or they to yours?'

'Squadron-Leader Posey once came to the door asking me to contribute to some charity or other.'

'The RAF Benevolent Association?'

'I believe so.'

'And did you contribute?'

'Certainly not. My family were in the Navy. Besides, the man's manner did not inspire confidence.'

Ginger's sudden snigger was cut short by one of her coldest glances.

'Now, my lady, to your knowledge, did your son ever receive either one of the Poseys in this flat?'

'Certainly not.'

'Or visit the Posey flat?'

'What an absurd idea. The man was a vulgar oaf.'

'I was thinking of Mrs Posey rather than the Squadron-Leader.'

'Out of the question.'

'And yet apparently Mr Winter was on quite friendly terms with Mrs Posey.'

'I should be very much surprised if that were so. They were not our kind of people at all.' And yet I had the feeling that, beneath the snappishness, she was not in the least surprised. Had there not been letters, little missives of love from Very among all the papers that Lady Winter had destroyed? It would have been in character.

'Then you are not aware that your son left Mrs Posey a substantial sum of money in his Will?'

'Absolute nonsense!' Cyril said loudly. 'I am quite familiar with the terms of the Will—there is no such legacy.'

'Did he not leave thirty thousand pounds to one Veronica

Jane Ashe?'

'Ashe? Lives somewhere on the Norfolk coast? Yes, I believe he did. What of it?' Poor fool, he wasn't even halfway there. But she was.

'I suppose you are going to tell us that Miss Ashe and Mrs Posey were one and the same person?' she said.

'Exactly so, my lady.'

'What of it?' Cyril said angrily. 'Probably sorry for the girl. A man's entitled to leave—'

'Be quiet, Cyril. Mr McQuade, are you quite sure of this?'

'Quite sure. Miss Ashe lived with Posey, but they were not legally married. It was she who owned the cottage in Norfolk.' He sounded absolutely certain—yet he had only my hearsay to go on. I felt a flash of the traitor's discomfort. I wanted to be well out of this.

'And what do you conclude from that, Inspector?'

'I conclude nothing. But taken together with certain other information we have, it is suggestive of a fairly close relationship between your son and Miss Ashe.'

'May I ask the nature of this "other information"?'

McQuade turned to me with his little smile. 'Mr Speke, would you mind telling Lady Winter what you related to me earlier this evening?'

Yes—I would mind. I had been caught good and proper.

'Well, Ivor?' she asked mildly after a long pause. And there was no hostility in her gaze, only that look of amused and interested enquiry I had seen so often on Vivian's face.

The blood ran to my cheeks. I couldn't do it.

'You bloody little snooper!' Cyril took a furious pace forward. 'Have you been poking your nose into—'

'Please, Cyril, restrain yourself.'

He hesitated, his fists clenched. 'I'd like to punch your head, you damned sneaking—'

'Be quiet, Cyril. At once.'

As he stepped back, anger in his face and stance but the grey hair quite unruffled, there seemed to me something unreal about the scene. The reaction had been too quick, too pat.

I made up my mind. I repeated exactly what I had told McQuade. I was not allowed to get away with it easily. Yet despite Cyril's repeated interruptions—'That's mere hearsay!' 'The woman must have been demented!'—and Lady Winter's unwavering gaze, I sensed that I held my audience less than spellbound. By the time I got to the end, I was sure that she had known about Vivian and Very.

After a silence, she said, 'Ivor, I don't dispute that you were told all that—but don't you think you might have been spun a tale by a highly neurotic young woman?'

'No,' I said firmly. I too could be laconic.

'You could have made it all up from start to finish,' Cyril said, then, catching my look of contempt, 'There's not one jot of evidence in the whole tarrydiddle.'

Suddenly McQuade spoke. 'Evidence of what, Mr Grayling?'

'What?'

'Whatever the nature of the relationship between Mr Winter and Miss Ashe, no one is suggesting there was anything criminal about it.'

'Well, no—of course not.' He smoothed his waistcoat and assumed a dignified tone, 'But I must say I would very much like to know what the point of all this is.'

McQuade made no answer, but took out of an inner pocket the long narrow parcel I had seen in Very's bedroom. He placed it on the small table before him and carefully undid the newspaper wrapping. 'Now, Lady Winter, I am going to ask you whether you are able to identify this knife.'

He lifted the final fold. And I recognized it at once. I had the same one at home—one of a set of five.

'. . . of carbon steel, made by Sabatier. The blade is approximately nine and three-quarter inches in length. . . .'

It was the most useful—the heaviest and best for chopping meat and dismembering chickens. I could see the pleasure on Vivian's face as he found they were on sale—*je prendrai deux batteries, une pour mon ami.*

'. . . observe a nick in the blade approximately two inches from the tip. And also that the lower rivet attaching the blade to the haft has at some time been replaced.'

Mrs Blaine is always complaining there isn't a decent knife in the house—I could hear him saying it now.

'No, I'd rather you didn't touch it, ma'am. Just examine it and tell me whether you recollect having seen it before.'

'It looks to me as though it might match the set that we have in the kitchen here.' Lady Winter raised her head. 'But I'm afraid I can't be positive about it. I don't have much to do with the kitchen utensils.'

But she knew all right—we all knew what was coming.

'Well, no matter. Your Mrs Blaine has positively identified the knife as the one that went missing on the night of Mr Winter's death. The new rivet was put in by her husband when the original became loose. It is very unlikely that there can be two such knives in existence.'

'Is it,' Cyril cleared his throat, 'is it the knife that. . . .'

'We cannot say for sure, Mr Grayling. There are a number of tests that will be carried out. But I think it very likely that this was the murder weapon. The page of newspaper in which it's wrapped is from the *Telegraph* of the relevant date. I am sorry, Lady Winter.'

She gave a quick shake of the head.

'Superintendent,' I said, 'where did you find it?'

'It was found in the top drawer of the desk in the Poseys' living room, along with a variety of other weapons.'

Cyril frowned. 'Are you saying this man—Posey—killed Viv—Mr Winter?'

'I would think it is the most likely explanation, yes.'

'But why?' He was still puzzled. 'From what Ivor here says, Posey only discovered that there was any connection between his wife and Mr Winter on Tuesday morning, when my letter arrived in Norfolk.'

'I don't think we'll ever know the certain answer to that question.'

'But you have a theory,' I said, 'don't you?'

'Theories are not much in my line. But I think we could make some reasonable assumptions about the sequence of events.' He looked at Lady Winter and she gave him a brusque nod.

'We have to assume,' he went on, 'that Posey found out about the relationship between his wife and Mr Winter before April 14th. Whether that relationship was simply friendly or something more—or possibly magnified by Miss Ashe into something more—doesn't matter. Because, however he found out—a note, an overheard phone call, an incautious word— Posey would put the worst interpretation on it. A jealous and suspicious man, he was also clearly unbalanced. Rather than confronting Ashe, he took steps to eliminate what must have

261

seemed to him an intolerable threat to his "marriage." He comes to this flat and on some harmless pretext or other—to borrow something most likely—gains entry to the kitchen. He may have come prepared with a weapon, but instead chooses the kitchen knife to hand. He uses it for the commission of the crime, then leaves and returns to his own flat and wraps the knife in newspaper and conceals it in the desk drawer. He says nothing to Ashe, and she may not even have known he'd left the flat, if she'd been asleep, say.

'As far as he's concerned, the problem is solved. He feels in little danger. When interviewed by the police, he points out how easy it is to gain access to the block of flats. As for Ashe, she may have been frightened and suspicious, but she says nothing. She—'

'Frightened,' I said, 'but not suspicious, I think. She was anyway frightened of Posey and additionally frightened that he might discover about Vivian. And grieving for Vivian. But I don't think she suspected Posey of the murder.'

'Why not?' said Cyril. 'She must have realised he was a violent man—all that business about shooting up tins of soup on the sea wall.'

'Baked beans,' I said. 'Yes—but she probably connected his violence with guns, not knives.'

Cyril snorted. 'Well, she wasn't far wrong there.'

'Nevertheless, Mr Speke, at some point over the long weekend or on Tuesday, Ashe became sufficiently alarmed to phone you. Have you any suggestions as to what caused her alarm?'

'I've been trying to think. It was about nine yesterday evening that she rang—and she was worried rather than alarmed, the way one is when one senses something amiss without having anything concrete to go on. She didn't know about your letter, Cyril—but Posey did of course. Perhaps it affected his manner in some way. To him, the legacy was final and absolute proof of her betrayal. But it also was a threat. I don't know anything about their finances, but Very—Miss Ashe—had no job and I imagine she was pretty much dependent on Posey, although of course she owned the cottage. Thirty thousand pounds would make her independent, if she chose. She had betrayed him, and now, with the means, might she not leave him? Yet he would have to tell her about the letter sooner or later, because there would be others—and he may have figured out that I, as a friend of Vivian's, would know and tell Very. He was in a quandary, he had to make up his mind to tell her or not—and what to do when he did. I don't know—he may only have given her a queer look or two or asked an odd question—but it was enough to worry her. And then after I told her on the phone about the possibility of the letter and urged her to leave at once, *then* she probably really did become alarmed.'

They were all staring at me—I had their attention now. I felt slightly sick.

'Go on, Mr Speke. And then?'

'Then?' I spread out my hands. 'So then Very can guess why Posey is behaving in an odd manner—he must have the letter, so he knows about Vivian. She, too, doesn't know what to do. She daren't challenge him. So she puts off making any decision until she has seen me. I don't suppose either of them slept much yesterday night.' I thought of them lying side by side in the pink bed, each wrapped in separate and solitary nightmare. If she wept, she wept silently.

'In the morning, Posey goes off. What was Miss Ashe wearing when she was found?'

'Heather mixture tweed suit with a Harrods label, high-necked mauve blouse of raw silk, mauve tights and dark plum-coloured high-heeled pumps.' Ginger rattled off the answer by heart.

'Yes. So she gets dressed to go out. Puts on the kettle for a last cup of coffee. Then Posey unexpectedly returns. He challenges her. They have a row. It all comes out....' The dialogue ran through my head like the soundtrack from a bad movie—in which I was the villain.

'... and then,' I said, 'he shot her—and shot himself.'

'Aye,' said McQuade, 'it was very likely something like that. We'll know a bit more in a day or two. Then we'll probably want to reopen the inquest. I'll let you know, Lady Winter, Mr Grayling.' He and Ginger got up together.

'Goodbye, Inspector.' She smiled—an old lady's smile, gracious but detached, rather like Vivian's. 'And thank you.'

'I'll show you out,' said Cyril, already moving towards the door.

'I must be going too.' I stood up. 'Perhaps you could give me a lift, Superintendent?'

'By all means, Mr Speke.'

Yet, as they filed out, I lingered.

'I'm sorry,' I said.

'Why sorry, Ivor?'

'I'm sorry that. . . .' Did she not know—the sorrow that crept into every nook and corner of our life? Did she fail to weep because, after all, her incurious heart, like Vivian's, was not acquainted with grief or guilt. 'I'm sorry that it had to end like this.'

'You think it sordid?'

'Sordid? No, not sordid. Unnecessary—a pointless waste.'

'You don't understand. It is not pointless. On the contrary. My son is avenged.'

A coldness passed through me. 'Is that what you wanted?'

'Of course. Do we not all want justice?'

'At such a price? No—no.'

'The price is always the same, Ivor,' she said with implacable serenity. 'Blood for blood.'

'There's too much blood!' I burst out. I turned and hurried from the room, half-blind, muttering a farewell, and found McQuade and Ginger in the hall—solid figures of sanity amidst the horror.

35 A Pale Sort of Paradise

'How is he getting on, do you think?'

The June sun shone yellowly and the cloudless sky had the special white-blue lucid beauty of early summer. The sea was plucked and puckered by the breeze like silk in a seamstress's hands, and two yachts—which must have come all the way from Brighton—cavorted about the red-funnelled Channel ferry trundling in from Dieppe.

I turned to Shep. 'Who?' I said with deliberate vagueness— I wanted to think as little as possible about the stranger in my

264

house.

'George, of course.' Shep smiled, immediately detecting my evasiveness. He was dressed in ragged jeans, an old grey sweater and sneakers with a hole in the toes. Perhaps he'd thought *we* were to go yachting—or was the informality intended to reassure Camrose?

'Oh he's all right.' Then I pulled myself together. 'As a matter of fact he's getting on pretty well. He's clean, neat and tidy, always punctual. Doesn't drink. Pays the rent on time. To tell you the truth, I don't see much of him. When he's not at his Eastbourne parks job, he's off working for one or other of the local people—most evenings and all the weekends. Judge Towner thinks the world of him and Mrs Helmsley-Clinch can't imagine how she managed before he came. He's a hard worker all right. You can see for yourself what he's done for my garden....'

'But?' The wind had blown Shep's hair into a fluffy grey halo, frivolously at odds with his habitual severity of mien.

'Well—he doesn't seem to have any recreation, for one thing. I bought a TV for his room, but I hardly ever hear it on. And for some one whose main concern is the fruits of the earth, he has odd eating habits—frozen pizza, chicken pie, baked beans, hot dogs, things like that. And I don't believe he's ever taken a walk just for the pleasure of it—he's never been up here, for instance, I'm sure.' I looked again towards the gently ambulant beauty of the sea, oddly irked at Camrose's neglect of what lay beneath his nose—yet he was at one with the locals, few of whom sailed or swam or paddled or even ate fish.

'You don't like him, do you?'

'Shep, I simply don't know—there doesn't seem enough of him to either like or dislike. I understood him being shy that day you took me up to see him at Leyhill, but it's got worse rather than better.'

'Has it occurred to you that he's frightened of you?'

'Is that what he said?' I had left them together for half an hour in the 'study' while I peeled the vegetables and put the meat in the oven.

'No, he didn't say it, but I think it may be true, all the same. It wouldn't be so extraordinary. You must remember he's lived in a very restricted environment for a number of years. Freedom is always a problem for released long-term prisoners.

All this is new to him. He needs security and stability, fixed points, clear time-tables—to assure himself of his place and position. Of course he's tentative; he's not ready for exploration, even to the extent of taking a random walk by himself.'

'You mean I'm failing him.' Perhaps, yet could I bring myself to invite Camrose for a walk on the Downs?

'No. As a matter of fact, he's very happy. He said a rather touching thing—"It's like paradise here, isn't it, Dr Keith?"'

'A pretty pale sort of paradise.' Damn the man—I didn't want to have to think about his humanity. It was all very well for him, but what about the dead girl, what about Anne Rourke—and her crippled mother and her fiancé, what sort of 'paradise' was left over for them? 'Shep,' I said, 'what happened to Mrs Rourke when she no longer had Anne to look after her?' When he didn't answer, I glanced at him—he was staring out to sea. 'Shep—what happened—'

'I heard you.' He turned back to me with a sigh. 'She had to go into a home . . . she couldn't manage on her own.'

'And the young man—couldn't he have taken care of her?'

'Pleasance? No.' He shook his head. 'I'm sorry, Ivor—Pleasance committed suicide after the trial.'

'Oh dear God. . . .' My heart plummeted like the little boy's red ball plunging over the cliff and down, down.

'Perhaps I should have told you, but I thought. . . .'

'What did you think?'

'I thought it might have prejudiced you against him.' He cleared his throat. 'Would it?'

'Does it matter? It's done now. I shan't abandon the bloke, if that's what you're afraid of.'

'No, I'm not afraid of that. Ivor—you have to look at it in perspective. It was an unfortunate occurrence, but—'

'Unfortunate?'

'—tragic, a tragic occurrence, but you can't blame George for that.'

'No, quite. I don't suppose the fate of Pleasance and Mrs Rourke came within the purview of the Parole Board, did it? And even if it had, you'd still have let him out. Not *his* fault. Nobody's fault. That's just the trouble, isn't it? Nobody gives a damn about the survivors of the victims.'

'There are agencies—'

'Balls! Bereavement counsellors? Come again.'

266

'Well, what do you suggest—what would you do?'

'I don't know, but I know what I wouldn't do—I wouldn't pretend that Camrose carries no responsibility for *all* the consequences of his act, the "unfortunate occurrences".'

'What good would that do to George?'

'Why should I want to *do good* to George?'

'Because we want to turn him into a decent, useful member of society. By rehabilitating him, we do to some extent repair the damage that he's done to the community.'

'I don't know about that. He's repaired the storm damage to my slate roof—I suppose that makes him useful.'

Shep frowned. 'You're being flippant. Surely I don't have to remind you that you've taken on a serious responsibility.'

'Well, I asked for it. I wanted to take Camrose—you didn't push him off on me.'

'Yes, but frankly your attitude worries me a little. I know you accepted him from the best of motives but—'

'Oh no. I took him on, but I didn't *accept* him—I don't accept him. And as to motive—as I told you at the time, it's a matter of life or death. I can't have any more killing, Shep, I can't stand that, I can't stand....' I looked at him—solemn, grey, awkward. 'Alright,' I said heavily, 'I can't stand any more guilt.'

In the silence a couple of seagulls yelped plaintively. 'Ivor, you don't still imagine that George is in any danger, do you?'

'Why not? The trap's baited and . . . oh, I see, the Avenger's disappeared into thin air, has he?'

'My dear fellow, his existence was never anything more than hypothetical, and now—'

'Now the police have got cold feet.'

'I wouldn't put it like that—they're keeping an eye on things. You can hardly blame them for being dubious—there's not an atom of evidence that such a creature ever existed. Oh I know, I know—but coincidence isn't evidence. I've never really doubted that Maynard committed suicide. And as for Latham—is it so unlikely that a man working by himself on a roof on a dark night should slip and fall?'

'And Soper?' I asked with quiet sarcasm.

'Once you remove two elements out of a trio of coincidences, you have—nothing. And now that Vivian's death has been proved to have absolutely nothing to do with it, it seems to me the whole theory has been put right out of court.'

'And that's the official view?'

'Yes. But I'm bound to say it's mine too.'

'You've rather changed your tune, haven't you? You were much more positive about the Avenger theory when you felt there was a possibility of Jerry having murdered Vivian.'

Shep's cheeks were suddenly touched with a colour not caused by the freshening breeze. He was silent for a moment—counting to ten perhaps. Then he said, 'Perhaps. One's judgment is never entirely independent of one's fears. I am not immune to that.'

Watching him struggling with his professional conscience, I wondered just how his judgment of Vivian had been affected by the affair with Jerry. Thinking about it clearly, it seemed to me far more likely that Jerry had led Vivian on than the other way round. It was not just that Jerry was batty, but Vivian was scrupulous about not getting into messy situations, about not hurting people, above all about the Law. It was inconceivable to me that Vivian had known the drugs she was giving him were obtained by false pretences—if indeed she gave him any drugs at all.

'... I felt about it,' he was saying, 'nevertheless, it doesn't alter the fact that Vivian's death had absolutely nothing to do with this other business.'

'And the "other business" had no validity at all?'

'Let's just say that it was a highly imaginative construction.'

The ferry had disappeared and the yachts were no more than flecks on the sea's surface. I shivered; we'd been standing still for a long time and it was getting chillier.

'Shep, are you a hundred per cent convinced that Posey killed Vivian?'

'Well, of course I am,' he said in a puzzled way. 'Surely you don't have any doubts. The circumstantial evidence is damning, the opportunity obvious, and the motive is clear and convincing.'

'It seems so trivial—meaningless.'

'Not to Posey. Look, we know now he was a borderline psychotic, committed twice, discharged from the RAF for savagely assaulting his CO, incapable of holding down a job for more than a few weeks—not to mention a history of petty

268

frauds and swindles, the peculations from the RAF Benevolent Fund. . . . The threat to his relationship with Ashe provoked a typically paranoid reaction—predictable if we had known something about him.'

'But I did know something about him. That day in Norfolk when he shot up the cans of baked beans, I felt in my bones he was a dangerous man—but I didn't predict what happened.'

'You came very close. Frankly, I think you were fairly lucky to escape with your life on that occasion, from what you tell me.'

'Lucky? Lucky for me—not so lucky for Very.'

'You can't blame yourself for that. You did your best to warn her and—'

'But if I hadn't, if I hadn't been so damned curious, if I'd kept my mouth shut, she'd be alive today.'

'Possibly. Today. But not tomorrow. As you rightly say, he was a dangerous man—and she must have known it. She must have known she was living on a tightrope. Sooner or later she would have slipped and then. . . .'

'Over the cliff,' I murmured.

'What?'

'Nothing,' I answered sadly. I lit a cigarette with difficulty against the wind. 'You know, despite what you say, I can't get it out my head that Vivian must have believed there was some connection between those three deaths—something more than an accidental connection. And Vivian had a trained legal mind—he wasn't given to wild goose chases.'

'Quite, but in this case I think we have to accept that Vivian was to some extent obsessed. The destructive nature of his own relationships with women may well have led him to identify with men who had violated and destroyed women in the literal sense. I needn't go into the mechanism of identification, and the various supporting factors—but the idea of quasi-Divine punishment probably attracted him a great deal. As I've said before, I don't think he was averse to the idea of death—either for them or for himself.'

'You still think he actually invited Posey—or whoever it was—up to kill him?'

'I think it a possibility—no more. But there is no way we shall ever know.'

The wind whipped the smoke from my nostrils and mouth,

and behind us a dog barked. 'And do you consider that I am equally obsessed?'

'No.' Shep shook his head. 'Obviously, your emotional involvement has been strengthened by your own particular problems and needs. And forgive me for saying so, but I think one of your needs is precisely for emotional involvement. But your motive for undertaking the investigation was perfectly rational—not least because you were asked to do so by Lady Winter.'

'And the "highly imaginative construction"?'

'That was to be expected, wasn't it?' He smiled his rare gentle little smile. 'Thank God I don't have writers as patients every day.'

'Am I still your patient?'

'No—no, of course not.' But it seemed to me he was measuring me for the couch—of course, I had upset him. 'Tell me, Ivor, do you still have that recurring nightmare of yours?'

'Not exactly.' I hesitated, restraining a smile—but I owed him something. 'I still have it—but it's developed rather.' Ever since Camrose had come, I'd had the dream two or three nights a week. The first time, I did not understand where I was—there was the valley, with its mephitic mists slowly crawling, now opening to reveal the tufted surface of the mire, now shutting out all visible feature, but no house. I was looking down, not up—as if everything were reversed. And then it came to me that I was *in* the house itself and standing at the open window—everything *was* reversed—and each time I staggered a little and clutched at the window frame for support and held on to it frantically and battled with the temptation to look directly down. And with each repetition of the dream, the temptation became stronger and my strength less, and there was the weakness of water in my knees and a breathlessness like the suffocation of an adolescent's first lust. But I knew I must not look—for to look would be to fall. And to fall. . . .

'Yes?' said Shep gently, 'And what would happen if you fell?'

'I don't know.' I shrugged uneasily. 'The unthinkable.'

'And what is the unthinkable?'

The sunlight hurt my eyes and the sweat was wet across my shoulders; I dug my shooting stick deep into the turf and gripped it tight and tried to speak.

270

He saw my distress. 'All right,' he said, 'don't try to answer.' And he took me by the elbow and turned me away from the cliff and we began to walk slowly down the long slope in the direction of Upper Leeching.

'I'm sorry,' I said after we'd gone a little way.

'Don't worry. Don't think about it, but don't ignore it. It will come. How are you, otherwise?'

'Pretty well.' And yet I resented the inquiry. I knew I'd raised doubts in Shep's mind—not about Vivian, but about me. And I guessed he was re-evaluating my fitness as a guardian or moral mentor. 'I've started a book—a real one, not that muck I was trying to write for months.'

'Excellent,' he said. His rubber-soled foot skidded on a patch of slick chalk—and only my hand saved him from a fall. 'Thank you, Ivor, thank you.'

'A nasty feeling, isn't it?'

'Yes it is.' He took two or three deep breaths. 'That is good news—about your book. Of course, all this will have given you a lot of material.'

'I'm not a journalist.'

'No no, of course not.'

'Another thing,' I said, relenting, 'is that for the first time in my life I'm free from what they call "financial anxiety." Vivian's money hasn't made me rich, but it does mean I can do what I like.'

'And what will you do with your new-found freedom?'

We had reached the point where the slope suddenly becomes much steeper and we could see the village of Upper Leeching peeping from amongst its leafy trees and my own house with its slate roof from which Camrose had removed all trace of moss. The windows gleamed in the sun and a lazy thread of smoke rose placidly from the kitchen chimney.

'I don't know,' I said. 'But what I do know is that I'm ready for a cup of tea.'

But Shep had no time for tea; he had to get back to London. I saw him directly into his car and—an odd thing to do—shook hands. At the last moment I remembered to ask after Jerry. She had been committed again, and it looked as though it would be a long stay this time.

When I got back to the house, Camrose was seated at the kitchen table eating cold baked beans out of a tin with a spoon.

271

'Hello, C—George. No, don't get up.'

'Oh hello, Mr Speke.' He was already on his feet.

'Hungry?' I managed a smile—the man had eaten a colossal lunch of roast beef and Yorkshire pudding, but that was not his food of course.

'I just come up to borrow that new pair of shears—the Judge's is busted.'

'I don't mind why you came,' I said—but it didn't sound right. 'I mean—it's your home, you know.'

I bent to unlace my boots. I couldn't stand the sight of the orange smears of juice round that tight little rosebud mouth.

Your home—I winced at the hypocrisy. After he'd gone I made myself a pot of tea and drank a cup looking out of the window and up the hill. Camrose was no home-maker—he was a destroyer of homes. I should have to be careful he didn't destroy mine; already his presence had taken much of my pleasure from it.

And I thought of the last time I'd seen Very, waving in the doorway of her cottage, and Posey grinning, and the baked beans dripping from the wall—and something gave a little lurch within me.

I had gone to her funeral. Apart from her solicitor, who introduced himself as 'Mr Sandman,' I was the only mourner. As we stood outside the crematorium on one of the few days of drizzle that May, he said, 'I wish I'd known you'd be here, I needn't have bothered to have come. People don't seem to realize that solicitors are busy men. The only relative appears to be an elderly great-aunt in the North, and in the circumstances one could hardly expect her to turn up. I was worried there would be no one at all—no one. And that wouldn't have done, would it?'

No one. And there were no flowers and no music, except for the obligatory hymn or two, neither of which I recognized. It was a perfunctory putting-away of this beautiful and pitiable woman.

Afterwards, as we stood in the porch waiting for the rain to let up so that we could make a dash for our cars, Mr Sandman glanced curiously at the traces of my grief. 'I take it you must have been acquainted with the deceased for quite some time?'

'I only met her three times.'

'Really, really? All the same—a great tragedy, so young,

although frankly not quite the sort of thing we are accustomed—'

I left him sheltering and walked off into the rain.

A great tragedy—and Very's only part in it had been Cordelia. Very was dead—and I was living with a 'rehabilitated' murderer and rapist.

And my poor fool is hang'd. Why should a dog, a horse, a rat have life, and thou no breath at all?

36 Farewells

Phil Wood was in ebullient form. He had just returned from a two-week trip to New York and was sporting a richly fake American accent.

'Whisky, with a bit of ice?' I asked him.

'Sure sure. Scotch on the rocks, that'll be just fine.'

'Aw, come on, Pops—why don't you lay off the hard stuff?' Isabelle mocked mercilessly. Phil threw a handful of peanuts at her, which Goldie immediately gobbled from the floor.

The darkness of my mood began to lighten. I'd had the nightmare twice in the night and had fumbled through the morning in a state of heady fatigue.

'May I explore?' Isabelle asked.

'Sure—I mean, yes, go ahead.'

Eleanor cocked a look at the ceiling. 'Is he there?'

'No no, that's all right—he's off gardening for the day.' I usually made rather a point of Camrose sitting down to Sunday lunch with me, but this time I'd shuffled him off on Mrs Helmsley-Clinch—it was odd how she had taken to him. If she had her way, I told them, people like Camrose would be automatically hanged—and doubtless drawn and quartered too, if possible.

Phil laughed. 'It's always been my theory that these female pillars of the Conservative Establishment are filled with sentimental mush inside.'

'What's he *like*?' said Eleanor.

'Ordinary. Quiet and shy—extraordinarily quiet. He's hardly ever around, but when he is, he's apt to pop up at my elbow without warning.'

'Like Jeeves,' Phil said, lighting a cigar.

'Not as useful.'

'Ummmm. No.' He shook out the match and blew gently on the glowing end of the cigar. 'Forgive my saying so, Ivor, but what you need is a good wife.'

'Oh but he's got one in prospect, haven't you, Ivor?' said Eleanor in her best shining silvery tone. 'Dilys, she's called—a local wench complete with burred r's and milkmaid eyes.'

'Phyllis. Alas, she's taken.' I smiled and started to cut up the mushrooms. 'She's getting married to our local publican in a couple of weeks.'

'How appropriate!'

I laughed. The total inappropriateness of a union between Phyllis and Hamish had stung me with a temporary pang of jealousy, then sadness, but now at last to mild mirth.

'I say, talking of weddings,' Phil said, 'shall we be seeing you at Marion's?'

'Oh Phil, darling!'

'What's wrong, my dear? There's no secret about it, is there?'

'So it's really on?' I carefully quartered a mushroom. 'When?'

'Next month,' Eleanor said quickly. 'We had them down to lunch yesterday. He's dark and attractive and rather nervous, but we liked him a lot, didn't we, Phil?'

'A sound bloke. Reminded me of you a bit as a matter of fact. In a better paying line, of course.'

'I don't think,' I said stiffly, 'that would make any difference to Marion.'

'Of course it does. All women are mercenary at heart, it's part of their charm. They wouldn't be women if they weren't. Don't get me wrong,' he said expansively, 'I like women, I admire women, I love women. But God forbid they should become like men. Men bore me. Sorry, Ivor, you're an exception. I count it my greatest blessing that I've got at least one daughter.'

'Oh Phil, haven't you ever heard of tact?' Eleanor said with indulgence rather than reproof.

'I don't mind,' I said—and it was true. I'd not actually thought of Henrietta for days—only my nightmares kept her absence alive.

At that moment, Isabelle came back into the kitchen.

'Oh I do love your little house, Ivor, it's so cosy and neat. But why don't you have a living room?'

'A sitting room, darling.'

'A sitting room, then?'

'Because I sit—and live—here. And I work here too.'

'Well,' she said, consideringly, 'I suppose it does make it easier to get at the food. Who's the girl in the silver frame on the chest of drawers in the little bedroom?'

'It's somebody called Anne Rourke.'

'Is that the one he murdered?'

'Oh Isab—'

'No, that's all right,' I said. 'Yes, that's the one.'

'How peculiar. It was a long time ago; wasn't it? I should have thought he'd have found another girlfriend by now.'

'I don't suppose he's had time yet,' said Eleanor. 'He's been in prison, you see, and there aren't any women in prison. Now, why don't you—'

'Why not? Don't women commit crimes?'

'Yes of course—but they're kept separate, the men and the women, I mean. Why don't you take Marigold for a little run in the garden before lunch?'

'Okay. It does seem silly, though, keeping them apart. Come on, Goldie. Can I take the kite?'

'No, darling, we'll do that after lunch.'

Lunch was a success. Phil ate and drank copiously and described his New York trip at length.

'I've brought it off, I think. I knew the Americans would come to heel as soon as we made a serious offer backed with immediate cash. They don't quite trust us Brits, you know—and if half the people I do business with are anything to go by, I can't say I blame them. Something remarkably refreshing about the Yanks, always was, although they're going downhill now of course. And nowadays New York is full of. . . .'

He had bought Isabelle a magnificent long-tailed kite from New York, and after lunch she and Eleanor went off to the

275

cliffs to fly it. No amount of persuading would make Phil budge, however, so we sat on drinking—whisky for him, wine for me.

'I've decided to give up the flat,' he said abruptly.

'Oh, why's that?'

'It was never really a justifiable expense. I told old Easton Camber it would make an ideal pad for him when he visited London, but he wasn't wearing that one. He's quite right of course. And naturally Eleanor's pleased. But I'm afraid it'll be a bit inconvenient for you, though.'

'That's all right. I shouldn't be using it much in future in any case. I've chucked the job at the *Gazette* and I'm resigning from the Club, so I shan't be going up very often.'

'Well, the *Gazette* I can understand—terrible wet pink rag— but the Club? I thought the Club was your lifeline.'

'I thought so at one time—but it's a pretty unreal sort of life to be tied to.'

'I know *that*. Ghastly bunch of bores. But . . . what's put you off? Vivian?'

'Vivian's probably at the root of it—but it's more than that.'

'Gilt worn off the gingerbread, eh?' He focused his attention on lighting another cigar. 'I must say—Ivor—I was damned relieved—when it turned out—that air force chappie—was the guilty party—ah, there we are!' He drew contentedly. 'Not that I was all that worried. After your call that night, I was in something of a blue funk—I admit it. Got completely squiffed. But in the morning I saw the light—went straight off to the police and told them all about that bloody little black whore. McQuade gave me a bit of a hard time of course—but they found her all right. So I was pretty much in the clear.' He drank some whisky. 'Of course, it doesn't exactly resolve your problem, I see that.'

'About what?'

'Specifically, about taking on this fellow Camrose. Or perhaps you think he no longer presents any danger?'

'I've never thought he's a danger, Phil. It's what might be in store for him.'

'Ah—then you haven't changed your mind. You still believe the Avenger is waiting in the wings?'

'I don't know. I'm not as sure as I was—and official opinion is against me, but—'

'Official opinion—pah!'

'—but I can't believe the death of those three men was merely some extraordinary kind of meaningless coincidence.'

'No—no.' He meditated over his cigar. 'In that case, your gaolbird guest is a bit of a time bomb, isn't he?'

'Yes—he could be.'

'Have you told him?'

'No.'

'Wise man. Ignorance is bliss. All the same, if I were you, I'd take a few precautions.'

I smiled. 'Such as what?'

'Increased fire coverage for one. A bit of protection for this place. You might get a dog. If it were me, I'd buy a gun.'

'I'd probably shoot myself in the foot,' I said, pouring some more wine.

'Well, it's your own funeral.' He attentively tipped a chunk of ash into the ashtray. Then he looked up at me with that frank, challenging expression which, in him, always indicated embarrassment. 'Of course, I had to have it all out with Eleanor—about Vivian. It's the only way, in the end.'

'Oh?'

'Dammit, you know what I'm talking about.' But he couldn't bring himself to say it outright. 'Mind you, I don't say it wasn't a bit of a blow—but, well, it's no good being prejudiced about it. It's all in the past now. I don't approve of double standards, never have. Any woman worth her salt is bound to kick over the traces once in her life. And in a curious way,' he cocked his head to see how I would take it, 'in a curious way, I respect Eleanor more. Odd thing to say, but it's true. It's brought us closer too.' He hesitated. 'As a matter of fact, we're going to have a child.'

'Congratulations.'

'Thanks. To tell you the truth, I'm rather looking forward to it. Might be a boy. Put him in the business.' He smoked in silence for a while. 'One can't really blame Vivian for fancying her, poor kid.'

'Indeed not.'

'Mind you, and I own it frankly, I never greatly cared for Vivian—and quite honestly I don't think Eleanor did either. More of a flash in the pan type of thing. Of course he was a brilliant fellow in his way, but I always thought there was something a bit flashy about him. I remember when I first met him, he....'

I got up and started clearing away the debris and didn't listen. I knew exactly what he was doing—he was 'putting it in perspective,' establishing a line on which he and Eleanor could agree and which in future I should be expected to toe. It had little to do with the truth, and not much to do with Vivian.

He was distancing himself too. His inner sexual privacy had been invaded, and from henceforth the barriers would be gently raised. We'd see less of each other in the future and, when we did, be less free, less easy. I had lost a friend.

And when Isabelle and Eleanor and Goldie came gambolling back, high on fresh air and kite flying, and ate a vigorous tea of Gentleman's Relish sandwiches and a specially baked Victoria sponge cake, I was making a distance myself. Our conversation was just a little too joyous and, finally, our farewells slightly too lavish. I thought I had managed it all very successfully, until Isabelle leaned out of the car window, put her arms around my neck and whispered, 'I think you're much the nicest of all Daddy's friends.'

37 Visitation

The announcement that Phyllis and Hamish were to be married had excited the village to incredulity and much ribald humour. Yet as the days went on, the amusement gave way to expectation—the wedding became an event to look forward to.

Hamish's esteem rocketed and his confidence with it—he was after all a human being. His little robotics tricks of speech and movement were smoothed by a flood of geniality.

And Phyllis—well, Phyllis who'd been generally considered on the way to spinsterhood, was redeemed as a creature of flesh and blood and, fair to say, prospects (for Hamish owned the Green Bough outright). He went on the wagon and lost twenty pounds in two weeks, and all talk of Beauty and the

278

Beast died on the lips. As the village readied itself, I too was busy.

I had taken Phil's advice to heart—not to the extent of purchasing a gun, but I put a fire extinguisher in every room and installed new locks on doors and windows and altered the hooks on the downstairs shutters so they couldn't be opened by a blade slipped in the crack. And one evening I walked over to Eastbourne and had a drink with Sheila Wantage at the Bilberry Tree and bought a year-old dog from a gipsyish-looking man in the bar. It was black and white and liver-coloured, with floppy ears and large brown eyes and it cost me ten pounds. I named it Vivian, only later to discover that in my innocence I'd bought a bitch. So I shortened the name to Viv. 'A good ratter,' the man had told me, which is perhaps why she didn't much take to George, treating him with a surly indifference.

To him, I explained my extraordinary precautions by pretending to have developed a chronic fear of burglars. He accepted this as perfectly natural and dutifully kept the house locked and bolted. He even reminisced about some of the burglars he'd known—the first time he'd ever referred to prison life. I accepted it as an opening and widened it assiduously so that one evening I was able casually to ask, 'That girl you have the photo of upstairs—what was she like?'

He almost choked over his pizza and turned white to the gills, the half dozen pustules on his neck glaring unnaturally red.

'She . . . she. . . .'

I ate a piece of ham. 'It is the one you killed, isn't it—Anne?'

'It was an accident,' he said thickly, swallowing at last.

'Come on, George, you don't have to pull that with me,' I said with a rallying smile. 'You were just aching to have it off with her—that's understandable. She wouldn't oblige, so you hit her and screwed her and then—'

'Don't talk like that!'

'—and then you felt pretty disgusted with yourself—and her—and you panicked and set fire to the shed.'

'It wasn't like that. I loved her.'

'We don't murder people we love, George.'

'I asked her to marry me, I begged her. I didn't mind about the child—I'd have loved it like it was mine. I told her that, but she wouldn't listen—she was stubborn.' The small rosebud mouth grew tight with disapproval.

'Maybe she didn't care for you very much?'

'She'd have learned.' He swallowed. 'There's nothing wrong with me.'

'Do you think it's as simple as that—any woman will come to love a man who screws her often enough?'

'Don't *talk* like that—*please*, Mr Speke!'

'Ivor.' I poured myself some more wine. 'Very well then—you tell me how it was.'

'I loved her. I always loved her, ever since we were little kids at school. I always told her we'd be married one day. She knew that—she knew she was mine. She had no right to—to. . . .' He looked down at the half-eaten slice of cold pizza.

'No right to have it off with some one else?'

'It's disgusting the way you talk,' he mumbled.

'Then let's just say she had no right to get involved with anyone else? Is that right?'

'Yes.'

'But she didn't see it that way?'

'No.'

'So you decided if you couldn't have her, nobody would?'

He didn't answer.

'George, isn't that it? You took her to the allotment to give her an ultimatum—marry me or you'll marry no one?'

He looked up. 'All she had to do was say yes.'

'But she said no?'

'She giggled.'

Laughter—the classically fatal mistake. Frightened out of her wits, all she could manage was a small frantic giggle.

'So you killed her.'

'If she'd just of said yes, none of it would have happened. We'd be happy, married with a little kid, maybe two.'

'But you killed the kid as well.'

'We'd have a little house, like this one, in the country some-where, an' I'd grow vegetables an' Annie'd do the cooking and I'd be showing the kid how to—'

'Did you love your mother, George?'

'What?'

'Did you love your mother?'

'You sound like all them psychiatricks.'

280

'Well, did you?'

'I hated the bloody bitch.' An honest answer at last.

'Why do you like gardening so much?'

'Well, it's peaceful like, calm.'

'The Judge says you're good—you take care.'

'You got to take care, haven't you? I mean, it changes all the time—you got to watch it and be ready for it. You can't plant and mulch and spray and prune just any old time. The Judge, see, he has trouble with his tomatoes; that's because he doesn't. . . .'

I'd never heard him so animated and fluent. Bateman and Maynard and Soper and Latham—all had at least one person who loved them, for whom the heinousness of the deed did not alienate the affection. But not Camrose. And yet—if Anne Rourke had been just a little different, or if he had fixed on another, more amenable woman—might he not now be a cherished husband and devoted father?

'George.' I interrupted his flow. 'Hasn't it ever occurred to you that people need concern and attention paid to them, just as much as tomatoes? Don't you think women need to be attended to and cared for and protected from the vagaries of the climate and the weather's mood? You can't *command* tomatoes to do what you want—or cabbages or dahlias or mulberry bushes—so why should you think you could order a woman to love you?'

'That's different.' He wore his familiar mulish look.

'Why?'

'Tomatoes don't give you no argument.'

I laughed—laughed at the bitter irony that such a man as this should be alive and Vivian dead. Here was work for the Avenger—why did he not come? For a moment my fatalism was penetrated, and I felt I could do the job myself. I longed for a burning—a bonfire of such trash.

Such savagery in myself disturbed me, and I took Viv for a long walk over the Downs to clear my head—and my heart. In a sense, George needed protecting from me; it is not good to live with someone who despises you—or whom you despise. I thought perhaps I should take up Shep's offer—get rid of George, hand him over to some more fit agency. I had taken him in to guard him, so I thought, from Vivian's murderer. But with Vivian's murder proved against Frank Posey (as I was forced to concede was more than probable), my act of guardianship had been robbed of meaning. Or it had taken on a more sinister meaning: Camrose alive and flourishing would make nonsense of the Avenger, prove the absurdity of Vivian's preoccupation and the futility of my own search; it was only the death of Camrose that would vindicate my friend. These thoughts turned in my mind and stuck me at the same spot in my nightmare. I waited restlessly for something I both feared and desired.

Watching Viv chasing from tussock to tussock in inept but joyful pursuit of rabbits, I envied her untrammelled freedom. There is something to be said for a dog's life—at least no crippling enmeshment of memories. I wondered whether I should ever be able to cut and run, like my father before me. I had written him that I'd resigned from the Club, and in response had received an unexpected, gruffly worded invitation to stay for a few weeks in the South of France. In his acerbic way, perhaps he was beginning to admit that he was a lonely old man. Tired of the chase at last, Viv was prancing and barking around me, pretending I was an outsize rabbit, but as I ran with her and rolled with her in the grass, I knew I wanted more than the companionship of a dog—or of an elderly gentleman in foreign parts.

Perhaps it was Phil's observation about needing a good wife, or the nuptial enthusiasm investing the village, that made me look forward to Goldie Grayling's visit with such expectation. She had lost weight—a good deal of weight—so that her belly had flattened and her face had regained that once-fashionable gauntness in which her eyes swam more huge than ever. She had bought an old farmhouse and stables not far from Cheltenham—'an utter shambles, darling, but we're doing it up in spanking style'. The other half of the 'we' was an old school friend and together they had started a riding school and were going to hire out hunters. I made some banal remark about fitness.

'Fit? I should think I am. I haven't got up at six every morning since I was a toddler, and I shift a ton of hay before breakfast. I hardly drink at all now—look, one measly glass of sherry. And Livia's made me stop smoking—she's allergic to it, poor darling. I've given up sex too—and do you know?—I don't miss it a bit.'

282

She talked on—about dogs and horses. They were training two promising chasers for a local magnate and had been left a whole flock or pack or herd—or whatever you call it—of dogs by the departing farmer, with names like Todd and Lob and Tinkums and Halibut. Animals are of small interest to me (so long as they're not being experimented on or hunted) and in talking of them the attractive hoarseness of Goldie's voice took on an edge of stridency, suitable for calling across hill and dale—and I remembered her father had been a general or an admiral and the family, county.

She must have seen my boredom and disappointment for latish in the evening she leaned across and put a hand on my arm. 'Poor darling, did you fancy me? I will if you like. I can easily stay the night. I'll tell Livia I met up with a chum in town.'

I smiled and shook my head. Such is the stuff of foolish dreams.

It was a salutary douche of cold water that helped me brace myself for the next day. Marion had phoned earlier in the week—at Eleanor's behest, I was sure—and was coming to lunch. I hadn't seen her for six years, except once by accident on the other side of Oxford Street. It was another piece of the past about to be given away.

38 The Letter of the Law

'I didn't mean that!' She stood there angrily, holding the cheque away from her. 'I don't want your money—and never did.'

'But you cashed the cheques.'

'Because you wanted it. It assuaged something in you. Oh Ivor,' and her tone softened, 'I was worried because it's so unlike you to forget anything. But I'm glad you did.'

'Oh.' Then, as she moved towards the stove, I lifted the lid, and she dropped the cheque into the fire.

'There!'

'There.'

'Come on,' she caught my hand, 'I like what you've done to this room, now show me the rest of it.'

The only place she spent any time in was Camrose's room. I had stripped it and repainted it in cream and apple green and sanded and varnished the floor and put down a circular cream-coloured rug. I had bought pine furniture—two chairs, the bed, a chest of drawers, a hanging closet, an armchair and a small table for the TV. I'd found two rather primitively painted seascapes in an antique shop in Seaford for the walls. It was the best I could do. Nothing of Henrietta remained. And, with the one exception of the photo of Anne Rourke, there was nothing of Camrose in the room, either.

'Whisky,' said Marion when we were back in the kitchen. I was foolishly surprised—when we were married she'd drunk nothing except the occasional glass of plonk. But of course she was a media person now, probably earning four or five times as much as me. And it showed in an assurance that had replaced the old hesitancy of movement. The brusque shake of the head that had sent her short cap of dark hair swirling and had been used to mask her vulnerability, had given way to a graver nod.

'You're staring, Ivor.'

'Yes.'

'Have I changed so much? No, don't answer. I'm sorry.' She frowned—then smiled. 'That's silly of me. Do you want to come to my wedding?'

'I don't know. Wouldn't I be *de trop*?' The idea pained me, although I was happy she'd asked.

'Not a bit. I shouldn't find it awkward. You'd like Raymond.'

'I don't know. It would make a nice change from funerals, but—'

Viv gave a *sotto voce* growl from her basket next to the stove, and I turned to see Camrose in the doorway.

'Oh hello, George, you're off early.'

'Well, there's a bit of a strike, like. We was told to down tools and come back tomorrow. Sorry, I didn't know you had company.'

'That's all right,' I said with strained bonhomie, 'it's your home, you know. Marion, this is George Camrose. George,

284

Marion, er—'

She gave me an amused look. 'Bland,' she said and held out her hand, 'Hello, George.'

'Pleased to meet you.' He shook hands and blinked his small grey eyes rapidly. With a little shiver, I realised that Marion's dark good looks and small, clean-cut features bore a distinct resemblance to that of the girl in the photo.

'Have you had any lunch, George?'

'What?' He turned to me, his cheeks flushed with more than just the sun and the wind. 'Oh that's okay. I'll be off down to the pub—I promised to help setting up the floodlighting in the garden. For the wedding party, that is. Mr Hamish'll give me a sandwich.'

'If you're quite sure then.'

'Yes. Well. . . .' He ran his tongue over his lips. 'Pleased to have met you, Miss.' He backed out and shut the door with unaccustomed clumsiness so it banged.

'So that's your lodger?'

'What do you think of him?'

'Creepy. What was he in for—child molesting?'

'Murder and rape.'

'Jesus. Not—not the girl upstairs?'

'So you noticed? Yes—that was the one. Anne Rourke, twenty-two, pregnant, about to be married—not to him, to someone else.

'Ivor. What are you doing? You weren't ever a one for good works.'

'It's a long story.'

'Well, tell me. I've taken the day off. But give me some more whisky first.' She tossed off what remained and held out her glass. 'It must have something to do with Vivian, I suppose.'

'Yes.' I filled both glasses and sat myself down. 'But it goes back a long way before that.'

She listened with that intense equanimity I remembered from the old days when I used to read aloud a short story or bits of a current novel.

I had told the tale to many different people in differently edited versions—yet telling it to Marion was harder than any of these. When we'd been married, we had made a private solemn vow never to lie about our feelings. I didn't believe that vow had been dissolved along with our marriage, but nor could I tell her the truth of my feelings about Vivian. So I related simply the facts.

She faced the window and had been staring up the hill, now she lit a cigarette and looked directly at me. 'You really don't see it, do you?'

'See what? What do you mean?'

'Don't be angry. You've got nothing to worry about now. There isn't any danger.'

'Oh,' I said, with a sudden bitter weariness. 'So then you share the official view. Just a series of unrelated coincidences. And the Avenger—a figment of Vivian's obsessional neurosis and his mother's thirst for blood and my feverish imagination. Yes, I've heard all that before, but what if—'

'Oh Ivor, do stop it,' she said in a tone of exasperated kindliness which I remembered well. 'Of course I believe in the Avenger, if that's what you want to call him. And the coincidences are clearly related—if only through Vivian.'

'Oh well—yes. . . .' I took a cigarette from her packet; in the old days, Marion hadn't smoked either.

'And through the women—the three he left money to, the kin of the murdered men.'

'Of course—that's what put me on their track. But isn't that rather circular reasoning?'

'You still don't see it, do you? You always were a lousy historian. Wergild.'

'Wergild?' It touched a chord somewhere in my memory. 'Isn't that something they paid to keep the Danes away?'

'That was Danegeld.' She blew some smoke into the sunlight. 'Wergild, in Anglo-Saxon law, was the compensation paid to the kin of the murdered by the murderer. As I recall, the price varied according to rank—so presumably Soper was of a higher status than the others, since his wife got more.'

'Marion—what,' I cleared my throat, I was having difficulty with my voice, 'what are you saying?'

'I'm saying that Vivian killed those men. He was your Avenger.'

I half-stood up—I don't know what I intended to do—then slowly sat down again. 'That's nonsense, Marion. Vivian wouldn't have hurt a fly.'

'They weren't flies. They were killers of women—and, not so incidentally, of children.'

286

'For God's sake—they'd been tried, convicted, punished. According to law. Vivian wouldn't have taken the law into his own hands in a thousand years. It was sacrosanct to him. Besides, it's just—impossible....'

But she wasn't listening to me. She got up and went over to the shelf of reference books I kept on the Welsh dresser. She came back with my Bible in her hands. 'It's a lot older than a thousand years—four or five, I should think. Let's see—yes, here we are. Exodus 21, twenty-two to twenty-five.' She sat down and read:

If men strive and hurt a woman with child, so that her fruit depart from her—and yet no mischief follow—he shall surely be punished as the woman's husband will lay upon him; and he shall pay as the judges determine.

And *if* any mischief follow, *then* thou shalt give eye for eye, tooth for tooth, hand for hand, foot for foot, burning for burning, wound for wound, stripe for stripe.

'The Mosaic Law—and Vivian was upholding it.' She glanced up. 'Ivor—don't look so stricken.'

'I didn't—didn't realize it was so—so particular....'

'Of course it's particular—the Jews weren't sentimentalists—and it fits your men exactly. The women were striven with and hurt and did lose their children and did suffer mischief—death. So the men had to die too—in the same way. There's a formidably ruthless logic to it.'

'But Vivian wasn't like that—he wasn't ruthless.'

'He loved women,' she said quietly. The statement hung in the air, like the cigarette smoke turning slowly in the sun.

'And children?' I said hoarsely.

'He couldn't have children. Low sperm count or something.'

'Oh.'

She snapped the Bible shut. 'For God's sake give me something to eat, or I'll collapse.'

It had always been like that; white-faced and cold and indrawn—food, warmth, love would become an immediate need without which she wilted, silent like a sad flower.

I was glad to have something accurate to do with my hands, for my mind was stumbling clumsily in the old mists of my nightmare. As I made the omelette and sliced tomatoes for a salad and opened the wine, I wondered whether her Raymond understood the necessity for rapid fulfilment.

The reward was an equally rapid response. Now, as she ate, she visibly flourished, like a TV commercial for magic plant food. I drank the wine, but I could eat nothing. As I watched her across the table, I thought of all the life we had shared—and the death that we couldn't share. I shied away into small talk.

'How do you know that bit from Exodus so well?'

She wiped her mouth. 'I'm not a vicar's daughter for nothing.'

'No—of course.' Her father had been a delight—a bright dark gnome of a man, full of wit and sardonic laughter, quite unlike any clergyman I'd ever met. He kept bees and thought me a rather pompous young man—as I expect I was. What would he have made of Raymond?

'I'm going to have a child, Ivor.'

'What?' I came back to her with a start. 'You're pregnant?'

'No,' she smiled, 'not quite yet. That's why I'm marrying Raymond. Oh, I like him—love him—but I'd be quite happy living with him, if it weren't for that. For a little while, after Henrietta, I couldn't see a child in the street without clutching and hurrying home to weep. And then I had other things—my job that got more interesting all the time, the occasional man, and I took up painting, did you know?'

'I didn't.'

'Yes, I even had a showing in Paris in January. Oh nothing grand—just a little gallery in the rue d'Orsel. I'm not terribly good, but I enjoy it. So for a long time I thought, why bother with children? I didn't want a replacement for Henrietta—I didn't have to prove I needed children. But then those feelings vanished too and I quite suddenly knew I simply wanted a child . . . do you see?'

I nodded, but turned my head away—I felt it as a stab of betrayal. Viv, in her basket, opened her great brown eyes and looked at me mournfully. 'Is that why you didn't marry Vivian,' I said in a cold mean little voice, 'because he couldn't have children?'

'You have been tactful,' she said dryly, 'not like the police.' She paused and I glanced at her, but she wasn't looking at me.

'Vivian was—a comfort. No more, but no less.' She reached for a cigarette and lit it. 'I don't think I was even that for him—no comfort, I mean. The more I knew of him, the less I knew him. He was in some absolute sense unreachable.'

'According to Shepperton Keith he was an obsessional neurotic, incapable of any real affective life.'

'Oh fuck Keith!' A contemptuous flash, a shake of the dark head. 'You don't believe that sort of trite psychological identi-kit.'

'I don't believe he was a murderer.'

'You don't believe in Heaven and Hell,' she said with such sharp fury that Viv started up with a throaty growl. 'You might at least allow him *his* despair—you've indulged your own long enough!'

'What the hell do you mean by that?'

'Oh God—I didn't want to get into this.'

'Well you're in it now.'

She gave a little flicker of a smile. 'Yes, I am, amn't I?' She took a sip of wine—then drained the glass in a gulp. 'All right—you're not an invalid anymore, that's one thing this business seems to have proved. Let's go back to the inquest, you—'

'Henry's inquest?'

'Henrietta.' She had always disliked my abbreviation. 'I don't know whether you remember exactly, but what you said then is engraved in my memory. "It's my fault," you said, "if I hadn't—"'

'Marion!'

'"—if I hadn't gone down to the garden to lend a hand to our neighbour and left the child unguarded, it would never have happened. There should have been bars on the window—they were to have been put in the next week. I accept that I am entirely to blame...." That is what you said, Ivor—that is textually what you said.'

'All right. You always did have practically total recall. I accept that. And it's true. It was my turn to look after her and I—'

'Your *turn*! You don't take *turns* at love. I was in the room, Ivor. I was on the phone and my back was turned to the window—but I was in the *room* when our daughter fell.'

'Yes, I know that, but I—'

'Don't say it!' She glared at me. 'That's what you did then—you took all the guilt for yourself and wrapped yourself in it like a mantle and wouldn't let me in. How I longed for you to say, "Marion, it was your fault!" But you wouldn't. You took away my guilt and robbed me of my grief and killed my love. And I had to get away to survive. I had to weep so I could live, remember so that I could forget, mourn to recover. But you didn't know how to mourn.' She stubbed out her cigarette.

'I think I did—sometimes I think I've done nothing else since.'

'No.' She shook her head—gently this time. 'You've suffered because you couldn't mourn. Mourning means forgiveness—forgiving yourself. And you couldn't do that. You couldn't forgive, so you had to punish yourself—punish, punish, punish. And Vivian was the same.'

'What do you mean?'

'Vivian used women to punish himself.'

'But you said he loved women.'

'Of course he did—it wouldn't have been a punishment if he hadn't. He used women to show him how unworthy he was of love. God knows what you imagine you've done to deserve such punishment—what sort of ghastly original sin you've committed. It's like a drug—you need more and more of it, more punishment, in larger doses, murdering yourselves with nightmare guilt until even that isn't enough and you have to start in on the rest of the world. And that was what Vivian was doing in the end—murdering the murderers, punishing them, murdering himself.'

'And me?'

'No,' she said. 'No, that's enough. I can't go on.'

'Yes, you can. You can't leave it there, Marion. Who have I murdered—who am I going to murder?'

She sighed slowly. 'I don't think you're going to murder anyone.' She lit another cigarette. 'But don't tell me you haven't had a glimmer of sympathy with Vivian's killing those men and—'

'I don't believe Vivian did kill them.'

She made an impatient gesture. 'Well then, your anonymous Avenger. And I don't believe you took this creature Camrose solely to save him from death—you're not that noble. If he died—if he were burnt, you'd see it as a kind of justice. It

290

would satisfy—and justify—the punisher in you. And perhaps the satisfaction would be more perfect if you too were consumed in the holocaust. . . .'

'Believe it or not, Marion—I do not want to die.'

'That's not the question.' She looked at me hard and straight. 'The question is, how keen are you on living?'

As I opened my mouth to answer, Viv sat up in her basket and gave a tremendous canine yawn.

'Fair comment,' I said—and we laughed.

'What does she want—food?'

'A walk, I think.' And at the word, she came over and licked my hand with her gravelly tongue and then went and stood at the door.

'I could do with a walk too. I'm feeling a bit—'

'Battered,' I said.

'Poor darling,' she smiled. 'Where shall we go?'

'Up to the Head.'

'All right—as long as I'm back in town by seven.'

'You shall be.'

Later, as we kissed farewell, she said, 'You know, perhaps it wouldn't be such a good idea for you to come to the wedding after all.'

'No, perhaps not.' And I smiled.

And quite uncharacteristically, she blushed.

'And no more cheques.'

'No more cheques.'

39 Giving Away

The day of Phyllis's wedding, as these days should be, was one of brilliant sunshine; in the morning it was so clear that when I took Viv for her walk up to the Head, the coast of France seemed almost within touching distance.

The ceremony itself was in the afternoon, and the church

was packed. Old Jeremiah Pleach was too tottery on his feet to stand for long, so Phyllis had asked me to give her away. I had hired a morning suit in Eastbourne and, having been carefully valeted by George, was for one of the few times in my life dressed to fit the occasion. Putting off the old and putting on the new (even if only borrowed) gave me an unaccustomed feeling of exhilaration. Leaving George behind to look after Viv (now very much in heat), I stepped away from the last few uneasy days of aridity and nightmare.

The Judge, who'd consented to be best man, was as immaculate as to be expected (by everyone, that is, except Hamish, who'd imagined he'd turn up in judicial robes and full wig). Hamish himself was resplendent in a white tail suit, white silk shirt and cravat, white shoes and a white top hat—in a Liberace sort of way, he outshone everyone. Except for Phyllis.

I collected her from the dark little cottage where she had spent all her life and which she was leaving now for the last time (she would live on the premises with Hamish, and Jeremiah was moving to his daughter's at Seaford). She wore a tight-bodiced gown of peach-coloured silk covered with a fine lace filigree and a small hat to match. I presented her with a bouquet of garden flowers that I'd got Camrose to make for her—pink and apricot and peach. Her creamily transparent cheeks were faintly flushed and her grey eyes alive with joy as I leaned over and kissed her before she lowered the veil. Perhaps we both felt a pang—I know I did—but it was dissipated the moment we crossed the threshold to walk the hundred yards up the street to the church in the benevolent sun, with half a dozen children clapping us on the way, and then up the aisle as the organ played the Entry of the Queen of Sheba.

For me the ceremony passed in a dream, which even Mr Brimbright's sanctimonious drone couldn't fret. He preached an eminently inappropriate sermon on the evils of war and the benefits of unilateral disarmament, which made the congregation shuffle a bit. But a foolish man has the right to be foolish in his own church (locally known as the House of CND). And he'd promised to switch on the floodlighting that night, so we couldn't be too cross with him. I signed the register with a flourish, amused to discover that Hamish's last name was Jones.

The Green Bough was entirely turned over to the wedding

celebrations—and Hamish had organized it with a lavish hand. Half the pub garden had been boarded over to make a gigantic dance floor, with a twelve-piece band ensconced in an immense red and white striped marquee (with three sides rolled up) which they shared with a dozen trestle tables laden with cold hams and turkeys and sides of roast beef, veal pies, steak and kidney pies, pork pies, great silver platters of oysters and others heaped with fresh shrimp and whelk, smoked eel, smoked salmon, smoked trout, huge boards of cheeses, a whole Stilton, bowls of strawberries, bowls of raspberries, and baskets of peaches and apricots—and flowers everywhere the eye could touch.

Apart from a few toutish-looking men—no doubt fellow publicans—and a bevy of swift-footed servers, the whole company was from the village. Anything—from champagne to cider—that anyone could possibly wish to drink was there in abundance. Judge Towner made a gracious speech, I as gently witty a one as I could, but Hamish was the hit of the evening (as in a trice it seemed to be)—he was a natural-born speaker; all the curious little mechanisms that grated in ordinary conversation, worked perfectly in oratory—he was funny, grave, vulgar, solemn, sentimental, and, by golly, eloquent all the way.

'He ought to be in Parliament,' Fred Fletching whispered to me, and I nodded. He held us all entranced, and when he finished there was a moment of silence before we came out of it and rose and applauded him. Hamish had been accepted.

The Judge and I were alike in our distaste for champagne, though we dutifully sipped it for the toasts, and were thinking of whisky when Hamish gave us a nudge. 'Hold on, gentlemen, I got something a little special for you I dug out from the cellar.' It was a case of Lafitte 1970. 'I think you'll appreciate that, gentlemen.'

'Dug it out of the cellar!' said Towner as we settled down to the first bottle. 'My eye! Sent down from Berry Bros & Rudd, if you ask me.'

I said, 'To hell with where it came from—let's see how much we can drink.'

We moved gently into a delicate haze of claret, and only the descending twilight suggested time passing. Jeremiah Pleach got magisterially drunk quite early and sang ballads of amazing bawdiness in a vibrant bass. I danced twice with Phyllis and once with Mrs Helmsley-Clinch who dropped me with a sniff when she discovered I couldn't waltz. The rest of it I sat out, content to observe.

The switching on of the floodlights in the garden revealed Old George in an embarrassing position with one of the waitresses by the far hedge. We laughed and Judge Towner filled our glasses from the third bottle.

'Where's Young George?' he asked. 'Haven't seen Young George all evening.'

'He didn't come.' I recognized the connection—if you wanted a little bit of something done on your acres, you asked Young George these days, not Old George. 'He's shy, you know—and he doesn't drink.'

'Shy? Shouldn't be shy. Valuable member of the community, that lad.'

'Ah—community!' There was a gentle hiccough and we turned to see Mr Brimbright smiling down at us. 'Glad to hear you use that word, Judge.'

'Ah, padre, sit down and have a drink.'

'Thank you, thank you.' He was undeniably wobbly on his pins and sat down with evident relief. 'Marriage,' he said, 'community...'

'Yes?' I prompted, pushing a full glass towards him.

'I like to think of marriage as the perfect affertation—affirmation, yes, affirmation of us all as persons in community.'

'Legally,' said Towner with exaggerated gravity, 'it's a contract between two individuals.'

'Oh no no no no. Individuals?' He grasped his glass and, raising it, gulped the contents down in one, as if to take away the nasty taste of the word. 'The salvation of individual souls,' he said in his best sermonizing tone rendered impressive by the occasional hiccough, 'implies that the individual remains an egocentric unit and takes on a God dimension.'

'Eh?' said Towner.

'A God dimension,' he said loudly against the band, 'which makes him demonic. Demonic.' He smiled. 'Not salvation. Quite wrong. What we have to aim for is the transformation of us individuals and of our cruel mass society in all its forms. All its forms so ... so ...' He hesitated and then came through with a final flourish, 'so that we become together persons in community!'

'Well,' I said, 'how about a little more of this transforming fluid?'

But Towner had had enough. 'I say, padre, I thought you were going to light up the church for the occasion?'

'Eh? What? Oh yes, of course. Dear me dear me. Old George was supposed to be doing it, but in the circumstances,' he gave a heavy wink, or, more charitably, an inebriated tic of the eyelid, 'in the circumstances, the duty falls upon my humble self.' He staggered to his feet, took a deep breath, and made his way very slowly through the celebratory throng.

'A true worker in the vineyard,' murmured the Judge.

'Somebody must have spiked his tomato juice.'

The band was playing the Blue Danube for the third or fourth time, bribed no doubt by Mrs Helmsley-Clinch who was waltzing majestically with Fred Fletching.

'All work and no play makes Jack a dull boy,' said Towner.

'Brimbright? I shouldn't have said he was—'

'No no—Young George, I mean. Have a cigar?' He proffered a massive silver case. 'No? By the way, what are your plans for the lad when the first six months are up?'

'God knows—depends what he wants to do. Why?'

'I thought of doing up that flat over my old stables—putting in a proper bathroom, that sort of thing.' He cut the top from a cigar and blew down the end with inflated cheeks. 'Make a nice place for a young chap, closer to the village and—'

And suddenly all the lights went out.

There was a general groan and then a great cheer.

'Must be the padre.' Towner struck a match and held it to his cigar. 'I expect the bloody fool stuck his finger in the socket.'

The consensus was that the floodlights of the church combined with those in the pub garden had overloaded the mains, but nobody cared. With amazing rapidity, Hamish produced lanterns, the soft light of which was far preferable to the former garish glare. And in any event it was time for the fireworks—this was Hamish's *pièce de resistance* and an extravagant and stunning display it was. Enormous catherine wheels whirred and hissed and the rockets zooming high into the sky must have been visible across the Channel and alerted half the

Coastguard. The faces of the watchers were like beautiful night flowers turned up to the heavens. Even Towner was impressed.

Afterwards, as though the fireworks had released some inner fire, an atmosphere of abandon descended on the party. Hamish and Phyllis performed a dance which in any other circumstances would have been considered obscene and, infected by their wildness, the villagers danced too with an intensity that had something primeval about it. Couples disappeared into the neighbouring field, old ladies swayed with half-closed eyes as in folk memory of an ancient ritual. And the Judge and I moved into that celestial state of dream where all women are fair and all nature benign.

40 Light in the Dark

It was late when I took the shortcut across the field, but the party had diminished only slightly. Just before I reached the clump of trees that hid the village from view, I turned and looked back. Whatever electrical fault had caused the blackout had not been repaired, and the only illumination in the whole swathe of countryside was the soft candlelit glow from the Green Bough. The band had reverted to Glenn Miller, and nostalgia invested the night and for a moment pricked my eyelids. Then I turned for home.

I was surprised to see a chink of light between the shutters across the 'study' window; but I realised that George must have lit the kerosene lamp. It was a kindly gesture, for Viv didn't like the dark and would whine and yelp if I forgot to switch on the tiny nightlight by her basket.

I was not wearing my cleated boots of course and I slipped and fell heavily in the driveway. I was dazed for a moment and lay vaguely gazing at the house. There was something not quite right—perhaps the strength of the light between the shutters—but suddenly I was up and running. As I rounded the corner I caught the smell of burning. 'George,' I cried, 'George!' and pounded furiously at the back door. It took me an age to find my keys, but at last I found them, unlocked the door and threw it open. The room was licked with small flames which, as I looked, joined and exploded in one great orange mass. I caught a glimpse of the lamp overturned on the floor, then fell back from the furious heat. The draught from the open door had released the full force of the fire and there was no penetrating now.

I ran to the front of the house and called up at the window, 'George—George!' The window was shut and behind the panes I could see a reddish glow—the stairs would be alight by this time, and the only hope of escape was by the window. I cast round for something to raise me that high, but it was a good twelve foot from the ground and I had no ladder of my own.

And then I saw a movement—and then again. It was Viv's face behind the glass—face and forepaws scrabbling uselessly until she fell back and tried again.

'Keep at it, old girl, keep at it,' I shouted. Frantically I prised a brick from the walkway and flung it with all my force. It was a lucky shot, hitting the central catch and throwing the two halves of the window wide. Immediately I could hear the deep roar of the fire, and then Viv jumped and got herself half across the sill.

'Come on, love, I'm here, I'll catch you...' God knows what I babbled as she struggled and heaved herself up. For a moment she stood uncertainly on the sill, looking back at the room now sharp with flame, and then she leapt into my arms and we rolled over and over together. I clutched her to me, smelling the singed fur, crooning comfort as she growled softly deep in her throat.

I stood up and shouted for George, as the smoke seeped from the slate roof. Surely nothing could live in that. I snatched up Viv and ran for the car.

As I drove at a crazy racing speed to the village I felt a queer wild triumph. I was right and they were wrong—Marion, Shep, McQuade, all the bloody officials. The Avenger had got to Camrose after all.

I trod on the brakes too hard and slammed into a stone post in front of the pub. I leapt out shouting.

'Fire! Fire!' I yelled breaking in on the general bemusement. It was Fred Fletching who reacted first and he was on the phone at once—but the nearest fire station was at Hawley and then Seaford, and neither could arrive much under twenty minutes. Ladders were fetched, although I knew no ladder could save George Camrose now, and men, cars and trucks raced to the scene.

My house was a terrible and beautiful sight. The roof had caught and was a mass of wreathing flame, shooting columns of sparks high into the air as a timber collapsed. Great gouts of fire spurted from the windows, licking the walls to the eaves, and the crackling carried in the night like the breaking of little bones. Slate tiles slid from the roof and smashed to smithereens on the walkway below.

'Stand back!' It was Hamish in the voice of authority and the crowd retreated with their ladders.

'He's in there,' I shouted, 'George is inside.'

'Well, he hasn't got a bloody hope in hell.'

But the spectators fell silent at the news, their faces blood red and wild as they watched the burning of my home, my goods, my chattels, the immolation of George Camrose, my ward and guard...

And then, carrying across the valley on the still summer air, came the shrill clang of the fire engines, far away yet and too late, too late for George, too late for the kill. Glancing round at the fire-red faces of the villagers, my neighbours, I was filled with a revulsion of horror—not at the avid stares or gaping mouths, but at my own half-savage satisfaction. I felt the fire in my own limbs, my own belly, my own head, as if the mania for retribution had joined me to the Avenger—he who perhaps now stood at the back of the crowd as I stood at the front—and made me one with him. I, who had taken in the wretched Camrose in order to save him, had instead delivered him into the hands of his executioner. What utter madness to leave him alone and unguarded on such a night! My duty to protect him had been duty to Vivian—to keep clear his name, his memory, his love. And now I had finally betrayed both.

The blood of guilt fired my cheeks and I stepped forward to the pyre.

'Keep clear there!' Someone gripped my arm and pulled me back. 'Don't be a damned fool—can't you see it's going to go?'

And as the first of the fire engines lumbered up the steep drive, the roof fell in with a roaring crash. The crowd moaned softly, then fell silent as men in yellow helmets jumped down with important cries and unwound hoses. I turned aside from the hissing as they began to deluge the embers and pushed my way through the spectators, ignoring murmurs and touches of sympathy, my head down, Viv faithfully beside me.

It was the dog's growl that made me stop suddenly and look up. The face in front of me swayed and flickered redly in the revolving lights of the fire engines.

'George!'

'Hello, Mr. Speke, I . . . .' He was panting.

'I thought you—you were in there.'

'Nao—I just run up the top of the hill to look at the fire-works and . . . .' His whine dwindled to nothing.

'Get out of my fucking way,' I said.

41 The Party is Over

'No,' I said, 'it was just a damn fool accident. He lit the kerosene lamp because he knew my dog disliked the dark, and the electricity was still out. He just wanted to watch the fire-works and join the party, and didn't think—or didn't care—that Viv can't stand being left alone. She must have got in a panic, jumped about and knocked over the lamp and—Bob's your Uncle.'

'Aye,' said McQuade, 'I'm inclined to that way of thinking myself.' Nevertheless—despite the protests of the Judge, who'd sat in on the questioning—he'd given George a rough going over.

'You're nothing but a bloody little pyromaniac, aren't you, laddie?'

'Naoo,' George had wailed. And in the end, we'd believed him. It was people he burned, I thought, not dogs. And he'd gone off in care of the Judge, where soon he would have a little flat of his own and become a fully fledged 'person in community'—more than I had ever been.

Some of the candles were guttering and outside the light was greying with the dawn.

'I'm afraid you rushed down here for nothing,' I said, 'a storm in a teacup.'

McQuade smiled faintly and drank some of Hamish's best malt. Roused out of bed by Fred Fletching's phone call, he wore an old black polo neck sweater and, with his hair slightly awry, he seemed almost human. 'I wouldn't precisely say that, Mr Speke.'

'Wouldn't you?' I said wearily. 'Why not? It's just another accident, isn't it—only this time without fatal results? Doesn't that prove what you thought all along—they were all just accidents?'

'May I have one of your cigarettes?'

'By all means.' I took the packet out of my pocket and pushed it across to him. I didn't want to smoke. The smell of burning hung about me, in my hair, my clothes. Perhaps I would never smoke again.

'They may have been accidents,' he said, lighting a cigarette from a candle, 'just as the inquests decided. Officially that's what they were and what they always will be.'

'But unofficially?' I said, my tiredness dropping away.

'Well now—I'd be surprised if no other explanation had occurred to a man of your imagination.'

I leaned over and poured some whisky into my own glass and drank it quickly. I was fully alert now, but I had to brace myself to speak, to hear what I didn't want to know.

'You mean,' I said carefully, 'that Vivian killed them?'

'It's a possibility. I don't say more than that. But it's a possibility.'

I got up and went to the window and threw it open. The dawn smelled fresh and the village was smudged with the soft light. The band had long gone home, the food had been eaten, the drink drunk, and upstairs the bridal pair were sweetly coupled—the party was definitely over.

I turned back to the bar.

'Do you believe it yourself, Mr McQuade?'

He shook his head—not in negation, but in doubt.

'And Lady Winter,' I said, 'do you think she believed it?'

'She came to it, Mr Speke—in my opinion, she came to it.'

'I see,' I said, 'I see.' So perhaps, at least at the beginning, she had not so much been deceiving me, as herself. And Vivian was his mother's son—a believer in blood for blood. 'But you've nothing concrete to go on?' I came back into the room. 'What about Posey—did he kill Vivian?'

'Oh aye, there's no doubt about that.'

'A coincidence?' I asked, trying to clear my throat of its thickness. I looked down at him and he stared back, the candles making small wavering points of light in his deep-set eyes.

'I'll tell you a very curious thing,' he said slowly, 'which I have never seen on a body killed as your friend was killed. There was a smile on his face—a tender wee smile, such as a man might make when he's got what he wanted at last.'

So perhaps Shep had been right in the end and Vivian *had* organized his own death, invited—encouraged—Posey to murder. And Frank, avid for anything concerning his neighbours, would probably have known all the gory details about Madeleine Hodder and Jenny Thrush—and the neatness of sixteen stabs would have appealed to his paranoid mentality. And if he hadn't known, Vivian could have told him. Or it might, after all, have been just a curious coincidence.

I shivered a little. 'Maybe then,' I said, 'he was happy.'

'Aye,' McQuade said, stubbing out his cigarette, 'maybe.' He stood up.

'Thank you,' I said. And we shook hands then.

Phyllis had made up a bed for me, but the last thing I felt like was sleep.

I whistled up Viv, and we left McQuade blowing out the candles in the bar and stepped out into the deserted street. We skirted the village to the West, taking the long route up to the Head.

Still absurdly clad in my morning suit and city shoes, I found the going tough and Viv was impatient with my slowness. We reached the top at last, just as the sun was rising, casting a pale glitter on the smooth surface of the sea. It would be hot again. But in the cool peace of the dawn, I thought of Vivian—not the Vivian who was all charm and kindliness and sardonic wit, not the clever barrister, the brilliant performer, but the man who had gently comforted me through a long

301

night of anguish in that little bedroom on Torcello and whose own anguish never showed but drove him at last to that most terrible and logical of all reparations: healing by death, healing by the infliction of death, healing by the acceptance of death for himself. Yet no one would be eased or healed by such condign punishment—not Ralph Duke or Maudie Gray or Gerald Price, and the dead girls would not even stir in their graves. And I? *I* knew what it was all about, for myself just as for Vivian. Marion was right, one can forgive everyone except oneself. Perhaps.

I moved close to the edge. A small onshore breeze ruffled my hair and below me the waves whispered against the cliff. But my head was clear and I felt no dizziness, no fear, not the least temptation to cast myself down. I looked up across the waters to the purple land on the other side, and I knew with absolute certainty that my nightmare had gone. I turned and called Viv. It was time to look at the ruins and plan the day.